To Bill

C3

Knave Takes Queen

KNAVE
TAKES QUEEN

by

PETER CHEYNEY

FABER AND FABER
24 Russell Square
London

First published by Wm. Collins Sons and Co. Ltd.
Reprinted in this new and enlarged edition in mcml
by Faber and Faber Limited
24 Russell Square London W.C.1
Printed in Great Britain by
Purnell and Sons Limited
Paulton (Somerset) and London

For

MY WIFE

All the characters in this book are fictitious, except Mr. Krasinsky, who, as everybody knows, exists.

Contents

Episode I.   Of Honoria Dove-Mellifleur   *page* 11

Episode II.   Of the Demise of Mr. Evelyn Sout   39

Episode III.   Of the Reclamation of Captain Kidd   58

Episode IV.   Of the Vengeance of Hyacinth Jones   97

Episode V.   Of Perfume and Sudden Death   112

Episode VI.   Of an Experience of Pierre Duchesne 142

Episode VII.   Of a Delay in the Post   162

Episode VIII. A Lady of Quality   191

Episode IX.   Of Pastoral Blackmail   210

Episode X.   Of the Dream of Erasmus Bellamy 241

Episode XI.   Of the King of Tarragona   260

An Introduction

⊂∞∽∾⊃

It was late when the Poet returned to his garret and found the portly and good-humoured figure, dressed in a smart suit of shepherd's plaid, sitting on a stool by the window.

"Good evening," said the Poet. "My name is Clarges—Adrian Clarges. May I ask, who are you?"

The portly gentleman rose and proceeded to take a pinch of snuff with obvious pleasure.

"Permit me to introduce myself," he said. "I am not, as you might believe, the bum-bailiff or even the man who comes about the rent. In fact you ought to know me very well. I am Imagination—Yours or Anybody's. I get about considerably."

"How very interesting," said Clarges with a sigh. "I must say that you seemed vaguely familiar. And I expect you know a great many nice women. You might introduce me to some when you've time."

The other smiled.

"I know some delightful women," he said, "but only when I'm with men. When I'm with women I know a lot of charming and very virile men. Incidentally, I think you've met some of your nicest women through me ... don't you think ...?"

"I suppose I have," murmured the Poet. "It's funny that I've never seen you before. By the way, what am I to call you?"

"Well . . . I'm not too particular," said the plump gentleman. "I have all sorts of names. Krasinsky will do as well
as any other."

The Poet sat down on the bed.

"I'm very glad to meet you," he said. "Dear Mr. Krasinsky. . . ."

EPISODE ONE

Of Honoria Dove-Mellifleur

CARRO

This is the story of Miss Honoria Dove-Mellifleur and of the extraordinary series of events which took place in and around the West Central District of London in the years 1890 and 1891.

The author takes up his pen with a certain reluctance that is easy to feel but more difficult to describe. He records these happenings because he believes that many a gentleman of the style and manner of Snells Dove-Mellifleur may learn something from the pages that follow.

It has been said that the record of the part played in the business by Doctor Horatio Fiddlebee was, in fact, libellous; that the doctor was honestly and sincerely acting within the confines of his professional duties and that the advice which he gave Snells Dove-Mellifleur regarding the mental state of his daughter was *good* advice.

I do not propose to argue this, or other, fine points in this business. It has been believed that the crux of the situation—with its attendant crisis in the life of Miss Honoria Dove-Mellifleur—was twisted, falsified and generally turned inside out through the machinations of Mr. Krasinsky. But be this as it may the fact remains that the eventual position seemed adequate to the happiness of the lady.

It is necessary that the reader should, without further waste of time, have some inkling of the background of events preceding this history. It is also necessary that he should know something of the Dove-Mellifleurs, their family traditions, their technique, their amatory inclinations and whatnots, and the atmospherics into which Honoria was projected by a Providence whose kindliness was somewhat delayed even if, in the end, it was handed out with that liberality so aptly described by the more vulgar citizens of London as "a basinful."

To the tremulous lady reader who turns each page with properly nervous fingers—the result of a hopeful fear that there may be overleaf something which she should not (in any event) be *seen* reading; to those delicately nurtured women to whom the overtures—even by post—of men not educated at (at least) one of the lesser Universities are anathema; in fact to all those of a sensitive nature who, owing to lack of inclination, time or other obstruction, have not yet been able to view some of the advices regarding the successful techniques for love which add such a lustre to the advertisement pages of the more popular American magazines, little can be said.

But—and I am sure that all sincere thinkers will agree—it is only because it has been considered necessary from every point of view that the story of Honoria should be laid, in its entirety, before a critical but, I hope, sympathetic world, that I have consented to record the facts as they were told to me by no less a person than Sophie Mulligatawny—Honoria's personal maid —whose ears have, for a long time, been attuned to the most difficult and draughty keyholes.

. . . . . .

Consider, if you please, the exterior of No. 435 Woburn Square in the year 1890. There was, about this place, at that time, an air of dignity, of grace and of extreme gentility. The oaken door, solid and ironbound, proclaimed to the world that the Dove-Mellifleurs still believed—(as did their ancestor Sir Ulk the Bastard who was split to the navel by an indignant Saxon at the Battle of Hastings, winning thereby their proud Motto—"Thus Far and No Farther")—in the strength and security of their portcullis. The whiteness of the doorsteps, bleached each morning by a retainer so old that he had forgotten practically everything worth remembering; the glitter of the doorplates in the sunshine which came often in those days to Woburn Square; all these things told their own tale; they proclaimed to a world which then believed in the essential *difference* of people who had both *birth* and *breeding* that the Dove-Mellifleurs still maintained that *savoir-faire*, that *je ne sais quoi* which prompted the whispered reply by another of their ancestors to Charles the Second's dying wish . . . "Look after poor Nellie" . . . a reply which, history has told us, caused the Monarch to pass hence with a happy smile and a slight quivering of one eyelid.

So much then for the outside of the mansion.

Within, nearly eighty years of age, but of a strength of body and intellect that was as amazing as it was obvious, lived Mr. Snells Dove-Mellifleur.

It is perhaps a little difficult to reduce to words an exact description of this gentleman, whose devotion to Queen and Country, whose taste in port, and whose general outlook on a world which he regarded as merely ordinary, were apt to stamp him as being of an extreme Victorian type. There was, it must be confessed, something a little *different* about Snells Dove-Mellifleur, some *nuance* of mind that separated Snells from his fellow-men.

But one thing was certain and it was this. It was that Snells Dove-Mellifleur had—ever since that historic night in the dark past when his lovely blonde and ineptly passionate wife, Geralda, had, with a toss of her head, ordered a locksmith to put two bolts and a burglar proof lock on the inside of her bedroom-door—been a changed man.

Never had Snells quite recovered from that never-to-be-forgotten night when Geralda lay dying, and when he, hovering about her bedside, had discovered, just underneath the coverlet, a more-or-less accurate tin-type photograph of the bronzed and stalwart individual who used to come to attend to the gas meter.

And never had Snells forgotten the last words of his departing spouse, words which constituted—especially having regard to the expression on her face—a *bon mot* which was not at all in good taste.

From that time he had shunned all feminine company and, what is more, he had brought to bear upon the whole business of the relationships of men and women a viewpoint which was as distorted as it was bitter.

There is little doubt that there was more than a touch of heredity in this. Mr. Krasinsky who, I am sure, was more aware of the mental workings of Snells than any other person, has said so and was it to be wondered at?

Was it not true that Snells' own father, Graypole Dove-Mellifleur, renowned in the political circles of his time, had sacrificed a distinguished, nay brilliant, career by rushing eagerly from an important Cabinet meeting merely because he had seen, out of the window, a young *modiste* wearing one of the new French bustles?

These things may help us to understand his attitude towards his daughter Honoria, to understand his attitude towards all those young (some of them personable and quite eligible) men who had, in the past, sought her hand in marriage.

For they had never succeeded in convincing Snells Dove-Mellifleur of their dependability as husbands. Each and every one of them had been sent packing about his business on some flimsy excuse. One was told that he was too inexperienced to bring happiness to the only daughter of the Dove-Mellifleur family, another that he was too experienced and not likely to stand the strain of the continued effort necessary to any man who aspired to satisfy the hand and heart of Honoria.

In this manner the years passed in the way that years *do* pass. Snells, whose greatest pleasure was to look appraisingly after his daughter each evening as she mounted the wide staircase after dinner, congratulated himself that the delicacy of her contours had not been wasted on some young and worthless suitor. Either the best or none at all said Snells, knowing that there would be no "best".

In mitigation of his attitude we must remember that he was supported and confirmed in it by his friend—the family physician—Doctor Horatio Fiddlebee. Whether such support was worthy is not for me to say, although it has been whispered that Doctor Fiddlebee was not entirely free from influence in such matters.

Fiddlebee—it has been said—was never quite the same man after the night on which he had been suddenly called in to perform a slight—but very necessary—operation on no less a person than Her Highness The Duchess of Sax-Gottblitz-Gefilter.

Trembling with nerves as he had approached the gracious torso, Fiddlebee had in one fell moment punctured his royal and anxious patient in the wrong place and his prospects as an Imperial surgeon for ever.

And this was not all, for the Duchess who, as a result of Fiddlebee's bungling, was unable to occupy her throne with any degree of comfort for some considerable period, had written him a personal note which, even allowing for the fact that she was writing in a language not native to her, was so terse, so much to the point that Fiddlebee had sold his instruments to a brother medico and never again took a knife in his hand except for the purpose of eating.

So much then for Snells Dove-Mellifleur, and so much for Doctor Horatio Fiddlebee.

. . . . . .

By this time the gentle and kindly reader will have created for himself the framework of the picture into which Honoria must now step. The atmosphere of the Dove-Mellifleur house, the respectable and cultured air of the neighbourhood, the very quietness of the tradesmen's boys when delivering at the back doors or down the area steps, will, it is hoped, form an adequate background for the appearance of the leading figure in the tragedy which must now unfold itself.

Honoria Dove-Mellifleur was forty-three years of age. She was tall but not too tall, and she possessed that roundness of contour which suggests, in the most delicate manner of course, that a beneficent nature when planning her had been concerned with the kindliest thoughts towards the male sex.

The fact that Honoria was forty-three must not be regarded at all seriously. In fact, it has been suggested by those who knew her well that like certain virgin wines she had improved in the maturing, that the impeccable modesty of her demeanour, the grace and kindliness which she meted out to all and sundry were the results of her forty-two summers superimposed upon a nature which, it must be confessed, was as ardent as that of a girl of twenty.

Honoria was intelligent and witty and cultured. She had intellect. It is, of course, possible that on occasion, in the privacy of her own room, she had wondered why it was that with all the women friends of her youth married and with families, she should remain in the single state, that no man had yet essayed to win her hand and with it those creature comforts for which men have struggled and fought so stubbornly ever since the far off day when the Serpent, with the very worst intentions, had taken it upon himself to advocate to the unfortunate but headstrong Adam a line of conduct that was in the worst of taste, even if we, in the light of our own civilised researches and knowledge, are able to understand and (possibly) sympathise with it.

It may be that deep within her heart Honoria realised the perfidy of her father. She may have known that Snells, an apparently kindly parent—but none the less a dog-in-the-manger so far as any marriage for her was concerned—had short-circuited the thousand and one young men who, driven almost insane by thinking about the charms of Honoria, had, after a short and one-sided interview with Snells, come to the abrupt conclusion that for them there must be other fish in the sea, and, as promptly, gone to look for them. If such thoughts had come to Honoria she had kept them to herself. She had, with the courage of the Dove-Mellifleurs, refrained from an undue criticism of her father's attitude.

Alternately, as has been suggested, it was merely that nothing had yet stirred Honoria to such a degree that her desire for knowledge of all those things which make life worth living had yet reached a climax.

It has been said that she was of good height and delightfully rounded. Her skin was as clear and as beautiful as that of a selected peach and the bloom on her cheeks as youthful. Her eyes were blue, but sometimes turned towards a peculiar and most attractive shade of violet as the evening progressed, and one who knew her perhaps better than most has written that on certain occasions her eyes took upon themselves a glowing tint of purple so enthralling that it was hardly believable. This matter, however, must be left just where it is in order that the bounds of extreme delicacy should not be outraged by thoughts of Honoria which, while being possibly excusable, are nevertheless not quite *de rigueur*.

Her person and carriage were most suitable for the fashions which a lady affected in those days. Her sense of dress was subtle and quite supreme. Her tiny and exquisitely shod feet, her slender and delicately moulded ankles which gave such promise of still greater beauty above, and the unconscious and quite lovely undulation of the hips when walking—the more attractive because of the air of supreme innocence which accompanied it; all these things conspired together to create a picture of superb, poised and glowing womanhood which made many a man who passed her on her daily walk in Woburn Square catch his breath in wonder.

And in some strange manner Snells took delight in the lovely picture. Honoria was something which he intended should be kept captive in the house until the day when the supreme beauty began to fade, the bloom to leave the peach-like cheek, the graceful and easy walk to turn into the *staccato* step of the elderly spinster and the soft lines of the full and delightfully shaped mouth to turn into the "rat-trap" of the "lady of a certain age" who is fated to die curious and slightly bitter.

It was, possibly, for this reason that Snells Dove-Mellifleur was generous towards Honoria as regards her allowance; in order that she might have all those subtle and intimate luxuries so helpful to the *amour propre* of a lovely lady. When Honoria had passed along the passage by his library door on her way out, Snells would often, on some excuse or another, stand in the hall sniffing with appreciative pleasure at the suggestion of perfume which her passing left behind.

But how deep are the workings of an inscrutable Providence? How clever the machinations of that extraordinary and cheerful individual Krasinsky who, apparently engaged on most days in the business of feeding two sparrows in Gordon Square, knew, by some astral means, of the circumstances which surrounded the Dove-Mellifleur domicile and those within it, and indirectly through whom—it is believed—the strange events which took shape from a mere beginning on the 23rd day of September 1890 and which were to repercuss so sharply in one direction and—one hopes—so delightfully in another.

.   .   .   .   .

We have disposed of Snells, of Doctor Horatio Fiddlebee, and we have (or have we?) endeavoured to acquaint ourselves with the *nuances* of the subtle, essentially feminine and wholly delightful *aura* of Honoria. Now whether we like it or not we must come to Lambert Whelks.

And, at this moment, it is not proposed to acquaint the reader with the business of Mr. Whelks, because his calling—except inasmuch as it provides undecorative *mise-en-scène*—is of no particular account.

His name, as is quite obvious to the more than cultured reader, is of no particular account and is merely reminiscent of a rather indifferent form of indelicately shaped shell-fish too often associated with orgies held by rough men in the Old Kent Road on Saturday nights, with vinegar. No, it must not be Mr. Whelks who holds the stage, it must be Lambert, and every woman who has a heart in her bosom (and what woman has not?) will agree with me that this is one of those cases in which all the difference in the universe lies between a Surname and a Christian name. Whelks, at the first sound of the word, can mean nothing but the crustacean above referred to, but Lambert—breathed gently by lips moistened with the tender juices of desire—can be a word of exquisite importance.

Very well then: Lambert Whelks possessed each and every one of those qualities which go to make a man. He was twenty-two years of age. He possessed a straight, slender and manly figure. His face was open and intelligent. He had good eyes, and his mouth, chiselled to a pattern which, by comparison, would have made that of Achilles look like a pathological case, was of such beauty that, too often, cooks and housekeepers in the neighbourhood of Woburn Square would put in a double order of mutton chops merely so that he should come round on the second delivery thereby giving them something to think about in that quiet period in the servants' hall when dinner has been cooked and served and there is nothing much to be done except to think.

And now the secret is out of the bag. It is divulged that Lambert Whelks was nothing more—and nothing less—than the butcher's boy.

But what a butcher's boy! From earliest childhood Lambert had been different not only because he desired to be, but because he *had* to be.

Placed, at the age of three and one half weeks, in a strong paper bag and suspended by an indifferent piece of string from the brass knocker of the Walter Bagrancy Foundling Home by a parent whose disinterest in Lambert may be surmised, he had, on the door being opened and the string broken, fallen out of the bag onto his head, a process which, far from causing him any harm, merely produced a bump which, in after years, was held by an eminent phrenologist to indicate a desire to travel.

Of his life in the Foundling Home nothing need be said, save that he was of a modest nature, a strong and controlled character and an ardent disposition coupled with an extreme disinterest in the more ordinary things of life. His inclination tended towards poetry, and, when he had graduated from the Foundling Hospital and was apprenticed to Swaythe, Family Butcher, of Ridgemount Place, he would in his spare time haunt the theatre gallery and absorb the Shakespearian drama until he knew six of the plays by heart.

But never, and I am adamant on this point because all records are agreed on it, never I repeat, although he delivered the meat, morning and evening, at the Dove-Mellifleur house, had he in attitude, gesture, word or even thought, shown even a realisation of the existence of Miss Honoria Dove-Mellifleur. How could he? How could a lady of good family, in the year 1890, even impinge on the consciousness of a member of the lower classes, a butcher's lad and a foundling?

This then was Lambert Whelks, as honest and as well set up a lad as ever handled an undercut of the rump, and, in thinking of him let us remember that a man may raise himself above his destiny and that although his background may have been over-decorated with suet he was also a student of Shakespeare and therefore well able, within the confines of his own soul, to escape from mundane thoughts of brisket to regions more in keeping with the nobler attributes.

. . . . .

The day of the 23rd September 1890 dawned brightly and beautifully as if it realised that it was an important day.

Towards the afternoon Honoria, who had just finished perusing a copy of Don Juan, and who was sitting at her window wondering about Lord Byron, observed the arrival of Lambert Whelks with the saddle of mutton intended for dinner that evening.

I think it may be said that this was the first occasion on which Honoria had ever really *seen* Lambert. That is to say she was on this day *conscious* of him. On previous occasions she had merely observed the arrival of the butcher's lad from Swaythe's bringing the meat.

But now she saw Lambert.

Possibly it was the influence of the Byronic rhyme that showed her the wave in the chestnut hair of the virile Whelks as with unconscious grace he dismounted from his cart. His very act of handling the saddle of mutton seemed to her almost medieval and certainly romantic in its intensity.

The suppleness and the grace with which he ran down the area steps were not lost upon the now interested and critical eyes of Honoria, and for no reason which she could understand she felt a wave of something interesting, exhilarating and even troubling in its intensity, come over her.

From that moment, although she did not consciously realise it, Honoria was a different woman.

When she went downstairs to pour the specially selected brand of Orange Pekoe tea which had for years graced the Dove-Mellifleur tea-table, Snells noticed the absence of the charming smile, the small generalities of conversation, with which Honoria had always brightened his tea-table.

I do not suggest that he was greatly concerned because, as has been suggested, Snells was a very selfish old man.

After dinner the restlessness of spirit which had come upon Honoria ever since she had seen Lambert Whelkes increased, and at eight o'clock that evening took upon itself such an intensity that she felt it necessary to leave the house and go for a little walk in order to attempt to analyse her own peculiar feelings, a difficult matter for a charming woman who was not in the slightest degree introspective.

Outside the house she stood undecided for a moment and then taking the Woburn Gardens key from her reticule, opened the gate of the gardens, locked it carefully behind her, and walked in the autumn twilight towards the antique summer house which stood in those days at the northern end of the Gardens.

The interior of the summer house was dark, and it was only when Honoria had stepped inside that she became aware of the perfume of a very good cigar. She gave a little gasp, for sitting on the rustic seat which ran along the farther wall of the summer house was a plump and placid gentleman in a shepherd's plaid suit, who bestowed upon her a beaming smile—no less a person than Mr. Krasinsky.

It is perhaps not necessary to add that Honoria was affected by the smile of Mr. Krasinsky in exactly the same manner as men and women have experienced from the earliest times.

There came over her an indefinable feeling of well-being and of comfort, and although she had been brought up under the strict regime which had distinguished the up-bringing of all Dove-Mellifleur women for generations, she found herself returning the smile.

"Good evening," said Mr. Krasinsky cheerily. "Miss Dove-Mellifleur, I believe. I am delighted to make your acquaintance."

Honoria inclined her head.

"Good evening " she murmured and without knowing why sat down on the seat not far from Mr. Krasinsky, who carefully stubbed out the end of his cigar and, leaving the summer house, pushed the butt end into the soil beneath a plant where the influence of the tobacco would be helpful. Then he returned to his seat.

"I have spent a great number of years, my dear lady," he said, "in considering the rather small and sometimes very delicate matters which obtrude themselves, sometimes not too happily, on the inner consciousness of entirely delightful women. This being so, it seemed indicated to me that I should be here this evening in order that you might ask any questions to which you were inclined."

Honoria began to listen to herself speaking. I say this advisedly, because it seemed to her that she was not speaking of her volition but rather that some mysterious and quite delightful force was speaking for her.

"That is very good of you, dear Mr. Krasinsky," (she never knew how it was that she came to know his name), "but I *am* very glad that you are here, because I *am* troubled. I will tell you why."

Honoria then proceeded to tell Krasinsky all about her life, all about the quiet happiness which she had experienced as the daughter of Snells Dove-Mellifleur until the early afternoon of that day, when, for some reason which she could not understand, the sight of Lambert Whelks had produced such an odd effect upon her.

Krasinsky listened amicably, nodding his head from time to time almost as if he did not understand and know every thought which had ever entered the head of Honoria.

When Honoria had finished her story Krasinsky began to speak. She thought that the words he uttered were clothed in a peculiar and sweet resonance of almost hypnotic power. Their effect upon her was almost anæsthetic.

She sat there, her pretty gloved hands folded in her lap, listening, knowing that in some indefinable manner her future lay bound up in the words of Mr. Krasinsky.

"Ever since the world began," he said, "all true women have been concerned with the business of love. It is most unhappy and quite unnecessary that any lady should be concerned through lack of it. It is true, however, that fate, often apparently unkindly, sometimes appears to insist that love should be absent from a life which needs it—one such as yours, dear lady—but this apparently means nothing. Usually fate is merely delaying the process until the subject is ripe for experience.

"The Victorian mentality has taught us all that a woman should first of all demand respect and then love. This is, of course, quite foolish. Ladies are not really interested in being respected by men in whom they find themselves interested. They desire to be loved with extreme warmth, passion, ardour and whatnot, and I have yet to meet a lady of any perception who finding herself well-loved bothered as to whether, in his heart of hearts, her swain respected her. Respect is something which a woman needs merely as a protection, an armour plating as it were against the lusty onslaughts of the more virile types of manhood who go about seeking prey in very much the same way as the ferocious native, lurking about in the South African undergrowth, springs upon the wild pig and plunges his sharp and quivering assegai into the unfortunate porcine without as much as a by your leave."

Krasinsky placed a forefinger and thumb in his waistcoat pocket and produced a pinch of snuff which he took with obvious pleasure.

He continued: "It is quite obvious to me that you are in need of that love, that ardour, that extreme affection which is every woman's birthright. Your preoccupation and uneasiness experienced this afternoon after a more than searching glance in the direction of Lambert Whelks, the butcher's lad, is indicative of the fact that the figure of this young man, occupied as he was in the mundane business of handling legs of mutton, became momentarily transformed by your subconscious mind into something *not* a butcher's lad but of infinitely more importance.

"Remove the leg of mutton from the virile hands of Lambert. Take away his blue and white butcher's apron, clothe him in fine raiment, and says your inner soul, there we have as fine a figure of a man as ever attempted to catch a ripe plum ready to fall into his mouth. Am I wrong?"

"No . . . indeed . . ." said Honoria faintly. "No . . . I do not think you are at all wrong."

"Excellent," said Mr. Krasinsky. "Therefore we have only to concern ourselves with the attainment of your heart's desire. We have only to concern ourselves with the future of two mentalities—those of your sweet self and Mr. Whelks—both of whom are yearning towards something which seems to be quite unattainable, something so sweet . . . so delicious that it makes one tremble at the thought of it. Do I err?"

"No," said Honoria, who was herself trembling at the thought of something which had just entered her exquisitely coiffured head, "No . . . indeed you do not, dear Mr. Krasinsky."

"Very well," said he blithely. "Let us consider love which, for all purposes of consideration, may be divided into two parts. First of all the purely practical part of the emotion which is something which I think you would not wish to discuss at the moment, and secondly—and this is important so far as you are concerned—the theoretical part.

"Of what does this theoretical part consist? It must be agreed by one and all that the theory of love consists of all that part of the business of love which falls short of a passionate and entirely practical onslaught against the beloved one. It consists of the uttering of endearing phrases, the writing of superb love notes, letters and billets doux, and it is through this theoretical process that a lady such as yourself . . . a lady of the extremest delicacy . . . may attain a certain mental satisfaction well worth the little trouble experienced in obtaining it.

"You will agree, I am sure," said Krasinsky, in the most honeyed tones, "that if on each and every morning or evening you were to receive a letter couched in the most delightful language, breathing in every word a passion so ardent, a love so superb, that it took your very breath away, you would be delighted and enthralled. The day, now so often boring and filled with routine, would take on a new shape. Your very household tasks and duties would each reflect a particular joy. In other words you would be transformed by the mere act of receiving such a letter, and of knowing that its glowing language referred to you, of knowing that you were lovely and adorable . . . that you were superb in every feminine way . . . that you were the difference between life and death to some young and ardent man. Am I not right, Miss Honoria?"

"Oh yes," gasped Honoria very faintly. "Yes . . . you are *quite* right."

"Excellent," purred Krasinsky. "Then all we have to do to ensure this happiness for you is to arrange that you receive such a letter each morning or each evening, whichever you prefer, and to place in your mind a definite picture of the writer of it."

He paused for a moment and then went on:

"I think I am right in saying," said he, "that there is no person who knows better than yourself the particular terms in which you would like to be addressed by a lover. No one can know more than you those *nuances* of expression, those delicate shades of ardent description which could and should be applied to you, than you do yourself. In fact, I would go so far as to say," said Krasinsky with a charming smile, "that the best and most proper person to write such letters would be yourself because you know more about yourself—have *thought* more about yourself in this connection—than anyone else. Is that logical, dear Miss Honoria . . .?"

"Oh yes," said Honoria. "I must admit it is very logical."

"However, there are two other points which we must consider," continued Krasinsky glibly. "First of all who is to be the signatory of the letters, and secondly the handwriting in which they are to be written. I will deal with the second point first.

"Obviously the handwriting must not be your own. The fact that you are to be the composer of the love letters to yourself means little, as in the writing thereof you will obviously superimpose upon your own thoughts of yourself the mental picture of the lover who you would wish to write you such letters. But quite as obviously the handwriting must *not* be your own. To open a love letter, delivered through the penny post and to find the contents couched in one's own handwriting would be a mistake.

"Therefore it will be necessary that you secure a typewriter—an instrument but lately invented, which is, I believe, most efficacious—and typewrite the letters to yourself. In this connection I would point out that Bendix the Stationer, of Gower Street, has such an instrument, second-hand, costing seven pounds, which you may care to inspect in the morning. It has a violet ribbon and beyond one or two minor defects is, I believe, in excellent condition. Do you hear . . .?"

"Oh yes," she murmured, leaning back against the side of the summer-house in a half-fainting condition. "Oh yes, I do hear . . . indeed I do . . ."

The voice of Mr. Krasinsky took on a beautiful and bell-like quality. It flowed straight into the mind of Honoria and implanted the words upon her receptive brain.

"Now," said he, "there remains only one thing to be decided and that is the figure of the man who is to be in your mind as the writer of these quite adorable letters which you will shortly be receiving. I suggest that there is one person quite suitable to our purpose. I refer to this Lambert Whelks who has, for some reason—although only a young man engaged in a possibly menial occupation—already implanted himself upon your perception and imagination merely because of the indefinable quality which comes to some men irrespective of birth, breeding or monetary status.

"So," said Krasinsky, and his words seemed to her to become fainter and fainter, to possess a strange and evanescent quality as charming as it was amazing, "dear Miss Honoria, it remains only for you to purchase the second-hand typewriter from Bendix, to spend an hour in the afternoon typewriting the most charming and delightful letters to yourself, posting them in the morning so that they arrive by the nine o'clock post in the evening, and opening and reading them after you have retired for the night. When perusing them you will of course conjure up a mental picture of Mr. Whelks—not in his butcher's apron of course, but dressed in such a manner as you consider suitable.

"And now," concluded Krasinsky, "I have said enough. Possibly it is time that you were returning to the house. You will find Bendix, the stationer, open at nine o'clock tomorrow morning.

"Good evening, Ma'am," said he, with a very subtle smile. "I hope you will eventually agree that I have been of some slight service. Perhaps you may decide to act upon my poor suggestions."

"Oh yes," said Honoria. "Thank you, Mr. Krasinsky. . . . I shall most certainly do what you say. Good evening, Sir."

But when she rose from the seat and tottered a little unsteadily from the summer-house—for she felt a slight agitation—she saw that Mr. Krasinsky had disappeared, that the evening was come and that the shadows in Woburn Gardens bore delightful and fascinating shapes.

.   .   .   .   .

It was in the early part of November that Snells Dove-Mellifleur became aware of the extraordinary change which had taken place in his daughter.

Of Honoria Dove-Mellifleur

Honoria was a different woman. She radiated a peculiar and amazing charm; a new virility, an almost unbelievable radiancy had come upon her that amazed and vaguely shocked him.

It has already been explained that Snells was a crusty and selfish old gentleman, and it must now be stated that so far as Honoria was concerned he was definitely suspicious. He watched her with the eye of an eagle. He observed every movement, every gesture. He scrutinised her goings and comings with a jealous and rheumy optic, and it was not long before he became aware of the fact that each nine o'clock evening post brought for Honoria an envelope, blue in colour, upon which her name and address were typed in violet coloured ink.

Secure in his library on the ground floor Snells wrestled with himself. His curiosity was fast overcoming that pride for which the Dove-Mellifleurs were famous. His mind, leaping off at the most impossible tangents, visualised circumstances attendant upon this business of a letter each evening which could only be ominous.

So it is not to be wondered at that one evening, furious, jealous and restless, he sneaked out into the hall, and before the tiny feet of Honoria had time to descend from her room to even the first floor, Snells, impatiently attending upon the postman's knock, had snatched the letter from the man's hand and retreated into the library where he had already prepared a steaming kettle which stood ready upon the gas ring used for making the hot toddy in which Snells and his friend Doctor Horatio Fiddlebee indulged at night.

With fingers that trembled with fear and age he held the back of the envelope towards the kettle. In two minutes the steam had done its work and Snells, his breath coming quickly, was reading the typewritten missive within.

It is not proposed that the gentle reader shall be made aware of the contents of the letter. Flesh and blood will not agree that the tender and delicious thoughts, the solicitous expressions, the ardent wishes and hopes expressed in the letter which was signed with the typewritten signature "Lambert," and which were intended *only* for Honoria, should be made public.

Of Honoria Dove-Mellifleur

I will only say that Snells Dove-Mellifleur, his face the colour of putty, staggered to the sideboard and poured himself out five fingers of Runciman's Fine Old Liqueur Brandy, swallowed it, and then, sticking down the envelope with a fearful oath, sneaked out into the hall and placed the letter in the receptacle used for the incoming post.

Within ten minutes the small page-boy used for cleaning knives and other menial businesses about the house, had been sent post-haste for Doctor Fiddlebee; and within half an hour that worthy gentleman, breathing wisdom, professional etiquette, a soupçon of old Jamaica rum not entirely obscured by the application of a Brompton Hospital Cough Lozenge, was closeted with Snells in the library, hearing, with ears that almost flapped with intensity, of the fearful and amazing happening which had come upon the family of Dove-Mellifleur.

"Damme, Sir," said Snells . . . "damme, I say. And how is a gentleman to deal with this! My own daughter . . . a Dove-Mellifleur at that . . . receiving letters of that sort—typewritten too—and her own father knowing nothing. And if I tax her with it what will she do? She might walk out of the house. There's been something odd about her for the last week or two that's been beyond me."

"Hum . . ." said Doctor Fiddlebee. "Hum . . ." He cleared his throat noisily. "This is a bad business, Snells," he said. "A very bad business . . . hum. . . . I remember a case very like it in the early days of my professional career. The lady concerned was a certain Lady Polkfus. She . . ."

"Damn Lady Polkfus!" exclaimed Snells with great feeling. "What do *I* care about Lady Polkfus. Damme, Sir, this is *my* daughter . . . Honoria . . . forty-three years of age come next quarter day, an' damme you begin to talk about Lady Polkfus."

He got up and began to walk up and down the library.

"You must advise me, Horatio," he said at last. "Damme, Sir, you're a doctor, you know all about women . . . you've had a great experience of women. You've brought 'em into the world . . . you've sent 'em out of the world, you've had to do with all their flims an' flams and whatnots. I need advice,

not reminiscences. I tell you, Horatio, I don't like it. Honoria
is at a damn dangerous age . . . an' she's got her own money
too . . . I can't touch it . . . an' if she gets ideas into her head
about this damned Lambert . . . *Who*," asked Snells, holding
his hands up to Heaven, "is this interloper . . . this . . .
this . . .?"

"Precisely," said Fiddlebee, helping himself to port. "Precisely . . . *who is he?*"

He changed his tone and took a soothing note into his voice.

"Listen to me, Snells," he said. "Before I advise you on this
portentous matter I must have time to think. I must go back
into my vast experience and cull such wisdom as I may from it.
But let me give you this advice now. Say nothing to Honoria
of having opened and read her letter. That would be fatal to
your hopes. Remember she may have realised ere now that
sundry young men whom *she* might have considered eligible
for her hand have been . . . er . . . sent packing, in the past, by
you. She might, shocked at what she would consider a turpi-
tude on your part, do anything. She might even kill herself."

Snells nodded miserably.

"Tomorrow night," said Fiddlebee, who, knowing nothing
at all about women, hoped, in the interim, to get advice from
someone else . . . "tomorrow night I will come after dinner
and advise you on this matter. Until then let discretion be your
master."

He helped himself to another glass of the Dove-Mellifleur
port, and took his hat and departure. Snells, returning morbidly
to the library, heard from the music room above the soft yet
vibrant voice of Honoria singing "My Lover Is Over The
Water."

I will not insult the delicacies of my readers by informing
them just what Snells said at that moment. I will only say that
his expression was coarse and unworthy of a gentleman of
breeding.

. . . . . .

When Doctor Horatio Fiddlebee left the Dove-Mellifleur
abode he began to walk slowly in the direction of Gower Street

where he lived. He was deep in thought and concerned greatly
with the present problem of Honoria.

First of all his reputation as a doctor was at stake. He knew
perfectly well that Snells, in asking his advice, had done so
with the idea of placing the responsibilty of decision upon the
Doctor. Then, whatever happened, it would be Fiddlebee's fault.

Horatio began to regret that he had been, on many previous
occasions, so very fulsome regarding his knowledge of the
mental workings of femininity. He wished that he had not
enlarged to such an extent upon his amazing experiences—both
as a doctor and a man—with the weaker sex. He realised of
course that in doing so he had been concerned mainly with the
hospitality and friendship of Snells, both of which had been
obtained by the recounting of sundry tales and experiences
which had not only flattered Snells' memory of his own treatment of his late wife Geralda, but which had also served to
sharpen the delight of the many glasses of port which the
Doctor and Snells were wont to drink in the comfort and
seclusion of the library.

Now, Horatio saw clearly, he must advise Snells and the
results of his advice must be *good*, otherwise . . . .

Just at this moment the Doctor, who was so engrossed with
his own thoughts that he was not looking where he was going,
bumped into an individual who was walking towards him.
By the light of an adjacent street lamp whose flickering gas jet
cast fitful shadows about the end of the Gardens, the doctor
saw that his *vis-à-vis* was a plump and good-natured individual
dressed in a suit of shepherd's plaid. An individual who
addressed him cheerfully.

"I must apologise for my carelessness," said Mr. Krasinsky,
for of course it was he, "but I was so entertained, my dear Sir,
by the colour of my own thoughts that I failed to see your
distinguished presence."

Horatio accepted the apology gracefully. For some reason
which he did not quite understand the appearance of Mr.
Krasinsky brought him a certain comfort. He stood there and
listened agreeably as Krasinsky continued:

"I did not see you approaching, Sir," said that worthy, "because I was so busily engaged in thinking about a strange event which has just happened to a friend of mine by the name of Wilbrox. Mr. Wilbrox is, I think I may say, one of the distinguished members of the Most Worshipful Company of Fish Filleters, and he has been greatly concerned with certain correspondence that his daughter Joanna has been receiving—correspondence, I may say, that reeked more of ardour than of discretion."

Horatio pricked up his ears. What a coincidence. What an amazing coincidence!

"I think you are very kind, Sir," he said pleasantly. "I find myself very interested."

So interested was he that he hardly noticed that Krasinsky had taken him by the arm and that they were walking towards Gower Street together, like old friends.

"My friend," continued Krasinsky, "was greatly concerned with the tone of this clandestine correspondence, but luckily, before doing anything about it—for his daughter was of a certain age and inclined to be headstrong—he spoke to me and I was able to solve the situation almost immediately.

"You see," said Krasinsky, smiling into the darkness, "my friend Wilbrox had never conceived even an inkling of the truth of the matter which was, of course, that his daughter was writing the letters to herself, and was quite delighted when I pointed this out to him. I was able to tell him that by writing these ardent missives, receiving and opening them with joy, the lady was successfully experiencing the true delights of the theoretical love without any of the chances, the dangers, nay the *perils* of the real and actual state.

"So, being wise, he said nothing of the matter to dear Joanna, and all is peace and happiness in their pleasant home."

Inside him the heart of Horatio Fiddlebee missed two beats. Here was the explanation of Honoria's mysterious correspondence. What luck that by this extraordinary coincidence this pleasant and suddenly found acquaintance had been able to make all things clear to him.

Of Honoria Dove-Mellifleur

Of course, Honoria was writing the letters to herself. His advice—like Krasinsky's—must be that she must not be interfered with, that she must continue to correspond with herself because while she was content to do that she was as safe as any lady could be.

The good Doctor chuckled to himself. There was not the slightest reason, he thought, why Snells and he should not steam open Honoria's correspondence from time to time just to see how her theoretical love affair was progressing! Such a process, thought Horatio, would add a pleasant tang to the winter's evenings in the library over a glass of brandy. Snells would like that too . . . it would take years off his age.

Fiddlebee realised suddenly that he was outside his own house. He realised also that, as suddenly, his luckily-found acquaintance had disappeared, and although the Doctor looked both up and down the street he could see no sign of a portly and retreating figure.

He found his key and opened his front door. He felt very happy. Tomorrow evening he would give Snells the benefit of his great experience. He would advise him and the advice would be excellent.

He felt almost impatient for the next day.

. . . . . .

I will, because of that delicacy which I trust has, ere now, made itself obvious to my cultured readers—especially those of the more *particular* sex—forbear from recounting how, during the following weeks, Snells Dove-Mellifleur stained for ever the fair *escutcheon* of his family by sneaking out into the hall every evening, meeting the postman, hobbling back to the library and, in company with Doctor Fiddlebee, steaming open the typewritten letters which arrived for Honoria with unfailing regularity.

An investigation, quietly conducted, had confirmed that the Doctor's theory was correct; that Honoria was typewriting the letters to herself. Snells, snooping about the neighbourhood, had unearthed the fact that Honoria had purchased from

Bendix the stationer a second-hand typewriter. Bendix was able to identify the instrument by the fact that the "A" was out of and above the true alignment, the "R" had the tail broken off and the "B" was set at an angle and slightly below the alignment. These discrepancies appeared in all the letters to Honoria, so there was no doubt about the matter.

Once the letters were steamed open, they were read, re-sealed quickly and put back in the hall for Honoria. Then the precious pair of conspirators, forgetting all delicacy of feeling, all virtue of breeding, in fact each and every manly, fatherly and medical quality, would, over four fingers of Blutops Blue Seal Rare and Tawny, chuckle and tee-hee for hours over the slightly exaggerated expression of affection which characterised some of the more urgent paragraphs of Honoria's amorous correspondence.

Each week the tone of the missives became more ardent, each month added lustre to the peculiar and amazing technique possessed by the writer of these letters. Holding his sides with suppressed laughter, Snells was forced to admit that Honoria had a lively and winsome imagination not entirely unlike that of her mother.

So the weeks passed, until one February night Snells, having purloined from the post-box in the hall the latest letter for his daughter, brought it back to the library and the waiting Horatio, steamed it open and, with the learned Doctor peering over his shoulder, read with joy and tears of laughter streaming down his face, the latest effusion.

The letter, which was as usual typed on blue notepaper with the violet-ribboned typewriter, bearing all the defects in lettering made plain by Bendix the stationer, expressed clearly that the time had come when Honoria must at once marry the writer.

I will not state exactly what the wording implied, but it made it clear that for the sake of the Dove-Mellifleur family, for the sake of Snells and for the sake of Honoria herself, the marriage must take place immediately and before an urgent and delicate *contretemps*, which the writer suggested would be due about June, took place.

Of Honoria Dove-Mellifleur

When the letter was re-sealed and back in its place in the hall, Snells and the Doctor, sitting opposite each other, were unable to speak for a good five minutes so convulsed with mirth were they.

"Did I not tell you so, my dear Snells," said the Doctor gleefully. "Did I not say that Honoria would allow this theoretical love-affair to progress to its true conclusion? And therein lies its charm. She has now hypnotised herself into the belief that there *is actually* some individual in love with her. She has written so many of these letters to herself that she must now, perforce, bring the *affaire* to its logical conclusion and suggest —as she does in this last letter—that . . . ahum . . . a quick marriage would be the best thing for everyone.

"In fact," continued the Doctor, leaning forward and wagging a fat forefinger at Snells, "I should not be at all surprised if she did not inform you that she proposes to take a trip abroad for a few months, there to experience, in her mind, the natural conclusion of her entirely unpractical and mentally clandestine association with this non-existent lover of hers."

Snells nodded. He could not speak for mirth.

"And," continued the Doctor seriously, "if she does, then you must agree. Not by any word or gesture must you allow her to think that we are aware of her pretty self-deception. It might affect her strongly. It might even unhinge her mind. You must allow her to believe in the *rôle* she is playing for which she has, apparently, so successfully cast herself."

And it was just as the clever Doctor prophesied. For, five days later, Honoria, delightful, trim and with a delicately mantling blush which Snells found entirely charming, presented herself one morning at Snells' desk in the library and informed him that she had come to the conclusion that she needed a change and that she desired above all things to go to Dieppe; that she would take with her Sophie Mulligatawny, her personal maid, and that her dear papa was not to worry about her because she would be quite safe and happy.

Snells, after a proper show of fatherly remonstrance and advice, allowed himself to be persuaded, and it was on the fourteenth of February 1891 that the carriage was brought to the door and Honoria, befurred for travelling, with the maid Sophie beside her, took an affectionate leave of her father.

When the carriage had driven off Snells returned to the library and over a morning glass of brandy, congratulated himself on the rare tact, the extreme parental feeling which he had shown to a daughter who, thanks to her own stupidity and his agile mentality—and that of his good friend Horatio Fiddlebee—was still unmarried and likely to be so.

.　　.　　.　　.　　.

On the following Sunday morning Doctor Horatio Fiddlebee received a note from Snells Dove-Mellifleur asking him to dine.

The Doctor was glad to go. First of all because the Dove-Mellifleur cook was good and roasted a joint in the manner which has since become a lost art, and secondly because he realised that Snells, with a mental licking of the lips, desired to review the whole of the Honoria correspondence and, assisted by the Doctor, to follow the mental processes of the lady throughout the history of her airy romance.

And so it was.

The beginning of their dinner was enlivened by many trite sayings, by nods and winks, chuckles and all those other gestures which even the most carefully brought up individuals adopt when discussing the more intimate business of their female relatives.

From the start the Doctor enjoyed his dinner. The soup was excellent—a strong consommé which was a speciality of Snells' cook. Then turbot with anchovy sauce and an excellent claret; then an entrée of cutlets and sautéd kidneys.

But it was when the roast appeared that both Snells and Horatio forgot Honoria for a moment and looked at each other in surprise.

For the beef was definitely not of the first class. It had that peculiar tang, that taste of stale tallow which associates itself with beef that has been hanging on the butcher's hook for too long a period.

"I must apologise for this beef," said Snells. "God knows what has happened to that damned Swaythe. During the last week or so I have complained time and time again about the quality of the meat he sends us. This roast is stringy . . . damme, Fiddlebee, it's more than stringy, it's sour!"

He pressed the bell and ordered the neat parlourmaid to ask the housekeeper to step into the dining-room.

When Mrs. Hinds appeared, covered in a certain confusion which invariably followed a summons to talk to Snells and a black glazed silk bombazine gown with a lace apron, Snells talked at length on the question of the meat. Mrs. Hinds listened attentively, her head slightly on one side, for she was inclined to deafness.

"I'm very sorry, of course, Sir," she said. "But I have carried your complaints to Swaythe. I went so far as to write him a note about it this morning."

"Hum . . ." said Snells. "And what did he say?"

"Mr. Swaythe himself said nothing," said Mrs. Hinds primly. "It's my belief, Sir, that he leaves much too much to that assistant of his. There was a time," continued Mrs. Hinds sternly, "when a complaint from me would have merited the attention of Mr. Swaythe himself. This afternoon the assistant wrote me a note which, Sir, while it apologised for the lack of quality in the meat we have had lately, lacked a great deal of the gratitude for past favours and further orders that Mr. Swaythe was careful to insert in any letter he wrote to me."

Mrs. Hinds sniffed audibly.

"Damme . . ." said Snells. "An upstart butcher, eh? I'll deal with Swaythe, Mrs. Hinds. Bring me his letter, will you? I would like to read it. I'll write to Swaythe myself . . . damme!"

It was but a few minutes before Mrs. Hinds returned with the letter from the butcher's. The offending roast had been removed and more cutlets ordered.

Snells, busy in the act of pouring out a glass of wine, did not look at the letter which Mrs. Hinds laid down at his elbow until she had left the room.

Then he glanced down.

From the other side of the table, Doctor Fiddlebee, following the direction of Snells' look, focused his own eyes upon the letter of apology from the butcher's shop, and the fork which was on its way to his mouth fell, with a resonant smack, upon the table.

Fiddlebee sprang to his feet and hurried round the long table, for everything about Snells Dove-Mellifleur—his attitude, expression, the colour of his face—*everything*, I repeat, prophesied apoplexy.

And as he fumbled to release the tight cravat that Snells always affected in the evening, the Doctor had time to read the letter, to discover what it was that had, in such a devastating manner, nearly strangled his friend.

He saw, with eyes that bulged from his head, that the letter of apology from the butcher's was typewritten upon blue paper with a violet ribbon. More, he noticed certain irregularities in the typewriting. He saw that the "A" was out of and above the alignment, the "R" had the tail broken off, and the "B" was set at an angle slightly below the true alignment. He saw that it was signed "Lambert Whelks."

.   .   .   .   .

"Good God!" said the Doctor.

But without any appreciable effect.

.   .   .   .   .

Nota Bene: I know that the more particular of my kind readers will be comforted to know that the records of the British Consul at Dieppe show that on the 1st March 1891, Miss Honoria Dove-Mellifleur, only daughter of Snells Dove-Mellifleur Esq., was joined in holy wedlock to Mr. Lambert Whelks. Snells was unable to be present, having died of a seizure some days previously.

Of the Demise of Mr. Evelyn Sout

C onsider, ye philosophers, the diverse and, occasionally, astounding characteristics of moonlight. To
the uninitiated it is but moonlight, but to your true
sage the qualities of the moon's essences are as variable as the
colours of the rainbow.

There is the moonlight of damp evenings following upon a
hot day. A false and tricky light withal, and one under the
influence of which many a swain has committed those not-
quite-indicated *faux pas* which result in memories akin to
stomach ache.

There is the sickly light of the new moon when, we are told,
we must needs turn our money over—if we are possessed of
money; or, if we have no money, we may sleepily turn ourselves over and, if alone, dreamily consider the possibilities of
a more interesting future; or, if not alone, more seriously
consider whether we have met our obligations like little gentlemen, and console ourselves with the thought that we may do
better tomorrow night. In any event we shall eventually go to
sleep—which is something.

But, my gentles, there is that moonlight, that hard, pale
night light, born often in November, which shows us a street
in such a manner that we fail to recognise it; which shows us
love akin to the picture on the cover of a film magazine; which
shows us ourselves so unprettily that we are fain to rush to

some half-forgotten woman in order to be assured that we are still possessed of something which is possibly not worth having.

And, to my mind—in spite of the remarks of that silly wiseacre Mr. Polpwhistle, the Coroner—I am convinced that this moonlight was primarily responsible for the mysterious and too-early death of my half-brother, Mr. Evelyn Sout, who, in spite of the fact that he had twice borrowed my name in certain money-lending transactions—without mentioning the fact to me—and in spite of the fact that he had plotted the seduction (successfully I believe) of my third and youngest sister Prunella—the one with the mole on her ankle—was very dear to me for no particular reason that I can think of.

. . . . . .

Police Constable McCulloch, inevitably lucky, was the individual who chanced upon the body of Mr. Evelyn Sout, lying at the entrance of Goppins Mews, which, as everybody knows, is but two stones' throw from Berkeley Square.

It was evidenced by the Constable that Mr. Sout looked amazingly happy; that he was smiling, and that he looked like nothing so much as a sleeping child. So said McCulloch, and, in spite of the long and rambling discourse of Mr. Polpwhistle who had a liver and a wife who slept alone—which discourse (after the manner of Coroners) meant nothing at all, a verdict of Death from Causes Unknown was returned.

Had it been at all understood that the last act of Mr. Sout "before handing in his dinner pail"—as he himself would have put it—was to push the little crystal bottle, which Señor Ramones de Puerta y Bostolitos had given him, down an adjacent drain pipe, then indeed, the verdict might have been different. But the fact remains that even the great toxicologist employed—a man who had found poison on seventeen occasions when none existed—failed to find any trace of anything in the stomach of Mr. Sout except two and one half pints of bitter beer, about four pounds ten shillingsworth of champagne, and a brown bead from a rosary, which Mr. Sout had swallowed under the impression that it was a coffee bean.

Of the Demise of Mr. Evelyn Sout

There the matter ended. Everybody was happy, and nobody went into mourning except three hundred and forty-seven money-lenders, and a housemaid who was romantic and who had been kissed on the backstairs by Sout one night in error.

But I have no doubt that the eventual responsibility lies, lightly enough, upon Mr. Krasinsky, and upon the particularly cold and pale moonlight which functioned on the night before the constable found Mr. Sout.

Which is, I am sure, as it should be.

. . . . . .

To those people who would suggest that any element of fear entered into the condition of mind of Mr. Sout on the 21st night of November 1927, a contemptuous reply is indicated. Mr. Sout was afraid of nothing, he was simply uncomfortable.

From the moment when he took leave of his host in Church Gardens, and proceeded to walk in the direction of Cavendish Square, a feeling of untowardness had possessed him in no uncertain manner. Occasional glances, out of the corner of his eye, had, it seemed, revealed to him the stout and good-humoured figure, dressed unmistakably in shepherd's plaid and wearing a massive gold albert, to which figure, for some unknown reason, Sout found himself fitting the name of Krasinsky.

And there was little reason for discomfort. The night was fine and cold, and Mr. Sout was bored only as much as was usual. Certainly he found the somewhat peculiar light of the moon a little difficult, for he saw that it appeared to scintillate upon the pavement in a somewhat strange manner. Mr. Sout found himself inclined to indications of a climax.

But it was only when he saw himself in a passage which he knew did not exist that Sout definitely came to the conclusion that some influence, possibly not earthly, was at work. The passage had, apparently, appeared somewhere in the middle of Grosvenor Square. Whilst being entirely aware of the Square, Mr. Sout found himself enclosed, adequately enough, in this ancient and narrow passage, the walls of which, so old and crumbly were they, seemed hardly able to support the weight of the antique oil lamps which jutted out, one on each side.

Sout, with a sigh, sat down on a doorstep, and was glad to find that he could light a human cigarette with an entirely practical match. Opposite him, leaning good-humouredly against a shop which purported to be that of a sword sharpener, was Mr. Krasinsky.

It has already been said that Mr. Sout was aware, for some reason entirely unknown to himself, of the name of Mr. Krasinsky. But what is perhaps more strange is the fact that Sout seemed (in as vague a manner) to know Mr. Krasinsky. Had you asked him he would have been unable to tell you just when and how he had made the acquaintance of this gentleman. He would have had difficulty in remembering anything to do with the fat figure in the shepherd's plaid suit. Yet in some strange and rather mystic manner it appeared to Sout that he had always known Mr. Krasinsky, and he was utterly convinced, for some mysterious reason, that Mr. Krasinsky knew all about him even to the colour of his most secret thoughts.

One might almost go so far as to say that, to Sout, Krasinsky appeared as a reflection of his own personality or conscience or what will you. And beyond this feeling Sout would have been unable to give any adequate explanation for the amazing feeling of comfort and familiarity which the person of Mr. Krasinsky produced.

"Well," said Mr. Sout . . . . "Good evening. . . ."

Krasinsky blew his nose.

"And to you," he said cheerily. "It would seem," he continued, "that you are fully aware, my young friend, that the continuous career of opportunist seduction to which you have accustomed yourself must eventually come to an end. Like the gloss upon your immaculate shirt front, the forces of time must needs take the gilt off the gingerbread. However, feeling, as I have always done, for the necessary comfort of mind due to one of your attainments, I felt it incumbent to allow myself these few words with you in order that the manner of your passing might be excellently planned."

Mr. Sout inhaled.

"Death," he said with a sigh of relief, "appears to be in the vicinity. Mine?" he queried hopefully.

Krasinsky bowed.

"No less a person," said he.

He became a trifle more serious.

"Knowing your admiration for the artistic finish, which I have observed on so many occasions, I feel that you may care to allow yourself to help in the unravelling of a somewhat tangled skein," purred Krasinsky, "and, in any event, I have no doubt that a slight search in the bureau drawer at the Merys' house may help with indications . . ." his voice trailed away . . . "Goodnight, friend," said Mr. Krasinsky.

Sout became aware that he was leaning against the railings in the middle of Grosvenor Square. He was also, and very decidedly, aware that he had not been dreaming. Also, about his nostrils hovered the scent of Paula Merys' particular perfume. Sout grinned and wandered across the Square, somewhat heedlessly.

It was somewhere at the back of Wigmore Street that the encounter happened. Turning a corner, a lady ran into him. Mr. Sout was aware of a contradiction—a Spanish accent (to which he was partial) and a blonde woman.

"Madame," he said, "you appear distressed. Can I help?"

"Consider, Señor," she replied deliciously. "I am alone in my house, and my small tiger—such a dear when on the chain —has broken loose and has already devoured a joint, one kitten and the canary. It would appear that I need assistance."

Mr. Sout replaced his hat.

"It seems," he said, "that this encounter is one of those planned by a not unkindly fate. They tell me that my method with tigers is admirable."

Possibly because his mind was still remotely concerned with the business of the ancient passage in the middle of Grosvenor

Square and of the somewhat cold suggestion of death, Mr. Sout's usually rapid perceptions failed to function in their normal manner. He hardly noticed that the mansion to which she led him was dark, and, as far as could be seen, deserted. More, it possessed that weird and indefinable atmosphere that goes with old and uninhabited domiciles. However, he followed her from room to room, absently looking in the corners which she indicated, and still more absently considering abstract possibilities.

It was on the second floor, where the intimacy of bedrooms affected somewhat the outlook of Mr. Sout, that he became fully aware of the charm of the figure which he followed. She walked with a quick grace, and the fleeting glances which she gave him over her shoulder from time to time, betrayed an exquisite beauty.

Eventually, as they stood in the middle of the floor of the last room on the corridor, Sout took a grasp of the situation and recovered his usual technique.

"Madame," he said, "I am no longer very interested in this absent tiger. I perceive clearly that I adore your figure."

She sighed.

"I am so glad of that," she said. "Señor, I must confess to you that my small tiger is safe and asleep as usual in the basement. He was but an excuse. I felt the necessity of your acquaintance."

Mr. Sout smiled.

"Your candour is delightful," he murmured, and reached out for her.

. . . .

It was as a neighbouring clock struck two that Mr. Sout awoke. He became aware that the electric light had been switched on and also that a tall and unmistakably Spanish gentleman was leaning on the foot-rail of the bed regarding him with an expression distinguished by its lack of benignity. The Señora, smiling in the most charming manner, slept peacefully.

The Spanish gentleman sighed.

Of the Demise of Mr. Evelyn Sout

"Permit me to introduce myself," he said quietly. "I am Ramones de Puerta y Bostolitos, and I observe that you have not only dishonoured my bed but also that you are wearing the top half of my best pyjamas."

Mr. Sout yawned.

"Your perception is acute, Bostolitos," he said. "Continue, for I feel that you have more to say touching this matter."

The Señora, smiling in her sleep, endeavoured to bite the left ear of Mr. Sout.

"Of course," said Bostolitos, "it will be obvious that I shall demand complete satisfaction. Perhaps you will be good enough to accompany me into the library?"

With some difficulty Mr. Sout disengaged himself from the arms of the Señora.

"Certainly," he said. "Perhaps *you* will be good enough to lend me a dressing-gown?"

Bostolitos nodded amicably, and brought the dressing-gown. Then, with a final glance at the lady who still slept adorably, Sout followed the Spaniard into the library.

"It will be evident to you," said Bostolitos, with a charming smile, when they were seated before the fire, "that I must kill you. Much more so because I have a decided feeling that this business of my wife going out and getting people to help her find her tiger is on the increase. She has already secured the assistance, during the past week, of a fireman, a film actor, and a policeman who was afterwards discovered in an exhausted condition in the area. However, this is the first time that I have been enabled to surprise her almost in the act, so to speak, and I therefore take the opportunity of revenge. How will you die?"

Mr. Sout took an interest.

"Really I have no decided ideas on the subject," he said. He lit a cigarette. "Can you make a suggestion?"

"I can and will," answered Bostolitos in the most friendly manner. "I am possessed of a remarkably fine poison, one which is absolutely tasteless, and which leaves no trace whatsoever."

He went to a cabinet and returned with a small and prettily shaped bottle, which he handed to Mr. Sout.

"Here it is," he said smilingly.

Sout turned the bottle in his hands.

"If I might request a favour," he murmured, "I should feel indebted. I consider that this hour—I notice that it is half past two in the morning—is a bad time for poisoning oneself. It appears to me that death should obtain about seven when the milkmen are going their rounds. Therefore, with your permission, I will postpone my demise until that time."

"I am happy to agree," said Bostolitos. "I take it then that I have your word that you will take this poison at seven precisely."

"Exactly," he murmured. "Now, with your permission, I will find my clothes and go. My salutations to the Señora, please!"

Ten minutes later Mr. Sout walked, quickly for him, in the direction of Knightsbridge. It had been little matter, so far as he was concerned, whether he died at two o'clock or seven o'clock, but in his mind had appeared, suddenly, a picture of the passage in the middle of Grosvenor Square, this passage which did not exist, but where the happy Krasinsky had informed him that a search in the bureau drawer might be beneficial. It had occurred to Sout that to die without examining this drawer might be to leave unsatisfied a curiosity which was one of his remaining assets.

He stood before the door of Paula Merys' house regarding its polished panels with something near to affection. He had always considered that there was about this house an air of dignity, and it seemed rather a pity that this would be the last time he should pass through that door. With a shrug he dismissed the thought, and after some ten minutes of tintinnabulation succeeded in rousing the butler.

"Good morning, Pevons," said Mr. Sout. "A spot of burglary is indicated. I find it necessary to break open her ladyship's bureau."

Pevons smiled wearily.

Of the Demise of Mr. Evelyn Sout

"Come in, Sir," he said. "Her ladyship is away, but I know that anything which you might do is quite in order."

He led the way upstairs.

Following the butler up the wide staircase, Sout found himself wondering where Paula Merys could be. That she was in London but a few hours before was a fact. However, the lady being of a like nature to Sout, it was not impossible that some wildcat scheme had suggested itself to her at or about the hour of midnight, when even the best people sometimes become subjugated by almost primeval instincts.

He had little difficulty in breaking open the bureau drawer, and stood regarding the mass of unnecessary oddments which a woman locks away. He ran his fingers through the pile, and withdrew his hand. A letter was caught in his fingers, a letter undistinguished except for the mediocrity of the notepaper and the handwriting thereon. Sout read a few lines, and then stopped. He jibbed rather at reading love letters—even the love letters of a country bumpkin.

He threw the letter back into the drawer, closed and locked it. Pevons, used by long service with Paula Merys to anything, waited patiently in the background. It seemed very definite to Pevons that something might happen, for he observed that Sout's mouth was twitching a little; that he was looking just as he had looked some two years ago when—as Pevons had discreetly described downstairs—there had been a few words between her ladyship and Mr. Sout.

Sout, for once somewhat undecided, considered the situation. He had controlled the twitching of his mouth, and found himself wondering why he had been foolish enough to be taken off his guard for one moment simply because she had aspired to an excursion into mediocrity.

He sat down. Pevons placed a tray somewhere near him and poured out a whisky and soda. Holding the glass in his hand, looking at it and not seeing it, Sout realised that, in any event, the laugh 'was on him'. *He* had started this damned silly adventure at Chobleigh; had found it necessary to try his amorous technique on some fool of a farm girl simply because it had occurred to him in those days—how far off they seemed—that it might annoy Paula. That was what the scene had been about. He remembered her, clearly, vividly, asking him to consider the feelings of the girl's swain . . . the poor bumpkin. Sout roared with laughter. He knew, quite certainly, just as certainly as if God or Mr. Krasinsky had told him, that Paula Merys was at this moment either with or on her way to the said swain—the uncouth idiot whose elementary effort at penmanship lay in the drawer. . . .

Sout came back to himself. Once more he found himself thinking of the passage in the middle of Grosvenor Square . . . of Krasinsky. Krasinsky had intended him to read the letter . . . some odd words came back . . . "the unravelling of a somewhat tangled skein. . . ." He drank the whisky and got up.

"Pevons," he asked quietly, "where might her ladyship be?"

Pevons regarded his finger nails.

"I do not know, Sir," he said.

Sout helped himself to a cigarette.

"Consider, Pevons," he said amicably. "It is not my habit to ask questions. More especially as I know that you are inevitably aware of your mistress's movements for the sole purpose of keeping the information to yourself. However, I must know. Where is she?"

Pevons coughed.

"Mr. Sout . . . Sir," he murmured. . . . "I really couldn't. . . . I couldn't."

"Pevons," said Sout. "This is a matter of life and death . . ." he smiled . . . "it is certainly a matter of death, my good Pevons," said Mr. Sout.

Pevons looked up. He was a man of experience, such experience as only service in families who can afford to do what they do not like can bring. He observed that the face of Mr. Sout was somewhat grim, and that a tiny bead of sweat poised itself on the right-hand side of Mr. Sout's brow. Pevons concluded that something had gone wrong.

"Her ladyship is at the Goat Inn at Yellerton, Sir," he said.

"Precisely," said Mr. Sout. "She met someone there . . . possibly, Pevons?"

Pevons coughed.

"There was a matter of telephoning, Sir. She took the light car. I ordered her room, Sir . . ." Pevons coughed again . . . "in the name of Mrs. Cannaught . . . a double room, Sir."

Sout smiled. So sweetly did he smile that Pevons was almost reassured.

"Excellent," he said. "You will be thanked for this. Pevons, I assure you that you have rendered adequate service to your employer. Where is the Stutz?"

"In the garage, Sir."

"Telephone Stands and tell him to bring it round. Then he can go back to bed. I'll drive myself. Ten minutes after I have left you will telephone the Goat Inn at Yellerton. You will speak to the night porter, you will inform him that he must immediately inform Mrs. Cannaught that a gentleman is on his way to see her on the most urgent business. I shall be there in forty minutes."

Pevons sighed.

"Yes, Sir," he said. "If I am asked for the name of the gentleman who is arriving, shall I give your name, Sir?"

Sout smiled.

"Certainly not," he said. Then he smiled more broadly. "Say *Mr.* Cannaught is arriving," said Mr. Sout.

Pevons inclined a hoary head and left the room. He walked slowly down to the telephone in the hall. He was most perturbed.

"My God!" said Pevons.

. . . .

The clock on the ancient church at Yellerton told Mr. Sout that it was fifteen minutes to four as the Stutz slid round into the courtyard of the Goat Inn. Sout, cold and bad-tempered, as a man may well be at that hour of the morning, realising that he had but three and a quarter hours to live, and a great deal to do in the time, jumped quickly from the car and entered the open door of the Inn.

Inside, in the hall, a drowsy boots half slept—propped most inadequately against the wall. Further back a tapering shoe, silhouetted against the flickering light of the hall fire, moved restlessly. The shoe was of green satin. Mr. Sout realised that Paula was waiting.

She rose from the depths of the armchair in which she had been ensconced and advanced to meet him. He was aware of a ravishing décolletée, a suggestion of perfume, but even more aware of the restlessness of spirit, the internal trouble of the mind which the proximity of this woman always brought. Her hair shone in the half light.

"Wake up and get some coffee, please," said Sout to the boots.

The man went off.

Sout moved to the fire. He was icy cold. After warming himself he turned to her.

"How charming you look," he said. "Tell me, was our yokel thrilled . . . did he appreciate . . .?"

She yawned prettily.

"Poor thing, he hadn't a chance," she said. "I allowed you to spoil his evening, Evelyn. I was aware that nothing but some matter of the greatest urgency could allow you to interfere so much with the advanced education of a young agriculturist. I have proof of that. Surely *nothing* could induce Mr. Sout to drive from London to Yellerton in a tail coat *sans* overcoat."

She leaned against the mantelpiece.

Sout stirred uneasily.

"Paula," he said. "You will realise that, given as I am to practical joking, there are moments when possibly my outlook might become serious. I am not drunk, I assure you, but strange things have happened this night. It became incumbent upon me to stop this obscenity with this ploughboy . . . ."

She laughed softly.

"Really," she murmured. "You realise . . ."

"I realise that I am possibly the cause," said Sout somewhat grimly. "I have no doubt that I shall eventually pay. However, be that as it may, you will return to town with me immediately. I shall drive you back just as soon as I have drunk the coffee which will presently arrive."

She yawned again, a deliberate yawn.

"Evelyn, you are wrong," she said smilingly. "Consider the feelings of my poor friend upstairs—so expectant—you know? Imagine him having negotiated himself into a pair of your pale grey crêpe-de-chine pyjamas (I was forced to borrow them, Evelyn—I felt he possessed only a nightshirt—possibly flannel), and then being left at the post. How inartistic . . . how could you, Evelyn? It would be cruelty to animals. You just couldn't do it."

Sout smiled.

"I could do anything tonight," he said. "And you will come back with me."

She saw that Mr. Sout's mouth was quite decided. She sat down and leaned back in the armchair.

He watched the shadows playing on her ankles. She stretched impertinently.

"Why, baby?" she asked.

He faced her. The head of sweat still poised on his forehead.

"Listen, Paula," he said. "I have been told tonight that some time the gilt must wear off the gingerbread. Your adventures must stop soon. This I feel was to be the last—this adventure which has not happened. In a month's time you marry, I believe, some fool of a man who is rich enough to buy you, fool enough to believe in you, to believe that the rumours—the half lies—are false. Come back with me now or I will make him believe that this, at least, is true."

She sighed.

"Oh, my sneaky Evelyn. What has come to you?"

He wiped his forehead.

"I am past caring," he said. "Get your wraps."

She laughed.

"Silly . . ." she murmured. "Do you think I could face the farmer's boy? Go get them for me."

Mr. Sout produced a smile and proceeded up the wide staircase. He entered the opened door in the corridor.

By the fire, glumly enough, sat Mr. Sout's silk pyjamas. Sout, passing quickly through the folding doors, caught up an armful of fur coat, bag and gloves from the room beyond. When he returned silk pyjamas was on his feet, his big blue eyes wide with questions.

By the door Mr. Sout halted and made a little bow.

"My friend," he said, "I congratulate you. The joys of anticipation without the sick headache of the anticlimax have been yours. Return to the farm. Your unsatisfaction will ensure a lifetime of most enviable curiosity. Goodnight!"

Silk pyjamas, from the window, saw the Stutz slide out into the high road. They found him crying in the morning.

Which is not entirely incomprehensible.

. . . . .

Mr. Sout, behind the steering wheel of the Stutz, was but dimly aware of the fur-wrapped, snuggled figure by his side. His thoughts, growing one might say more ephemeral, and certainly less earthly, with each mile which the car gobbled, were concerned solely with the carrying out of the dim idea which was becoming more apparent with each minute. The idea of providing an entirely new career for Paula Merys.

He was concerned only with the reclamation of this lady. For—although this may seem improbable to any who knew Evelyn Sout—the approach of his end was clarifying his brain to such a degree that he realised with the vision of the near dead that he loved her. To inform her of the proximity of his demise would be foolish. She would believe him tipsy, or at best engaged in one of the amusing episodes for which his career had been infamous.

Also, the fact that he was plotting something for her would be sufficient to set her against any scheme in the most marked manner.

Of the Demise of Mr. Evelyn Sout

A certain happiness came slowly to Sout. He began to see that much lay behind the chance meeting with the stout Krasinsky in the odd passage in the middle of Grosvenor Square. Krasinsky took new shape in the mind of Sout. He became a veritable ally.

It was so simple. Sout now realised with his newfound and almost clairvoyant intelligence that Paula loved him. He realised that they had loved each other for many years, but that the atmosphere and environment—the half cynical attempt, so fashionable in this 20th century, of getting the worst of life—had eluded any possibilities of this love coming to a charming fruition. They had been the children of their age, and they had also been the losers. Happily, he saw that, with luck, he might at least cut Paula's loss.

The first thing was the smashing of the ridiculous match which she had made with the bourgeois coalowner, who, with his bought title, his bought mansions, and his but lately acquired manners, was buying her as a fitting ending to a career of opportunism. But—and this was lucky—this enterprising Lord Easterbasin would have value for his money. Let him once know that Paula Merys had been the mistress of Sout (whom he hated with the hatred of a successful profiteer), and he would discard her with the despatch of one who could easily purchase some more fitting adjunct from the shopwindows where our saleable feminine aristocracy dwell.

And it needed but a telephone call. Sout thrilled at the idea of the telephone call. This would, effectively, make an end of the Easterbasin business. She would be furious of course, but her anger would be assuaged by the shock of Sout's immediate suicide, a shock which he felt would produce in her a new frame of mind and one which might easily lead to a more appropriate manner of life.

Also, he knew that his death would bring to her the realisation that she loved him. He knew this, and, almost subconsciously, connected the knowledge with Krasinsky.

He felt that these results would compensate him for the trouble which he had been put to on this important night. He could carry out his promise to Bostolitos and, at the same time, 'unravel the tangled skein' which the cheerful Krasinsky had suggested could do with a little disentanglement.

So that when the car stopped before the Knightsbridge house, Mr. Sout was humming a tune in the most cheerful manner.

He took her key and opened the door. Then, hat in hand, stood waiting for her to pass.

She smiled—a trifle wanly Sout thought. She was cold.

"I suppose, Evelyn," she said, "there will be an explanation at your convenience. There must be a joke in this somewhere, and I should like to enjoy it too."

Sout grinned.

"My dear," he said cheerily, "this is the best joke in the world. Tomorrow, I am certain, you will appreciate it. In the meantime, be happy."

"Do you want breakfast," she asked. She looked at her wrist. "It is five o'clock," she said.

"Is it?" smiled Mr. Sout. "Then, paradoxically enough, it is too late for me to breakfast. I have much to do in the next two hours, and my excitement over a certain climax at seven o'clock disturbs my appetite. Goodbye."

She made as if to hold up her mouth to be kissed, but retracted.

"No," she said. "I will not kiss you until I know the joke, my Evelyn."

Mr. Sout smiled and made a little bow. Then he turned on his heel, and made off rapidly.

She stood on the step, looking after him, for Mr. Sout walked as handsomely as any man.

.   .   .   .   .

Arrived at his rooms Sout bathed, shaved and changed his clothes. He was a little particular about the choice of a lounge suit. His man, Dort, aroused from slumber, wondered—if Dort *ever* wondered—what was afoot.

This business completed, Sout realised that it was near six o'clock, and time when a profiteer peer might, adequately enough, be aroused from slumber. Dort was sent off to get coffee, and his master, with a quiet smile, took off the telephone receiver. Mr. Sout was almost too happy.

He was surprised at the rapidity of the response, more surprised at the steady, brusque voice which answered him.

"Yes, who is it?"

Mr. Sout drawled.

"This is Sout," he said. "May I apologise for disturbing you at this early hour? That *is* Easterbasin, isn't it?"

"Yes, it is. And it isn't early. . . . I start work at five."

"Dear me. How nice for you," said Mr. Sout. "Easterbasin, I want to talk to you about your marriage. I'm interested in you, Easterbasin—you remind me of a strange fish. Possibly I dislike you, but I cannot allow you to marry Paula Merys."

Sout imagined the grin at the other end of the telephone.

"I don't see why I should discuss it with you," said Easterbasin, "but since we are discussing it, why?"

"Badly put, my Easterbasin," said Sout. "Badly put. Surely if you do not see why we should discuss it you should not ask me my objections. However, I will assuage your curiosity. The fact of the matter is briefly this. I think that you are entitled to a square deal, my Easterbasin. You have made lots of money you have agreed to pay an adequate price for the lady in question, but, my Easterbasin, she has sold you. Yes, indeed she has. Since your engagement there have been so many odd little affairs, not including, of course, myself, who, I think, might be regarded as what the housemaid calls a 'steady'. See?"

"I see," the voice was steady enough. "Are you lying, Sout?"

"Not at all," said Mr. Sout. "You see, I've come to the end of my tether. One can't go on for ever. I'm departing this life in about fifty-five minutes' time, and I sort of wanted to do somebody a decent turn before I went. . . . Understand?"

"Ah," said Easterbasin. . . . "I see, suicide . . . hum. . . . Yes, well, if you do it I'll believe you, and, by the way, you might send me a note first, just confirming what you've said."

Sout grinned.

"Certainly," he said. "You want something to show her. Something to indicate that you have reasons for desiring the cancellation of your contract. I'll send Dort round with it now, and I'll make it pretty strong too, Easterbasin—. I'll do you proud. By the way, why not marry Elizabeth Polfexen? She's awfully nice, old stock, and very hard up. Consider it."

"I will," answered Easterbasin. "Well, goodbye. Pleasant voyage. They tell me chloroform and prussic acid are very good."

"Thanks," said Sout. "I've got something better. Goodbye."

He hung up the receiver.

It was with a certain amount of humour that Sout wrote the letter to Easterbasin. He knew that it would be shown to Paula. Indeed, he wrote it for her especial benefit. Her adventures extending over the previous six months were set out at length and lost nothing by Sout's method of telling. He imagined her thoughts as she read it. Easterbasin would present her with the letter as a parting gift. Sout guessed that the merchant peer was not sorry to get out of his contract. He must have surmised things.

And the effect on Paula. That letter *and* Sout's suicide would provide an adequate shock for the lovely lady. She might do anything. But whatever she did he had no doubt that the atmosphere created by the whole business would suffice to make her shed her present attitude to life and to take things a little less amorously.

Sout sealed the letter, rang for Dort and sent him off with it.

This done, he lit a cigar and, putting Bostolitos' little bottle in his breast pocket, he went out.

It was ten minutes to seven when he wandered into Goppins Mews. Goppins Mews appealed to him. The sun was glinting prettily on the windows. Somewhere in the dairy that was in the Mews someone was singing and there was a cheery rattle of milk cans.

Mr. Sout sat down on the pavement and leaned against the wall. To his right was a drain pipe. Mr. Sout agreed to push

Bostolitos' bottle down this pipe after he had taken the draught. This would adequately close the matter so far as Bostolitos was concerned. He sat there, the bottle in his hand, looking at the sky.

A clock struck seven. On the last stroke Mr. Sout removed the silver stopper and drank. The stuff tasted good . . . he leaned back contented . . . the sunlight began to fade a little, and near by he could hear laughter . . . such adorable laughter. He found himself happier than ever before, and the faces which persisted through the fragrant mist which was enveloping him were laughing.

The face of Krasinsky loomed cheerfully, that of Bostolitos was pleasantly concerned, and Paula—how delicious—with such a very charming smile. . . .

Mr. Sout died.

EPISODE THREE

Of the Reclamation of Captain Kidd

༄

I

It was on the evening of the 22nd of June 1938, which, if
you care to remember, was one of the most delightful days
known to our unequal climate, that Mr. Julian Falange,
who had arrived only that afternoon from Paris by aeroplane,
considered it necessary to take a walk in the purlieus of Ridgemount Gardens.

And in case anyone should be unaware of the peculiar
atmosphere which existed—and which, in fact, still persists—
about that neighbourhood, I would point out that it is the only
place which still contains numerous Victorian ghosts in the
architectural line, the consideration of which—even although it
be unconscious—has been known to produce a certain placidity
of mind and a quietness of step and demeanour not particularly
noticeable in any other part of London.

First of all a word about Mr. Falange. He was tall and immaculate and slim. His clothes were well-cut and of that
peculiar quietness which is so obvious. Everything about Mr.
Falange was as it should be. His face was thin and dark but it
was of that thinness which is so very attractive to women—
whether they have husbands with plump countenances or not—
and the darkness of his face was not a darkness of colour but of
aspect. On examining the features of Mr. Falange carefully,

one could not fail to note that his complexion was, in fact, of a normal hue, but that a particularly saturnine expression which suited him very well gave the impression of darkness.

His eyes were of a dark brown, under black lashes. His hair was, of course, black, and his figure elegant. Mr. Falange walked in a manner that suggested he was possessed of great reserves of energy and which also indicated by its ease that he did not care particularly at that moment to use them.

His hands were delightfully contradictory inasmuch as the span from the wrist to the beginning of the fingers was long, but the length of the fingers themselves was short. So that the effect created by his hands was one of great artistry and still greater strength.

On the corner of Ridgemount Gardens, where it nears Tavistock Square, Mr. Falange stopped for a moment and bought a box of matches from a woman who was standing in the gutter. He gave her a florin and forgot to take the matches. He then continued walking in the direction of Russell Square and thence to Bedford Square, where he walked round and round with a certain lack of interest that betokened that his mind was elsewhere and that his own physical whereabouts meant very little to him.

As I think it necessary that the reader be acquainted with the condition of Mr. Falange's mind, I will state immediately that it was concerned with two ladies and a picture which he had viewed early that morning in the Lapellere Gallery in the Rue Henri Martin, in Paris.

For reasons which he could not quite elucidate, Mr. Falange found himself entwining, as it were, his memory of the picture[1] with that of the faces of the two ladies, of which I think it best to make an explanation now so that I do not fall into the error of confusing issues.

It must be stated that Mr. Falange was in love with both these ladies and whilst some of my readers may consider that such a

---

[1] *The picture that Falange had in mind was Gaston Arpallard's 'Monsieur Le Capitaine Kidd' done, in oils, from memory in 1703.*

process is impossible I would point out that it is my duty merely to record facts, and it was a fact that Mr. Falange loved them both.

I do not mean by this that—for instance—he loved one because he liked her mind or her manner of speech or her character or her eyes—and in this connection I would like to state that many a woman has found herself well-loved only because she possessed one such attribute—or her ankles. I mean that he loved them both—ardently (perhaps I should say passionately), with genius (the infinite capacity for taking pains) and absolutely comprehensively. When he was with one he remembered poignantly the other and loved her all the more for her absence, and when he was with them both, and this had happened on several occasions, he found himself wishing deeply that he could be alone with either of them—he did not mind which.

This explanation, however, does not dissolve any of the difficulties with which Mr. Falange found himself beset at this moment. There were other and more practical considerations to be contended with.

The first lady—the Comtesse Laienne de la Nuences—was of a description which is almost beyond the powers of a writer to reproduce.

She was tall and lissome and of the most exquisite figure. She was of an artistic[1] temperament, and radiated a certain purity of spirit which was as interesting as it was unexpected. She played several musical instruments and has, I believe, composed one or two very agreeable songs.

She was of a sweet disposition. She was especially generous in her mind, and she possessed that ability to charm anyone— even women—which is so seldom encountered in these days. Her voice was low, and when she spoke her words came very slowly, each one of them having its true pronunciation and cadence accentuated in the most delightful manner. One very

---

[1] *Samuel Kibitzer of Kolossal-Kibitzer Films offered her ten thousand dollars a week if she would discuss a film contract with him at supper one night. She accepted the offer of supper, and a week's salary, but for some reason never played in the production.*

famous diplomat—who was some years afterwards discovered in an empty beer cask in Vienna—it was supposed that he had committed suicide through love of her—said that when listening to her he forgot all the cares and worries of a mundane world and desired only to continue to hear that delicious voice with its ability to turn the most ordinary word into a veritable caress.

The Comtesse was thirty-one years of age, and lived near Paris with her husband, who whilst being some forty-two years her senior still took a bright and nearly ceaseless interest in her activities, and had sometimes interrupted a shoot at his place in the country to dash straight off to Paris to see just what she was doing at that moment without even stopping *en route*, at the château, to put his gun away.

It will be easy to understand therefore that the ardent nature of Mr. Falange, thrown into juxtaposition with such a charming personality, had reacted in the only way it could react. He adored the Comtesse. He had said that he would die for her. More, he had said that, if necessary, he would challenge the Count to a duel and kill him in order to gain possession of such an adorable creature.

The second lady who had created havoc in the heart and mind of Julian Falange was Mrs. Fernandina Drax-Pelisse, an Englishwoman of the most striking attainments and qualities.

At the age of seventeen Mrs. Drax-Pelisse—whom I will call Fernandina hereafter—had imagined herself deeply in love with an ensign in a regiment of Foot Guards. The young man, amused, and no doubt flattered at her effusion of temperament which was of course unknown to her parents who were very strict—had encouraged her in what he considered to be an innocent flirtation but which she took most seriously.

The result was stark drama. On his regiment being ordered to India and his departing without so much as a written good-bye, Fernandina had gone straight out and married an unemployed glass-blower who lived in Seven Dials giving a false age and name for the purpose.

It is true that she was soon afterwards rescued from this terrible *contretemps* by her parents, but there is no doubt that it left its mark upon her, for thereafter she was unable to look at a glass ornament without a delicate shudder.

Fernandina had been married three times after this. Her second marriage was to a half-pay Captain in the Navy, who, well-satisfied with her *dot*, had consented to overlook the glass-blowing episode. Her third marriage—three months after the death of the gallant Captain—to a man who used to look after sea-lions in a travelling circus, was the result of a quarrel with her father, and her fourth and presently existing marriage, made a few months after the death of her parents, was to a stockbroker who, whilst being very senior to his spouse, was well-supplied with this world's goods.

It will be seen by the observant reader that Fernandina's temperament was ardent even if it was concealed beneath a superbly poised exterior. She herself would say that although her marriages had been mixed in quality yet each one of them had contributed something to the making of her character and personality.

Her pretty method of pursing-up her lips and making a gentle hissing noise—much more delicious than it sounds—when affected was, one imagines, a legacy from her union with the hairy, but nevertheless skilled, artisan whose boast was that he could "blow a glass pot, jug, jar or bottle with any man in England"; her quite charming and rather nautical sway, when walking, was learned, it is believed, from the naval husband. Her supreme carriage and poise of the head was, there is no doubt, due to the happy months she spent watching sea-lions balancing balls on their noses before being issued with their well-earned modicum of salt fish.

And only her last marriage—the one to the stockbroker—seemed to have contributed little to her mental and physical make-up, and there is no doubt that her husband's devotion to the ticker tape, his continuous and suspicious watch on the market prices, a watch which, I regret to say, sometimes took in his wife's activities, had created in Fernandina a hidden yearning for the bigger, more active things of life. Let us face it—her last husband was killing her soul!

She was of middle height, well-rounded, but not *too* plump, and of the most charming and affectionate disposition imaginable. When her husband returned home suddenly, as he sometimes did, she would run to meet him in the hall and throwing her arms round his neck would not release him until she had heard the back door of the house close gently.

Her hair was of the most lovely shade of Titian red, and her superb complexion and ever-ready smile produced in the beholder a sensation of loveliness difficult to describe.

She was intellectual but never allowed this to be obvious to anyone, and it is said that more than one great man, faced with an important problem, had often hurried to take the advice—given in clear, cultured and lively tones—of Fernandina Drax-Pelisse.

Consider, if you please, the effect of these two vibrant and delightful personalities on a nature as ardent, as forceful, as weak and as reckless as that of Mr. Falange, who, by the way, had much more money than was good for him. Having done this, consider too the fact that early that morning he had received two notes—one from each of these ladies—each one asking him to visit the Lapellere Gallery and inspect the portrait of Captain Kidd because—as each lovely writer said in her own charming words—it was the living image of himself.

II

There was, at this time, in the neighbourhood of Bedford Square—it was on one of those little streets immediately opposite the British Museum—an Italian café owned by an olive-skinned individual by the name of Delgarati. It was a small and interesting place, often empty, but used by students and people with not much money to spare.

One was waited on at this place by the proprietor's daughter, an amply bosomed tight-waisted daughter of the south, whose flashing smile and brilliant teeth overcame the disadvantages of an overdone *escalope* or a table-knife whose acquaintance with the washbowl was of the slenderest.

It was at nine o'clock that Mr. Falange found himself outside this place and it was at that moment that he decided to go in and to read once again the letters from Laienne and Fernandina which had produced in him such a discomfort of mind.

He seated himself at the table in the farthest corner, ordered the coffee, and, taking the letters from his breast pocket, began to read the first, which bore the signature of Laienne. Looking at it he found himself wondering about the romance of modern travel which had permitted him, that morning, to stand regarding the portrait of Captain Kidd in the Gallery in the Rue Henri Martin, and which, this evening, separated from France and Laienne by the English Channel, to be seated in a little café in London. He thought that he had not, in his lifetime, allowed himself to be sufficiently romantic, that the fortune which had come into his possession when he was twenty-five had affected the medieval urgings of his mind, stilling the passionate ambitions to do this and that which had stayed with him during his earlier and poorer years.

He lit an expensive cigarette and leaned back. There was no one in the café, for the girl had gone downstairs into the basement after bringing his coffee. Falange began to think that it was an extraordinary thing that both Laienne and Fernandina—whose letters he had received in Paris that morning—should have both, at almost the same time, concluded that he ought to inspect the portrait of the buccaneer Kidd. Why had both these delightful women thought of Kidd and why did they connect the portrait in their minds with himself?

Of course he was very like Kidd. He had not failed to compare the saturnine expression, the hot eyes, the impression of thwarted yearning with which Arpallard, the artist, had imbued the portrait, with the memory of his own face which he saw each morning when shaving.

It was impossible not to note the similarity of contour of the two faces. The high cheekbones, the flexible inclination of the mouth—a mouth that could curve itself easily under the influence of some charming thought or set itself into the cruel straight line so indicative of the sadistic instinct—the well-shaped, correctly squared off chin, which aligned itself in the proper manner with the cut of the upper lips, the sensitive nostrils which could expand as easily at the nearness of a woman as at the spectacle of a batch of unfortunate captives walking the plank to fall, accompanied by the vulgar laughter of a buccaneer crew, into the hot and shark-infested Caribbean waters.

Mr. Falange gasped at the immensity of the thought that had come to him. The explanation was obvious. Both the ladies were interested in art; both of them had heard of, had seen, Arpallard's portrait, both of them had been struck with the unique similarity between the features of the pirate Captain and Mr. Falange, and both of them had straightway sat down and, taking pen in hand, had written at once to inform him of their discovery and to ask him to inspect the portrait for himself.

Falange forgot his coffee and concentrated on the letters, reading them with a new mentality. Laienne's letter, which he read first, breathed its usual warm wishes, touched on the loneliness of the writer, deprecated the increasing gap between the minds of herself and the Comte, whose eccentricities were now becoming more boring than amusing, suggested that life would be easier and more interesting for a woman if it could be lived in an earlier century "when men were indeed men and inclined to take what they wanted. . . ." And then, after some more warm wishes and an expression of unhappiness at not having seen Falange for some time, "because of the controlled forcefulness of his personality which always brought to her the realisation of something lacking in her life . . ." indicated that he might find the inspection of the Kidd portrait amusing.

The letter concluded with the hope that she would see him soon and an intimation that she was suffering from a certain curiosity as to what circumstances would bring them together, whether these circumstances would be merely conventional or was it possible that something might suggest itself to him. . . .

Of the Reclamation of Captain Kidd

Mr. Falange put the letter back into his pocket and concentrated on the missive from Fernandina. The style was a little cooler, a shade more poised, but the sentiments expressed were akin to those of Laienne.

Fernandina spoke regretfully of the increasing calls which her husband's business affairs made on him, of the loneliness which must come upon a woman who could have no possible interest in the fluctuations of Associated Coconuts and Minerals. She mentioned the fact that she had found difficulty in sleeping well since she had last seen Mr. Falange and went on to say that this was no doubt due to her habit of lying awake at night and thinking about the more charming things of life.

She ended by regretting the passing of the days when convention could be spurned with advantage by those men who had carved for themselves reputations on land and on sea, whose forcefulness of character, whose essentially masculine instincts had planned for them the success of their campaigns and their affairs of the heart.

Then came the paragraph which said that the writer felt that Falange should visit the Lapellere Gallery and see the portrait of Kidd which, the letter went on, " . . . breathes a certain something that one cannot distinguish, but which produces in me the same feeling, the same tightening of the breath, the same quite attractive sense of *fear* that your own proximity brings . . . but perhaps it is wrong of me to say that. . . ."

Falange put Fernandina's letter with the other in his pocket. His mind went back to the Gallery and the cynical expression in the dark eyes of the pirate which had seemed to grow more strong as he gazed upon the portrait.

Falange found himself wondering about Kidd. It was of course true that Kidd had come to a bad end. He had been hanged on Execution Dock. But what experiences had been his before he had been sent kicking his heels at the end of the rope?

Was it not possible, thought Falange, that during the split second before the rope was stretched taut Kidd's mind, racing with the intensity of its last effort to remember, had run the gamut of all those adventures on the high seas, all the spoil and treasure, all the tastes of the strange liquors drunk in the hostels set behind the fringes of Tortuga and Hispaniola Islands?

What lovely ladies' faces had rushed pell-mell through the soon-to-die mind of the buccaneer . . . what delicious moments in carved oaken cabins set in the sterncastles of wicked sloops like Kidd's last ship, the sloop *Adventure*. . . .

Falange sat upright with a jerk. Was not this a coincidence of coincidences? Was it not strange that it was only at this moment that he had remembered that his own yacht at this moment, lying at Southampton, was called *Adventure*?

Here then was the explanation. Both Laienne and Fernandina had been struck with the same thought of him. Both of them, sick at heart, dismayed at the proximity of their too elderly husbands, both yearning for the adventure which life had withheld from them, had realised that in him, Julian Falange, there lay the same possibilities, the same forcefulness, the same cruelties, the same ability to grasp life by the throat and choke from it the desired sweetness, as were embodied in the resourceful mind and virile body of Monsieur Le Capitaine Kidd.

But he realised too that each one had been thinking only of herself. Laienne saw herself seized and carried off. . . . Fernandina saw *herself* seized and carried off. Neither of them realising that the truth of their theory lay in the fact that Captain Kidd would have carried them *both* off. . . .

Mr. Falange began to smile slowly. Strangely enough he began to smile in exactly the same manner as he imagined Captain Kidd would have smiled in like circumstances. Then he lit a cigarette.

He waited a minute to allow his idea to settle. He would of course have to think out details. But his mind was made up. Laienne desired to be carried off by force. She should be. So should Fernandina. Each of them would believe that her suggestion about the Kidd technique had reacted to her own advantage. Each of them would be amazed when she found that the other had also been spirited aboard *Adventure*, but they should not make this discovery, thought Falange, until they were in the Kidd atmosphere, until afar off lights of Hispaniola could be seen beneath the evening mist.

Then what would happen? Falange grinned cruelly. Having asked for Kidd and got Kidd, both of them would use every womanly artifice to escape from a situation which they would describe as villainous and love all the more because of that fact. Falange saw himself rolling from the forrard cabin where Fernandina would be incarcerated until she was "prepared to be reasonable", to the after state room where Laienne would pound upon the panels and, enthralled with a new found and wholly delightful fear, pray to be released.

He made up his mind that he would walk a little round Bedford Square which he found a quiet and restful place, and work out, at his leisure, the finer points in his plan of piracy.

Having done this he would telephone to the yard at Southampton and get them to prepare the *Adventure* for sea, after which he would send two wires, one for Laienne and one for Fernandina, giving them each a rendezvous to come aboard.

Each delightful lady would, on receipt of the wire, congratulate herself on her victory, would see the charming episode concluding in the (she would think) quiet divorce from her husband and a new lease of more exotic life as Mrs. Falange.

And of course each would be wrong. For, in due course, Falange would return them to their complaining spouses, who could rest content on the assumption (obvious to a gentleman) that each dear lady had been adequately chaperoned by the other.

He walked cheerfully in the direction of Bedford Square, his mind busy with interesting details. He found that life could be exhilarating, that he was not at all bored, that, on the contrary, he was extremely happy.

For, as he said to himself . . . "Mesdames, you want Captain Kidd, and by all the salt in the sea, you shall have him."

And, if this thought brought a cruel twist to his otherwise charming mouth, I am as certain as I have no doubt you are that both ladies would have preferred it so.

III

It was on the corner of Bedford Square and Bailey Street that Mr. Falange encountered Mr. Krasinsky, who was sitting on a wide door-step endeavouring to light the stub of a cigar with an ineffective match.

Falange, always good-mannered, supplied the deficiency with his lighter, and then, for a reason of which he was quite unaware, sat down on the step by the side of Mr. Krasinsky.

That one thanked him and blew a large puff of very sweet smelling smoke onto the night air. Falange noted that the night was appreciably warmer.

Without more ado Krasinsky began to speak. Falange, who loved softness in certain moods, was struck with the superb modulation of the voice to which he was listening.

"It was on such a night as this," said Krasinsky, "that an old friend of mine—a man of delightful if somewhat forcible and occasionally repellent attributes—I refer to no less a person than Captain William Kidd, who was, as you have doubtless heard, a famous buccaneer—took it upon himself to embark upon an adventure which, so foolhardy it was, led to his ultimate undoing, although that undoing was, it appeared, of his own wish.

"The fact that he was hanged meant nothing at all," continued Krasinsky, "because in those delightful days many a good man was hanged for the vaguest of reasons, none of which would, possibly, be considered adequate today. I have no doubt," he went on, "that had Kidd been the type of man to have committed *felo de se* he would have done so; as it was, it was much easier for him to return to England and present himself at Execution Dock with his neckerchief already arranged for the hands of the individual detailed to push him off the ladder."

Of the Reclamation of Captain Kidd

He took a pinch of snuff and paused for a moment.

"I believe," he went on, "that you are considering a trip to those waters on which Kidd was wont to sail?"

Falange smiled into the darkness.

"Yes," he said, "I am. I propose to emulate your late friend the pirate without securing any of the disadvantages under which he seemed to labour, such as the Execution Dock episode, which has always seemed to me a drab and untimely ending to such a glorious and adventurous career. However, it appears that Kidd thought it was worth it."

"Indeed he did," said Krasinsky. "It always appeared to me that he thought his career was worth just that particular ending."

Falange lit a cigarette.

"It seems to me, Sir," he said, "that you are an authority on the life—and death—of Captain Kidd. Strangely enough I was only this morning viewing Arpellard's portrait and thinking that, in appearance at any rate, the Captain was rather like myself."

"Precisely," said Krasinsky with a little smile. "I think that he was greatly akin to you in many things. In fact," he continued, "I would say that towards the end he found himself faced with very much the same collection of circumstances which seem to surround you at this moment. I think," said Krasinsky, his voice growing fainter and fainter, "I would like to tell you something that might be of help to you."

"I should love to listen to you, Sir," said Mr. Falange, "with one proviso, and that is that it is essential that I catch the midnight train to Southampton and that before I do so I despatch, from the station, two telegrams. But I shall be delighted to listen to you, providing I am able to do those two things without fail."

Krasinsky turned to him with a charming smile.

"Dear Mr. Falange," he said, "I would not stop you. Only would I tell you of the adventure which befell my good and very vital friend Kidd, an adventure that may have some bearing on your own mind."

Of the Reclamation of Captain Kidd

He turned his head towards the gardens in the middle of the Square, and Falange, following his gaze, was amazed to see the gardens begin to disappear. Krasinsky's voice grew fainter and more sweet. A smell of salt water—a suggestion of humid breeze came to Falange's mouth and nostrils. Before his widening eyes the houses, the lamp-posts, everything faded. . . .

.   .   .   .   .

The sun had sunk into the waves like a faded green cheese. Already the shadows were lapping at the side of the ship and the twilight hovered like violet velvet. The sultry heat of the afternoon, first giving place to a false promise of an evening breeze, had returned in a still pall that hung in the shrouds.

Kidd, fancy in plum velvet with fresh Mechlin lace at his throat and wrists, a bloodstain on his breeches, a fine Spanish cutlass in a silk baldrick, and silver buckles to his shoes, walked on the stern-quarter with the quick and angry step of a tiger. Time and time again he wiped his mouth—hot and acid from a draught of bitter wine—on a morsel of lace torn from a woman's gown that he used for a kerchief.

His face was dark and thin; his eyes, quick and bloodshot, gazed out over the still waters first towards Tortuga where the mist hung like a shroud, then back to where the new lit, flickering lights proclaimed the line of Hispaniola Island.

He muttered and cursed, his tongue flicking in and out like a snake's tongue, the high heels of his shoes tapping upon the deck.

Tom Senecal—a sweet pirate—come out of Bolt's Head on the Devon Coast, in a blue seaman's kilt and a soiled silken shirt, his head tied in a bandana like any Bahamas cut-throat, kicked his great seaboots athwart the wheel, grinning into the falling darkness with a crooked smile and black teeth like the devil on a feast day.

"Sink me an' burn me, Cap'n," he says, spitting into the sea. "I say that they have the heels of ye. As clean a pair as ever a fat son of a Spanish square-rumped carvel showed a sloop like

71

this, an' here we lay close-hauled, in an oven of sweat, waitin' on a ship that has run past us.

"Master Kidd," says he, still grinning, "the hands do say that this venture is the maddest that ever ye tried. They do say that the *Bonaventura* has run us past last night i' the mist, run past without lights, knowin'—an' how should she not—that this place is as thick with French pirates as Savannah flies on a dead man's carcass."

Kidd swung upon him, his eyes acid and glittering. He swore a fearful oath.

"The hands do say this and that," he growled bitterly. "These dogs of sea-lice do say that I am made a dolt by a fat Spaniard who could not sail under my stern if Saint Christopher himself blew his paunch dry to give her wind. Rot 'em," he roars. "Let them have a care o' themselves, the mangy mutineering gobs. Let 'em have care or by the blood upon my breeches I'll trice the rum-swilling jacks up by the thumbs from the yard-arm until their arms be longer than their guts. Let 'em remember 'tis a privateer this ship, with a letter of marque and me the Master with a commission under the Great Seal in my sea chest. . . ."

"Soft, Cap'n," says Senecal, his mouth more atwist. "Maybe the King will not like his name upon the commission when he sees it next. As for privateering, well, Master Kidd . . ." He hummed a little tune.

"Was it privateering," he says, "to sink the sloop *Windflower*, an' she under English colours last sennight? An' the women we took out of the *Marqueterie*—were they not English, and their husbands who walked the plank—mind ye not, Cap'n, how we wagered upon which one a shark would fancy first?

"Cap'n," says he, "the hands do say that we be a pirate ship, an' if ye be not the worst of us, then I was not born in a caul an' breeched on sailor's rum."

"Blast my lights and heart," says Kidd, "I'll be what I may as takes my fancy, but no scupper-rat shall have me by the tail, pirate or not. Let 'em mind their manners. . . ."

Of the Reclamation of Captain Kidd

From out of the waist of the ship came trolling the hoarse voices of Lim Ryles and John his brother.

> *"Ho sing of a quean in Plymouth Town . . .*
> *An' a sonsy rig was she,*
> *With eyes hot blue an' a tress of brown,*
> *For a salt gob from the sea.*
> *So haul in close for Plymouth Town*
> *For a sight o' jades like she.*

> *"O blow me a kiss from the north or the south*
> *An' a dram of Jamaica to stop up her mouth,*
> *O blow me . . ."*

Kidd dragged a pistolet from his gold-bound pocket and jumped for the quarter rail. Senecal saw the spark from the flint, heard the sharp cry from Lim Ryles as he fell by the mainmast.

"I'll have no songs aboard this scow," roars Kidd. "Blast my lights, shall I lay here waiting like any fool for a ship an' pray silence from a crew of loose-scuppered, drunken, roaring, bastard dogs of no account? Splice your mouths, ye sea-scabs, or by the shades of Hades I'll top 'em for you with a leaden slug."

Senecal's boots clattered to the quarter rail as Thomas Hayle dragged Lim Ryles to the side and cast him into the sea. His breast-bone and heart were smashed by Kidd's shot. John Ryles went off away muttering. . . .

Kidd spat upon the deck.

"Lay in to the coast, Tom Senecal," he cries in a sharp voice. "Catch what wind ye may an' lay in off Monte Christi. 'Sblood," he says, "I'll know whether I be a fool or not. I'll have 'em if I land an' drag 'em out of their husbands' arms."

Senecal cried out:

"Come up, ye lice," he roars. "All hands to stations. The Cap'n would go ashore an' see some fine ladies for ye. Round up there, you lazy sea-gobs. . . . Come away there."

He whistled through his fingers. Forward, the quartermaster,

Jabez Fauls, answered him shrilling upon his quartermaster's pipe for a wind.

Kidd passed into his cabin, crashing the door upon its iron heel. Senecal looked after him, then clattered down the port quarter stairs to the waist.

"Come up, my hearty sea-dog," he says to John Ryle, "an' if a shark eats his supper off your brother what care ye? An' you singin' of a Plymouth quean . . . sing now, blast ye," he roars.

His grin shone out like a lantern.

"This sloop *Adventure* is a ship o' song," he bellows. "Of warm blood, sweat, an' mangy cockroaches . . . so haul away, my merry jail-sweepings. This be a ship o' joy an' sweet Jamaica rum. So sing, my hearties, an' damn my liver, mop up the blood of that sweet sea-dog Lim Ryle who has departed from us with a lead slug in his middle.

"Into the scuppers with the red juice, my bonnies . . . haul away there. We be for the coast for a cargo of sweet rum an' ladies. Close-reef your breeches, ye sons of scuts, for there be fine furbelows comin' amongst ye. . . . Haul away O."

IV

The moon lay upon the water when Kidd put off in the long-boat. The sloop, close reefed, rode on a single anchor under the lee of Dead Man's Cay east by south-east of Tortuga.

Kidd sat in the stern sheets, his black brows frowning. By him sat Senecal whose mirthless grin flickered about his mouth. Five picked men were in the boat—all true pirates with years in the boucan trade behind them. Henry Glyss from Salop. William Bless and Gregory Mayliss from London Town, John Somers and John Delwer out of Devon, both with a price on their head for the killing of a King's Port Officer.

Each man had a Spanish musquetoon, a powder horn, twelve slugs, a cutlass and a sailor's knife. Senecal wore a trim hanger taken from the master of a French ship and a pair of pistols in his breeches waist.

Of the Reclamation of Captain Kidd

Kidd was freshly dressed. He wore black velvet and silver, Spanish seaboots, fine lace at his neck and wrists and a red feather in his hat. He had a gold-tilted Toledo hanger and a pistol in his sash. He carried his French pistolets one in each side pocket. They were loaded with a split ball to make a torn wound.

Kidd took a draught at the rum bottle and handed it to Senecal, who passed it round. Each man lay on his oar for a long swig, wiped his mouth with the back of his hand and spat into the sea.

"'Tis the sweet life," says Kidd. "I tell ye, Senecal, if I get these fine ladies aboard *Adventure*, 'tis five thousand Spanish dollars I'll get for each of 'em . . . an' get 'em I will. . . . Stap me," he says, "if we cut the throats out of their bridegrooms this night to get 'em, 'tis that shall be done. Haul away O."

"Aye, aye, sir," says Senecal. "'Tis the joy of a bridegroom to have his gullet slashed on a sonsy night like this be . . . and 'tis some sweet hanging for us an' maybe some drawing an' quartering with the breath still in us if King's ship lays in Hispaniola Water, waiting on us like a damned fat hold rat that smells a juicy corpse. Haul O, boys . . .!"

"Muffle your oars, ye dogs," says Kidd. "We be in the shallows by Christi Head. An' if ye must talk, speak in whispers. I would not have them know that Kidd's with 'em."

Senecal looked to the priming of his pistols.

"Where to when we land, Cap'n?" he says. "How will ye play this quarry? Is't the sudden shot through the casement an' grab what we may with the devil after the hindmost or will ye speak 'em fair?"

"Oars in and let her ride upon the water, boys!"

"I will speak 'em fair," says Kidd. "I will speak 'em like a dove on the yardarm on Christmas night. Such poetry will I quote 'em that they'll come to me like African love-birds with a dream of a fat worm . . . an' if it be no they say," he hisses. . . . "Well, rot me, I'll slash 'em and eat the hearts out of 'em like they tell of Morgan. . . ."

Senecal chuckled.

Of the Reclamation of Captain Kidd

"There was a pirate," he says. "There was a sea-gentleman for ye. . . . At Bahamas I was with him, Cap'n, the night we took the Shalot House. Rot me," he says, "but Morgan had the breeches off every man an' roasted 'em over their own fires till their sterns sizzled like fat capons . . . an' they made him knight for't. Sir Henry Morgan . . . ho . . . ho, my merries, 'tis a full span of rope at Execution Dock or the King's accolade, an' no man knows which may be his in this pirate trade."

The boat grounded upon the shingle. Kidd's eye, keen as an eagle's, scanned the beach that ran like a white ribbon around the island bounded at its top by the heavy palms.

"Harry Glyss," he says. "Make a long painter to the beach. Make it fast to the palm trunk yonder. Then stay at the beach top. If ye see aught fire your musket, run for the boat, and make away back. Bless, Mayliss, Somers and Delmer, take your muskets an' work round to the back o' the Skull Hostel. Stay quiet and come not in. Myself and you, Senecal, will go see Mistress Blackamoor at the Skull like any two quiet sailor-men with a thirst for good rum.

"There we shall drink and find where our cooing doves be lying. When we are gone from there ye four come after us, keeping in the shadows like ghosts. Let me not see ye or hear ye. Do ye mind me?"

"Aye," they said. "We mind ye, Cap'n."

Glyss got out of the boat and splashed through the water paying out the painter. Senecal, flopping over the side like a porpoise, waited on Kidd, his shoulders bent.

Kidd, standing in the stern sheets, mounted himself on Senecal's broad shoulders pick-a-back.

They splashed towards the shore.

There Kidd and Senecal waited until the five were gone, Harry Glyss to his post beneath the palms, where he stood leaning on his musket and chewing plug, the other four working eastward to the path through the trees leading to the back of the Skull Hostel.

Kidd took a pinch of snuff and flounced his neck lace with a scented handkerchief. Senecal stood, his feet apart, grinning like an ape at the moon.

"Come away," says Kidd, and marched off through the silver sand.

. . . . .

They stood beneath the palms. Away over the clearing, bright in the pale moonlight, the casements of the Skull Hostel stood open; through them—ever and anon—came a burst of drunken, roaring song.

Kidd put his hands in his breeches pockets and waited.

"How do they sing?" he says. "Be they King's men . . . hearken to the song . . .?"

Senecal, his head cocked on one side like a drunken parrot, listened for the next chorus. He looked at Kidd with a grin as from the open doorway came the refrain. . . .

> "*There was a man on Guana Cay . . .*
> *Ho there, my sweetheart . . .*
> *Who never moved by night nor day,*
> *Throw me a line, my sweetheart,*
> *With a noggin o' rum and a cask o' gin,*
> *With his eyes put out an' his skull stove in,*
> *An' the tide lays out an' the tide lays in,*
> *Ho there, my sweetheart. . . .*

> "*Ho give me a noggin of juniper gin,*
> *Ho there, my sweetheart. . . .*
> *An' the tide will wash me clean o' sin,*
> *Waitin' for my sweetheart. . . .*"

"Pirates, Cap'n," he says. . . . "'Tis a song of Morgan's. 'Tis the *Esmeralda* barque hands, Flint's boys."

Kidd looked at the moon. He stood there waiting, his back against a palm. Presently through the open doorway of the hostel came a sailor lurching across the clearing. As he staggered into the shadow of the palms, Senecal, quick as a cat, stepped softly behind him, seizing him by the arms, spread-eagling him. The man cursed drunkenly.

"'Sblood," he mutters, "'tis Kidd!"

Kidd smiled as sweet as a maid.

"The same, my hearty," he says, "an ye would live, speak fast. Yester e'en a Spanish carvel *Bonaventura* hauled in on Hispaniola Water. There were two fine gentlemen aboard with their ladies. Where be they now?"

Senecal released the man, who stood stupidly, his hands hanging by his side, a dribble of rum still in the corner of his mouth.

"They be at the Palisade House, Cap'n," he answered hoarsely. "Tomorrow they journey to the Fort at Santiado to join with their friends."

"Ha!" said Kidd, "an' who takes them?"

The man cocked his head towards the Skull Hostel.

"Flint," says he. "They ha' paid Flint five hundred crowns for safe escort."

Kidd nodded.

"An' Flint," he says, "an' the boys inside—what do they do?"

The man grinned feebly.

"Drunk as the devil," says he. "Flint took a ship but five days ago—a Frenchman bound for Puerta." He hiccoughed drunkenly. "We put the crew over the side," he says, "an' the sharks had 'em almost before they hit the water. Then we scuttled her. She sank out by Silver Bank—her mainmast showing still."

He hoisted his breeches.

"Goodnight, Cap'n," he says. "Watch out for Flint." He hiccoughed again. "He likes ye not an' still he fears ye like all the devils in hell."

Kidd looked again at the moon.

"I fain would trust ye, my hearty," he says, "but I fear me if I let ye loose you may talk to that sweet Cap'n of yours, whom I like not. So we'll quieten your mouth for you."

He stepped aside as his mate drove his knife into the back of the man's neck. Then, when Senecal had dragged the body into the bushes, he turned on his heel.

Of the Reclamation of Captain Kidd

"Come away," says Kidd. "This be an easy play. We'll take these cooing birds."

Senecal shrugged and wiped his knife upon his breeches' seat.

"An' Flint?" says he. "What will he do? He may not be so drunk, Cap'n, that he cannot cut us off ere we make back to the beach."

"No?" says Kidd. "Hearken to them—as drunk as paladins. Give me an hour an' we'll have our ladies as safe an' snug as ever in their lives."

He strode off through the palms towards the Palisade House, his hands in his breeches pockets, his head sunk into the lace at his throat. Two paces behind him, humming a bawdy song, came Senecal.

At the end of the palm fringe, where the white, sandy road led up towards the wooded foothills, waited Kidd's men, leaning upon their muskets. A quarter of a mile away to the east the lights of the Palisade House showed bright against the half darkness.

They straightened up as Kidd and Senecal came out from the thicket. A mile away to their left the soft breakers broke upon the white beach and the moon lay upon the sea like a silver dagger.

"Mind me now," says Kidd. "This thing is nothing so it be done right. Flint an' his crew are at the Skull as drunk as Plymouth sots. 'Twill take them a day to get their senses trim."

He took a snuff-box from his pocket and took a pinch daintily, flipping his lace cravat with his handkerchief.

"Work up behind the Palisade House," he says. "Be easy now an' do not sneeze nor snuffle. When ye come to the back of the house walk twenty paces. Two of you fire your muskets an' two your pistols. Then shout with all the oaths that come to ye an' make as if a fight is on. But while you shout, reload your pieces. Mind ye that.

"Flint hath made a bargain with these Spaniards," says he. "For five hundred Spanish crowns he gives them a safe passage to the Settlement Fort at Santiado, telling them that he is

79

the only pirate this side o' Hispaniola Island an' he being in their pay they think themselves sweetly safe from all.

"So when they hear the musketry an' the shouts they will straightly think 'tis some of Flint's crew in a drunken quarrel. An' as the din grows stronger they will, with such servants as they have about them, come out to ye, thinking to bid ye gone.

"Hold them in talk. Speak them fair for a little space. By this time we will have the women. Do ye mind me?"

"Aye, aye, Cap'n," they said.

"When a little time is passed they will come back into the Palisade House and find the women gone. Senecal will have them, bearing them back to the boat. Then march back as quickly as ye may, and wait upon the boat for me.

"Now get ye gone, an' the devil's luck go with you."

They went off. Kidd, with Senecal behind, walked towards the front of the house. They waited there, quiet, outside the wooden gate of the Palisade until from behind the house came the noise of muskets and drunken shouts. Then Kidd, picking his time, blew out the gate-lock with a pistol shot and walked towards the door.

Then more noise from the rear, more shots. Senecal, who had made his way round the side of the wooden building, ran back.

"They ha' gone out, Cap'n," he says. "Two Spaniards with much grey in their beards, an' lanterns, an' three serving men."

"'Tis well," Kidd replied. "Get ye behind the house, an' come back swiftly upon my whistle."

Senecal went off. Kidd walked to the entrance door and beat upon it with the butt of his pistol. In a minute it opened. In the hall, a lantern in her hand, stood a serving woman. Kidd pushed her aside, strode into the hall, crossed it and entered through the open door of the room on the far side.

The women rose from the supper table at which they had been seated. They were alone. Kidd swept off his hat and made a courtly bow. His eyes, glittering, came back to their faces.

They stood there, beautiful and cool. One, tall and raven-haired, looked at him with quiet and smiling eyes. The other, a short, sweet thing with flaxen hair and soft blue eyes, stood at her elbow.

"Señor Cavalier," says the raven lady in soft Spanish. "I am the Condesa Sophia Miratolos, and this lady, my cousin, the Señora Maria Aviera y Piras. Our husbands will be here in a little while. Till then be seated, Sir."

Kidd's eyes swept over them. He spoke fast in their own language.

"Ladies," says he. "I am Kidd ... perchance you have heard o' me. I have ta'en your husbands by a trick an' even now my men carry them back to my ship to hold them till a ransom be paid.

"What will ye do? Will ye come with them or will ye wait here, trusting yourselves, husbandless, to Flint and his measly crew o' sea scabs in the morning?"

"Oh, Sir," says the raven one. "I have heard much of pirates but I fear not you. You seem a courtly gentleman."

Her eyes scanned him from top to toe.

"Maria," she whispers, "we have a duty to our husbands. We must straightway join with them."

"Come quickly then," says Kidd. "For if we be not fast to the beach, Flint an' his crew may try a fight. So wait not for your cloaks, ladies. 'Tis a lovely night an' the soft breeze will not so much as stir your tresses or blow too harsh upon the beauty of your faces.

"Come away, I would not have Flint essay to earn his five hundred crowns by your protection, for if he does I will pistol both your husbands when the first shot be fired."

"La," says the flaxen Señora. "You are a hard pirate, Señor Captain, but I would not shorten the days of my husband—and they be not too many now—by so much as one."

Outside Kidd whistled. Senecal came running.

"Conduct these ladies to the boat," he says. "I will tarry here for a while. Ladies, this is my mate, Tom Senecal, who hath a name for courtesy and kindliness that is known in every port in the West Indian seas. Away with ye all."

Senecal, grinning at Kidd's grim jest, led them away. Kidd,

standing by the Palisade gate, watched the two women, with Senecal behind, gain the shelter of the palms. Turning, he walked quickly back to the house, his hands on his French pistolets in his side pockets.

The hall was in darkness. Presently he heard voices, then a door opening. Then the lanterns. Two gentlemen and three others came from the back of the house and went into the dining room. Kidd, pressed against the wall in the darkness, let them enter the room; then, as they stood wondering at its emptiness, and before the serving maid could speak, he came behind them, his pistols out.

"Señors," he said. "I am Kidd—a sea-gentleman of no sweet repute. This noise and musketry tonight was but a ruse, and by now your sweet ladies are already on their way to my ship under guard."

They stood looking at him. The Spaniards were of sixty years or so, and richly dressed. One spoke:

"Señor Kidd," he said. "Five hundred crowns have we paid to one Flint, a pirate upon this island, for safety and a guard tomorrow when we proceed to the Fort at Santiado. He will take this act harshly from one in his own trade."

Kidd laughed.

"Flint is no more than a yellow dog," he said. "A mangy cur who calls himself pirate when there is none there to say him nay!"

He put one pistol back in his pocket and poured himself a glass of wine from a decanter upon the table.

"Gentlemen," says he. "Ye will save time an' breath if ye do but list to me. I have your women an' they be sweet, fresh, young an' lovely—like I was told of them. Great luck for ye to win such wives, or maybe bought they were, with a dowry, in the fashion of your country.

"So ye shall pay another one for them. In three days' time I sail back here. If ye agree to what I do desire then ye will set a light—a red light—in the top room of this Palisade House on the third night. When I see this I will set off from my ship in the long boat with an armed crew an' your lady wives—

both without a hair o' their heads touched by so much as a pirate's hat feather.

"Ye shall await me on the beach with ten thousand Spanish crowns—five thousand for each wife—an' I will give 'em back to ye. Well, how say ye?"

The second husband spoke.

"Sir," says he, "I have heard tell of you that you be a swift and merciless pirate, and that a hundred ghosts do wait on you at night. How shall we know that you speak truth, and what will be our lot if we do not do your will?"

Kidd took another glass of wine and laughed.

"Sir," says he, "I have no need to lie. Here be five of ye. I have two pistols, one for each of ye, and your three servitors I will e'en kill with my hanger if need be."

He seized a bunch of grapes and pressed the dark fruit into his mouth, his eyes lively for a movement from any of the five.

"You will do my bidding," says he, "or by the Shades of Hell my crew shall throw the dice for your lady wives as is our custom with women—it being reckoned under the law of sea-gentlemen that women are booty and therefore to be shared under equal chance. An' when the crew be tired of 'em they can go over a plank an' a shark can woo 'em like many another pretty lady ere now.

"If ye say no I will pistol you both straightway."

The first Spaniard spoke.

"Sir," he says, "it shall be as you say. On the third night we shall, with our own efforts and with help from our friends at Santiado, give this money. We shall put the light in the casement for you to see. But I do entreat you that when you bring our newly-wed wives back to us they shall be unharmed, nor hurt in mind by coarse pirate talk, or other thing."

"'Tis well," says Kidd. "Ho," he roars, "I will bring 'em back to you as sweet an' singing as any love-birds—for ten thousand Spanish crowns. But, gentlemen, try no tricks with me. No ambuscades, no talk with Flint, or blast my lights your wives shall be mistresses to a drove of pirates. Goodnight to ye, sweet Señors!"

He came out of the fringe of palms upon the beach. In the moonlight the long boat showed dark, riding upon the water. Senecal stood at the painter's end, a pistol in his hand. In the sternsheets of the boat, Kidd, striding down the beach, could see the figures of the two ladies.

"Here be a pretty pair," he says to himself. "As sweet a pair o' women as ever I did see . . . 'tis almost a mortal sin to sell 'em back to such greybeards as they have for husbands."

"Lay on your oars," cried Senecal. "Here be the Cap'n."

Kidd sprang athwart Senecal's shoulders to save his feet being wetted. He got into the boat.

"Welcome, ladies," he says. "Lay on, my hearties, an' mind your song for we have sweet women with us. Haul away O. . . ."

"*O there was a quean in Plymouth Town . . .*" trolled Senecal, and the crew took up the song. The long boat crept over the placid water.

"Haul away, ye sea-scuts," cried Kidd. "Here be ten thousand crowns worth o' woman—sweet cargo for any pirate, an' when the sun be up Flint shall have news o' me. Pull hard, my hearties. . . ."

The moon went behind a cloud. Back in the Palisade House two courtly Spanish gentlemen, very grey in the beard, with inkhorn and parchment, wrote a fair list of their friends at Santiado setting against each man's name the sum they might beg or borrow for ransom for their wives.

v

Close hauled the *Adventure* sloop lay off the Silver Bank not a half mile from the spot where Flint's Frenchman showed six feet of mainmast.

The moon was full and glittered upon the water. Kidd, in a white satin waistcoat sewn with gold under a black velvet full-skirted coat, leaned against the stern-castle gallery rail, looking over the water, humming a tune.

He heard the sound of the main cabin door, set under the

gallery, as it shut. Then came soft steps beside him. Kidd turned to see the Condesa.

She wore a blue silk cloak thrown about her and over one shoulder. Her face was white and sweet in the moonlight. Her eyes, resting on Kidd, were soft and, he thought, unlike those of a captive held for ransom.

"Well, madame," says he, "an' have ye aught for complaint?" He smiled at her, showing his white teeth.

"Sir," she says, dropping him a mock curtsey. "Never have two ladies been so well kept by pirates."

She sighed.

Senecal in the mainmast shrouds searched the coast line with a long spyglass.

"Sir Captain," says the Condesa. "It is most strange that when a time comes for something hoped for one wants it not. Is it not strange that our hearts—mine and that of Maria, who even now weeps in our cabin—which were so stoutly set upon our return to our husbands on Hispaniola Island, now are heavy at the thought of leaving this brave ship, which three short days ago we had not even seen. . . . is it not stranger?"

"My faith," says Kidd. "It is not. This ship *Adventure* is a pretty ship, as fast as a whale in flight, an' a very devil for running under their sterns in a fight. Ten guns aside hath she an' two fine swivel guns. She is a pretty sloop i' faith."

She sighed again.

"Señor Captain," says she. "Out of the air comes love and when it comes it will not drive away. But three nights ago I hated you—and Maria too—hated you with all our hearts and minds, that you had taken us by that trick from our new husbands and our duties as their wives. Now, when we tell you that the thought of parting saddens us you talk to me of guns and pretty sloops."

"'Sblood, lady," says Kidd. "If ye are sad 'tis but because you like the ship. I too have felt sorrow at leaving a stout, swift ship to walk upon a sun baked island or to ride in a pannier cart or on some trotting mare."

He heard her little foot tapping upon the deck.

Of the Reclamation of Captain Kidd

"Señor Captain," says she. "Of all the fools in Christendom you are the greatest. Must you force my modesty to tell you that it is not this silly ship which hath us in its toils, not its mast nor its sails nor its guns?"

"'Odds blood," says Kidd. "What is this talk?"

"Sweet Kidd," says she. "Maria and I have not known your world. Brought up from infancy in a convent's close, we knew no man, no love until that day when our two husbands carried us away like bales of merchandise bought with a dowry welcome to our parents.

"Until three nights ago we had not seen a man except the greybeards of our fathers' houses. Then with the moonlight on the sand, with the wind sighing in the palm trees, with a splash of musketry and shouting, you came, taut, trim and straight, a cursing, hot-eyed man who worked his will on all who stood before him.

"By Saint Katherine," says she, "'tis sorry but 'tis very true that both Maria and I are set upon you so, upon your pistols and your cursing, your strange oaths, your sanguine crew, your rum, gin puncheons and your knives, your vagrant songs, your laughter and your whistling for a wind when no wind comes, that we do straightway say that we will stay aboard this sloop *Adventure* and be as sisters to you rather than go back to Hispaniola and our husbands."

"Now blast my lights," roars Kidd. "What's this? Sweet love aboard the sloop *Adventure*? 'Tis treason and 'tis mutiny. No woman should be in a pirate barque save she be in tears the whole day through and in the long night pursued from stem to stern by hungry pirates. Or else for ransom. Sisters forsooth!"

He turned away. There was a little sweat upon his forehead. She came close behind him.

"Sweet Pirate," says she. "You who are so apt for concealment, who hides his ship so cunning behind some jutting cape or rock to spring out upon unhappy prey, are now concealing nothing. An' if ye like us not as sisters, 'tis well. Let Maria be your sister. I would be more. . . ."

Of the Reclamation of Captain Kidd

"Hell's scuppers!" cried Kidd, like a mad lion. "Ho, Senecal there . . . does the light show?"

"Not so much as a flint's sparkle," says Senecal. "Not a whisper o' light."

"See . . ." whispered Sophia . . . "Sweet Kidd, our husbands want us not. There is no light. Set sail and haste away with us. You have but lost ten thousand crowns and gained a sweet family of women who will make life a song for you."

"Madame," says Kidd. "Have ye ta'en leave of your mind? I am but the master of this ship—a pirate ship, an' if ye stay aboard 'tis the law o' the sea that the crew as well as I must dice for ye. Get ye gone to your cabin . . . get ye gone. . . . Ho, Senecal! See ye the light?"

"Not so much as a twinkle," cries Senecal. "Not a whisper of a touchhole match."

She threw her arms about Kidd's neck. He, pressed hard against the sterncastle gallery, fought to free himself.

At last he tore himself away.

"Vixen," he mutters. "Away to your cabin . . . or by the splicing of the shrouds I'll set you in irons."

She threw him a deep curtsey.

"Sir Captain," says she, "I am your slave and willingly obey." She stood before him, looking into his eyes.

"You will not send me back, sweet Kidd," she whispers. "You will not break a lady's heart—and you a wicked pirate. . . . Goodnight to you, sweet Kidd . . . sweet pirate lord. . . ."

She tripped away.

Kidd swore an awful oath.

"Ho, Senecal!" he roars . . . "the light, in God's name is there no light?"

"Aye, Cap'n," cries Senecal. "There she shows . . . 'tis but this minute lit . . . all hands to stations, haul away, give her each inch of canvas, show a leg, carrion . . .?"

Kidd leapt to the waist and up into the shrouds like a monkey. He tore the spyglass from Senecal's hand and focused it upon the shore. There, he saw the ruddy light twinkling. He breathed a sigh of relief.

Senecal looked at him wryly.

"Faith, Cap'n," he says. "Mayhap ye ha' ta'en more aboard this ship than ever ye bargained to get."

He licked his lips.

"An' they be sonsy sweet wenches," he says. "'Tis a pity their husbands want 'em so, an' we with so much gold already in the ship."

Kidd went to the sterncastle and stood looking over the quiet waters.

The *Adventure*, with all canvas set, swung into a breath of breeze, the steersman, tacking for every catch of wind, started a song.

In the waist Senecal, leaning upon the bulwarks, his head cocked on one side, picking his teeth with a dagger point, watched Kidd, his eyes a'twinkle.

VI

Twelve men, heavily armed, manned the longboat as she crept towards the shore. In the sternsheets sat Kidd and Senecal —each with a pair of pistols, and the two ladies.

On the sandy beach stood the Spaniards, their beards marking them easily from Flint and forty more who stood beside them.

"Blast me, 'tis Flint is with 'em," says Senecal. "A trick . . . lay on your starboard oars, pull her round, boys!"

The longboat, drifting easily, lay thirty yards from the shore. Kidd stood in the sternsheets.

"Ho, Spaniards," he roars. "What trick is this? By my dam's lights and liver, Flint, if there be so much as a word out o' your queasy mouth I'll come ashore an' tear your heart out. What be this play?"

Flint came down to the water's edge.

"Ho . . . Cap'n Kidd," he yells. "This be no trick . . . no ambuscade. I want no trouble with you, Kidd. So put your pistols up. These gentlemen would speak with ye."

One of the Spaniards began to speak. His voice, weak and quavery, would not reach across the water to the boat.

"'Sblood," cried Kidd. "Will ye speak for him, Flint? He mouths like any sucking dove so that we hear nothing except the tremble in his guts. Speak ho . . .!"

"I'll tell ye all," sings out Flint. "These Spanish gentlemen say they have not the money to get back their women. Their friends at Santiado will not e'en put a clipt doubloon i' the hat for them . . . an' why? They ha' told them t'would be madness to buy back the women after they ha' been in your ship for three days an' three nights . . . their friends ha' told 'em stories of ye, Kidd . . . an' your ways with women. . . ."

"'Tis a foul lie," roars Kidd. "They ha' lain on my ship like any ladies in a convent. No man has touched 'em."

The Condesa Sophia arose and stood beside Kidd. She showed sweet and slim in the moonlight.

"He lies, dear husband mine," she cried dolorously. "What we have suffered from him in his pirate ship is not for words from me. Oh, my poor husband. . . . O my sweet lord. . . ."

Kidd, livid with anger, pulled her down.

"'Tis a foul lie," he roars . . . "a double-damned lie to keep me from ten thousand crowns. I'll land an' flay the lot o' ye!"

"Ho . . . ho . . . ho . . .!" roars Tom Senecal. "Saint Christopher be praised, here be a sweet lady who likes pirates. . . . Ho . . . ho . . . ho . . .!"

"Get ye back, Kidd," cries Flint. "They will ha' none of their wives now, an' you ha' done me wrong by your play of three nights since. And killed a man o' mine—one Jeremy Coggs—by a knife stab.

"Is this your method with a brother o' the sea? Well . . . I ha' John Downey's crew from the barque *Rockaway* that lies by Samana, an' I ha' Bindy Jones' sweet cut-throats from Yaqui—here ye see 'em, an' if ye land we'll hang ye as high as seven devils. . . . Get ye away, Kidd . . . get ye gone. . . ."

"Hell's torments," says Kidd. "That I should hear this talk from Flint."

He stirred Sophia with his foot.

"O lying jade," he says . . . "what ha' you done to me?"

She looked at him and laughed, her eyes shining. Maria, beside her, squeezed Senecal's arm gently in the dark.

"About boat," roars Senecal. "Haul away back, boys . . . with a long pull . . . haul away O. . . ."

He began to sing:

> "*There was a man on Guana Cay,*
> *Ho there my sweetheart. . . ."*

Kidd swore a fearful oath.

"I will ha' blood for this!" he says.

VII

The lantern swung on its chain from the roof of the stern-castle cabin. Kidd, his arms upon the table, a cup of strong wine in his hand, his wig awry, and one foot beating a tattoo upon the wooden floor, scowled across the board at Senecal.

The mate took a fat black grape and squeezed it into his mouth. He threw the empty skin over his shoulder.

"Here be a pass, Cap'n," says he. "Here be a pretty pass. The crew are laughin' at ye . . . they say that this is the drollest venture that ever they did see, with Flint promising you a halter, if ye land, and those two greybeards with sorry jowls tellin' ye they ha' not won the ransom for their wives.

"An' sweetest thing of all to hear that sonsy wench stand in the boat an' lie like any jade. . . . 'O what we have suffered from him in his pirate ship . . .' says she . . . 'Oh my poor husband. . . .' Hell's anchor an' the pair of 'em with not so much as a hand touch from a pirate's fingers, lyin' aboard like two sweet angels. Oh she's a sonsy wench."

He looked at Kidd, his eyes twinkling.

"Master Kidd," says he, "'tis the law o' sea-gentlemen that women taken are part o' the ship's booty, that they be diced for, an' that the winner can have 'em or sell 'em as he thinks best. The men say that this is the law an' that this shall be so."

"Ha . . ." says Kidd.

He swore a foul oath.

Of the Reclamation of Captain Kidd

Senecal shrugged his great shoulders.

"Cap'n," he says, "this is a mort o' trouble for ye. Mayhap these pretties be but Jonahs bringing ill-luck and mutiny on this ship. Put 'em over the side, says I, put 'em over in the jack-boat an' let two o' the boys set 'em back on Hispaniola. Then all will be well . . . if ye pay out the crew in Spanish Crowns for their share o' the women."

Kidd swore again, rose and strode from the cabin. Up the quarter galleyway he went. On the sterncastle, looking at the moon, laughing, stood the two women.

"Ladies," said Kidd, "you ha' ta'en it upon yourselves to mar my plans. Condesa, that lie ye told your husband sets you in jeopardy upon this ship, an' here ye stand laughing like two birds that know not that the huntsman is upon 'em. What say ye now?"

"La, sweet Kidd," says Sophia. "How easy is this thing. An our husbands had bought us back they would have paid ten thousand crowns for us. Is this not true?

"I hear you have great treasure in this ship. Well, is it not easy? Take ten thousand crowns from your store and pay your crew. Then we belong to you and to this sloop *Adventure*. With you we shall sail the seas and see the fighting, hear the clash of cutlasses, the roar of cannon. We shall see good ships strike their colours surrendering to you."

"Lady," says Kidd. "Not one split silver dollar would I pay for ye. I like ye not an' less since this last trick."

She came close to him.

"You lie, sweet pirate," says she. "For I have seen a light come in your eye on my approach that tells me there is something soft in your heart for your Sophia."

From out of the waist of the ship came a growl of voices. That of Martin Dills, from out of Gyra, came above the rest.

" 'Tis the law o' pirates," says Martin. "These women be fair booty o' the ship. Let Master Kidd then pay for 'em an he wants 'em or let us dice for 'em. An' 'tis the last I'm for. Each man aboard hath already five hundred crowns in treasure for his share in the hold. Let's have the women!"

Kidd leapt for the rail. Senecal, a pistol in his hand, came up beside him.

"Ye scum," roars Kidd. "Ye mutinous scabrous dogs. Sweepings from Plymouth offal-butts. Will ye give me orders!"

Old Mason, pirate, cook and carpenter spake up. His voice a silver quaver.

"Ho, Cap'n," he says. "'Tis the sea-gentlemen's law. We'll have it. Either the women or the money, which ye will; an' seein' that we have good store o' money let it be the women. Prithee, Cap'n, let it be the women!"

"Dogs," bellowed Kidd. "These ladies are my charge. I gave my word that no harm comes to them aboard *Adventure*. This word I keep although ye howl like all the dogs o' hell!"

"Easy . . . Master Kidd," says Senecal in a whisper, his mouth agrin. "Easy now. . . . They want but one spark, an' they'll have the ship from us. Speak 'em fair, Cap'n. Speak 'em sweet. . . ."

The Condesa Sophia came to the rail beside Kidd. Below, muttering, surging in the waist, the crew looked up and waited.

"Señor Captain," she hissed—her voice trembling like a husky flute, "I speak for myself and for my cousin Maria. We know the law of pirates. It is the law of all ships a'sail under the black flag that the crew shall throw dice for women taken as booty. We are two gentlewomen and we stand upon our rights. Either you pay these good pirates the ten thousand crowns for us, or they shall throw the dice for us. Make quick your choice or I will proclaim you as a false pirate and no sea-gentleman in every port in the West Indies."

A great cheer came from the crew.

"Here be a sonsy wench," cries Mason. "Here be sweet ladies o' quality with a mind to see a bargain proper kept."

"Blast my light," mutters Kidd. "This is no ship for an honest pirate who would be a gentleman to women. Vixen," he says to her, "you think to force my hand, to bend me to your will. Either I shall pay for ye an' keep ye close or ye'll make mutiny aboard my ship, knowing I will not give ye to those dogs as wagers.

"'Tis well," he roars. "Ho, Mate, give them the money. Take ten thousand crowns out of my store, let each man have his share. But scurvy dogs," he mutters to himself, "I will be revenged upon ye all for this. I will bring death and despair upon ye.

"Senecal," says he, "I have sailed upon these seas these seven years and men have feared my name. Now this sweet wench has made a mock o' me. Strutted before my crew and made a jeer o' Kidd. On Hispaniola, Flint makes greater mock and when this story goes its round there's not a rum shop in the Bahamas from Caya Coco to Samana Point that will not split its roof tree with foul mirth at me.

"Lock me these two sweet ladies in their cabin," says he. "Keep 'em close. Let no man look at 'em. I have a plan to cool their loving hearts. Hell's keel-bolts, I am dead wi' angry blood!"

"Goodnight, sweet Sir," says Sophia.

She threw a pretty curtsey to the deck, Marla with her. Their eyes were alight with laughter.

"Come away, wenches," says Senecal. "Come away. . . . Ye ha' done well this night . . . too well if I know aught."

VIII

The moon was full. *Adventure*, close-hauled to the wind, lay off Monte Christi. Kidd, moping in his cabin, strode up and down in silent rage.

He stopped his pacing as he heard the jack-boat come to the ship's side. In a minute, Senecal, his boots a'clatter, came in.

"I ha' seen 'em, Cap'n," says he. "I found 'em in the Palisade House at dinner. I have told 'em all."

"Ha . . ." says Kidd. "What then?"

"I spoke 'em fair," says Senecal, sitting upon a chest. "Says I . . . 'These women be as pure as doves, fair Señors. No man hath touched 'em an' they have wrought much trouble in Kidd's ship. He would be rid of 'em.'

"They shook their heads," says Senecal. "But when I did tell 'em that ye would pay with the women ten thousand Spanish crowns if they would take 'em back, then 'twas a different tale. The long an' the short o' this, they did agree. They'll take 'em an' I'm to land 'em from out the jack-boat, in the shallows by the Head, in one hour's time, with ten thousand golden boys in bags with 'em to make the bargain right."

"'Tis well," says Kidd. "Now list to me, Senecal, when ye do put these vixens in the boat with the ten thousand crowns, take with ye your own share of treasure that is stored aboard this ship. And come not back. Join up with Flint or Bindy Jones or any of the pirate crews that lay upon the coast."

"Splicings o' Hell," cried Senecal. "What is this? Ha' ye got madness come upon ye, Cap'n?"

Kidd shook his head.

"You ha' been good mate to me, Tom Senecal," he says. "But my mind is set. No longer can I sail upon these seas an' have bold sailors tremble at my sight. These lovely wenches have made mock o' me. There's not a ship in the Bahamas but will split to the keel with laughter at this tale of what two silly women did to Kidd.

"I sail for England on this very night," says he. "I ha' a wife in Plymouth whom I ha' not seen this seven years. I liked her not but after this mort o' trouble the very sight o' her will be like sweet English ale after the bitter wine o' this Sophia wench, the which has poisoned me an' split my crew."

"'Tis mad ye are," says Senecal. "Show but your nose in any English port an' they'll hang ye as high as a black pennant. They'll swing ye off Execution Dock as sure as my name's Senecal."

"Mayhap they will," says Kidd. "Then be it so. I have stood murder and a sinking ship; quelled quarrels in these isles, killed men and captured treasure. I will not be a mock for any man. Now get ye gone."

Senecal took a cup of wine and drained it.

"Cap'n," says he, "I am a faithful pirate an' I'll do what ye say. An any man shall make a mock o' you I'll split him to the middle and hang his heart upon a palm tree. Farewell, Master Kidd, Farewell, brave Cap'n!"

He strode away singing of the man on Guana Cay. Kidd heard him load the jack-boat, call the women.

IX

The jack-boat grounded in the shallows by Monte Christi Head.

Kidd, standing in the waist of the *Adventure* sloop, watched the lantern light as Senecal carried the boat's painter up the beach.

"This *Adventure* is no treasure ship," he muttered. "That jack-boat be the treasure ship. In her goes my store, my faithful mate, an' that sweet vixen who hath boarded me, ta'en me, sunk me like any cheap merchantman feared of any pirate."

He bawled:

"Set sail . . . bring her round . . . all hands to tend her. Come on, my bonnies, we be for England. Haul away . . . dogs!"

Catching the night breeze *Adventure* swung about. Kidd, in the sterncastle, his spyglass set upon the beach, saw Senecal's lantern, like a twinkling firefly, moving towards the palms. He watched the light.

•　　•　　•　　•　　•

Mr. Falange awoke with a start. He found himself looking across Bedford Square at a street lamp on the other side of the gardens which twinkled rather like a lantern. He yawned, wondered how it was that he came to be asleep on a door-step, and then remembered.

He got up and stretched. Mr. Krasinsky, still smoking his cigar butt, looked up at him, the kindliness shining in his eyes.

"I had a most extraordinary dream," said Falange, "I dreamed a most colourful episode in the life of Captain Kidd. The reason is, of course, obvious. We were talking about him."

"Precisely," said Krasinsky with a sigh. "It is possible that you dreamed of those odd circumstances which led to the return of Captain William Kidd to England and his eventual hanging on Execution Dock.

"But," he continued, rising and flipping the ash from his cigar, "I would be interested to know whether this dream of yours has, in any way, affected your own plans, dear Mr. Falange. You will remember you had an idea about two ladies . . . and your yacht *Adventure* . . . are you of the same mind now?"

Falange smiled into the darkness. Then he looked at his watch.

"Thank you for reminding me," he said. "It is twenty minutes to twelve. I have just time to get to Waterloo Station and to send off the wires before catching my train for Southampton.

"Good night, Mr. Krasinsky," he said.

He walked away into the darkness of the square.

Krasinsky addressed the moon.

"There is not the slightest doubt," he said cheerfully, "that history like everything else repeats itself almost monotonously."

He sighed and sat down again on the doorstep.

Driving down the Tottenham Court Road, in a taxi-cab, Mr. Falange thought adventurously of Laienne, of Fernandina and of the moon lying upon the still sea-waters like a silver dagger.

Of the Vengeance of Hyacinth Jones

ℭℳℳℭ

There comes a time on Winter afternoons when the brightness of the day takes on an aura of grey, afflicting certain people with a sadness associated with the twilight.

It was at such a time on a November afternoon that Mr. Lucien Grey (who believed that he was a poet) walked across that part of Hyde Park which presently becomes Kensington Gardens.

Mr. Grey found himself very unhappy. That this state is common to all poets is well known, but Lucien had additional reasons for his unhappiness; firstly, a matter of rent, which he was unable to pay, and secondly (and more urgently) over a matter of love—or lack of it; for Mr. Grey's nature vehemently desired love, but a love of a special kind; no ordinary love would serve.

She must be a lady of importance, and one on whom such adjectives as *svelte*, *soignée*, and *chic* could be hung. Also she must (of course) dress with an exquisite taste, and smell sweetly of a rare perfume when you approached near enough.

I have no doubt that the reader, being sophisticated, realises immediately the condition of mind of Mr. Grey. It is a mixture of ideals, magazine covers, loneliness, and a certain spiritual hunger common enough to youth which follows some artistic bent.

It must not be denied that Mr. Grey had looks. He was also distinctive in appearance, and his clothes hung well upon his slimness.

He sat down on a seat and regarded the emptiness of the Park about him. A little distance away he could hear the sound of motor horns and other business, and he reflected that the hour was approaching, when, if one had money with which to dine, one considered dressing for dinner. Mr. Grey proceeded to allow himself a dream (one which he used often) in which he saw himself, immaculately garbed, waiting at the foot of a staircase which was wide and imposing.

Soon, down the staircase towards him, came a beautiful lady. She was a picture of elegance and her grace in moving was, in the highest degree, seductive. As she neared the bottom of the staircase Mr. Grey saw himself turn away with a certain assumed diffidence, and he thought that she would pass him without a word. But she did not. She stopped suddenly, and, as Lucien half turned towards her, caught him by the hand. Her face (an oval of the most exquisite complexion) was strained, and her mouth (I have no words to describe the tremulous delicacy of her mouth) was trembling.

"Lucien," she murmured (her voice held a note of suppressed passion) . . . "Lucien, you cannot continue to treat me thus . . . flesh and blood cannot bear it. Adoring you as I do I can no longer endure your coldness. I must leave tomorrow morning, but I entreat you to endeavour to give me, at least, some sign of friendship, otherwise life will become insupportable."

Mr. Grey saw himself regard her with a (possible) softening of the hard lines about his mouth.

"Avara," he said firmly, "you must realise that friendship is useless to me. It must be all or nothing . . . and I object to nothing."

"*Dieu*," she breathed. (Why she should have breathed '*Dieu*', I do not know, but Mr. Grey did . . . probably she was French.) "*Dieu* . . . can it be that you love me a little . . . oh Lucien. . . ."

Mr. Grey did not reply to this immediately. Of course, he could have said with promptitude that he *did* love her, after which the whole business might have concluded with certain arrangements between the parties which (surely) would be of no interest to the reader. But no—Mr. Grey wanted his money's worth. After all, when such a woman tells one that she adores one, even if only in a dream, one must prolong the joy of anticipation—thus would Lucien have argued. And for this reason he proposed to hold things in abeyance for a while. So he withdrew his fingers gracefully from her palm, and leaned against the balustrade.

"I will not deny, Avara," he said, "that you stir me occasionally . . ." (Here, Mr. Grey wished that he had not used the word 'stir,' it made him feel rather like a cup of tea) . . . "No, I will not deny this . . . but you must understand . . . I am not as other men. . . ."

He sighed.

"Oh, my beloved," she whispered. "Is not that the reason for my love?"

She came nearer to him. The perfume she affected became obvious to Mr. Grey, and he felt that he was weakening.

"Lucien," she said, "can you bear to see me suffer thus? Have you no pity?"

Then Mr. Grey (who was sorely affected in this dream of his by the beauty, perfume and proximity of the lady, which last, in these petticoatless days, can be a very trying business), murmured something quite inaudible and crushed her in his arms.

They stood, their lips clinging, for a long time, until in fact Mr. Grey thought that he needed to breathe (he wondered why it is that women, when kissing, never seem to require breath), and for this reason, and also because of the sound of approaching footsteps, they released each other.

With a superb movement she regained her poise, and Lucien saw himself following her towards the dining-room, a slight and cynically humorous smile playing about the corners of his mouth.

.   .   .   .   .

Here Mr. Grey awakened from his dream because of a decided bump. He turned and saw that a newcomer had taken the far end of the seat. This newcomer Lucien had little difficulty in recognising as one Krasinsky, whose business it appeared was to be everywhere, and to know everything which happened, and a great deal which did not. Lucien wriggled a little uneasily for he was certain that the aforesaid Krasinsky would be cognisant of the dream which he had so rudely interrupted. In this supposition he was right, for, without further ado, that worthy began to hold forth:

"Consider, my Lucien," said Krasinsky, "that the things we most desire would appear to be entirely dependent upon our age. To you, the proximity of the lady whom you were, but a moment ago, embracing so ardently with your mind, was, I have no doubt, wholly delightful. At the same time I would like you to understand that twenty years hence your attitude towards such things will be one of extreme nonchalance and you will be all the more concerned with a cure for chronic indigestion, brought on, I have no doubt, by late suppers and aggravated by clandestine love affairs necessitating hurry at a time when a man should be deliberate."

Mr. Grey sneered. Men have a habit (a foolish one, I think) of sneering at Mr. Krasinsky.

"Why should I consider my state of mind in twenty years' time?" said he. "Krasinsky, you are a fool."

"Possibly," said Mr. Krasinsky. "Yet, having acquaintance with the minds of most men, I have found that these minds are, in the main, occupied with women. Things, in this respect, are as bad as ever, and civilization invariably brings with its train of appalling evils one good thing—a more rarefied atmosphere in the perpetual competition between wives and mistresses. Although why a wife should compete with a mistress I do not know; for the very necessity for competition would appear to prove that the wife has already lost what she possessed and has therefore nothing to gain. Her opportunity for competition should, surely, precede the appearance of the mistress, which is impossible, as in that event she would have nothing to compete with. So we see that in any event wives must perforce experience continuous connubial difficulties, their only hope being to be mistresses and wives simultaneously, which is a great strain on the imagination, but whereby they may possibly gain on the swings what they are like to lose on the roundabouts."

Here Mr. Krasinsky fumbled in his waistcoat pocket with a very white and plump forefinger and thumb and presently produced a pinch of snuff which he took with great equanimity and an absence of sneezing.

"This being so," he continued softly, "there can be no ideal of matrimony, which is a bad thing, for observation has shown me that the ideal is inevitably the only good thing about matrimony, the other attributes to the marital state being arguments about money and a disinclination to want to do things at the same moment.

"However," said Mr. Krasinsky (giving a crumb to a sparrow with great gentleness), "I do not wish to discuss these sorrowful things with you, but because I saw in your dream of some minutes ago an inclination for love I feel it my duty to tell you of the happenings which befell a young poet of my acquaintance some time ago, and which will doubtless prove to you how extremely bad it is for a man to get everything he wants, and how the only hope for happiness is to get nothing, in which case one is never worried as to what one should do with it after one has got it."

.   .   .   .   .   .

"Figure to yourself then, my dear Lucien," continued Krasinsky, "that my young friend and erstwhile companion, Hyacinth Jones, was, like yourself, a somewhat unsuccessful poet. This unsuccess he attributed to the stupidity of publishers in general and one in particular—a Mr. Verdant Pastures, upon whom my unfortunate Hyacinth had inflicted four hundred and sixty-three different stories, plays, novels, books of poetry, and other things, and of which the said Pastures had purchased but one effort, which was an article on how to dye white blouses pink with green ink which had been written (in a moment of despair) by Hyacinth's landlady, and had been included (with an unpaid laundry bill) in his bundle of manuscripts by mistake.

"Understand that he was not without a certain comeliness. He was a charming young man, and, in spite of the somewhat shabby condition of his clothes, possessed an air; for his mother had been a Lanruoye of Burgundy, whilst his father was a prepossessing commercial traveller with ways of his own, whose marriage with the noble lady had been unduly hastened or perhaps one should say made necessary by a slight *contretemps* which is no part of my story. He also possessed an extensive vocabulary and a quick brain. He suffered, however, from certain fits of depression which would descend upon him without warning and which reduced him almost to tears, and it was at these times (as with you, I think, my Lucien) that he urgently desired that intensive sympathy of a charming woman which alone can make a fit of depression worth while.

"It was on just such an evening as this that he was walking slowly across Bedford Square. He was depressed beyond endurance, two manuscripts having been returned to him that morning, and his landlady having informed him in a few well chosen and succinct words that unless his rent was forthcoming almost immediately, his room would be preferable to his presence.

"Candidly, his sense of humour, which had always been of the greatest use to him, was becoming slightly worn. His head was aching (due, no doubt, to absence of food) and he desired nothing so much as a feminine bosom on which he might weep gracefully. This desire, however, seemed to him likely to go ungratified.

"It was at this moment," said Mr. Krasinsky with a charming and reminiscent smile, "that he encountered me—quite by accident, so to speak, and in the same circumstances as obtained just now when *we* met.

" 'Ah, it is my Hyacinth,' said I, extending my hand. 'I am delighted to see you. I trust that things are progressing.'

" 'Damn you, Krasinsky,' said Hyacinth Jones with some heat. 'You know how things go with me. The only matter which remains for my contemplation is whether I shall presently walk over some convenient bridge into the river, or whether I shall use my braces to hang myself with. I would die, being absolutely sick of this too appalling existence.'

" 'You are, as usual, entirely wrong, my delightful friend,' I told him. 'For I think that you are upon the threshold of a somewhat staggering experience. Also, be good enough to remember that courage is not always (in spite of the dialectics of the effulgent Napoleon) associated with an overfull stomach. The things which you find so necessary are not so distant as you imagine, but whether you really require them, or whether you require only the desire for them is another matter. However, being yourself, with a little *aplomb* I am assured of your success. My benedictions.'

"And with these entirely cheering remarks, I disappeared—at least so far as he was aware, but from the position of vantage which I use on these occasions I watched him very carefully, mainly I believe in order that today I should be able to give *you* the benefit of his experience.

"Hyacinth, with something that sounded like a curse or a sob, crossed the road to the pavement which runs on the left hand side of the Square. His eyes were cast down upon the ground before him; his head, now aching so badly that it seemed made of lead, hung heavily upon his shoulders. Suddenly he looked up and stood, petrified, and trembling with a feeling so delicious that it seemed almost unendurable.

"A few yards away a large car faced him. It was unattended, the chauffeur having, evidently, been despatched upon some errand. The interior of the car was lit by some soft light, and reclining against a purple cushion was a lady.

"She possessed," Krasinsky continued, giving another crumb to the sparrow which was now affectionately perched upon his left knee, "a beauty so entirely mysterious that it would be foolish for me to endeavour to use the unworthy medium of words to describe it. But her appearance was of such wonder that Hyacinth's breath was stopped for quite two minutes.

" He stood for this time reluctantly considering moving away and thereby losing this lovely picture. Then, as he gazed, the lady (who was quite oblivious of his presence) made a movement to leave the car. She leaned forward and protruded a foot and ankle of great allurement in search of the step. Unfortunately, as she did so, she pulled the door toward her by mischance, and sinking backwards, found her foot imprisoned between the door and the frame.

" She gave a little cry which had hardly escaped her lips when Hyacinth was beside the car. He pulled back the door, freeing her foot, and knelt upon the step, a picture of concern, his hat in his hand.

" 'I am greatly indebted to you, sir,' she murmured.

"Hyacinth said nothing. Spellbound by a closer view of her beauty he was unable to speak. He knelt, gazing at her like one in a trance, and it was only when, under this prolonged scrutiny, a colour appeared in her cheeks, that he was able to find his tongue. He began to speak, but his own voice sounded strange to him, and the words which issued from his lips appeared to come of their own volition.

" 'Madame,' said he, 'understand that I adore you with a passion so intense that it appears to be strangling me. Your wonderful eyes have gazed at me out of a hundred dreams. Your mouth, of such seduction that the thought of kissing it qualifies me for a lunatic asylum, has been the one thing I have lived for. You will please understand that I realise how utterly impossible it is that you could ever reciprocate. I am a poor and unknown poet, whose only possessions are his dreams. But I have seen you, and now I can at least die with some semblance of satisfaction that my life has not been entirely misspent. For die I must. Life would be too execrably impossible should I continue living, knowing that you were in the same city, in the same country, in the same world, and that you were unattainable. I go to hang myself from the banisters with my best braces, which happily are white, thereby endowing my demise

with an air of unmistakable purity. My last thoughts shall be
of you. Adieu, Madame,' quoth Hyacinth, the tears rolling
down his cheeks. 'Adieu. . . .'

" 'One moment, Sir,' she murmured, inhaling from a jewelled
smelling salts bottle. 'One moment . . . Am I to understand
that you consider death through love of me? Is there no
alternative?'

" 'None,' replied Hyacinth with sad determination. 'As you
cannot be mine there remains only death. Once more, adieu. . . .'

" 'I wish that you would not be in such a hurry,' she murmured faintly, having recourse once more to the jewelled
bottle. 'Will you be good enough to enter the car and to discuss this matter from a logical point of view?'

"Hyacinth obeyed. As she made room for him a breath of
the scent she wore made his brain reel. He sat, gazing before
him, unutterably lost in emotions too poignant for his
physique.

" 'It would appear, Sir,' she continued, 'that you intend
to place me in a situation of the utmost difficulty. Either I must
surrender myself to you (in which case *I* am undone), or you
will proceed to hang yourself (in which case *you* are undone)
and this last, I am assured, would cause me much mental
torture in the future. Indeed, I doubt whether I should be
able ever to forget it. It also appears that you are not entirely
unattractive, in fact I consider your eyes to be quite nice, and
I do not doubt that you possess other good points which might
be apparent at some future time. Also, I admire your modesty,
which sent you, post haste, to hang yourself before you even
permitted yourself to consider whether or not I might consent
to the first part of your proposition.'

"Hyacinth found himself almost senseless. Could it be that
this wonderful creature was agreeing to fall in love with him?
His voice trembled as he replied:

" 'Madame, I did not consider that you might possibly care
for me in such a short time. It did not seem feasible. . . .'

" 'It is not feasible,' she murmured. 'That is why the idea
is so attractive. However, I beg that you will allow me a little

time in which to consider this matter fully, and to make such arrangements as may be necessary. Will you therefore be good enough to write your name and address on the writing pad which is hanging on your left—there is a pencil attached— and I will give you my word that you shall hear from me tomorrow. In the meantime may I hope that your idea of suicide is absolutely dismissed?'

"Hyacinth, having written his name and the address of his garret on the pad with fingers which shook, managed, somehow to descend from the car, and stood, his hand upon the door, regarding her with eyes filled with such wonder that they looked as if they might burst at any moment.

" 'Madame,' said he, 'I cannot believe at this minute that all this has really happened. I feel that tomorrow I shall awake and find that I have but dreamed. Therefore I entreat you, if this be really true, that you will allow your letter to reach me in the early part of the morrow, as I feel that my sanity will last only till then.'

"She smiled. A tantalising, slow and delicious smile.

" 'You shall have my letter in the morning,' she said. 'In the meantime this may help you to remember that I really exist and that you have not dreamed.'

"She held towards him a tiny handkerchief.

"Hyacinth took it. Suddenly he became aware that the chauffeur was back in his seat. He bent over her hand, and in a moment found himself gazing at the rear lights of the car as it sped away."

. . . . .

"I do not consider that it would be at all good for you, my Lucien," continued Krasinsky, "for me to make you fully aware of the contents of the letter which my (possibly) lucky young friend Hyacinth received on the following morning from his lady (who by the way was the Comtesse Eriane de Meriacca—a place not far from Majorca, not unduly noted for love, garlic, and other strong condiments), but I will tell you that this missive was such that he almost expired in the most extreme paroxysms of delight. Neither do I propose to excite

your juvenile mentality with a description of his next meeting
with her, which took place on the same evening at a charming
flat near this very Park, which abode she used (I believe) as a
retreat from the mundane cares of this world, and as a place for
the due consideration (in appropriate quietness) of those things
which are so essential to the well-being of any right thinking
lady. Let it suffice that under the guidance of her inspiration
the soul of my friend Hyacinth assumed such Brobdignagian
proportions that it became almost too big for his convenience.

"He commenced to write in the most exquisite manner. At
first he found difficulty in finding a vehicle for the charming
thoughts which continuously assailed him, but eventually, at
the Countess' suggestion, he wrote in that intimate style (so
popular with our too-journalistic aristocracy when describing
the merits of somebody's face cream), the actual story of his
first meeting with the Countess, and having polished it to his
own and her complete satisfaction, took it, with a pardonable
assumption of success, to the publisher, Mr. Verdant Pastures.

"Mr. Pastures, who, I regret to say, suffered from an enlarged
liver, and who had, on that very morning, experienced a slight
disagreement with his spouse over a matter (entirely personal)
which he considered important, and she a nuisance, was not as
encouraging as Hyacinth had hoped.

"He perused the manuscript, and then sitting back in his chair
and gazing at Hyacinth in the offensive and superior manner
so dear to publishers, said:

" 'It is apparent to me, Mr. Jones, that something has happened to you which has, at last, enabled you to write coherently.
At the same time the incident described in this story is so
absolutely foolish that I fail to see how you can imagine that
a man of my intelligence would ever hope that the public
could believe it. Such an happening could not, in any
circumstances, take place. It is not only impossible it is also
improbable. Take it away.'

" Hyacinth flushed.

" 'Mr. Pastures,' he said, 'I perceive clearly that you are a
fool. This happening, far from being impossible or improbable,

actually took place a short time ago, and has been the cause of the most excruciating happiness to me. I regret that your lack of imagination allows you to see no further than your too unsightly nose.'

" Mr. Pastures sneered.

" 'I do not believe you, Mr. Jones,' he said. 'Firstly because you are too provincial to speak the truth, and secondly because I do not believe that any lady possessing beauty worth consideration would be so short-sighted as to succumb to your entirely inexperienced charms. However, as I am a man of my word, and of the world, I should like to tell you that if you will arrange that this lady whom you so poetically describe, and who in the circumstances is surely interested in your artistic welfare, shall come to me and inform me personally that the incident is true, I give you my word that I will publish your story.'

"And with this retort and a leer which reminded Hyacinth of nothing so much as the hot glance of a lustful codfish. Mr. Pastures rang his bell and requested that the enraged poet be shown to the door.

"The hate which possessed the soul of the young lover could not be described. At first, the most charming blandishments administered by the Countess, to whom he rushed post haste with the tale of the perfidy of Pastures, were insufficient to assuage his appalling wrath, and it was only after continued effort on her part that he was eventually reduced to a state where he could tell her of the too impossible condition upon which the publisher had agreed to publish the story.

" 'Consider, my beloved,' said Hyacinth. 'Consider the terrible suggestion that I should allow you to go and inform this execrable Mormon that my story of our first meeting is true. Imagine my allowing you to talk to this beast whose Midas-like ears would flap with excitement. Consider . . .'

"But at this moment Hyacinth found his mouth most effectively stopped.

" 'My adored one,' said she, with that passionate intensity which he found so captivating, 'realise that your love having become superb, it is essential that your art should be of the same quality. Therefore you will please leave this matter to me, for I feel that with some thought I may solve this difficulty. In the meantime I would point out to you that you have not kissed me for sixteen seconds.'"

.   .   .   .   .

Krasinsky continued:

"It was two weeks after this," said he, "that my young friend experienced a great shock. Strolling one day in the Strand, he purchased a copy of the Pastures' Magazine—*Love in Idleness*—and was amazed to find, printed in the most effective manner, his story. A horrible, sickening fear seized at his heart. His brain reeled, and it was with the utmost difficulty that he staggered into a telephone box.

"In quivering tones he telephoned his mistress, the very sound of her voice intensifying his agony.

" 'Eriane . . .' he gasped, 'I have just observed that the beast Pastures has published my story. What does this mean . . . can it mean . . . does it mean . . . that you . . . that you . . . ?'

" 'Light of my soul,' she cooed, 'do not disturb yourself. It is true that I have gone so far as to inform Mr. Pastures that the incident so beautifully recorded by you, my beloved, was true. But do not distress yourself unduly. Walk quietly here, counting ten before using any really strong expressions. Do nothing immediately. You will be so much more reasonable in my arms.'

"Hyacinth hung up the receiver. Red lights danced before his eyes. The death of Pastures would alone suffice to right this business. But on second thoughts Hyacinth came to the conclusion that death would be too good. He hurried, running in his anxiety, to the Countess, thinking with intense passion of new methods by which the entrails of Pastures could be most slowly and painfully destroyed.

"Arrived, he gazed at her with tears of sorrow and pride coursing down his flushed cheeks.

" 'Adored one,' he said eventually, 'what can I say to you?

What admiration can I bestow on your wondrous courage which enabled you to do this thing for me and for my art. From you has come my first success. But at what a price! My soul shudders as I imagine you, blushingly, stammeringly, telling him . . . the words stumbling unwillingly from your tongue.

" 'Now I shall deal with him. Love and art are assured to me. There remains only the satisfaction of revenge to be desired. I shall kill this creature . . . in cold blood I shall suffocate him with his own blotting paper. I shall . . .'

" With a gesture she stopped him, and drawing him to her side, couched his head on that place intended by a beneficent Nature for its reception.

" 'Sweetheart,' she murmured, 'you do not desire revenge, because I assure you that you do not need it. Your vengeance is already satisfied. The unfortunate Pastures is dead. He died, most unwillingly, of apoplexy at breakfast on the morning when I told him that your story was true.

" 'You see, Beloved,' she continued with a caress, 'I forgot to tell you that Mr. Verdant Pastures was my husband. . . .' "

.   .   .   .   .

Mr. Krasinsky drew a fat cigar from his pocket, which he lit with gusto. The shadows were already thick upon the green sward of the Park.

Lucien Grey bestirred himself.

"What happened then, Krasinsky?" he asked.

Krasinsky yawned.

"Hyacinth married her," he answered, "and took over the publishing business of the deceased Pastures. I should have thought," continued Krasinsky with a small smile, "that this was obvious to you."

"Obvious to me," echoed Lucien.

Then a thought struck him.

"Heavens!" he exclaimed. "It is he! The appalling publisher who returns all my best work is named Hyacinth Jones! it is— it must be the same!"

"Exactly," murmured Krasinsky. "Precisely. . . . It was for this reason that I told you of this happening. History," ruminated Krasinsky, "would appear to repeat itself, and I happen to know that the Countess Eriane—his wife—will be visiting in Bedford Square about this hour. If, by any chance, you happened that way at this time . . . who knows . . ." murmured Mr. Krasinsky, "who knows? Surely anything might happen on a night of this description. . . ."

But the seat was empty at the far end. And Lucien Grey was already running, breathing quickly, in the direction of Bedford Square.

* * * * *

Krasinsky stretched himself and sighed. Then he rose from his seat, and wiping his mouth delicately with a suède glove which he produced from his waistcoat pocket, walked softly in the direction of some trees.

On a seat under these trees sat a young and unsuccessful poet, immersed in a dream. His name was Arnault d'Esperance, and he looked up with an annoyed expression as Krasinsky sat down with a bump.

"Consider, my Arnault," murmured Krasinsky reflectively, "consider . . . this dream of yours. . . ."

Of Perfume and Sudden Death

༺⁘⁘⁘༻

I

Those people who are interested in the meteorological influences on crime will know of the effect of bad weather upon potential criminals. Just as any young policeman with a year's service knows that it is upon wet and foggy nights that individuals, leaving the welcome shelter of the public house and experiencing the inclemency of the weather outside, proceed to fight upon the pavement on the slightest provocation; their numbers being as three to one compared with those on the days when the weather is dry and mild.

It may be considered therefore that the fact that the Christmas of 1927 produced much snow in England had something to do with the murder which took place in "The Cloisters" and which was known as the Perfumed Murder for reasons which will presently be obvious. "The Cloisters" was, I should explain, a short and attractive passage—since pulled down— in the neighbourhood of Gordon Square, not far from the University College Hall, at the end of which, turning the passageway into a *cul-de-sac*, was the charming two-story house occupied by one of the characters in the episode which I am about to relate.

It will be remembered that two days before Christmas the snow lay very thick in London, and it was at eight-thirty

Of Perfume and Sudden Death

o'clock in the evening that Mr. Everard Forsythe, who had eaten a light but satisfying dinner, left his apartment in Bedford Square for the purpose of keeping an appointment to talk to his friend Mr. Hugo Melander.

I have always believed that an expert writer is able to show by the *actions* of the characters in his story the mentality and psychiatric processes of the people who pass across his pages, but in this case doubting my own ability I propose, in order that the purpose of the visit of Everard Forsythe may be made plain, to show what was in his mind and to give some indication of the backgrounds of both himself and Hugo Melander.

These two were very good friends, but just what being good friends means to you or to me is a matter which only we ourselves know. In some friendships there exists a tinge of dislike, envy or jealousy, some secret mental reservation existing in the mind of one or other of the friends which introduces a humour of spite into an otherwise perfect friendship.

The fact remains that there had come upon Everard Forsythe, during the two weeks previous to this time, such an accumulation of small jealousies, worries and suspicions, that he had felt it necessary to arrange to discuss his feelings with Hugo Melander in order that this mildly malevolent aspect should be eradicated from their friendship.

They were both about the age of thirty-five, both good-looking and both sufficiently blessed with this world's goods not to have to worry about the more mundane aspects of existence.

Forsythe was a composer of sorts, best described as a good amateur. Some of his work had been successful, and I believe his "*Chanson Jeunesse*" gave great pleasure to many radio listeners during the years 1925 and 1926.

Hugo Melander was a poet, and I think a good one. He published his own work in slim green and gold volumes (privately subscribed), most of which seem strangely to have disappeared. I believe one of the few complete sets in existence at the present time is in my possession.

The essential difference between the two men was the peculiar and almost magnetic attraction which Melander possessed, and which seemed to Forsythe to have such an uncanny effect upon his women friends. This attraction may not truly have existed, because the majority of women who knew Melander were not inclined to discuss him intimately after the events which I am about to relate had happened. But the idea that he had this attraction was strong in Forsythe and was I have no doubt responsible for the jealousy which existed in his mind.

It is not suggested that Melander possessed any of the attributes of a Doctor Jekyll and Mr. Hyde. He was slim, charming and good-looking. He possessed a mentality of the first order, but there was a lurking cynicism in the twisted smile which he adopted on certain occasions, a caustic expression of tongue and a cynical gleam of humour which Forsythe had noticed showing in his eyes on such occasions as they had talked together about women, especially certain women.

Had Forsythe been wiser, had he possessed the ability correctly to analyse himself, he would have realised that the one rift in the lute between himself and Hugo Melander was the fact that he was essentially jealous of the open admiration which Carola Cheshunt showed for his friend. He would have admitted that he was deeply in love with this charming girl and desired above all things to marry her.

He would have admitted too that the only reason he had not taken some steps in this matter or given any voice of his sentiments to her was the fact that there lurked in his mind a suspicion that she possessed more feeling for Melander than is usually evidenced between men and women who are merely friends.

Then again this suspicious side of Forsythe's nature questioned whether a friendship of an ordinary sort was possible between a man of the type of Melander and a girl of twenty-five, as charming, as open and as natural as Carola Cheshunt.

As Forsythe walked down Bedford Street, the snow crunching under his thin evening shoes, he experienced a certain mental satisfaction, due no doubt to the fact that he had eventually summoned up sufficient courage to decide to talk straightly to Melander. If it is wondered why it had not been possible for these two men, who were friends, to discuss such a situation casually and openly on some previous occasion, it must be remembered that the business of deciding just who finds most favour in a woman's eyes is more delicate and more difficult when the two men concerned are as close as Forsythe and Melander were.

And, thought Forsythe, it was not really a matter only of Carola. Two other feminine personalities intruded themselves on the canvas with which his mind was busy. They were Mrs. Vanessa Lorenzo, a dark, junoesque and passionate beauty, and a Mrs. Robina Gallery, a charming, poised and superficially casual lady whose fascination was so much greater than her forty years, and whose ability to charm is too well known to anyone who has met her to need further discussion here.

It had seemed to Forsythe that there existed between both these ladies and Melander that same odd dropping of the voice in conversation, the same whimsical and almost too affectionate smile on parting, the same *something* which, he desired ardently, should not exist where Carola was concerned.

But insofar as both Mrs. Lorenzo and Mrs. Gallery came into the question he had no qualms but merely curiosity. Both these ladies were well able to look after themselves. They were both truly experienced. Vanessa Lorenzo had buried two husbands, and Mrs. Gallery one. Their knowledge of life—and love—could be described as superb.

In other words Forsythe had not the remotest objection to Melander using—if he wanted to use—his peculiar and charming technique on these two ladies, who could either accept it if they desired or rebut it with their own equally charming wisdom. But the situation, he considered, was very different in the case of Carola.

If Melander desired to marry her, well and good. Let the point be established and let both contestants for her hand start from scratch. But if he did not and was merely amusing himself —as Forsythe feared—by languidly working up to some innocent climax desired by what might be described as an over-developed sense of the theatre, a climax which, interesting as it might be to Melander, could bring nothing but unhappiness to Carola, then this mischievous process must stop. Forsythe had made up his mind to this.

By now he was in Gordon Square, and turned into "The Cloisters". At the end of the passage, through a crack in the curtains behind the upper floor windows, he could see the light shining in the dining-room. He stopped and stood silently for a moment contemplating the charming exterior of the odd little house, bestowing a more than grudging admiration for the superb manner in which Melander, with his developed sense of the artistic, had furnished and decorated his home.

At this moment, thought Forsythe, Melander, with dinner over, would be sitting at his dining-table. The softly shaded wall lights would be reflecting on the carved oak panelling that formed the sombre background of the dining-room. Probably the gramophone would be playing softly.

Moving towards the door of the house Forsythe congratulated himself on having selected this evening for his discussion with his friend. Melander had sent his housekeeper away for Christmas and his man Sparkes was at the theatre with a ticket supplied by Forsythe. Melander was alone and no visitor would disturb the conversation, so important to Forsythe, which was about to take place.

On the doorstep he stamped the snow from his shoes and opened the door of the house with the key which, as Melander's friend, he had been given two years before. Inside, appreciative of the warmth and comfort of the hall, he took off his coat and muffler and hung them up. Then, lighting a cigarette, he walked slowly and quietly up the stairs.

Now and for the first time he began to feel a little afraid. Supposing Hugo was not inclined to be serious, supposing he was to treat Forsythe's case in the evasive, nonchalant and semi-humorous manner which he chose to adopt on occasion? Forsythe shrugged his shoulders and opened the door of the dining-room. As he thought, Hugo was sitting at the head of the antique refectory table.

Of Perfume and Sudden Death

"Good evening, Hugo," said Forsythe, and stopped in his tracks. A little gasp came from him, for he saw that Hugo Melander was no longer of this world. His two hands were on the table before him. His handsome face was twisted in a grotesque mask of death, and the slim triangle of his once white dinner shirt showing between the lapels of his black velvet coat was soaked darkly with his own blood.

Forsythe, with a coolness that surprised himself, walked to the top of the table and stood looking down at his friend. He saw that Hugo was able to sit upright because the arms of the high-backed carved oaken chair in which he was sitting supported his elbows, and that his slim white hands lay flat on the table before him.

Forsythe saw too the handle of the long *stiletto* protruding at an angle from under the right shoulder blade of his friend, and almost simultaneously looked towards the spot on the wall where it was usually kept.

Quite suddenly he realised that the gramophone in the corner was still playing *Debussy*, and with a little despairing shrug of the shoulders he walked across the room and turned it off.

.   .   .   .   .   .

I suppose there must be a great number of people in this world who think that they have a *flair* for the detection of criminals. Everard Forsythe was one of these. For a long time he had considered himself to be an amateur detective of no mean ability, had had, in fact, words upon this very subject with Hugo Melander who, with a characteristic lift of one cynical eyebrow, had said that so far as he was concerned his sympathies were invariably with criminals, against whom the dice were so unfairly loaded in these boring days.

And whilst Forsythe found himself profoundly shocked by the death—in its nastiest form—which had so suddenly come to his friend, yet almost in the same breath he experienced a strange delight in being the discoverer of the crime; in being in a position in which he could begin an exclusive examination into the circumstances surrounding the death of his friend, an examination which, he hoped, would eventually bring the killer to the gallows.

Having turned off the gramophone (which was one of those instruments which re-winds itself and supplies itself with new records from time to time without much attention), Forsythe looked about the room in search of some clue or indication which would set his mind working on the right line. But he had hardly done this when he stood still and began to sniff, because there was in the atmosphere, quite distinct to his sensitive and appreciative nostrils, a definitely attractive odour —that of an exquisite, but rather heavy, perfume.

He sat down in the chair at the end of the table opposite his dead friend and began to smile to himself. It seemed to him that the police would not have to look very far for the murderer. At the same time he realised that by the time he had summoned them the smell of the perfume would have disappeared and the only witness to its ever having existed would be himself. He thought with a rather grim smile that counsel for the defence would soon make short work of him and his perfume clue.

He realised too that no English jury would, in a thousand years, consent to find a murderer guilty merely because someone arriving soon after the crime had *thought* that he could recognise a perfume worn solely by the killer.

The "other side" would, no doubt, produce the manufacturer of the perfume who, in the witness box, with a self-satisfied smirk, would indicate the thousands of bottles of his particular perfume that were sold in the world each year, taking good care (having been carefully coached beforehand) not to mention that very few of these bottles were sold in England. No, thought Forsythe, there was no reason for him to mention the perfume to the police. *He* knew it was there; *he* knew the woman who wore it, and *he* knew that he must now prepare, by other and independent evidence, to build up a case against her, a case which would eventually be so strong that she would pay the penalty for the death of Hugo.

Sitting there, looking at the poor corpse who sat so

straightly at the top end of the table, Forsythe was certain that he knew just how Hugo had come to die in that odd position. Someone whose presence in the house did not surprise him, someone who had been in his bedroom, the door of which was set in the wall directly behind his chair, had stolen out and, with a little affectionate laugh, placed one arm round his head, and over his eyes, asking him to guess who it was.

Hugo had placed his hands flat on the table as children do when their eyes are covered, and was probably waiting quite cheerfully to be kissed when the point of the dagger, already taken from the wall by the murderess, had been deftly inserted under the right shoulder blade and pushed easily and straightly into Hugo's heart.

But the murderess—for Forsythe was, of course, aware that Hugo's killer had been a woman—had made the mistake so very common to the inexperienced criminal. Being used to wearing the perfume she had accepted it as part of her physical make-up; had forgotten that it was as much a part of her as her gloves or hand-bag. She would have been too clever to leave her gloves or hand-bag behind, but she was not sufficiently astute to realise that for a certain period a suggestion of her perfume might remain to definitely establish her presence in the room.

Forsythe sniffed again. It seemed to him that the odour was almost stronger than before. He got up and walked round the table and into the bedroom. There he stood in the darkness sniffing. Yes, the perfume was there too. He switched on the light and moved about the room trying to find some position in which the scent would be perceptibly stronger. Eventually he came to the conclusion that it hung equally on the air, and went back to his chair in the dining-room somewhat disappointed.

It was obvious to him that there was *too much perfume*. And then, with a sudden smile, realised that he was right in this supposition and that there *was* too much. Someone had deliberately planted perfume in the room, had sprayed scent about the place or dropped a spot or two from a bottle with the deliberate intention of establishing the presence in the room of the person who normally wore the perfume.

Forsythe knew that the usual wearer of the scent wore just the right amount—just enough to be attractive when one approached near enough. Her mere passage through the room, or her presence there for a little while, would not implant this scent upon the air in the strength which, at the moment, assailed his nostrils.

His smile became broader. *Because he knew the murderess was still the same person.* Knowing her and her agile mentality, Forsythe understood perfectly well how she would reason. She would say to herself that it was possible that some time during the evening—but only after dinner (therefore she knew his, Forsythe's, dinner time, and that he would not be with Hugo until after dinner, and she could only have learned these facts from Hugo himself) he would be coming to the house. She had thought it possible that Hugo might have informed Forsythe that she was coming and so had definitely *over-established* her own presence there by spraying or dropping some of her scent about the dining-room and the bedroom.

She knew that he was intelligent; that he would recognise that there was too much perfume; that he would come to the conclusion that some other woman, someone who had reason to be jealous of her, someone who would be infuriated at knowing that she had been with Hugo, had deliberately sprayed the place with her rival's perfume in order that she might be suspected.

And in order for this plan to be successful she would have put herself in a position wherein she knew that the other woman possessed a bottle of her perfume which had been used for this illicit plan and had been obtained for the sole purpose of throwing suspicion upon her.

"Very clever . . ." murmured Forsythe to himself. "Very clever . . . but too clever. And all that remains for me to do now, dear Vanessa, is to establish the fact that you have given —possibly as a Christmas present—a bottle of your own particular perfume to the woman you desire me to suspect.

"And," he concluded, selecting a cigarette from his case, "I shall find that the lady to whom you gave it is Robina Gallery. I am certain of that, dear Vanessa, as I am that you murdered Hugo. But I'm not going to tell on you yet."

And with this thought Everard Forsythe walked across to the telephone and proceeded to ring up New Scotland Yard and tell them about the murder—which, to tell the truth, was a process that he had always yearned to experience.

II

It was on the morning of the 24th December, after leaving Scotland Yard—where he had made a statement concerning the finding of the body of his dead friend, but carefully omitting all mention of the perfume—that Forsythe decided to interview both Mrs. Lorenzo and Mrs. Gallery.

The authorities were already beginning to take the view that the murder had been committed by some person outside the immediate circle of Melander's friends and acquaintances. With extraordinary rapidity the Detective Inspector in charge of the case had checked on Melander's background in the past, had discovered that, at one time in his life, he had known a somewhat peculiar circle of foreigners in London with whom he had had dealings of one sort and another. There had been talk of a girl in an Italian confectioner's, and the police officer—hypnotised no doubt by the fact that the dagger which had killed Melander had been of Italian origin—was busy checking on these far off details.

Before going to Scotland Yard Forsythe had telephoned Carola. He had not spoken to her for her maid had informed him that she was prostrated with grief. Her parents, greatly concerned, had summoned a physician who apparently feared a complete nervous breakdown.

A little sadly Forsythe realised that he had been right about Carola. She had loved Hugo dearly and the news of his death had struck her down completely.

In any event Forsythe had made up his mind that he would

not attempt to see her until he had solved the mystery of his friend's death and brought the murderess to justice. He knew that the sight of her grief would force him to talk before the time was ripe, and, at this moment he thought, his evidence was not yet sufficiently strong to enable the police to arrest and convict Mrs. Lorenzo.

It was quite impossible to think about Vanessa without realising that she was by nature a murderess. Everything about her indicated that if necessary she would kill. Her quiet and decisive method of speech; her complete ruthlessness of character; her ability to know exactly what she wanted and just how she was going to get it; her cool, unblinking, green eyes that looked so searchingly. Her caustic humour; her strong, slim and cruel hands. . . .

He remembered the rumours that had attended the death of her first husband who had died so strangely in the Argentine.

Forsythe thought to himself that it is an ill wind that blows nobody any good. Deep within him there was the idea that if he could successfully avenge the murder of Hugo then that very process would enable him to marry Carola. She would turn to him in her grief, with a certain gratitude, as Hugo's friend. After the first shock was over and she had begun to realise that after all one must go on living, her very disinterest in life would bring her more closely to the man who had been so close to Hugo and who had so successfully brought his murderess to justice.

What Melander had lost on the swings Forsythe was likely to gain on the roundabouts.

·　　·　　·　　·　　·

Vanessa was lying down on the long sofa before a brisk fire. Close at hand was a tea-tray. Forsythe thought that she must be one of the most attractive women in the world, that she was a superbly proportioned animal and that the lights in her lovely red hair produced by the flickering of the fire created the effect of an irregular halo about her head.

As she poured the tea, he noted with appreciation the

exquisite modelling of the hand and arm, the perfect co-ordination of movement.

She looked at him smilingly, her green eyes unblinking.

"My poor Everard," she said, "I hardly know what to say to you. How terribly you must feel the loss of Hugo, more especially"—and she made a moue—"having regard to the manner of his passing."

She sighed.

"There are times," she went on, "when words seem quite inadequate. This is one of them—it is one piece of sugar, isn't it, Everard?"

Forsythe smiled.

"You know, Vanessa," he said, "that you are a supreme actress, but do you think you delude me?"

She put her hands behind her head and stretched luxuriously. Everard noticed that the green of her rest-frock matched her eyes.

"I never try to delude anyone, Everard," she said.

He nodded.

"I am a great believer in truth, Vanessa," he said. "I think truth *can* be a most effective weapon. At any rate I think it is the only proper weapon to use against such a charming and clever person as yourself. I know *you* killed Hugo."

She laughed, a rich trilling little laugh.

"Aren't you delightful, Everard?" she said. "But I am inclined to agree with you that truth is a good weapon, almost as sharp as that dagger that killed Hugo, which—as the newspapers so dramatically point out—had razor sharp edges."

She moved her arms, and with a lithe movement swung down her legs from the sofa. She sat facing him.

"Let me tell *you* some truth, dear Everard," she said. "You who seem to believe that *I* killed Hugo. Well, I wish I had. I've wanted to kill Hugo a dozen times. Given the right circumstances, given an opportunity for murdering Hugo with a really good chance of not being found out, I think I should have done it a long time ago."

Her eyes smouldered.

"I loathed Hugo," she said. "I loathed him because I loved him so much, because he could be such a necessity and because he was the only man who has ever treated me casually. However," she went on calmly, "that is neither here nor there. But, Everard, I should like to hear your reasons for believing that I killed Hugo."

Forsythe took a cigarette from the box by his side and lit it.

"The perfume gave you away, Vanessa," he said. "I smelt it directly I got into the room. It was your perfume, there isn't another woman in London wears it. My first thought was that you had been there, but immediately I knew that your presence in the room wouldn't leave so strong a scent. It became obvious to me that somebody had deliberately planted the stuff about the place."

She nodded smilingly.

"So that you should smell it," she said, "when you came."

"Precisely," said Forsythe. "And they took good care that I should smell it. Directly I realised," he went on, "that the perfume was too strong, my thought was what you intended it should be—that somebody, someone who had a motive to kill Hugo, someone who knew that you were a close friend of his, someone who probably guessed that you either had been or still were his mistress, had deliberately left your scent about the place so that you should be suspected."

She took up her tea-cup.

"How delightful you are, Everard," she murmured.

He went on:

"I know that you were still the murderess. You're a clever woman, Vanessa, but you forgot that I am rather intelligent myself. I knew at once that you had sprinkled a little too much of your perfume about the place so that I should think that someone else had planted it. Just as I shall presently find out," he went on, "that someone has a bottle of your perfume; possibly you sent one to somebody as a Christmas present."

She put her cup down and looked at him. Forsythe thought he saw a little hatred in her eyes.

Of Perfume and Sudden Death

"You know, Everard," she said musingly, "you're not an unclever person, are you? It's a most extraordinary thing, but I *did* send someone a flask of my perfume as a Christmas present. Doesn't that thrill you? I sent it off to them on Thursday afternoon to make certain that they should get it. Carola was here when I did it. She can prove it. So they would have received it yesterday morning, just in time for Hugo's murder."

Forsythe nodded.

"Tell me something, Vanessa," he said. "You said a little while ago that you would have liked to have killed Hugo because he treated you casually. I don't think that reason is adequate. I think you had some other, more sudden, stronger reason for desiring Hugo dead."

She took a cigarette from the tea-tray. Everard walked over to the couch and lit it for her. Through the flame of his lighter he saw the little smile about her mouth.

"Oh yes, my dear," she answered, "I would hate you to think for one moment that I am trying to reduce my motives for having *wanted* to kill Hugo. As a matter of fact," she went on, "last night would have been the ideal time for me to have *wanted* to kill Hugo. You know of course about Carola? Robina Gallery told me a few days ago that she thought that Hugo and Carola were going to be married, and that is a thing for which I could not forgive Hugo. I mean"—she gave a little shrug—"Carola is a dear child, a charming, frank, pretty girl of twenty-five, as inexperienced of everything in this world— including Hugo's rather peculiar mentality when applied to sex—as it is possible to be."

Forsythe nodded. It had been as he had thought.

"I think I could have forgiven him for anything but that," said Vanessa with a little sigh which sounded rather artificial.

Forsythe drew on his cigarette.

"Have you got an alibi, my dear?" he asked.

She looked at him with wide eyes.

"An alibi! Of course I ought to have an alibi for last night, oughtn't I? Well, my dear, I am afraid I haven't one. In

125

point of fact," she went on, "it is going to be quite difficult for me if the police should want to know where I was last night, and I expect they will when you've had time to talk to them at length."

Forsythe smiled grimly.

"You admit you were with Hugo last night, Vanessa?" he said.

"Definitely," she replied. "I went to see Hugo last night and I went to see him for the purpose of being very rude to him. I saw him and I was rude to him. I told him many things which I thought would be good for him to hear. After which I left him, smiling rather strangely from his seat at the top of the table, apparently quite oblivious of my presence and concentrated on one of the *Debussy* records."

Forsythe smiled.

"So you two had a slanging match," he said. "Was he very rude to you, Vanessa? Did it take much to make you kill him, and by the way, you did it very cleverly too. After he told you that he and Carola were going to be married, you pretended to accept the situation, you began to walk about the room— you know that habit of yours. It was quite easy for you to take the dagger from the wall. And then you put your left hand over his eyes and made a little joke, and he put his hands flat on the table in front of him and you killed him. You remember of course, Vanessa, that your first husband—the one in the Argentine—died of a stab wound?"

She nodded.

"That was a terrible thing," she said coolly. "Poor Juan . . . But, my dear Everard, strangely enough—and I can't quite understand this myself—Hugo, who could be so quietly, so cuttingly, so fearfully insulting if he wanted to be, was quite nice to me. Last night he wasn't a bit insulting. Tell me, Everard," she said smilingly, "when do I expect a visit from the police?"

He smiled.

"Not for the moment anyway, Vanessa," he said. "You see, I have not told them anything about the perfume. They're on the wrong track. Apparently they've discovered something about Hugo. Something to do with an Italian girl, a few years ago. They think that one of her friends may have been responsible. I don't intend to tell them anything about you, Vanessa, until my case is complete."

She nodded.

"I see," she said softly. "Well now, Everard, since you're such a believer in truth perhaps you'll let me help in building up this case against myself. I think it would be most amusing."

She threw her cigarette end into the fire.

"Aren't you going to ask me to whom I sent that flask of perfume?"

He smiled cynically.

"I know," he said. "You would naturally send the perfume to the other person who might have a motive for removing Hugo. You sent the perfume to Robina Gallery."

"But how marvellous you are, Everard," she said, with a little smile that showed her teeth. "I did. It was to Robina that I sent the flask of perfume, and now all you have to do is to find out about that, and another nail is knocked into my coffin."

She got up, stretched once again.

"It is awful that they still hang women in England, isn't it?" she said. "You know, Everard, you ought to be a little concerned about trying so hard to get me hanged. You might regret it one day. But still I must say I do understand your motive."

"Which is?" queried Forsythe, rising.

"You will have Carola," she said. "The unlucky thing was that she loved Hugo, who would have made her a very bad husband, whereas you, my friend, would be a supreme mate. At the moment Carola is of course prostrated, but knowing that perfectly straight, frank, juvenile and clear-cut mind of hers, you are well aware that if you succeed in avenging Hugo's death, and after she has got over the shock of this thing, the logical sequence is that she will rebound into your arms.

"In other words, my dear, you will lead Carola to her marriage bed over my dead body. A rather mixed metaphor when you come to consider that I shall be swinging at the end of a rope. However, I promise not to haunt you both."

Forsythe grinned.

"You've got a supreme nerve, Vanessa," he said. "There are moments when I almost admire you."

She smiled.

"Come and admire me again soon, Everard," she said, "but I must turn you out now. I've a dinner engagement tonight. *Au revoir*, dear Everard."

III

Forsythe arrived at Mrs. Gallery's house at seven o'clock. He found her at her desk.

They shook hands without speaking. He noticed that her eyes were very tired and that they were red. Robina had been crying a great deal, he thought.

He wondered just how much there had been between Robina and Hugo and just how much of the Vanessa-Hugo *affaire* was known to her. Robina was essentially self-contained. She was what is known as the best type of Englishwoman. Yet the generations that had gone to the establishment of her poise were unable to prevent her wearing a suggestion of her heart on her sleeve today.

"You'd better have a cocktail," she said. "I suppose it's much better to go on doing the ordinary things and not think too much about it. By the way, have you been to see Carola yet?"

He shook his head.

"I thought it wasn't indicated at this time, Robina," he answered. "But I shall see her soon."

The maid brought in the cocktails. Robina moved over to the fireplace.

"Carola's quite done in," she said. "I telephoned this afternoon. Of course I guessed that she and Hugo were to be married. I've seen it coming for a long time and, poor child, so far as she is concerned it seems that life is quite finished. She'll get over it of course. Given enough time people can get over anything and she's a brave girl."

Forsythe smiled a little grimly.

"She would have had to be brave to marry Hugo," he said. "I should have thought that even as brave a girl as Carola would have funked *that* jump."

"She didn't know very much about him," said Robina. "Of course she thought she did. All women do—as you well know, Everard. But I believe she was worrying a little. She came here yesterday morning—I feel now that she wanted to see me about Hugo, but it was too early for me. I was still in bed and I sent her away. I shan't forgive myself for that."

Forsythe drank his cocktail.

"I shan't go to see her until I've got my case complete against Vanessa," he said. "I know she killed Hugo. That's what I came specially to talk to you about, Robina."

She looked out of the window. The snow was falling fast.

"I agree with you," she said. "It was the sort of thing that Vanessa would do, and, odd as it might seem, the sort of thing that Hugo would expect her to do."

He lit a cigarette.

"What do you think happened last night at 'The Cloisters'?" he asked.

She smiled a little grimly.

"I'm pretty certain that I *know* what happened," she answered. "I know that Vanessa made up her mind to see Hugo and have it out with him. Everyone knew that Vanessa only *seems* a cool person, but I know that she can get into the most fiendish rages. She'd probably spent the day pacing up and down like a caged tiger—hating everyone—Hugo, Carola and herself, but especially Hugo. I told her some days ago that I thought those two were planning to be quietly married.

"She made up her mind to tell Hugo just what she thought about him. She probably rehearsed it before she went—you can imagine Vanessa walking about selecting the most cutting phrases, picking out all the things which would annoy Hugo most and show him what a fearfully weak and lousy person he really was.

"Unfortunately for her—and for Hugo—she found him in the wrong frame of mind. He probably laughed at her. He could be terribly cynical when he wanted to and instead of losing his temper he probably amused himself by baiting Vanessa. You can see him doing it, can't you, Everard?"

He nodded. He could!

"That was a bit too much for her," continued Robina, "so she killed him. Of course she had a justifiable grouse against Hugo, but so had a lot of other people—myself included."

Forsythe raised his eyebrows. She laughed mirthlessly.

"Don't let's pretend, Everard," she said. "You know perfectly well that I had been Hugo's mistress too. I don't think that Hugo realised his own weird powers of seduction and their effect on the women who were subject to them. He had not the ability to realise that what was an amusement to him might have been something rather serious where the women were concerned."

Forsythe stubbed out his cigarette.

"Scotland Yard are on the wrong track," he said, "I haven't told them all I know—yet. They're chasing after some Italian fellow—a man who was engaged to one of Hugo's earlier conquests. They think he might have done it. But that won't be for long. Quite soon I'm going to hand them Vanessa on a plate."

"She did it," said Robina. "I know she did it."

"Precisely," said Forsythe, "and she's going to try to hang it on to you. Did you guess that too, Robina?"

"No," said Robina. "Is she really? Well, I'm afraid that she's going to find the process a little difficult. Naturally she would try to make out a case against someone else. She's quite clever, you know, Everard."

"I know that," he said. "She's got a bit of corroborative evidence against you too, Robina—that flask of perfume she sent you."

Robina looked surprised.

"What flask of perfume?" she asked. "I've had no perfume from Vanessa. What *are* you talking about, Everard?"

Forsythe was silent for a moment. He was wondering just why Robina should deny that she had received the perfume from Vanessa.

"Sit down, Robina," he said, "and listen carefully to me. When I arrived at Hugo's place last night—it would be about twenty minutes to nine—and discovered his dead body sitting there so very dramatically at the table, I realised that there was a distinct smell of perfume on the air and also that the perfume was nothing but Vanessa's *Lilas d' Amour Noir*. But there was too much of it. Obviously it had been planted in the place by Vanessa to make it appear that somebody was trying to hang the murder on to her.

"Almost immediately it struck me that Vanessa had done this herself for an obvious reason. She knew that she had already sent someone a flask of the perfume—it was necessary to her plot that she should be able to prove this—and she told me this afternoon that she despatched a bottle of *Lilas d' Amour Noir* to you on Thursday night."

Robina shrugged her shoulders.

"Well, I haven't received it, that's all," she said. "I suppose it must have gone astray in the post."

"How could it?" asked Forsythe. "Things don't go astray in the post, Robina."

"I still say I haven't received it," she said with an air of finality. "And even if I had received it or supposing I was to say here and now that I had a dozen bottles of it, then all I can say is that Vanessa must be fearfully optimistic if she thinks that such a process would prove that I had murdered Hugo. It's ridiculous on the face of it."

"Possibly," murmured Forsythe. "But Vanessa is not so concerned with proving anything as in shifting the suspicion from herself. She realises that in a murder investigation two suspects are better than one. Each one of them has fifty per cent more chance of getting away with it."

Robina helped herself to a cigarette and poured more cock-tails. She brought Forsythe his and carried her own glass over to the fire. She sat down and smoked slowly for a few moments, drawing the smoke right down into her lungs.

"Everard," she said eventually, "I told you that I knew Vanessa had killed Hugo. I will tell you how I know.

"Last night I suddenly decided to see Hugo. I intended to warn him that I expected some sort of trouble from Vanessa and that if she did not succeed in making it for him she would try to score off that poor child Carola. It was quite a nice night —cold and snowy of course but I rather liked that. I took a cab to Gordon Square and walked the rest of the way. As I came up the west side of the Square I looked at my watch and saw that it was a quarter-past eight. Then, just as I was about to cross the road, I saw Vanessa. She was approaching 'The Cloisters' from the King's Cross end of the Square. I saw her turn in to 'The Cloisters' and I was fearfully annoyed, but I knew that no good would accrue from my going in too, so I walked back to Bedford Square and took a taxi home.

"You arrived and found Hugo dead at say between eight-forty and eight-forty-five and I saw her go in there at between ten minutes past and a quarter past eight. So there you are!"

Forsythe finished his drink.

"As you say, Robina, there you are," he said. "At the same time you have to realise that your story doesn't make things very much worse for Vanessa. You say that you were almost arrived at 'The Cloisters' and went away because you saw her going in. That situation will suit Vanessa very well. She will promptly say that you, knowing that she was probably going to call on Hugo, waited for her, saw her enter the house, waited for her to leave and then walked over and killed Hugo. After which you proceeded to sprinkle her perfume about the place."

"That's all very nice," said Robina primly, "except, as I told you before, I haven't any of Vanessa's perfume. So please don't go on talking about it as if I had."

Forsythe saw that Robina was a little annoyed.

"I rather wish that you *had* got it," he said. "The logical sequence of events is that you *ought* to have it because it would have been logical for Vanessa to have sent it to you."

"Don't be a damned fool, Everard," Robina rejoined somewhat acidly. "In a minute you'll be accusing me of having stabbed Hugo."

A moment or two elapsed before he replied. During that time he thought:

After all why shouldn't Robina have killed Hugo? *Why not?* He definitely did not like her denials of having received the flask of perfume because he was certain that Vanessa had sent it. That was the obvious thing for Vanessa to do.

But he said:

"Don't be an awful mug, Robina. I know that such a thing is impossible. But don't you see what Vanessa is trying to do. She's drawing red herrings all over the place trying to create situations implicating you and hoping that she'll get away with it in the process. The joke is," he added somewhat bitterly, "it looks rather as if she will."

"Rubbish," said Robina. "She'll get away with nothing after I've told the police about her visit to 'The Cloisters' last night."

Forsythe thought: "Well, why haven't you told them already, you've had ample time." He said:

"Just take things easy. There'll be lots of time for you to talk to the police. Hugo was only killed last night. Besides, I rather fancy that I'm going to solve this thing in my own way. I have a feeling that I'm going to be the one who is going to bag poor old Hugo's murderess."

She looked into the fire.

"Poor old Hugo . . ." she repeated. "I wonder if he really was 'poor old Hugo' or whether he didn't ask for everything he got. He was quite charming and rather clever and fearfully amusing, but he couldn't differentiate between people—especially women. Women were just things that existed for Hugo to amuse himself with. I don't believe that he ever had a serious thought about anybody or anything. Well . . . life caught up with him."

Forsythe got up.

"It was death that caught up with him," he said with a wry smile. "Well . . . so long, Robina. I'll drop in and see you to-morrow if I may, and until then keep your chin up."

Outside he walked slowly back to his flat in Bedford Square. He was thinking very deeply. He was thinking that her denial that she had received the perfume was something which made him suspect *her*.

He realised suddenly that except for the differences in appearance and character between Vanessa and Robina each of them had as strong motives for wanting revenge on Hugo, each of them had a key to the house and each of them had been to "The Cloisters" at an operative time the night before.

And he had only Robina Gallery's word that she had not gone in.

IV

It was close on midnight when Forsythe put on his golf shoes and a thick overcoat and walked round to Gordon Square in the snow.

He was not quite certain as to why he was walking there. He had no intention of entering Hugo's house but he thought that the atmosphere of the Square might help him in the solution of the mystery which puzzled him.

He walked round the Square and, almost opposite the entrance to "The Cloisters", came upon a portly individual dressed in a suit of shepherd's plaid who was leaning against the railings, smoking the butt end of a cigar and looking up at the moon.

Forsythe wondered why he was wearing no overcoat and how such a very good-natured expression could exist on the face of any man on such a cold night.

"Good evening, Mr. Forsythe," said the overcoatless one, raising a billy-cock hat an inch or two from his head, and then replacing it at an angle. "Good evening, Sir. May I introduce myself? I am Detective-Inspector Krasinsky, and I am very glad to make your acquaintance."

Forsythe murmured the appropriate things. He was thinking to himself that this meeting was perhaps lucky.

"I am very interested in this case of murder," continued Krasinsky with a smile. "Of course there are people murdering each other all the time and one should not take the thing too seriously. Yet, believe it or not, there are certain aspects of this murder which interest me strongly. Such as, for instance, that business of the perfume. . . . Shall we walk round the Square?"

Forsythe stepped out beside his newly found acquaintance, Somehow he found that he was not surprised that this rather strange Detective Officer should know about the perfume, in spite of the fact that he, Forsythe, had said not one word about it to anyone in authority. Also he felt rather relieved at the prospect of talking the thing over with this sympathetic person.

"Tell me, Inspector," he said. "Who do *you* think killed Hugo Melander?"

Krasinsky waved his cigar stub in the air.

"It doesn't matter," he said. "The thing is that you are the person who is, in my opinion, best fitted to carry out this investigation, because I believe that you have the whole thing at your finger ends. In fact," he went on, smiling into the darkness, "I can definitely tell you, Sir, that it will be through you and through you alone that the murderer of Hugo Melander will be brought to the gallows, and I would like to congratulate you on that fact in advance."

Forsythe felt a glow of pleasure.

"That's very nice of you," he said. "But I find it difficult to believe you just at this moment. I have been worrying very much all the evening as to who had the strongest motives for killing Hugo. Both Vanessa Lorenzo and Robina Gallery had such motives. They had opportunity. They had front-door keys, and they both went out with the intention of seeing Hugo. Either of them or both of them might have done it."

"Precisely," said Krasinsky, with a glowing smile. "Yet, my dear Sir, I am afraid that you are not making sufficient use of the facts that are already at your disposal. The whole case against the killer of your deceased friend is, or should be, at your finger-tips, on information which has already been supplied to you; because you must realise that even if the beautiful Mrs. Lorenzo and the charming Mrs. Gallery are potential murderesses there is also no doubt that, in this matter, they were both speaking the truth.

"I have always found during an experience which has lasted for several thousand years," continued Krasinsky, "that simplicity is the essential condition of mind necessary for the solution of murders; that and the ability to seek and find the one incongruity which either proves or disproves the rest of the evidence, be it direct or circumstantial."

Forsythe nodded in the darkness.

"Therefore," said Krasinsky, his voice becoming rather fainter, and his presence seeming to be a little less clear to his companion, "I would suggest to you that a little concentration on the business of the perfume from every possible angle might help you in the solution of this mystery.

"That it will help you," he concluded, "I have no doubt whatsoever, because, as I have already told you, it will be through you and you alone that the killer of your friend will be brought to justice. Good night, dear Mr. Forsythe."

With a start Forsythe realised that the mysterious Detective Inspector, who knew so much about everything connected with the case, had disappeared. He realised that he was standing leaning against the railings in the exact spot at which he had met Krasinsky. He began to wonder if he had not actually imagined this meeting and whether the portly figure was not merely a figment of his rather overwrought mind which, concerned so deeply with the nuances of crime, had conjured up this ghostly assistant.

He shrugged his shoulders and began to walk back towards Bedford Square, and, as he walked, he smiled a little, because into his mind had suddenly come the incongruity which Krasinsky had particularly referred to. An incongruity that was so very obvious that Forsythe had never even thought of it.

Of Perfume and Sudden Death

Rather vaguely Forsythe considered that Detective-Inspector Krasinsky must be an extremely efficient police officer whether he existed or not!

V

It was Christmas night and Forsythe sat at his desk in his comfortable sitting-room in Bedford Square and concentrated on the letter he was writing. It was nearly finished when the telephone bell rang.

It was Carola Cheshunt. Her voice was low and steady, but it seemed to Forsythe that it required an effort of will to produce each word.

"Carola . . ." he said. "What is it? What can I do for you? Are you *very* ill?"

"I'm all right, Everard," she said, "except that I feel all the time that it would be so sweet to die. I never knew that there could be such misery in the world. I've been walking about for hours. At first the snow seemed to comfort me but now I'm tired of it."

"You must go home, Carola," said Forsythe.

"I will Everard," she said. "But I want you to do something for me first. Please, Everard. You still have the key to . . . to Hugo's house?"

"Yes, Carola," he answered.

"I want to see it just once more," she said. "The last time I was there it was on such a wonderful afternoon and the sun was shining through the window on to the oak table. Hugo was so sweet that afternoon. I'm going away tomorrow. They've told me that I'm to go on a cruise—somewhere where there'll be sun and laughter . . . doesn't that sound funny now? Sun and laughter. . . .

"But I want to see Hugo's room just once more before I go. I know that I shall feel him there . . . sense his presence and perhaps feel better for thinking so at any rate."

"Very well, my dear," said Forsythe. "I will go there immediately and wait for you. I shall be waiting in the hall when you arrive. Just knock quietly."

"I will do that," she said.

Forsythe finished his letter quickly, slipped into his over-coat and went downstairs. He found a taxi on the rank and ordered the driver to take him quickly to the Cheshunt house, to wait for him there for a few minutes and then to drive him to "The Cloisters" in Gordon Square.

.   .   .   .   .

Forsythe paid off the taxi outside "The Cloisters", walked quickly through the arched passage to the front door of Hugo's house and let himself in. Inside the place was cold, Forsythe thought, and smelled of death.

He closed the front door quietly behind him and went straight up to the dining-room. As he opened the door he was not surprised to find that the room was lit and that Carola was sitting in Hugo's chair at the top of the table.

Her face was as white as a sheet. Her eyes, usually so inno-cent and wide, were half-closed, almost slanting with a peculiar hatred. The red rims about them accentuated their glitter.

Forsythe sat down and faced her. He put his hands on the table in front of him.

"Carola . . ." he said. "This is how Hugo was sitting when you killed him. He was sitting just like this, wasn't he?"

She nodded. Then she began to laugh. A peculiar, hard, brittle laugh.

"Just like that," she said. "Just like that . . ."

Her fingers began to play with her handbag that lay on the table in front of her.

"You've been a long time," she said. "Where have you been?"

Forsythe smiled.

"I went round to your house, Carola," he said. "I took a chance on your doing what I thought you would have done. I told your maid that you had asked me to bring you the bottle of *Lilas d'Amour Noir* that you had in your drawer with your other perfumes and things. She found it. It was there all right."

"Damn you, Everard," she said. "Do you know where I got it from?"

Her voice was almost shrill with anger.

"Yes, Carola," he said. "You stole it from the table in the hall at Robina's when you went to see her on Friday morning. You knew Vanessa had sent it. You went there early knowing that she would still be in bed. You knew the packet would be on the hall table and you knew there would be lots of other packets and presents there. You knew it wouldn't be missed. Robina never even knew that it had arrived. Her maid probably received twenty Christmas gifts that morning."

She looked at him. Her eyes were straight on his and never blinked. Forsythe, fumbling for his cigarette case, wondered if she were quite sane.

He got out a cigarette and lit it.

"I never even began to think straightly about the murder until last night," he said. "Then I began to look for incongruities. First of all I took it for granted that both Vanessa and Robina were telling the truth. I knew that Vanessa was right when she had said that she sent the perfume to Robina and that Robina was right when she said that she'd never received it.

"I realised that Robina was right when she said that Hugo couldn't differentiate between people—especially women. She said that women were just things that existed for Hugo to amuse himself with. Well . . . that applied to you too. You'd gone the same way with Hugo as Vanessa had gone . . . as Robina had gone . . . but you had more to lose. And you thought he was going to marry you until a few days ago when he told you he didn't intend to—that I could have you. I know now why he laughed when I telephoned and told him I wanted to have a serious talk with him. He was going to give you to me as a Christmas present—after he'd finished with you!"

She made a little noise in her throat and a grimace. It was a fearful grimace.

"It was all so obvious," Forsythe went on. "And I was such a fool. It was obviously you from the start, but you'd fixed it marvellously. I must congratulate you on that, Carola. When I smelt the perfume just after I found Hugo dead—in that chair where you are sitting—I hadn't enough sense to realise that whoever had left that perfume about the place had left it *for me to smell*. In other words the murderess knew that I was coming to see Hugo.

"Well, quite obviously Vanessa didn't know. If she had she wouldn't have come round at the time she did knowing that I was due to arrive at any moment. Robina didn't know, and she went away without even coming into the house when she saw Vanessa.

"But you knew that Vanessa was coming. She told you that she intended to go and have it out with Hugo. You didn't say that you were going to be there or that Hugo had told you that I had arranged to see him soon after half-past eight.

"But you were here in this room when Vanessa arrived, and Hugo hid you in the bedroom. You heard just what Vanessa had to say to Hugo. And I'll bet she said an awful lot. Then you realised that you'd just been one of a crowd. That annoyed you, didn't it, Carola?

"Hugo got rid of Vanessa quickly. He had to with you in the place. She could only have been here for ten minutes or so.

"And then you came out and got the dagger and played your little game with Hugo . . . the lovers' game that you had played before. You put your hand over his eyes and you killed him. You had the stolen flask of perfume in your handbag. It was premeditated murder, Carola.

"After you killed Hugo you sprinkled some scent around the place, enough to make me believe that it was Vanessa planting it to make me believe that it was Robina who had been here. Then you went quickly before I got here. You must have had only five minutes to spare. But it was nicely planned."

She began to smile. Forsythe thought it was a ghastly smile.

"It's still well planned," she muttered thickly. "I've been to see Robina this afternoon. I got the story of your visit from her. You haven't told the police about the perfume. And nobody knows that I've a key to this house; that I was one of the women who had keys to this house. Do you see what I'm getting at, Everard?"

"Not quite, Carola," he said.

She spoke quickly. The words came tumbling over themselves.

"You found Hugo," she said. "Well, why shouldn't *you* have killed him? Vanessa and Robina know that you wanted to marry me—there's your motive. You've said nothing about the perfume."

She got up, fumbling with her handbag.

"I'm going to kill you, Everard," she said. "You know too much. I'm going to shoot you. No one will hear, and then I'm going to put the pistol in your hand and leave you here and they'll think you killed Hugo and came back here to commit suicide. Vanessa and Robina will tell how you've been trying to hang this on to Vanessa and how you had begun to pretend that you almost suspected Robina. They'll *know* you did it. Do you hear, you poor fool!"

She took out the pistol.

Forsythe began to smile. He was thinking of the letter he had sent to the police, of the bottle of *Lilas d'Amour Noir* with Carola's finger-prints on it that was even now on its way to Scotland Yard. He realised what the mysteriously evanescent Detective-Inspector Krasinsky had meant when he had said that it was through him that the murderess would go to the gallows.

He sat back in his chair and looked at her. He was still smiling bitterly as she pressed the trigger.

Forsythe slumped forward over the table.

"Poor Carola . . ." he murmured as he died.

EPISODE SIX

Of an Experience of Pierre Duchesne

ᘒᘒᘒᘒ

M r. Pierre Duchesne was a man of parts. He was tall and of an extreme slenderness, and when about the age of thirty was still so supple that he could touch his ear with his toe.

Also he was particularly fond of hanging good clothes upon himself, and was given to the blandishments of exquisite ladies to such an extent that he had acquired certain possibilities of conversation.

His hair, which had receded from his forehead, but still gave evidence of having once curled, gave him an appearance of wisdom and broadness of outlook. His eyes were like most eyes but occasionally took it upon themselves to be humorous.

His mouth, by far his best feature, was inclined to be humorous at the corners, yet possessed a certain lack of mobility—indicating a sense of justice—but could easily become quite tender in appearance—a phenomenon induced by the turning up of one corner, the turning down of the other and a certain petulant droop at which Mr. Duchesne was an expert.

It was a fine wintry night, and Gower Street had an immaculate air of mystery which attracted him. As he walked along (for he lived in these parts), a black soft hat upon one side of his head, his coat open, and the moonlight reflecting upon his shirt front, this Duchesne pondered upon the possibilities of life and more especially upon himself, in whom he was inordinately interested.

Now you must understand that this walking down Gower Street was a serious business and not to be taken at all lightly. First Duchesne walked as if the street belonged to him and had been designed for his own especial benefit. Secondly, he would regard divers houses and buildings with an open contempt as if—because their shape displeased him—they had no right to be there; and thirdly, because this walking down Gower Street decided for that night his state of mind. For, mark you, should the weather be rainy—rain annoyed him for it spoiled the shape of his clothes, and he had no money for cabs—then he would, on arriving at his rooms, conclude that he was misunderstood, unappreciated by the public who read his writings, and—carrying his mind back to some departed love affair—decide that his heart was broken. On the other hand—if it were a fine night, as this one was—with a touch of frost and a bright sparkle of moonlight—then he would swing along, smiling at the shadows, full of schemes for the betterment of the world, and would consider, pleasantly enough, plans for the possible undoing of some fair lady.

By now it will be realised that Mr. Duchesne was sufficiently like other young, romantic and impecunious writers to merit no further description.

You must know that the far end of Gower Street is bisected by Ridgmont Gardens and Tavistock Place. The architecture of the houses about this spot, together with the fact that some trees grew there, was extremely pleasing to Pierre, and whatever the hour of the night he would stand upon the corner and approve the situation in a condescending manner.

Upon this night, as he stood at the corner, he took it upon himself to visualise a scene in a story which he was writing, and on which he intended to work on arriving at his rooms. The space between Gower Street and Tavistock Place became in his mind a smooth field of green with a dash of silver from a good moon, and there, facing each other, stood Umberto Venaissin—most resplendent in white velvet—and, at the regulation six paces, Porro di Ugolini, fat and gross in his black and gold, a sneer upon his face and his rapier point flicking, as if it already desired acquaintance with the bowels of his opponent.

Vanaissin drew himself up to his full height. He smiled, and his white teeth glistened. . . .

"Listen, Ugolini," he said bitterly. "Before I kill you, you shall give me the satisfaction of your regret. . . ."

Ugolini laughed harshly.

"My poor dapper fool," he sneered. "I have no regrets. The favours of your ladies bestowed upon me in the past are but as appetisers to the repast of what you leave behind when I kill you!"

Celleri, Ugolini's second, interrupted gracefully:

"Gentlemen, in God's name ha' done with insults and kill each other, if possible. . . . We are cold, and I have an appointment at dawn. . . .

A hand touched Duchesne upon the shoulder and he turned to find Krasinsky. He blinked and came back to life . . . and Gower Street.

He was annoyed to encounter Krasinsky at this time, not because he really disliked the plump gentleman in the shepherd's plaid suit, from whom most of the salcable ideas that had kept the wolf from Duchesne's door had come, but, because Krasinsky, who seemed to have a good idea of Duchesne's mental worth, had, of late, made a habit of appearing at inconvenient times and adopting an attitude of gentle criticism rather like that of a kindly parent who, endeavouring to set a wayward child upon the right road, occasionally feels it necessary to guide a little more forcibly than is convenient to the child.

"Krasinsky," murmured Duchesne with a pained smile, "you have interrupted a literary dream of mine. . . ."

Krasinsky laughed.

"That is my prerogative and amusement," said he. "But I have a warning for you, my Pierre, and one which . . ."

Duchesne moved impatiently.

"Have done with your broodings, Krasinsky," he said with a show of temper. "Since when have you also usurped the attitude of my conscience?"

Krasinsky took snuff noisily.

"My friend, there is still time for your undoing," he remarked with a smile.

He wagged a fat forefinger.

"Mark you," he continued, "there is that which awaits you tonight which may well . . ."

Duchesne interrupted impatiently.

"I will not listen to you, Krasinsky," he said. "You have the ability to make me feel unnecessarily petty; also, you sometimes endeavour to spoil the colour of my thoughts. Get you gone!"

Krasinsky adjusted his hat and disappeared. Left to himself, Duchesne, his duel scene relegated to the limbo of lost pictures of the mind, continued on his way, endeavouring, rather vainly, to adjust his viewpoint to the work in hand, a viewpoint which was suffering somewhat from the mental mauling of Mr. Krasinsky.

He arrived at his house, and taking the door key from his pocket, loosed it, and allowed it to dangle upon its slender chain, whilst he regarded, with the critical eye of one who considers himself a judge of atmosphere, the gloomy forefront of his abode. The door, massive and gloomy, seemed in some indescribable way to shut him out from something eminently desirable. He considered it unhappily, comparing its temporary bleakness with the attempted warning of Krasinsky.

He cursed silently, opened the door and stepping across the threshold into the dark hall beyond, stood transfixed. Before him, he knew, lay the wide staircase leading to his rooms, and towards him, from the floor above, and seeming (in some strange manner) almost visible, came a faint perfume of violets.

No ordinary perfume this, but something remotely sweet, heralding or containing some power that caught his breath and caused his quickened brain to race, seeking vainly for some possible association. He stood, for a moment, sniffing, like a dog who sees a ghost, then carefully, and for some unknown reason, silently, he mounted the stairs.

At the first landing, but four stairs from his study door, he paused, and endeavoured with an attempt at scientific cynicism to rid himself of the mystic and strangely pleasurable feeling which possessed him. Then, with a shrug, he mounted the four stairs quickly, flung open the study door, felt for the electric light switch, and pressed it down.

Nothing happened. No light came. Duchesne, removing his fingers from the switch, felt a great tiredness come over him; he found that he was disinterested in whether he had an electric light or not, that he desired only to reach the armchair by the table and sit down.

He walked round the table and seated himself in the chair. He felt petulant, annoyed, and he believed that Krasinsky was responsible for this.

Then, suddenly, the electric light came on of its own volition, and Duchesne gave a gasp of astonishment.

No description of mine, no matter how analytical, could describe with justice the exquisite beauty of the lady who sat, nonchalantly enough, upon Duchesne's club fender, swinging a dainty shoe, which, with its attendant silk-clad ankle, peeped discreetly from the folds of her voluminous gown. Let it suffice that she was of the type which is, of necessity, the mistress of all men's minds, for she possessed that personality so rarely adaptable to all mental masculine processes. Duchesne, his sang-froid gone, recognised her—recognised her gown (a creation of some Italian mind which lived with the Borgias)—and sat, gaping like a bumpkin, his hands trembling, his relaxed face muscles permitting his eyeglass to fall to the floor and smash into a dozen crystals.

He closed his eyes and opened them expecting to find her gone. She was still there. He moved in his chair, thinking that movement would dispel this vision. Then, with the return of some little courage, he closed his eyes, straining the lids together, his mind made up that he would, simultaneously with their opening, crash his fist upon the table and once and for all dispel this dream.

He opened his eyes. He banged down his fist. She was still there! But as he looked, she moved, and, as if awakened from some pleasant musing by his noise, turned her head slowly and regarded him.

"I am so glad that you have come, Pierre," she said.

Duchesne wilted. His tongue, sticking in no uncertain manner to the roof of his mouth, refused to function. His mind, very frightened, refused to concentrate its undivided attention on the plain business of speaking.

However, he could see, and when eventually the power of speech returned he was so taken up with the study of the exquisite colouring of her gown, the rise and fall of her bosom, and the gentle directness of the appeal in her eyes, that he had no wish to speak. It was only the discovery of the fact that he was becoming mesmerised by the sound of his own breathing which brought back to him some portion of his normal sanity.

"Will you not speak to me, Pierre?" she said. "Dear Pierre. . . ."

Directness of attack had always been one of the salient points in Pierre's rather peculiar character, and, mark you, if any of you are inclined to judge him somewhat too harshly, I would remind you that not every man has been surprised by such a wondrous woman at such an hour of the night, and, if you put yourselves in his place, you may find it in your hearts to produce some little admiration for his sang-froid.

Realise, if you please, that he knew that she could not possibly be of this world, and although he was perturbed by a slight trembling at the knees, and although he felt acutely the loss of his eyeglass, which had always lent him great moral support upon delicate business, he was still himself. In fact, the drooping smile which he affected upon urgent occasions had already appeared upon the corners of his mouth as he rose and seated himself with appreciable calmness upon the other end of the club fender.

He leaned towards her slightly, noticing that the firelight played upon her hands in exactly the same manner as it would upon yours or mine, and this fact, combined with the almost imperceptible movement which she made towards him, and the aforesaid gentleness (if not something more urgent) in her eyes, together with his own impertinence, prompted him to speak.

"You are quite amazing," he said. "Very beautiful, and I seem vaguely to remember you. In fact," he continued, gaining a little more courage, "I believe that I'm already rather in love with you!"

She laughed. Then, with a quick and entirely feminine movement, she came quite close to him. Her fingers laid lightly upon his hand, felt of flesh and blood; her breath, warm and comforting upon his chin, was most unspiritlike and human. She regarded him for a moment, waiting for him to speak, but he sat silent, a trifle confused by her proximity and the gentle pressure of her fingers.

"You are entirely sweet, Pierre," she said. "And very *young*. In fact, I know of no other man, who, returning at midnight to his rooms, and finding there a lady whom he knows only by thought, and who died some centuries before his birth, awaiting him, could, without preliminary inquiries, make such a cool declaration of love. However, I shall in a moment assuage your curiosity. In the meantime, I should be grateful if you would hold me in your arms for a few moments, for, believe me, this transition business between our world and yours is very cold, especially having regard to the climate and the extreme width of our skirts!"

Pierre obeyed with alacrity, his mind seeking some possible explanation for this entirely impossible happening. However, he found, at the moment, other and more important points to be considered, and gave himself up whole-heartedly to the business in hand.

After a little while she spoke:

"It would seem, Pierre, that your pulse is already working a trifle too quickly for the cool consideration of the business

which has brought me all this long way to talk to you. Therefore, with your permission, I shall sit in your big armchair,
whilst you, if you please, will remain here. Nay,"—she laid a
finger upon his already expostulating mouth—"I will have no
argument."

She slipped away, and sank gracefully into the armchair,
whose black cushions enframed the lace ruff about her throat.

Thus seated, she regarded him quietly.

"Do you understand, my friend, that there is and always
has been a time and a place for all things, and, just as children
are instructed to eat plain bread before their sweetmeats, so
must you earn your dinner. I will brook no interruption, and
if you find the study of my poor self too great a strain for your
amatory consciousness, then possibly you will look somewhere else that is less disconcerting."

Duchesne came to the conclusion that his silence would help.

"I will not say one word," he said, "except to tell you that
I will do anything you ask."

She twisted the ring upon her finger.

"There can be no doubt, Pierre," she said, "that I love you
very dearly. No other reason could have forced me to undergo
the extremely inconvenient and almost barbaric ritual necessary to enable me to return to this earth in order to hold
this converse with you. This, and the discomfort caused
to me by your writings and your possibly forgivable habit of
rummaging about in disused corners of the British Museum,
have brought me here tonight."

Duchesne stared.

"My writings! My rummaging about in the Museum!
What in the name of goodness do you mean? I . . ."

She interrupted. One slim forefinger upheld.

"Listen, Pierre, I will explain. It was in a disused corner
near the North Library in the British Museum that you
originally found the copy of that ancient book called '*The
Reckoning at Paloma.*' Very well. It was as a result of reading
these closely-printed pages originally written down by my
extremely gross lord, that you conceived the idea of writing

the unfinished story which now lies upon your table here. It is of this story that I would speak with you. For in plotting out this story, your mind, fresh upon the somewhat mystic description of happenings which you had read in '*The Reckoning at Paloma,*' shaped certain leading characters.

"In your mind's eye you saw these characters very clearly. You observed their features exactly. You heard their voices, and, in my case (for as you know I am the Margarita di Astoli of your tale), you spent an unnecessary and possibly—to you— exciting time over the possibilities of my figure. Of my own feelings during this process I say nothing at all!

"Eventually, we were all complete. Ugolini, Venaissin, and the rest of us. But,"—she leaned forward, her eyes gleaming— "what you did not know was the fact that we, as you saw us, had actually existed—nay, more, the story which you thought had originated in your brain was, in fact, partly true of us in our own time and in our own beloved country. Indeed, I firmly believe that some devil had actually selected you to bring us to life again, which you did, for you must know, Pierre, that when an author conceives characters who have actually lived in bygone centuries, then these unfortunates are compelled to leave their sweet rest and carry out the actual circumstances into which his mind and story drags them.

"Figure to yourself the inconvenience! How annoyed we all were! Venaissin, bored to tears, has been walking about in white velvet for three whole weeks—he who changed the colour of his suit three times a day, and even more often when he had business after nightfall.

"The language of Ugolini has been deplorable. He has invented no less than seventy-five new oaths of the most appalling variety, and has devised six hundred and twenty new tortures to be used on you directly your span of life is finished and you join us. And then—Listero—our aged and useful apothecary and chemist—who, in your story you have made a sweet and doddering old gentleman! Listero, who in our days spent his whole life in inventing strange and efficacious draughts for the use of ladies at inconvenient moments, and who died with pleasure at finding what you in these effete days would call 'the real goods,' what have you made of him? Naught but a dear old man giving sweet and motherly advice to erring virgins! For shame, Pierre!"

She paused, her bosom heaving with suppressed emotion. Duchesne, his fingers nervously gripping the edge of the club fender, gazed at her in wonderment, realising that she was speaking truth, and that there are more things in Heaven and on earth than are known to the British Broadcasting Corporation and other etheric meddlers of the moment.

She rose suddenly and seated herself beside him, placing her small hand over his. Pierre, experiencing a slight and chilly trembling of the stomach muscles, found that contact with this wonderful ghost robbed him of his power of speech, so he endeavoured to say nothing and found the process easy.

"I must not be unkind to you, my dearest one," she continued. "You were not to know. Had you, in these so-called civilised days, the services of some of our really great soothsayers, I have no doubt that many of these happenings, seemingly so inexplicable to you, would be made plain. However, I am here to tell you how this appalling mistake may be put right, and I know that you will do whatever I tell you. You would not hurt me any more, would you, Pierre?"

Duchesne found his soul gradually slipping out of his mouth. His breath came in great gulps and he sounded like nothing so much as a case of incipient pleurisy.

"Margarita, I will do anything . . . anything . . ." he gasped.

"Very well," said she smilingly. "Here is the remedy. On your table there, is the unfinished story. Last night you ceased your writing at a climax. At the moment, in your tale, Ugolini has carried me off and I am incarcerated in an upper chamber in his tower at Paloma. Venaissin (in white velvet as usual— God! How he hates you for that, Pierre) accompanied by a half troop of di Vona's Horse, is thundering on the tower door. You intended to round off the story as follows: Venaissin and Ugolini agree to fight for me, and this duel of course ends in the complete victory of Venaissin, who, with his usual urbane courtesy, carries me, a willing (and luckily, still virginal) sweetheart back to Milan, there to be married."

She stopped speaking and gazed at him for a moment.

"Oh, Pierre, you must realise that this cannot be," she continued after a moment. "I *hate* Venaissin . . . I have always loathed him, although I have never had cause to make it apparent. The man I love is Ugolini, and here you are planning to make Venaissin kill him and carry me off. Surely there was never a worse position. You must write the ending as *I* tell you, Pierre! Ugolini must kill Venaissin, throw his body—white velvet and all—out of the window and drag me back to the upper chamber."

Duchesne found his tongue at last.

"Margarita, it is impossible," he spluttered. "Realise what a wonderful fellow Venaissin is in *my* story. He has all the arts and graces of your times, he is a noted duellist, his affairs have always been marked with the utmost discretion, and then, when you have realised all this, consider Ugolini—a bandit, a hog, a wine-swilling cut-throat *condottiere*, noted through the length and breadth of Italy for his grossness and cruelty. How in the name of all that is merciful can I make him kill Venaissin and have you at his mercy?

"Another thing," he went on breathlessly. "What about my public? Be reasonable, Margarita. It is a tradition of the historical, romantic writer that the hero wins the heroine and the villain gets a kick in the pants. Venaissin is the hero. He *must* win you, and Ugolini *must* get what is coming to him. Any writer who allows a low fellow like Porro di Ugolini to get away with anything is simply asking for trouble."

She snuggled closer.

"It must be done, Pierre," she whispered. "I know that Porri di Ugolini is a fat and a rather gross old thing, but I'm very fond of him. I'm tired of slim young men, and I want Porro to get me. He has got such a way with him. Please . . . please . . . Pierre, do as I ask you."

Her head was close against his shoulder.

He struggled in her toils. But no! It was impossible! He

could not do as she asked. Who would buy a story in which
the hero is killed by the villain—and what a villain? No! It was
impossible. The financial aspect of the situation smote Pierre
like a well-aimed brick.

"Margarita, my very dearest Margarita," he said. "I entreat
you to listen to my explanation, for it is absolutely impossible
for me to do as you ask. This story is being written for a
certain Syndicate. The synopsis has been passed by them, and
if I alter the ending as suggested by you, they will, naturally
enough, refuse to buy it from me. Incidentally, I am very
hard up. I always am. I *must* have that money. No, Margarita,
it breaks my heart to refuse you but I cannot do it. Venaissin
must kill Ugolini and take you back to Milan. Anyhow," he
added as an afterthought, "he will take you back to his
mother's house, and where do you think Ugolini would have
taken you? Think of that, Margarita."

She pouted.

"Damn Venaissin's mother!" she said with spirit. "She is a
silly old cat, and a man who gets a woman for the express
purpose of taking her to his mother for approval is a fool
anyway. No, Ugolini's methods, whilst being possibly a little
more forcible, are, I am told, proportionately more interesting.
I want Ugolini to win and you must make him win. . . . Please,
Pierre."

Duchesne turned and looked straight at her.

"Listen, Margarita," he said, "I am being paid two hundred
pounds for this story. Supposing I do as you ask. What
happens? You will disappear quietly and contentedly, and I
shall remain here and endeavour to negotiate with the broker's
men who will be in these rooms in a week's time if I don't
get my fingers on that £200. That's the position . . . you
see?"

She nestled still closer, her eyes downcast.

"Oh, Pierre," she murmured, "I didn't know it was as bad
as that. But, Pierre . . . I had something else in my mind. I
thought that . . . that supposing you re-wrote the end of the
story as *I* wanted it . . . supposing you did this tonight when

I am gone (for I must go in a minute), then tomorrow you would ask your Syndicate if they would buy the altered script. If they refused, you need not worry a bit, for you see I should know all about it, and I could do this: Ugolini has a really wonderful emerald. I'd get that from him and bring it to you when I come tomorrow night. You could sell this stone, which would more than repay you for your loss over the story."

"When you come tomorrow night!" gasped Pierre. "Margarita . . . *are* you coming tomorrow night. . . .?"

She blushed—most effectively.

"If you rewrite the story tonight, Pierre," she murmured, her head hidden on his shoulder. "If you do this . . . I will come tomorrow night . . . and . . . and I shall not have to hurry away . . . so quickly . . . Pierre . . ."

Duchesne, his mind frozen into complete calmness by the necessity of quick decision, thought rapidly. Either he was mad or he was not mad. If he *was* mad it didn't matter anyhow. If he was not mad, why not accept the proposition, the emerald, and (his mind wobbled here somewhat) anything else which was included in the deal.

"Margarita," he said quickly. "Margarita, I will do it!"

The last word was only adequately out of his mouth when Pierre Duchesne found himself kissed. A kiss such as a million poets struggling in the abortive paroxysms of unrequited love have endeavoured vainly to describe. He closed his eyes and when eventually he opened them he found himself alone— entirely alone, except perhaps for a reminiscent suggestion of a violet perfume.

.   .   .   .   .

I need not tell you that there was little sleep that night for the fortunate (or is it unfortunate) Pierre, his mind vaguely troubled with the perfume which seemed in some inexplicable manner to cling to his pyjamas. However, the night, like all other nights, passed eventually and left him fatigued and still wondering.

Of an Experience of Pierre Duchesne

He found that the sun shining on the flat asphalt of Gower Street went ill with his uncertainty of events of the night before. Also, the comparison of the physical attractions of Margarita di Astoli with the sight of the more practical exuberances of the young ladies who go to the Royal Academy of Dramatic Art, to learn how to try to be actresses, exhausted him. At one moment the whole of last night's conversation would seem as definite as the four o'clock muffin man. At another, he found himself cursing his soul with wonderful vehemence for even considering the belief that this wondrous woman would carry out her promise to return that night.

Incidentally, he mused, supposing (just for the sake of argument) she did return. Pierre pondered, somewhat diffidently, upon the possible disadvantages of a really intimate conversation with a lady whose appearance in Bloomsbury was possibly connected with somewhat weird demonstrations performed in some dark place by the aged and peeved Listero, which demonstrations were, he presumed, aided by a smell of brimstone and the sacrifice of an astral cat, or something of that ilk. Time and time again he flung the subject from his mind, and, time and time again, like a theoretical boomerang, it returned with added strength and hit him for six over the boundary. Even a close inspection of his unpaid tailor's bill proved abortive, and the formal (and optimistic) request for a 'cheque by return' seemed to be written with ink composed of essence of violets.

Imagine, then, his state of mind when that night, somewhere about the time of midnight, he walked, with a step intended to be casual, down Gower Street. Again it was a wondrous night. A little colder than the night before, he considered. He allowed himself to dally with the idea that the temperature would matter not so much in the circumstances which (if everything he had ever believed to be logical were untrue) might possibly accrue. His mind, so taken up with the consideration of the weighty matters which had nearly unhinged it during the day, failed to allow his eyes quickly to observe the protruding figure of Krasinsky upon the corner of Tavistock Place, and it was only when that gentleman hailed him that Duchesne, with a slight start, came to his everyday senses.

"Dear Pierre," commenced Krasinsky, his nose shining with good humour. "I entreat you to listen to me. Last night I endeavoured to warn you against circumstances which might well be worth your considered opinion before allowing yourself to be gathered further into the silken web of unforeseen happenings. Will you listen to me for a moment?"

Pierre Duchesne gazed across at the trees which so adequately garnish the Catholic Apostolic Church on the corner of Gordon Square—a Church which (by the way) battles so bravely to preserve a vestige of atmosphere for Bloomsbury against the sordid coffee stalls of Euston. Krasinsky noticed his mouth, usually so firm and decided, was trembling. Fit company for the fingers which fumbled nervously with his watch chain.

"Go away, Krasinsky," he said decidedly. "My mind is made up and I will have none of you. Of your sincerity I have no doubt. None but a sincere man could wear such a suit of shepherd's plaid. But I tell you that your point of view goes ill with the things which are, at the moment, consuming my curiosity. Goodnight!"

Arrived at his house, his door key in his fingers, Duchesne, feeling rather like a member of the Swimming Club, which (for some icy reason best known to itself) dives into the Serpentine on Christmas mornings, wondered whether it would be possible, even at this juncture, to effect a retreat. His stomach, cold enough from nervous distortion, egged him to withdraw, but his remaining common sense urged him forward, knowing that unsatisfied curiosity is the worst evil that can befall one. At last, with something that resembled a sigh, he opened the door and stepped across the threshold.

Once there, his fears departed. As on the previous night, down the wide staircase came stealing that wonderful perfume which stilled all doubts and fears, and promised only wonders with no account of the reckoning. He *knew* that she was upstairs in his study—that she was sitting upon the club

fender gazing into the fire with eyes whose soul-melting softness was for him only. In one quick moment there came to
him the instantaneous realisation of all that would happen.
His fingers could almost feel the hard polished surface of the
emerald which lay in the palm of her hand, a palm so small
and white that it seemed made solely for the capture of kisses.
He cursed himself that, for a moment, he had considered the
financial aspect of the question, whilst in the same moment
his brain assured him of the wonderful profit of the deal!

His heart was beating to the immediate danger of his ribs as
he ran quickly up the stairs . . . his fingers trembled upon the
door knob. He flung open his study door, his eyes focusing
upon the glint of the firelight upon her hair . . . the glint of the
firelight on the emerald which lay in her hand. His mind swam
into an ecstasy of delirious joy as he crushed her in his arms
and found her mouth upon his. . . .

.   .   .   .   .

There are certain mornings when it would appear to us
that there is a conspiracy on the part of the entire universe
to contribute in some indirect manner to our own especial
happiness. This business, caused, I have no doubt, by an
essentially satisfied condition of our mental and physical beings,
commended itself to Pierre Duchesne most forcibly on the
morning after the events which I have so barely described to
you. As he sat upon his club fender, the very cream floating
upon the surface of his coffee seemed to smile. The sun shone
in Gower Street and some mysterious charm imbued the
somewhat dingy furniture with an appearance reminiscent of
the ideals of Mr. Drage.

Pierre, gazing before him, swung in his fingers a violet waist
ribbon. A wondrously resplendent ribbon with a pile un-
touched by time although obviously of great age. Upon the
corner of his table lay the emerald, its sun-caught surface
blazing.

Duchesne glowed with the intensity of his secret. A secret
so marvellously wonderful that already he visualised its

amazing effect-to-be upon his domination of lesser spirits in the future. The world was merely an oyster.

A knock upon the door brought him back to the realisation that there were still human beings in the world, and the sight of the homely and perhaps somewhat too ample countenance of the maid who entered, reminded him (by comparison) of the mystic beauty of Margarita.

"Mr. Krasinsky," said the maid, and clattered off.

They stood gazing one at the other. Each smiling and concerned with the effect of his own thoughts on the other. Pierre spoke first:

"Welcome, outwitted one," he murmured. "And do you, who surely consider that all things are known to you . . . know? If so, let your lecture be still-born. Never will I be warned by any man in the future. No . . . not even Krasinsky!"

Krasinsky's smile was like a sunrise.

"I came only to congratulate," he said. "Only that . . ." and his voice was as smooth as cream. "Figure to yourself, my Pierre, that I am no man to endeavour to take the gloss from our little life, and I behold that the ribbon in your fingers, also the emerald upon the table, may or not may out-value any small ideas of mine. However, like the philosophers who eat heartily before the consideration of great things, you, having eaten, may perhaps let your mind drop from its celestial floor of feathers and listen."

"Speak on," said Pierre. "For there is nothing in the world which can hurt me. My soul is charged with so much happiness that it can outweigh all sorrows."

Krasinsky pondered upon this.

"Even so," he said eventually, "the outlook must be gloomy . . . For you, my Pierre, trapped as you are . . ."

Pierre laughed.

"How . . . trapped?" he asked. "Have I not this ribbon and the emerald?"

Krasinsky permitted himself to be morose.

"The inadequate pondering upon facts, and complete indifference to certain philosophers, have contributed to the

inevitable ruin of many young men," said he. "Of this I have
no doubt whatsoever. The flash of a woman's skirt has been
the undoing of many a stalwart young fellow. So be it. At the
same time, Pierre, allow me to bring to your notice several
salient facts which may have escaped you. Do you realise that
this story which you had written—this unfinished story which
you, so gallantly, completed for a consideration or considerations which, I have no doubt, seemed to your businesslike
and passionate nature more than sufficient—is one which you
have not examined completely.

"When you originally wrote your story, you selected a hero,
my Pierre, built upon something which you found originally
in the British Museum—the book called '*The Reckoning at
Paloma*' but only slightly built upon that. You know that in
your own mind *you* were Venaissin. . . . Venaissin that immaculate duellist . . . whose affairs, so marked with discretion,
were but a mirror of your own desires. Margarita . . . who was
Margarita but the lady upon whom these desires of yours
(*and Venaissin's*) were centred? Well, my Pierre, my clever
one, do you not see?"

"See what?" demanded Pierre, bravely enough, although a
little sickness crept upon him.

Krasinsky took snuff.

"Pierre," he said, "it would appear that you have been
swindled. Do you not see that our sweet Margarita, in giving
you these things which you consider to be ample proofs of
affection, did but carry out the original ending of '*The Reckoning
at Paloma*'? Consider these things. She has to rid herself of
Venaissin in order to obtain Ugolini. You would have made
Venaissin conquer. She desired him dead. So, little friend, she
came, sold this emerald (together with other things of which
mention is forbidden by reason of my extreme delicacy) in
order that Venaissin might meet the end which she had
destined for him, and in killing him what, O thoughtless one,
did you do to Pierre? These matters and other continuations
of these things may interest you in the future."

Pierre raised his head which, in some unaccountable manner,

had sunk upon his breast, and observed that Krasinsky was gone.

For some reason known (possibly) to itself, the sun had departed, and he shivered a little. Also he observed, somewhat dully, that the ribbon in his fingers looked like nothing so much as a worn suspender which one associates with cheap corsets, and the sparkle of the emerald upon the table was only the glint of an imitation jewel such as may be purchased for a few shillings.

He looked in the mirror, and discovered that his face was tired. His reflection bored him and he moved to the window, opening it so that the somewhat stale scent of violets might leave the room. He looked up Gower Street, and then down, and it seemed to him that the day was like any other day that had gone, and not unlike any day that might come in the future.

In the distance the disappearing figure of Mr. Krasinsky reminded him of some distantly remote lessons in perspective.

. . . . . .

Pierre Duchesne awoke with a start. He felt very cold. His brain, revolving like a squirrel in a too-small cage, endeavoured vainly to think where he was . . . what had happened.

Suddenly, with a great sigh of relief he became aware of the fact that he had been dreaming; that he had returned home and that when he had endeavoured to switch on the electric light nothing had happened.

He rose and walked over to the switch. He moved it up and down. His sanity returned when he found that it would still not produce light. He struck a match and looked at the clock on the mantelpiece. It was four o'clock—and the episode of Margarita from beginning to end had been nothing but a dream.

Pierre walked to his bedroom and procured a candle. He lit it and brought it back to the dark sitting room. On the table were the unfinished sheets of the story. . . . He smiled to himself . . . it should be finished as originally planned . . . in spite of the dream.

He opened the window and looked out. Down the street, walking slowly and with a certain hilarity of step, Pierre saw the portly figure of Mr. Krasinsky departing into the shadows.

He closed the window. Then he sighed deeply. In the space of a few hours he had dreamed two whole nights and one day into his existence.

He sighed again.

"Thank you, Krasinsky," he said softly. "Thank you very much . . . *dear* Mr. Krasinsky!"

Of a Delay in the Post

It is without any morbid intention that the story of the deaths of Mrs. Viola Trequin and her chauffeur, Vals Schrot, is resuscitated.

It will be remembered that the bodies of this lady and Schrot were found in a leafy lane not far from Balkin Hall, where she lived with her husband Ferdinand Trequin. It is a regrettable fact that they were discovered in what is usually called a compromising situation, which fact may have well supplied a motive for murder, if murder it was. Also it may be said that there were details which would corroborate this theory.

There is the butler's story. The butler said that Mrs. Trequin ordered the car at three o'clock, and Schrot brought it round. That she had said that she would be returning to the Hall about four o'clock and would like tea served in the library.

He said that whilst she was talking to him the postman arrived with a large sealed envelope, which she took from the man.

Varness said that she opened the envelope and stood there reading the documents which were inside it; that he waited a few feet away thinking that she might have some further instructions for him, and that he could not fail to notice the expressions of surprise, of anguish and of intense rage, which followed each other across her face as she read. Varness said that by this time Schrot had brought the car round and stood waiting with the door open.

Then Mrs. Trequin put the envelope or package—whichever it was—under her arm, and, looking very white and troubled, went through the double doors and stepped into the car.

Varness said that he could not fail to notice that as she got into the car she put her hand on Schrot's arm with what seemed to be an affectionate gesture. He noticed it particularly because he had never seen her do such a thing before, and because she was a lady of a distinctly cool and reserved nature who was not likely to do such a thing. Schrot then got into the driving seat and the car disappeared down the drive.

Varness said that some four or five minutes afterwards Mr. Trequin came in and asked where his wife was. Varness told him. Trequin said nothing but turned on his heel and walked away down the carriage drive. This would be about five minutes past three.

The bodies of Viola Trequin and Schrot were found in a leafy glade not ten minutes' drive from the Hall. They were discovered at seven o'clock that evening by James Peebles, a rustic, who was taking a short cut to the village Inn at Southing. Medical evidence showed that in both cases death had occurred probably between a quarter past three and a quarter to four. It seemed possible that Ferdinand Trequin had by accident taken the same route as the car, and had come upon his wife and the chauffeur in an attitude which he considered rather too intimate for his own dignity and esteem; that he had shot the supposedly guilty pair.

This theory, however, was never provable because Trequin had never been seen from that day to this, and so no one has been able to ask him. No one ever discovered what was in the mysterious envelope or packet which had annoyed Mrs. Trequin so much and which she had taken with her when she left the Hall on the afternoon of her death, and it was believed that either she had destroyed the documents—possibly thrown them into one of the ponds near the lane—or else Trequin had taken the papers off with him.

A .38 Colt pistol was found in some bushes quite near, and the finding of this pistol showed that there was a remote possibility that Schrot had first of all shot his mistress and then turned the gun on himself, living for a few moments afterwards, during which time he had thrown the weapon into the bushes. The fact that his finger-prints were on the butt of the pistol supported this supposition.

On the other hand the position in which the two bodies were found gave very little credence to this theory, and it was generally believed that Ferdinand Trequin had murdered his wife and his chauffeur.

Briefly, this is an outline of the events which occurred on that lovely September afternoon.

.   .   .   .   .   .

It was in 1936—some three years after the tragedy—that I met Plimbell in the bar in the West End and we drank some cocktails together.

Plimbell had a certain difficulty in recognising me owing to the fact that while I was in France I had grown what I considered to be a rather attractive beard. He is one of those men who for some reason best known to themselves think that a beard is a funny thing.

Plimbell worked on a Sunday newspaper as a crime specialist, and in course of conversation brought up the Trequin affair. He knew that I was interested in that sort of thing and asked me whether I had ever formed a theory about it. Plimbell had covered the story for his paper and was able to give me a fairly good description of the appearance and general characteristics of the parties concerned.

He said that Viola Trequin was still a very beautiful woman at the time of her death. She was forty-three years of age, but looked a great deal younger. She was amusing, very well liked by people of her own class, and a great favourite with the villagers at Southing. Everyone agreed that there was something very fascinating about Mrs. Trequin and that she radiated an extraordinary sex-attraction which, strangely enough, was belied by the almost ice-like attitude which she adopted towards men in general.

Ferdinand Trequin, who was thirty-five years old when the killings happened, was—said Plimbell—a bit of a mystery. He was a good-looking fellow and must have been even more handsome when he was a younger man. He had met Viola Maninway—as she was then—in 1918, soon after he was demobilised from the Army, and they were married a few days afterwards. Plimbell said that he had seen a picture of the wedding, that they were a damned good-looking pair and that even if she was eight years older than Trequin—who was then exactly twenty—she certainly had something in the way of looks and figure.

Schrot, the chauffeur—the third figure in the tragedy—was a young fellow of eighteen. He was a Scandinavian, a tall, superbly proportioned, blue-eyed fellow with a charming complexion and a still more charming smile. Apparently quite a few of the Southing girls had tried to get friendly with Schrot, but the chauffeur, said Plimbell, wasn't having any. He just stood them off.

I asked him if he thought that there had been something on between Mrs. Trequin and Schrot, because it seemed to me that the most possibly theory was that Ferdinand Trequin had come upon them in the middle of a spot of fun and games and shot them out of hand. Plimbell said that this might be so—Trequin was a first-class pistol shot—but that he thought that there was a very remote possibility that Schrot might have killed Viola first and then shot himself, throwing the pistol away as he died.

Plimbell was certain in his own mind that the cause of all the trouble was the big envelope containing the papers that Mrs. Trequin had opened in the hall and carried off with her. Had these papers been found there might have been some hope of a solution. He said that Mrs. Trequin was not the sort of woman to take a tumble in the hay with a good-looking chauffeur on a summer's afternoon. He was quite definite about that. First of all she was of a cold nature where men were concerned, and secondly even if she had conceived a sudden passion for Vals Schrot she was not the sort of woman to take a chance of being discovered *in flagrante delicto* by selecting a spot near a country lane and a time when there was a good chance of someone passing by.

Plimbell went on to say that the crux of the whole business was the envelope that had arrived. Something in that envelope had made Viola Trequin see red, and anything that happened afterwards was a direct result of something that she had read. Personally, he was certain that Ferdinand Trequin had killed the pair and then gone off with the envelope.

I was very interested. I wanted Plimbell to go on talking, but he was getting tired of the subject. There was a young woman sitting at the end of the bar, taking bites at a cocktail cherry on the end of a stick. She was sitting on a high stool and her attitude, combined with the cut of the neat blue suit she was wearing, was, Plimbell said, worth a fiver to look at any time.

There and then I made up my mind to go down to Balkin and have a look round. I was fearfully interested in the whole business and I thought it would be amusing to spend a few hours down at Southing and drink a pint of bitter beer at the Inn, talk to the villagers and generally see what I could find out.

I thought it would be rather amusing to walk down that lane and imagine what had happened. I'd read a lot about the business in the newspapers at the time of the "Balkin Hall Tragedy"—as they called it—and I expected that I'd get some sort of a "kick" out of it.

By this time Plimbell was deep in conversation with the young woman at the end of the bar. I grinned goodbye at him and went home.

II

Next afternoon at three o'clock I was leaning on a five barred gate at the top of Four Acre Hill. It was a marvellous afternoon, hot and sunny, and an occasional breeze swayed through the bluebells that were growing all over the place.

Away over to my right I could see Southing village, and old Hinkles—the village handy man—pushing his barrow round into the stables. The sun was shining on the sign hanging outside the Wheatsheaf and there was that quiet buzz of insect life that one can hear on a quiet summer's day.

On my left hand side, down in the valley, I could see—over the east wall of Balkin Hall—the wonderful splash of colour formed by the flower gardens. The Hall itself, brown and romantic, the hillside rolling up behind it with Tarney Woods topping the rise, formed a background to a superb picture.

I began to think about the Trequins. It was on such an afternoon as this that Viola Trequin had read the contents of the envelope that, according to Plimbell, had caused so much trouble. I wondered what she had thought when she read it. What pictures had sprung into her mind as a result of looking through the papers inside, which, according to what Varness the butler had said at the inquest, looked like a "lot of buff Army Forms pinned together and stamped with rubber stamps."

I opened the gate and walked towards the spinney, and into the thickly hedged lane beyond, towards the little clearing where the bodies had been discovered by Jimmy Peebles. I had talked to the old man before lunch and after his second pint he had opened up considerably. According to Jimmy, Schrot and Viola Trequin must have thrown discretion to the winds on that summer's afternoon after Schrot had parked the big car in the gateway at the end of the lane. Jimmy had said with a grin that if he hadn't seen the car and recognised it he would never have turned into the lane, and that would have been not so good for Jimmy, who had been telling the story with its accompanying free pints at the Wheatsheaf ever since, although, he informed me glumly, people weren't so keen on listening these days as they were. . . .

I sat down on an old tree stump on one side of the little clearing and filled my pipe. I was alone when I bent my head to light it, but when I raised it and threw the match away I saw that there was a rather extraordinary-looking old boy sitting in the hedge on the other side. He was an odd-looking bird. He had on a shepherd's plaid suit with a gold albert that looked as big as an anchor chain stretched across his waistcoat. He was wearing a very old-fashioned bowler hat, and in one hand he held the stub of a cigar. As I looked at him he put a finger and thumb in his waistcoat pocket and proceeded to take a pinch of snuff with obvious pleasure.

Then he smiled across at me. There was something rather nice about the cut of his round face. I wondered what the deuce he was doing there. He didn't look like a country man and he didn't look like a town bird either. I thought it funny that I hadn't noticed him before.

"Good afternoon, Sir," he said. "I'm sorry if I have disturbed your reverie, but to tell you the truth I've been lying here considering the beauty of the countryside and, I am afraid, dropped off to sleep."

He paused to examine the end of the cigar stub. After a close scrutiny he put it into his mouth and lit it with a single match that he produced from his coat pocket.

"This spot, as you may be aware, is an historic spot," he continued smilingly. "This is the place, Sir, where the bodies were discovered. Possibly you have heard something about it?"

"I've heard a great deal about it," I replied. "In fact I'm rather interested. I'm one of those people who are interested in crime and the atmospherics of crime. I like to go to places where crimes have been committed. Sometimes I get ideas...."

"Precisely, my dear Sir," said he heartily. "I'm rather like that too. In fact I'm afraid that I've been doing the same sort of thing myself for a very long time. My name," he continued, smiling still more broadly, "is Krasinsky."

I thought it an odd name, and I thought too that he was an extremely attractive sort of old bird. There was something fearfully experienced about him . . . something very trustworthy . . . on which one couldn't quite put one's finger. I'm not very good with strangers but for some odd reason I found myself believing that I'd known this strange portly person with his incongruous name for some time, and the more I looked at him the more this absurd thought persisted.

"I appreciate your curiosity and interest in the tragedy that happened here," he went on, "and the joke is—if there is a joke—that I am the only living person who knows the truth of the business." He blew a very good smoke ring and watched it. "I know the whole story . . . every bit of it."

"That's interesting," I said. "I've been making some enquiries about the leading characters in the 'Balkin Hall Tragedy' round about the village and in the neighbourhood generally this morning. But I haven't learned much. I suppose it would be asking too much . . .?"

He smiled across at me. There was something very friendly in his smile.

"Not at all, my dear Sir," he said. "Not at all. As a matter of fact I should be delighted to tell you the whole story. I will do so immediately."

I settled myself comfortably on the tree stump. My pipe was drawing well. Somehow—I couldn't think why—I was certain in my mind that this strange old fellow was going to tell me the truth.

He lay back restfully against the green bank. For a moment there was that peculiar unsilent silence that comes to the country on such an afternoon as this was. There was the twittering and cooing of birds, the soft buzz of a bee that was very busy in our neighbourhood, and a quiet rustling of leaves when a breath of the summer breeze came through the lane.

I looked at my wrist watch. It was four o'clock. I began to think that whatever happened I mustn't miss my train at six-thirty, and then, in the same instant, realised that I didn't very much care if I did miss it; that I wanted, very badly, to hear what my new-found friend had to say about Viola and Ferdinand Trequin and Vals Schrot.

I got up and lay down on the warm grass with my back against the stump. I closed my eyes. Then Krasinsky began to talk.

· · · · ·

Of a Delay in the Post

"It was on a warm summer's afternoon in August 1916," said Krasinsky, "that Lieutenant Ferdinand Donneton (he changed his surname to Trequin by Deed Poll in 1918, just before his marriage, at the wish expressed in the will of a relative) walked down the main street in Paris-Plage with that unconscious and vaguely grandiose air which distinguished him.

He was eighteen years of age and had already experienced one year's active service as an infantry officer; but this experience, far from coarsening what might best be described as an idealistic and romantic nature, had merely served to superimpose upon his true character a superficial attitude of toughness which he had adopted in very much the same way as one puts on an overcoat in the cold weather.

He was tall and slim. He had an air. He was one of those lucky men whose style and appearance is such that they look good in any sort of clothes. His uniform was spick and span, and he wore a voluminous "G.S." waterproof cloak which, intended by the Ordnance Department to provide protection in the front line trenches, added—as he well knew—a romantic touch to his khaki.

Donneton was happy, and this is not to be wondered at, because he was taking a ten days' course at the Machine Gun School at Camiers, which, situated not far from Paris-Plage, allowed the young officers—and there were some hundreds of them—who were attending the course, to sample the sea air of the watering place and to indulge in a little quiet drinking, undisturbed by the chatter of machine guns, the bellow "stretcher-bearers this way!" and the other normal and uninteresting accompaniments of front-line warfare.

It is necessary that something should be known of the character of Ferdinand Donneton. He was a mixture of ideals, caution and evasive modesty where women were concerned, but possessed an intense curiosity about them, which, had it not been controlled, might have got him into some difficult situations.

And his year in France and Flanders had not enabled him to satisfy this curiosity. He was—and how he would have hated to admit it!—entirely inexperienced in the matter of women. He had never possessed one, because, in England, before joining the British Expeditionary Force, he had had no opportunity, and, on arrival in France, he was sadly disillusioned by the discovery that most of the ladies who were available were not of a type that appealed to him, mainly because they seemed entirely unselective and regarded one khaki uniform as being very much the same thing as another.

His idea that service abroad was to be a mixture of fighting the enemy with intervals of making love to charming, *chic* and cultured ladies, who, for reasons best known to themselves, were unable to withstand the sex-appeal of Ferdinand, had proved itself to be quite erroneous ; and this fact had produced in him an intense disappointment, combined with an obstinate consistency of attitude which proclaimed—but only to himself—that if he could not have the sort of woman he wanted then he would have none at all.

So he had had none at all, and his curiosity—always intense—was now sharpened to an almost unendurable degree. Ferdinand desired nothing so much as to be entirely familiar with the more subtle *nuances* of the art of selective love-making under the best possible circumstances and with the best possible lady. But nothing had ever happened to solve this difficulty.

Yet nobody would have believed him to be inexperienced. On the contrary the rakish angle of his hat, the air with which he carried his cane, the set of the aforesaid "G.S." cloak which, on *his* shoulders, looked almost medieval, all stamped him as a young gentleman who had made the most of his opportunities and who knew very much more about the so-called weaker sex than most of his contemporaries.

Thus do appearances give the lie to the proverb *"le style c'est l'homme."*

Half way down the street, on the corner of the Rue Persse, deep in conversation, he saw the figures of two friends, Infantry officers who were at the Machine Gun School—one, Conelly, a subaltern in an Irish regiment, the other—McLeod, an officer in a Highland Battalion. These two men, both of them slightly older than Donneton, and whose units were brigaded with his, were cut to the pattern of those youthful infantry subalterns whose "fighting life", as we well know, averaged a matter of about thirteen weeks, and who naturally endeavoured to crowd as much into that time as they could.

Donneton joined the group.

"Hello," said McLeod. "Possibly you can help us, Donny. I've been having an argument with this mad Irishman here."

Donneton smiled as he lit a cigarette.

"I'll bet fifty francs it was about women," he said.

"Right first time," said McLeod. "Conelly says that we're all wrong in our ideas about French women. He says that it isn't the apparently passionate type that falls most easily. He says you want to find one who looks cold, austere and a little bit distinguished, and they fall about six times as quickly as the other type. I say no. What do you think?"

"I don't know," said Donneton. He grinned at Conelly. "But if I were you, Conelly," he said, "I wouldn't let any ideas like that run away with you in this part of the world. This place is in the French area. It would be too bad if you tried out your theory and made a mistake. You might find yourself in for a court-martial. I'd take it easy if I were you."

"All my eye, dear boy," said Conelly, his Irish eyes twinkling. "I've been out here eight months and I haven't made a mistake about a woman yet."

McLeod said: "Perhaps you've been lucky."

Then both he and Conelly looked at Donneton who was looking down the street, his eyes almost popping.

"Can you see what I see?" he murmured.

They looked. Walking towards them on the other side of the street was a woman. She was about thirty years of age. She had all that *chic* which French women are supposed to possess. She was quite superb. Her face was oval, her features delicately carved and about her eyes were those blue shadows suggestive of tiredness which can add such attraction to the face of a certain type of woman.

Of a Delay in the Post

"A wonderful woman," said Donneton. "Do you notice how she puts her feet on the ground, and what exquisite shoes!"

He sighed and then saw the look in Conelly's eyes.

"But she is not for you, Conelly, my boy," he said, "or for me—or even for McLeod whose kilts have fluttered the hearts of more French ladies than ever you or I will wot of."

Conelly drew on his cigarette. His eyes were very bright.

"Why not, Donny?" he said.

"Listen," said Ferdinand. "Isn't it quite obvious to you that that woman is what is commonly called a 'nice' woman? Isn't it also obvious to you that she is a woman of good class, and haven't you learnt by now that a French woman of good class can be a very tough proposition? If you tried to start any funny business she'd probably walk straight round to the provost-marshal's office, my friend. No; she is not for you, Conelly. You'll have to content yourself with thinking about 'Mademoiselle from Armentieres.' That's as far as you'll get."

Conelly, with a sudden gesture, threw his cigarette away.

"Rats, Donny!" he said. "As for you, McLeod, I'll take that bet you were offering when Donny joined us. . . . You : I was wrong about the type of French woman who falls easiest. *That* was the type I was talking about."

He indicated, with a look, the woman who had now passed.

McLeod said: "Don't be a fool, Conelly. Even if you won fifty francs it wouldn't be worth the risk."

Conelly said: "Is the bet still on or isn't it? Are you backing out?"

Donneton said: "Don't be a bloody fool, Conelly. It's asking for trouble."

Conelly grinned. Then he put his stick under his arm, walked across the road quickly and after the woman.

McLeod said: "My God, he's going to try it! What a damn fool!"

Donneton took out his cigarette case and lit a cigarette. He was watching Conelly as he overtook the woman. He saw Conelly speak to her, saw the look of intense surprise, followed by one of indignation, which crossed her face.

Then: "Let me handle this, Mac," he said, "otherwise that damn fool will be for it."

He walked quickly across the road. The lady was telling Conelly all about himself. She was telling him that he was a cad in very quiet, precise and cutting French. She turned and looked at Donneton as he joined them.

Donneton clicked his heels and saluted. He put a great deal of reverence and respect into that salute. Then he began to speak in rather bad, halting French, but in a very low and attractive voice.

He asked pardon. He pointed out to Madame that if she believed that his brother officer had intended any rudeness whatsoever to her, might he be permitted to point out to Madame——

The lady, who had been studying his face intently, said Yes he might be permitted to point out to her why an officer should have the effrontery to make such an appalling suggestion as his friend had made. She would be interested to hear. Her voice was very cold.

Donneton said, with a little deprecating smile, that he asked Madame's pardon but she was still mistaken; that he, Donneton, was in a position to know that she was wrong. He would like to point out to Madame that as she had approached them on the other side of the road his friend, Conelly, had remarked that here was the lady on whom he had been billeted some months before when he was staying in the town, that he was certain that it was she, that he must say good afternoon to her.

Donneton pointed out that both he and their mutual friend had told Conelly that they believed he was mistaken, but he had persisted that the lady had been his hostess.

Anything which had annoyed Madame, Donneton went on with a charming smile, was merely the result of the execrable French of *Monsieur le Lieutenant* Conelly, who in no circumstances would make an indelicate suggestion to any lady.

She took a very long look at Donneton. She looked for a moment straight into his eyes, then she looked him up and down. Then she smiled a very small and somewhat cynical smile. Then she said:

Of a Delay in the Post

"*Mon Lieutenant*, I accept your explanation. It is perhaps as you have said."

She inclined her head towards Conelly.

"Good afternoon, Sir," she said. "I hope that you will not make any more mistakes whilst you are here in Paris-Plage. It might not be agreeable for you."

Conelly saluted, threw a quick look of thanks at Donneton, turned on his heel and walked back across the street to where McLeod, a wry smile on his face, awaited him.

Donneton touched his hat. He said to the woman:

"I am grateful to Madame for being so understanding. Madame is very kind."

He saw that there was a suggestion of warmth in her eyes. She said to him:

"*Mon Lieutenant*, I am going to the tram. I wish to go to Etaples. Perhaps if you could find it convenient to escort me to the terminus I should not be annoyed by other gentlemen who might believe that they also have been billeted on me at some time or other."

Donneton said he would be enchanted. They walked down the street together towards the tram stop.

Conelly and McLeod stood on their corner, looking after them.

"Well, I'll be damned!" said Conelly.

.   .   .   .   .

"Trequin—for I propose to call Donneton by the surname which he afterwards took—was never quite certain as to whose suggestion it was that he should accompany Madame to Etaples," Krasinsky continued.

"The journey—as you will doubtless know—takes about half an hour, and during that time he had ample opportunity for studying, out of the corner of his eye, the outline and general characteristics of the lady he was accompanying.

She was slightly above middle height, and her eyes were grey-blue. They were cold, but could brighten perceptibly when she wanted them to. Her face was quite delightful and

175

Trequin was especially taken with her mouth. It was a superb mouth. It was deliciously shaped and gave evidence, when she smiled, of a peculiarly tremulous quality which enchanted him. Sitting beside her in the tram, answering in slow and carefully thought-out French when she spoke to him, and endeavouring to avoid the eyes of a burly Australian officer who was sitting opposite and whose interest in his companion's ankles was of the frankest and most complimentary kind, Ferdinand cursed quietly to himself about the unattainability of the one woman who had attracted him since he had been in France.

When she spoke to him—and most of the conversation consisted in questions from her about the war and its progress —and turned to him for the purpose, Trequin found himself almost hypnotised by the cool glance from the long-lidded grey-blue eyes which were so delightfully shadowed by that appealing tiredness which is so much more effective than any "eye-blue" that comes out of a box. On these occasions he would find himself unable to continue to look at her and would be forced to look straight in front of him at the Australian officer, who, from time to time, permitted himself to grin at Trequin in a sympathetic manner.

The tram arrived at the Etaples terminus. Trequin got out. Something closely resembling a shiver went through him as he took her hand to help her down from the tram step.

He walked with her to the pavement. There she stopped and held out her hand. He took it, pressed it gently and saluted.

"I am under a great obligation to you, Madame," he said. "I shall always remember this tram journey. Whatever happens to me I shall remember this afternoon."

She looked at him. Trequin thought that the grey-blue eyes were not quite so cold.

"*Mon Lieutenant,*" she said—in a very cool, quiet and entirely normal voice. "It gives me great pleasure to look at you. My name is Madame Ferasse-Mousqueton, and I live with my husband at the Villa Bleue, which is at the end of the Paris-Plage promenade. Sometimes we live here, at our house in Etaples, and sometimes my husband's business keeps him here for two or three days, during which time I stay at the Villa with my maid.

"One imagines," she continued as if she were discussing the most ordinary of topics, "that you are at the Machine Gun School at Camiers. It may be that you will be free after five o'clock. It may be that tomorrow, for instance, you will walk down the promenade and discover for yourself the Villa Bleue.

"Having done this, you may be sufficiently interested to look at the balcony which runs round the front and side of the house. Possibly you will see, hung over the balcony at the side, a white shawl. If you do see such a shawl then, if you desire it, you may come to the Villa and take tea with me, and I should like, very much, to show you an interesting game that I have invented.

"If on the other hand you see, thrown over the front of the balcony, a blue shawl, you will, if you please, *not* approach the place as this signal will mean that my husband, M. Ferasse-Mousqueton is at home and he is not partial to young men such as yourself. *Mon Lieutenant*, I wish you good afternoon."

She smiled. Trequin watched her as she walked away. His heart was thumping like a steam roller."

. . . . . .

Krasinsky blew an almost perfect smoke ring. After which he threw away the stub end of his cigar. For a moment he watched a thrush which returned his stare before flying away. Then:

"At ten minutes past five on the next afternoon," continued Krasinsky, "Trequin, possessed of a most peculiar sinking feeling in the stomach, walked down the Paris-Plage promenade in search of the Villa Bleue.

His mind, having concerned itself with nothing but Madame Ferasse-Mousqueton since the previous afternoon, was quite chaotic. Uncertainty had reduced him to an almost total wreck.

For he could not make up his mind about this entirely delightful person who had said that she liked to look at him. Nothing about her indicated that she was the type of woman

M   177

who would permit herself an *affaire* with a casually met young officer. Her method of speech, her cold eyes, her absolute poise and the entirely normal and matter-of-fact manner in which she had introduced her husband into the conversation inclined Trequin to the belief that the idea that anything passionate was possible where this lady was concerned was entirely incorrect. No, the probability was, he reasoned, that her husband, like so many middle-aged French gentlemen, was bored with the sight of the continuous stream of British officers who thronged the base camp at Etaples and, when possible, descended on the bars and cafés of Paris-Plage.

Madame herself, thought Trequin, was perhaps lonely. Most of her friends were away at the war. Her husband was probably concerned, in some way or other, with French national service. This, said Ferdinand to himself, was the truth of the matter. She was merely being gracious to him because he had endeavoured politely to straighten out the fearful *gaffe* that Conelly had achieved.

Across the lawn that bounded the shore side of the promenade he saw the villa. The name 'Villa Bleue' was painted on the white gate. On the side balcony, casually thrown, hung a white Spanish shawl.

Trequin looked round him. There was no one in sight for the villa was at the end of the promenade and a good hundred yards from the next house. He walked quickly across the road, through the white gate, up the short flower-edged gravel path and knocked on the door.

A trim maid opened it immediately. She closed the door behind Trequin, took his hat, cane and cloak, deftly folded the cloak, laid it on a chest in the hall and with a little gesture indicated that he should follow her.

Across the hall was a door. The maid opened it. "*Monsieur le Lieutenant,*" she announced quietly, and Trequin saw, sitting behind the tea table, which was set before the opened French windows looking out over a lawn, Madame Ferasse-Mousqueton, who, with a quiet smile, wished him good afternoon. Her eyes —very blue this afternoon—regarded him almost gravely.

Of a Delay in the Post

He sat down opposite her. He found a great difficulty in finding anything to say. He knew that she realised the fact; that she was rather amused by it.

Very seriously she asked him how he liked his tea.

.   .   .   .   .

The maid took the tea-things away.

Madame rose and walked to the escritoire on the other side of the room. Trequin, a little more at ease since tea, but still a trifle scared of something which he did not quite understand, watched her.

He was a little worried, a little annoyed with himself. All the technique, the opening and closing gambits which he had thought out for use on such an occasion, had departed from him. He found that his mind was particularly blank and consented only to wake up with a jerk and answer when he was spoken to.

She came back. She carried a square pad of drawing paper and two pencils. Trequin noticed that the pad and the pencils were quite new. She put them on the table.

"*Mon Lieutenant*," she said, "this is my game. It is an amusing game. Each of us takes a pencil and one begins to draw an animal of some sort. I suggest a horse. The beginner draws a little of the horse; then the other player continues the outline and each takes it in turn to add to the picture. The idea of the game is to force the other to complete the drawing—you will find it takes more skill than one would imagine.

"The player who is forced to finish the complete picture of the horse loses the game and must pay a forfeit."

Trequin nodded agreement. He was rather at a loss for words. He was wondering exactly what Conelly or McLeod would have thought—and said!—could they have visualised him, sitting there, drawing pictures of horses.

A little breeze had sprung up. Madame closed the French windows. Then she sat down opposite Trequin and drew an inch or so of what he imagined to be the backbone of the horse. Then she pushed the pad towards him.

Of a Delay in the Post

It was Trequin who finished the drawing. He laid down his pencil and looked at her. She was regarding him sombrely.

"*Mon Lieutenant,*" she said. "You have lost. You must pay a forfeit. Shall I tell you what you must pay?"

Her voice was so quiet, so almost disinterested that he thought the forfeit would probably be *ten centimes* or something equally childish. He hoped sincerely that this game would now finish.

"If you please, Madame," he said.

She began to smile. He could see her small and perfect teeth between the tremulous lips. She got up and came round the table. She stood by him.

"*Cher Lieutenant,*" she said softly. "You are so frightened, are you not? But you must pay your forfeit. I desire," she continued, and he could see her eyes changing colour, "that you shall embrace me—*immediately*!"

He got up. He stood there silently. He found himself suffering from some kind of mental paralysis that made him feel rather like the village idiot.

And it was only when he felt her mouth on his that he realised that the only truly delightful possibilities in life are those which—up to the very last moment—seem to be impossible.

. . . .

Trequin's eight days passed quickly. Each day was an adventure in which the crucial moment depended upon whether the white shawl hung over the balcony at the Villa Bleue. Sometimes, when Monsieur Ferasse-Mousqueton was safely ensconced in his office in Etaples, Trequin and Madame would investigate the lesser paths that thread through the woods between Paris-Plage and Camiers. Every hour which he spent with her seemed to him to be imbued with an excitement almost indescribable. He was thrilled to watch her walk, to listen to the soft cadences of her voice, to remind himself that he had possessed this delightful person whose quiet gravity formed such an adequate comparison with the complete abandonment with which she could surrender.

Of a Delay in the Post

If ever a man was absolutely seduced it was Trequin. At odd moments, sitting alone in his tent, at the Machine Gun School, he would wonder what the devil was going to happen when the time came for him to rejoin his regiment. The idea of not seeing her for a long time was almost unbearable and he was glad to dismiss it from his mind as quickly as possible. That life would be intolerable without her was quite obvious to him and already he was considering ways and means to make a return to Paris-Plage possible in the near future.

On the last morning at the Machine Gun Course, when orders for rejoining units were read out, he realised with a shock that within the next two or three days he would find himself in a front-line trench somewhere on the Somme front. Vaguely he began to realise why soldiers sometimes deserted — a process which he had never before been able to understand.

When the morning parade was dismissed he considered the awful possibility that a blue shawl might today be hanging on the balcony; that he might not even be able to see her before he left that night. The very thought brought to him an extraordinary unhappiness which persisted until the sight of her car, parked down the Camiers Road, in a spot where he must see it on leaving the camp gates, brought a sudden and delightful thrill.

They said goodbye to each other on the corner of the little wood that lies behind Paris-Plage. Trequin was glum and silent. He leaned against a tree smoking a cigarette and looking a picture of abject misery.

"My dear," she said to him softly, "it is quite unnecessary to be so despondent. A soldier should be one who smiles continuously and who takes a woman into his arms merely as an interlude to warfare."

She smiled at him.

"You would like me to consider you merely as an interlude?" demanded Trequin in execrable French.

She came close to him. From his knees upward her body was pressed close against him. After a moment she drew away.

"Ferdinand," she said. "You will listen to me, if you please.

You will try to understand that what I am saying to you is for your own good; for your own happiness. Because you have known nothing of women before, this loving interlude of ours seems to you to be the most important thing in your life. You are wrong, my dear friend, quite wrong. It is merely a part of your life just as the battle of the Somme will also be part of your life, and, probably, a dozen other women."

He stopped her mouth with his hand.

"You were the first. Why should you not be the last?" he asked.

She smiled at him.

"Dearest child," she said. "After you are gone you will think so differently. All this intimacy, this business of being together, will be done and finished. In a week my memory will become fainter. In a month I shall be—just a memory . . . something that you will remember now and then."

He crushed her against him.

"You are a liar," he muttered. "A beloved liar. I shall never forget you. After you any other woman will serve only to make a bad comparison. I must come back to you. We cannot finish here . . . like this! It is inhuman and it is impossible."

She asked him for a cigarette. He gave her one, took one for himself and lit them. She stood before him, the smoke curling up gently from her mouth.

"*Cher Lieutenant*," she said. "We shall see. In a week's time I shall write to you. Four or five days after that—wherever you may be—you will receive my letter. By then you will have been away from me for nearly two weeks. My memory will have faded just a little.

"Very well. You will reply to my letter, will you not? And I shall know by your reply whether you still think of me; whether I am so important to you as it seems to you at this moment. If I am then we must plan. It must be your business to remain alive so that you may come back to me. But I do not think that your letter will tell me that. I think it will be a charming letter but that is all. Already the hand of time will have rubbed a little of my writing from your memory."

"We shall see," said Trequin. He looked at his wrist watch.
"I must go," he muttered like a surly child.

"Go then," she said. "But go smilingly. Remember that you are now very experienced."

For a moment her eyes glowed with delicious naughtiness.

"Dear friend," she said. "If you forget me greatly, you will please to remember that it was I who made out of you a very charming lover."

She threw her cigarette away.

"*Cher Lieutenant*," she said. "*Adieu*."

She turned from him quickly and walked away. She disappeared among the trees. He remained there for a moment hopelessly wondering what he should do, and then, with a despairing shrug of the shoulders, he set off down the path towards Camiers.

He never saw her, or heard of her again.

.   .   .   .   .   .

"Trequin," Krasinsky went on, "was wounded in the early part of 1918. He was badly hit and realised that his fighting days were over. He left hospital some four or five weeks before the Armistice and met Viola Maninway a fortnight later.

He had not been at all concerned with women since the episode of Madame Ferasse-Mousqueton. The fact that she had never bothered to write to him as she had promised had filled him with a bitterness as deep as it was unreasonable. He believed that she had been amusing herself at his expense, and had not the intelligence to realise that in any event *he* had lost nothing over the romance.

In fact he was, in his heart, still deeply in love with Madame. No woman he had since met had ever thrilled him to the remotest degree. By now Trequin looked *very* experienced—a veritable *beau sabreur* where women were concerned—for his two and a half years of active service had strengthened his character and added to his appearance, and many charming women would have been glad to have penetrated behind the attitude of superficial but charming cynicism which he used so effectively.

Of a Delay in the Post

No one who knew him at all well—or thought they knew him well—would have believed that the amatory experience of this tall, still very young and distinguished-looking individual was confined to an eight day *affaire* with one woman. Only Trequin himself knew that since Madame he had never met any woman who possessed an iota of her charm, her experience, her personality or her passion. He resented the fact that, having introduced him so adequately to the arts of love, she had dismissed him from her mind, probably because—he thought bitterly—she was concerned with the attentions of other young and still unknowledgeable men, who had possibly stolen down the promenade at Paris-Plage whilst he was in the Somme Battle, with their hearts fluttering and their eyes skinned for the sight of a white shawl hanging on a balcony. Young men who, *in their turn*, having learned *their* lesson in love, might pass on to make way for the next.

I have said that he met Viola Maninway at the end of nineteen eighteen. They were married within three weeks. Their reasons for marrying were amusing and very different. Viola desired to have Trequin for a husband because she, like Madame Ferasse-Mousqueton, believed him to be absolutely inexperienced where women were concerned and Trequin, having found out which way the cat was jumping, allowed her to believe just what she wanted to believe for two reasons. First that she reminded him in feature, physically, and in some aspects of character, of Madame, and secondly because she had money and he was broke.

Trequin did not marry her only for her money. He would not have done this. He married her because certain things about her brought back to his mind the woman with whom he had spent the happiest hours of his life. It would be true to say that the affection for Viola which came later on was soon afterwards leavened with an increasing irritation that she should look so like Madame Ferasse-Mousqueton and yet fail so dismally in all matters relating to the passionate side of love. Viola was a fraud. Everything about her—thought Trequin—everything of her cool, poised and quietly smiling self, promised the superb passion which Madame could achieve at the mere raising of an eyelid. But the promise was not kept.

Viola, who was eight years older than Trequin, had come of a family which believed itself to be essentially *moral*. She had been taught from the beginning that "sex" was a thing which was really best avoided if possible; that if it could not be avoided it must be suffered with the best available grace; that it was really rather a nuisance.

Viola at twenty-eight, rather shocked at the behaviour of some of her friends during the war period, had made up her mind that if and when she married it should be to a man who had not left behind him a trail of mistresses whose only dissatisfaction was that they *had* been left behind. When Trequin appeared she almost sprang at him. Here was a man who looked well, who spoke well, who had had a not undistinguished war service, and who was fit to be her mate because (as she thought) he had never had the opportunity of discovering whether he was fit to be any woman's mate.

Of such is the kingdom of 'pure' women.

Viola was repressed— I believe that is the word— because she was afraid to be anything else. After she was married to Trequin she did not want to be repressed and if Trequin had helped it may be that everything would have been well. Trequin, however, did not want to help. He was bored with Viola because she had not, immediately after marriage, turned herself into a Madame Ferasse-Mousqueton. Foolishly, he did not realise that that process could have been achieved very easily had he taken the slightest pains in the matter.

But, obstinately, he felt disinclined to take pains and, although *he* did not understand it, the reason was not at all mysterious. Underneath his superficial cynicism Trequin was a dreamer and he was still—in the uncharted realms of his mind—continuing his *affaire* with Madame.

Naturally, Viola's self-esteem began to suffer. The passionate love which had been at Trequin's disposal turned to a mild anger, then a dislike, then an almost passionate hatred.

And, at the crucial time in this business of passionate hatred, Trequin engaged Vals Schrot as chauffeur, and the fat was in the fire.

.   .   .   .   .

Viola bought Balkin Hall in 1930 and they took possession of the place on her fortieth birthday. She had imagined that living in the heart of the country might make her more content.

The chauffeur, Schrot, was engaged by Trequin through an agency. He was a fine young fellow, of good education. His father had been a sea captain who had been drowned at sea, and his mother had died soon after. A strange, lonely person was Schrot.

It was of course indicated that he should fall in love with Viola, who was fond of being driven about the countryside. The chauffeur was a young man of quick perception, and it was not long before he realised exactly what the situation was between Trequin and his wife. Vals, who was in his own way idealistic and chivalrous, kept his amatory yearnings to himself, until one afternoon, too strongly affected by the atmospherics of a long drive, and the proximity of Viola (they were using the two-seater), he had allowed himself to make a halting and passionate declaration of love.

Viola was slightly amused and afterwards interested. She resented the attitude of Trequin who, in these days, had developed the habit of walking about the woods all day, potting at rabbits with his .38 automatic—which he invariably carried in his coat pocket for that purpose—returning at night to eat his dinner, taking a walk to Southing Inn and then going straight to his room on his return.

So far as he was concerned Viola might not have existed.

However, she was woman of the world enough to know that nothing stays put; that a situation either develops or goes backwards. She knew that her business was to send Schrot packing about his business, and when she decided not to do this she was perfectly well aware that one day something would happen.

It did. It happened in the early part of 1933 on a January day, the day on which Viola became her chauffeur's mistress in fact as well as fancy.

Trequin—who was no fool—had already sensed that *something* was afoot between his wife and the chauffeur but he did not realise that the something was quite so definite. He thought that Viola was amusing herself with a mental flirtation with the good-looking youngster and much he cared.

Shortly before the day on which Jimmy Peebles found the bodies, Trequin observed that the breech action of one of his pair of automatic pistols needed oiling. He gave the pistol to Schrot to clean. It was a ten shot pistol with four cartridges in the clip. Schrot cleaned the gun and had it in his side pocket for return to Trequin on the day that the envelope arrived."

.　　　.　　　.　　　.　　　.

Krasinsky plucked a blade of grass and began to chew it. I noticed that his teeth were very white and young-looking for a man of his age. After he had chewed for a few minutes he went on.

"Now we come to the operative day," he said. "The day of the murders.

Trequin went out immediately after lunch and walked into Southing. He intended to walk through Tarncy Woods as usual. One of his shoes, however, was rubbing and he walked back to Balkin Hall to change them. He entered by the side door, went to his room, changed his shoes and left the Hall by the side entrance. As he did so he heard the car drive off.

For the first time he felt vaguely curious as to where his wife might be going. He walked round to the front and found Varness in the hall. He asked him where Mrs. Trequin was and the butler said she had gone for a drive and would be back in the region of four o'clock.

Trequin walked down the drive. He had made up his mind to go to Tarney by way of the Spinney. He cut across the fields, walked through Two-Acre coppice, into the Spinney, and was about to go through the gate when he saw the top of the car showing over a nearby hedge which bounded the lane. He wondered why of all places Schrot should have parked the car there. He turned round and walked quietly towards it. It was the saloon car and it was empty, but on the rear seat, where Viola had left it, was the envelope.

He opened the door and picked up the envelope. It was addressed to Captain Ferdinand Trequin (or Donneton) at Balkin Hall. Trequin pulled out the papers inside and examined them. Then he sat down on the car step feeling very odd.

The packet of papers consisted of a letter written in French. Attached to the letter were a dozen "orderly room memos", stamped with the battalion stamp and signed by the adjutants of a dozen battalions in Trequin's regiment.

The letter of course was the letter from Madame Ferasse-Mousqueton—the letter which she had promised and which he had never received. It was the kind of letter which Madame would write. It suffered from no repressive instinct and it told of things that were intended only for Trequin.

Quite obviously she had, by mistake, addressed the letter to the wrong battalion; Trequin's battalion was the first Battalion of his regiment, she had addressed it to the eleventh. The eleventh battalion was in Egypt, where the orderly room had opened it, read it (Trequin, with a fearful oath, visualised this process) before attaching an official memo which said "Not serving with this battalion. Try 9th Battalion at Mudros."

And so, from one battalion to the other, this passionate missive had by the grace of chance and the extraordinary efficiency of the British Army Postal service, gone to eleven battalions to be read and chortled over until, eventually at the end of 1918—two years after it had been written—it had reached his own battalion whose orderly room note said: "Evacuated as a casualty. Forward to Pay Agents."

There was an accompanying note from the Pay Agents. They had received the letter and accompanying memos in December 1918, but they did not know where to forward the documents. Trequin had given them no notice of his change of name from Donneton to Trequin. His account with them was closed. Their letter, apologising for the delay in forwarding the original letter and official correspondence, explained that they had never until a few days ago been able to trace him, that it was by chance that they had discovered that the Captain Ferdinand Trequin of Balkin Hall was the Captain Ferdinand Donneton whom they had known.

A very solid and dull kind of rage possessed Trequin. His life—as he saw it—had been entirely ruined through this delay in the post. But above everything a fury swept through him because Viola had read Madame's letter. Some instinct told Trequin that, at that very moment, she was discussing the matter with Schrot, seeking sympathy for the love which had been denied her because of this wraith from out of the past. He knew that she had stopped the car, and ordered Schrot to park it in this odd place so that she could unburden her soul to him.

He put the letters in his pocket, got up and walked quietly down the lane.

He heard their voices before he saw them. He knew by the sound that they were in the little clearing bordering the east side of the Spinney. He pushed through the hedge and came upon them.

They were lying on the grass. Viola, her back to him, was in Schrot's arms, sobbing bitterly. As Trequin broke through the hedge, the chauffeur raised his head and saw him. Immediately Schrot's hand went into his coat pocket and reappeared with Trequin's newly oiled pistol. Trequin saw that the chauffeur's face was livid.

Trequin began to smile terribly. He drew his own pistol from his pocket. Schrot raised his hand, fired and missed, as Viola, with a little scream, turned over towards Trequin.

Trequin was still smiling. He looked like a devil. He took two carefully aimed shots. He shot Viola and the chauffeur between the eyes with two perfect shots. They were dead immediately.

Trequin stood there for a moment looking at them. Then he put his pistol back into his pocket, took his handkerchief out of his pocket and walked over to them. Using the handkerchief he took the pistol, holding it by the barrel, out of Schrot's lifeless hand. He threw it into the bushes.

Then he turned away. He walked across the fields towards Lenderbury. He went on walking. Every two or three miles he stopped and sat down and read Madame's letter. Then he began to walk again. . . ."

.   .   .   .   .

Krasinsky plucked another blade of grass and began to chew it. I raised myself up and realised that leaning up against a tree stump is a good way to give one a very stiff back. I looked at my wrist watch. I thought that if I wanted to catch that train I must be moving.

We both of us got up and brushed the odd bits of grass from our clothes. Krasinsky put his finger and thumb into his waistcoat pocket and took a pinch of snuff delicately.

"I'm much obliged to you, Mr. Krasinsky," I said. "I've had a very interesting afternoon. Thank you!"

He smiled at me. There was something awfully nice in his smile. Then he turned towards the gate that leads up to the Long Fields beyond the Spinney. He threw me another smile over his shoulder.

"Good-day to you, Mr. Krasinsky," I said.

He waved his hand to me.

"And good-day to you . . . Captain Trequin . . ." he called out cheerily.

He turned through the gate and I began to walk, in the summer sun, towards the station at Southing.

EPISODE EIGHT

A Lady of Quality

❧

For a long time I have desired to make public the story of Mr. Marcel Woodpecker who worked in a stockbroker's office in the City of London, of Miss Eulalia Swansdown, and of the rather peculiar events which happened as a result of these two being in love with each other.

First of all a word about Mr. Woodpecker. He was young, idealistic, charming, and he thought that Miss Swansdown was the most supreme and perfect person in the world, as indeed I have no doubt she was, for she was most certainly beautiful. Also she was tall and slim and delicate. Then again, she was curved in all the right places. Besides this, she had melting eyes which, when occasion demanded, could be *not* so melting, and she was full of character. In fact I think I may go so far as to say that she was too full of character for Mr. Woodpecker.

It has been said of course that women of character do not like always to have their own way, but Marcel had apparently not heard of this saying because he always gave in to his Eulalia. When they went out in the evening he would ask her to which cinema she would like to go. She would ask him to make a suggestion, but always he would leave her to make the decision. In everything that happened between them the same situation arose, and she was bored with it. Marcel presented to her a picture of a rather weak, yielding and amorous young man, when what Eulalia really required was a strong, tough and not so yielding young man. Each one of my feminine readers will, I am sure, understand exactly what I mean.

To cut a long story short, things came to a head one night in no less a place than Messrs. Lyons' Corner House café near Piccadilly Circus, when Eulalia told Marcel all about it.

She said in her soft and charming but decided voice: "I would like you to understand that I consider you to be an utter and complete push-over. You have no mind of your own. You do not realise that, no matter how much a woman may like her own way, there are moments when she desires above all things to be dominated by the man who loves her. Why don't you dominate me? At least why don't you *try* to dominate me?"

Marcel said wearily: "I don't know, except that I think I love you so much that I can refuse you nothing."

Eulalia looked at him with a certain frigid contempt. She said: "Nuts . . .! Can't you imagine how impossible it would be to be married to a man who gave way in every little thing?" She looked at him darkly. "My father, who lived happily with my mother for many years, always said that his rule in life was to allow his wife to have her own way about nothing, but merely to delude her that she was having her own way about everything. The operational word," continued Eulalia, "is 'delude'. I am very fond of you, Marcel. There are lots of things I like about you, but you are too weak. So I am going to suggest that you try to do something about it. I'm going to suggest that we do not see each other for a month, during which time you might take a correspondence course in how to be the complete lover, or how to get tough, or something like that. Do you understand me?"

Marcel nodded dumbly. He presented a picture of the utmost pathos. He said: "I understand perfectly, Eulalia."

She looked at him a little bitterly. "I suppose you are going to do exactly what I want, aren't you, my sweet?"

He said: "Of course, darling. Didn't you ask me to?"

She said: "You are the damnedest fool. If you had any sense you'd have thrown that ice-cream at me. Goodnight to you. Ring me up in a month's time."

She got up. She swept out of the restaurant, leaving Marcel disconsolately looking at the ice-cream which, appropriately enough, was a raspberry one.

He pushed it away from him; began to consider how a man of his mentality, characteristics and make-up could possibly turn himself into a tough he-man type in four short weeks. He had not the remotest notion how this might be done.

Despondently, he began to read his evening newspaper. He read an article which stated that if one was worried or faced with a problem which one desired to work out, there was nothing better than a long, solitary walk in the country. Marcel thought this would be a good idea; that he would try anything once.

So the following Saturday he took a train thirty miles out of London and began to walk across a footpath that led from the remote railway station. He walked for a long time, but as far as acquiring any strength from the countryside, or walking, was concerned, he found that the process seemed to be failing utterly in his case. Tired and dispirited he sat down on a sloping and grassy bank from which a few primroses coyly peeped.

He was so intent on looking at these flowers that he neither saw nor heard the arrival of Mr. Krasinsky, who sat down on the bank opposite Marcel, and said: "Good afternoon. I believe you wanted to see me. My name's Krasinsky. I think we've met before somewhere."

Marcel sat up and regarded Krasinsky with curiosity. He said: "I cannot remember whether I have met you, Sir, but I am very glad that you seem to know me. I do not think I dislike you. On the contrary——"

"No one ever really dislikes me," said Krasinsky. "Although sometimes they think they do. I have been called all sorts of things—conscience, memory, unfulfilled desire. Actually, I am all of those things. I get about the place considerably without bothering to take a conveyance because, living in people's minds, I am always where I want to be. Or rather," said Krasinsky archly, "where they want me to be."

"How very interesting," said Marcel. "How funny that I should read that article in the evening newspaper and take a walk merely for the purpose of running into you. I suppose one might almost call you fate?"

Krasinsky shrugged his shoulders pleasantly. "Why not? You can call me anything you like, my dear Mr. Woodpecker, but I'm very glad that we have met this afternoon because, sensing the position between yourself and your lovely Eulalia, I thought perhaps you might like to hear a story which would possibly help you a great deal. Would you care to hear it?"

A strange hope crept into Marcel's heart. He said: "Mr. Krasinsky, I should like very much to hear it."

Krasinsky sighed. A sparrow which was fluttering about in the vicinity, settled on his left shoulder.

He said: "Not so very long ago there met, in a place in the country not a thousand miles from here, four personalities. The first—Cyrus K. Chavenix, who was a Colonel in the American Army and a very tough egg—or at least he thought he was."

Mr. Krasinsky blew a smoke ring from his cigar and watched it sail away in the summer's air. "Chavenix was one of those people who believed he was fitted to give everyone advice about their lives. He was a great believer in Colonel Chavenix. Disguised under a somewhat forthright disposition, was a slight bitterness of character which he had acquired after half a dozen unsuccessful affairs with ladies with whom he thought he was in love. He was a burly and good-looking man and believed at this moment that he was very much in love with the second character in our story whose name was Miss Georgia Garland—a pretty enough name for anyone, I think," said Krasinsky. "She lived in a most delightful cottage on the edge of a large estate in Somerset. Miss Garland, I should point out, was very pretty. Indeed she was beautiful. Everyone liked her. Even the ladies of the district admired and respected her. She was full of sweetness; she dressed supremely; she had a charming disposition. Can I say more?" asked Krasinsky.

"No, indeed," said Mr. Woodpecker. "I am sure you can't. She sounds a most interesting person."

"She was and is," said Krasinsky. "I have told you that Colonel Chavenix was very much in love with her—or thought he was. But she had no such delusions about Colonel Chavenix. She knew she was not in love with him, but she admired certain traits in his character. She thought he was honest and friendly and vaguely stupid! You understand all this?"

"Every word of it. I am very intrigued. Please go on."

"The third character in my story is a writer by the name of Roland Giradot," continued Krasinsky. "This writer was as romantic as his name. He was a man of some forty-five years of age, who had written several not too successful novels, and was in that part of the country recovering from a wound which he had received in the early part of the war. He too had fallen in love with Georgia Garland. Indeed he worshipped the very ground she walked on. He regarded her with a certain awe. In point of fact, I could go so far as to say," said Krasinsky with a smile, "that he very often trembled at the knees when she approached, this trembling being produced by her proximity. The odd sensation caused by the most attractive perfume which she wore, and which made the nostrils of Roland Giradot dilate like a war horse, often reduced him to a state in which he found himself almost unable to talk.

"The fourth character in my story," Krasinsky went on, watching with a benevolent smile the sparrow fly away from his shoulder, "was a person—a very tough person indeed—called Red O'Malley, about whom I shall have a certain amount to say later. I can only bring this preamble to a conclusion by saying that Roland Giradot, who knew that Colonel Chavenix thought himself in love with Georgia, loathed the Colonel with a loathing that is almost indescribable. He thought he was a make-believe soldier, because, as I should point out, Colonel Cyrus K. Chavenix had never fought anybody on any battlefield at any time. He was an instructor at a School of Arms in the neighbourhood and spent his time teaching other and younger men how to deal ferociously with the enemy at such times as *they* might encounter him. It might also be guessed that Colonel Chavenix had the most amazing contempt for Mr. Giradot whom he considered to be a push-over, a snake in the grass, a weakling, a person of no individuality or character, and certainly not a person to be allowed to approach within miles of Miss Georgia Garland.

"Her attitude", continued the check-suited sage, "was just the same towards each of them. She liked them both. She thought they were both very nice people. She allowed both of them to take her out. And so there was this extraordinary triangle, consisting of a delightful and charming woman and two men, both of whom were in love with her, often meeting and, whilst bathing in the smiles of their beloved Georgia, regarding each other with a quiet and secret dislike, with baleful side glances from Giradot and cynical wise-cracks from Chavenix.

"It was on a lovely spring afternoon," recounted Krasinsky with a sigh, "that our delightful and beauteous heroine, Miss Georgia Garland, went for a walk in some woods near her cottage, and there she encountered Mr. Giradot. He was wearing a well-cut check country suit and a terrified expression.

"Georgia stopped and looked at him in amazement. She thought that possibly he had been bitten by a snake of some sort. She said: 'Mr. Giradot, is anything the matter? Are you ill?'

"There was a pause; then he said desperately: 'I think I am. I think I am very ill and I have come to this state because I must tell you that I am madly in love with you. Life without you would be utterly impossible. Please, Georgia, will you marry me?'

"She said: 'Oh dear . . .' and sat down upon a convenient felled oak tree which abutted the path. She thought of saying 'this is so sudden', but before she did so, remembered that it was a conventional remark, so she contented herself with saying 'Oh dear . . .' again.

"Roland Giradot seated himself by her side, allowing a good twelve inches between them for the sake of propriety. He said miserably: 'Do you think you could ever think of me as a husband?'

"Georgia considered the matter. She said: 'Really, I don't know. I think it's terribly nice of you to want me to marry you. I think you are a very very nice man.' She went on hurriedly: 'In fact I think you are one of the nicest men I've ever known in my life, but I *do* think I'd like to consider this. May I, please, Roland?'

"Roland said: 'That doesn't sound so good for me, does it? A woman ought to know whether she wishes to marry a man or not. She ought to know it at once.'

"Georgia sighed. 'So I've heard,' she said. 'But do you know, for the life of me I couldn't answer your question immediately? But I promise you I'll give you my reply in two or three days' time, and in the meantime I would ask you please not to be too upset or to let your imagination run away with you.'

"He said: 'Very well. Perhaps I can come and see you then?'

"'Yes,' she replied. 'I'll telephone you. Then we can talk about it.'

"He asked: 'May I walk back with you to the cottage? I promise you I won't worry you. I'll leave you at the door.'

"She said kindly: 'Of course . . .'

"They walked back together.

"That evening at cocktail time," continued Krasinsky, "Colonel Chavenix, as was his wont, arrived for a cocktail, bringing with him two or three young officers from the school. He took his opportunity when the rest of the company were engrossed in conversation to take Georgia outside in the charming garden at the back of the cottage. When they were there, he said: 'Listen to me, Georgia, it looks like you're worrying about something. What's wrong? Why don't you tell Papa?' I should point out that he used to talk like this because it gave him an easy sense of familiarity; made him feel rather a man of the world.

"She said: 'Well, you know, I am a little worried. I went for a walk this afternoon and I met Mr. Roland Giradot. He proposed to me and he's such a nice man I'm not quite certain what to do.'

"Chavenix made a sound indicative of the utmost contempt. He said: 'For God's sake . . . that push-over! . . . Listen, Georgia, don't you ever take a chance on marrying a guy like that. He ought to have a lily in his hand. He's so meek he can't be true. He's one of those quiet, pleasant guys, but he's not the man for you. You want somebody more my type.'

"She said: 'Quite. . . . But promise me you won't propose to me again. You've done it twenty-four times, and I'm so tired of saying no to you, because there are some things about you that I like very very much.'

"He said: 'Aw . . . hell. . . . I suppose you think I'm jealous. Well, I'm not.'

"Georgia said: 'I'm sure you're not.' She knew perfectly well he was. She went on: 'Tell me, Cyrus, why do you think Mr. Giradot would make such a bad husband?'

"He shrugged his shoulders. 'I could think up a dozen reasons, baby. But this one's good enough. Look at his books. . . they stink. They're full of whimsy. This guy writes about love affairs and what-have-you-got. Have you ever read any of his poetry? Boy, does it stink to high heaven! How a guy that writes stuff like that can be allowed to exist I don't know.'

"Georgia said weakly: 'That's as maybe, but a lot of people like his books, you know.'

"He shook his head. 'Don't you believe it, kid. I tell you the sales of his books are so low they could get under a snake's belly. And that's a thing you've got to consider. This guy is a professional writer, see? He's a writer of romance that nobody wants to buy. I suppose you didn't ask him what his income was? How's this mug going to keep you? I reckon you're better off as you are. Maybe if you get married to him, he won't earn any money for himself because he can't, and he'll spend the little you have if he can. Take my tip and lay off, Georgia. This mug is not for you.'

"She said: 'This is all very interesting, Cyrus, but I don't think you ought to judge a man by the books he writes. According to you I should consider marriage only to a man who wrote in a much more tough way; who made a lot of money because his work appealed to the public, irrespective of his character or anything else. Is that what you're saying?'

"He looked at her sideways. 'Listen, kid,' he said. 'The sort of guy you ought to marry is the sort of guy whose books I read. You ever heard of Red O'Malley?'

"She shook her head.

" 'I'm going to tell you something, baby,' said Cyrus wistfully. 'This guy—I don't know who he is but I've read a lot of his books. And are they good! Tough, exciting books. I like 'em so much that I wrote him a letter at his publishers and said I thought he was a hell of a guy.'

" 'And did he answer it?' asked Georgia.

" 'I'm comin' to that,' said Cyrus. 'He not only answered it but he told me he was down here in this part of the world three or four months ago. He told me that he'd seen you down here; that he wanted an introduction to you. He wanted to meet you because he said you were the only woman he could ever love in his life. He said he was making plenty dough. He said if he came around here would I introduce him to you? He'd got the idea because I'd written to him and said how swell his books were.'

"Georgia said: 'Dear . . . dear . . . this is most extraordinary. Are you telling me, Cyrus, that you want to introduce me to a gentleman—this Red O'Malley—whom you have never seen —with a view to my marriage, just because you like his books?'

"Cyrus said: 'Listen . . . maybe you're going to think I'm being jealous again—jealous of this Giradot guy. Maybe you think I'm suggesting this merely because I don't want you to marry him. All I say is you ought to give this guy, Red O'Malley, a break. Never mind about Roland,' he continued under his breath, 'I'd pay good money to ditch that guy . . .!'

"Georgia said: 'I think you would. I think you're very

jealous, Cyrus. Anyway, if you're so keen on this I'm quite prepared to meet Mr. O'Malley on one condition.'

"He asked what it was. She said: 'On condition that you allow me to telephone Mr. Giradot and tell him all about it. I think it would only be fair to him. And when I meet Mr. O'Malley I want to meet him by myself. I don't want to have him introduced to me by you.'

"She went on: 'You know there's a dance on at your School of Arms next Thursday night? Tell Mr. O'Malley that if he's waiting in the shrubbery at the back entrance of the School at eleven o'clock I'll go out and talk to him. Then I shan't have any false impressions. The day afterwards—Friday—I'll make up my mind. Either I'll decide that I like Mr. O'Malley and want to see more of him; that I don't like him and that I'll marry Mr. Giradot; or that I don't like him and I won't marry anybody. Don't you think that's the best thing for me to do?'

"Cyrus said: 'It sounds a bit screwy to me, but I never argue with a woman. I don't give a hoot what happens as long as you don't marry Giradot, and,' he continued, 'you can tell him I said so.'

"With that the gallant Colonel picked up his hat; put it on his head at its usual jaunty angle; gave her a very American salute and disappeared.

"Georgia sat down and sighed. In spite of herself she was rather intrigued with Mr. O'Malley."

.   .   .   .   .

Krasinsky asked: "Don't you think this is a rather interesting story, Mr. Woodpecker?"

Marcel sighed. "Indeed, yes . . . it's most interesting. But I don't see what it has to do with me."

"You will," said Krasinsky with an arch smile. "That I promise you. Listen. . . . The following Thursday night was one which will be for ever remembered by Georgia, Colonel Cyrus K. Chavenix, Mr. Roland Giradot and especially by Mr. Red O'Malley, because all sorts of interesting things happened on that night.

"First of all at the time when the festivities began ˮatˮ the School of Arms, where a dinner and dance was held for the local ladies and gentlemen by Colonel Chavenix and the American members of his School of Arms, it was a lovely spring evening. Afterwards, there were changes in the weather and atmosphere at which," Krasinsky continued with a sidelong glance at Marcel Woodpecker, "I am not surprised. However, I will endeavour not to deviate from the important matters I have to discuss with you.

"I will only say that the belle of the ball was Miss Georgia Garland, dressed in an ivory satin dinner frock with the new tubular draped effect so popular in Paris at the moment, I believe. She was what is commonly known as the cynosure of all eyes. Many a young American heart beat faster. Her lovely complexion, auburn hair, contrasting with the colour of her frock, beneath which tiny gold sandals twinkled, caused almost as much trouble as the enemy.

"As for Georgia herself, she felt most peculiar. Something told her that she was playing with fire; something told her that she was being very foolish indeed to make this appointment to meet Red O'Malley, of whom she knew nothing except that he wrote very tough books indeed, in the shrubbery at eleven o'clock. She felt diffident about the appointment; wished at one moment she had never made it, and at the next moment found herself vaguely excited with this adventurous idea which was so much outside the scheme of her usual simple life. At other times she found herself wishing that she had accepted Roland Giradot's offer of marriage, and then a moment afterwards would feel very angry with Colonel Chavenix for having created this situation.

"All of which will indicate to you," said Krasinsky with a wise smile, "that Miss Georgia Garland desired very much to be in love with somebody and to be loved in return, the only thing she was uncertain about being who the lucky individual was to be. Don't you think she sounds charming, Mr. Woodpecker?"

"Indeed I do," said Marcel whole-heartedly. "She sounds to me rather like a lady in whom I am very interested."

"Quite so," said Krasinsky. "I will proceed. At a minute to eleven several things happened almost simultaneously. First of all our beautiful Georgia left the ball-room; walked along a passage-way into a smaller room and through the french windows on to the lawn at the back of the house. She walked across the lawn in the direction of the shrubbery. Suddenly, and without any warning whatsoever, the spring moon disappeared behind a cloud and for some unknown reason the area of the grounds surrounding the School of Arms was bathed in darkness. Indeed," Krasinsky continued, "Georgia could hardly see her hand in front of her face. But she knew where the shrubbery was and she hoped by the time she arrived there the moon and a little light would have re-appeared.

"She was wrong. As she stepped into the shrubbery and felt the leaves of a large rhododendron bush press against her in the darkness, a hand was placed on her arm and a voice, low, tense and masculine, said: 'Georgia, my darling . . . what d'you know, kid . . .! This is Red, and I don't mean maybe. . . .'

"When I say," said Krasinsky with a smirk, "that Georgia was alarmed, it hardly describes the situation. She stepped backwards, but her retreat was impeded by a large oak tree, and before she could move a masculine arm went at once about her neck and she found herself very definitely kissed. You may be aware, Mr. Woodpecker," said Krasinsky, "that there are kisses and kisses. This, I should like to point out, was definitely a kiss! It did something to Georgia. In fact, it altered the whole course of her life. She found herself becoming quite limp.

"She gasped a little and said, with a vague idea of placating the proprieties: 'Mr. O'Malley . . . you must not do that. I don't like it . . .' which, I assure you," said Krasinsky, "was a lie. In the darkness she heard a soft chuckle.

"O'Malley said: 'Well, if you don't like it, baby, you've got to learn to. Here's lesson two. . . .' Our delightful Georgia found herself embraced most ardently once again.

"The voice said: 'I'll be around to marry you soon, and I don't mean maybe. There isn't goin' to be any argument about this, honey. I know what's good for you. Now go back and do some more dancing with that so-called tough guy Cyrus Chavenix or that push-over Giradot. I'll be seein' you! And here's one for the road.'

"The last kiss," said Krasinsky, almost rolling the words round his tongue, "very nearly decimated Georgia. The unseen Mr. O'Malley disappeared into the darkness, and she found herself leaning against the oak tree gasping a little, endeavouring to summon up sufficient concentration to go back to the School of Arms.

"It was perhaps one of those tricks of fate that as she came out of the shrubbery and began to cross the lawn the moon came out from behind the clouds and the night became quite beautiful again."

.   .   .   .   .

"The following day," recounted the check-suited sage, "Georgia, who found herself in a state of rather peculiar bliss, made two telephone calls. One was to Colonel Chavenix; the other to Mr. Roland Giradot. She told the gallant Colonel that she would like to see him on the following Monday. She apologised to Mr. Roland Giradot for not being able to keep an appointment she had made with him for that day—when she had promised to give him her answer. She asked him also to come to her cottage on the Monday afternoon for tea. Then she packed an over-night bag; telephoned for a hired car; drove to the station and took the train for London."

.   .   .   .   .

"At half past three on the following Monday afternoon Colonel Cyrus K. Chavenix arrived," said Krasinsky, "at Georgia's cottage. The gallant Colonel found himself in a very peculiar frame of mind. He was beginning to think that his astuteness had rather repercussed on his own head; that he was in fact hoist with his own petard.

"Georgia received him in the most charming way. She looked utterly delightful in a navy blue taffeta coat and skirt which set off perfectly the most delightful organdie blouse.

"She said: 'Cyrus, I can't tell you how very pleased I am to see you, and to feel at this rather important moment in my life that I am surrounded by my friends.'

"Cyrus grunted a little. He sat down in a chintz-covered armchair in the room, which was splashed with the afternoon sunlight, and looked at Georgia with amazement. He realised that something had happened to her. Her eyes sparkled; her milky complexion radiated happiness. She looked quite supreme.

"He said: 'You know, Georgia, I'm not so sure that I like what's been going on. I'm an old friend of yours, baby, and my instinct tells me you've been up to something.'

"She nodded gleefully. She said: 'I've been up to all sorts of things, but I won't talk about them at the moment. I think we'd better wait till Roland Giradot arrives and then we'll have tea and we can have a *lovely* talk.'

"The gallant Colonel grunted once again," said Krasinsky, "and lighted himself a Chesterfield cigarette. He was about to indulge in a long lecture, about what he was not quite certain, when Georgia's maid announced: 'Mr. Giradot'. He came into the room, wearing a well-worn but very attractive suit of country tweeds and a pre-occupied air that seemed to indicate that he was not quite certain in which direction he was pointing. At Georgia's invitation he seated himself in the armchair, brother to the one in which Chavenix was ensconced. Then tea was brought in."

Krasinsky sighed. "I can't tell you, Mr. Woodpecker, of the extraordinary atmosphere which encompassed these three people. Here was Georgia, dainty and demure, seated behind the tea-table pouring out. On one side of her was the burly form of Colonel Chavenix, who bore on his face an expression of pained dissatisfaction. On the other side sat Mr. Giradot, looking rather unhappy and extremely meek.

"Georgia said: 'My dear friends, because I *know* you are my dear friends, I am so glad to see you here this afternoon. I wanted you two to know before anyone else that I am to be married.'

"Mr. Giradot said nothing. He only succeeded in looking a little more helpless. The Colonel sat upright in his chair. He said: 'O.K. So you're going to do something silly. You're going to marry somebody.'

"Giradot said in a quiet voice: 'Is it silly to marry anybody— except you, I mean, Chavenix?'

"Chavenix scowled. He said: 'Look, you keep your trap shut. I don't like you, Giradot.'

" 'That has always been obvious,' replied Giradot.

"Georgia raised her hand. She said: 'You two must no quarrel. Each of you in his own way is sweet. You, Cyrus, are big and burly and full of good intentions and you just dislike anybody whom I like because in your heart you are very jealous, and because you think you are what you would call a hell of a guy. And as for you, Roland,' she said, turning in his direction, 'you are just so meek that you creak. You ask me to marry you in a rather hopeless sort of way as if you considered the idea was really impossible but something that you ought to get off your chest.'

"Chavenix said: 'What did I tell you? Didn't I always say he was a big hum? Just another English mug.'

"Georgia said: 'Please be quiet, Cyrus.'

"Cyrus said: 'That's all very well—about being quiet I mean—but I reckon that we're entitled to know who you're goin' to marry anyway.'

" 'Of course,' said Georgia. 'How foolish of me.' She smiled at them both—a lustrous and charming smile. She said brightly: 'I'm going to marry Mr. Red O'Malley—a most delightful man. You remember, Cyrus, you very kindly arranged that I should meet Mr. O'Malley—with whom I believe you had had correspondence, because you liked his books, but whom you had never seen—in the shrubbery, at the School of Arms dance last Thursday. Well, I did. But I did not see him because it was awfully dark at eleven o'clock that night. But when I went into the shrubbery,' said Georgia haltingly, a slow blush mantling her cheeks, 'I became aware quite definitely of his presence. In fact,' she said, intertwining her fingers at the memory, 'I found myself embraced in no uncertain manner by Red. He didn't ask me if I'd marry him. He told me I was going to. I liked that.'

"There was a pause. The Colonel shrugged his shoulders hopelessly. Mr. Giradot sat looking straight in front of him, a bemused expression on his face.

"Georgia went on: 'Naturally, the next morning I was very intrigued with the idea of Mr. O'Malley—this forthright and rather tough gentleman who had so much . . . what do they call it . . . a most peculiar word . . . I believe it's "oomph" . . .! I made up my mind that I ought to do something about it. I made up my mind that as I was toying with the idea of marriage I ought to find out what sort of man this Red O'Malley was. So I went up to London the next day and I made my investigations. I found out who were the publishers of the O'Malley books of which you are so fond, Cyrus. I discovered who Red O'Malley really was.' She sighed. 'I was utterly delighted.'

"Chavenix said: 'Look, honey, are you sure you're not makin' a mistake? Maybe I like this egg's books. He's tough and I like tough eggs, but maybe when you've married him you'll find you don't like them so tough.'

"Georgia said: 'That's just it. I discovered that he wasn't entirely tough. I discovered that he had quite a different side to his nature. I discovered that he could be quite sweet and charming and all the things that a woman likes sometimes. He seemed to me to be a man of great imagination. I decided to marry him. Does that make you very angry, Roland?'

"Roland said nothing. He sat looking at the carpet in front of him. He looked like nothing so much as a man who has been hit smartly on the head with a sledge-hammer. Cyrus stubbed out his cigarette butt in the ash-tray on the table beside him.

"He said: 'Look, Georgia, I gotta do something about this, so I'm goin' to tell you the truth. When I told you that I'd read O'Malley's books; that I thought he was the sort of egg you oughta marry, I only said that because I wanted to get you away from that Giradot egg over there.'

"Giradot looked up. 'That's very nice of you, I'm sure. Thank you very much.'

" 'You don't have to thank me,' said the gallant Colonel. 'Nuts to you, Giradot. . . .!'

"Georgia said: 'Dear . . . dear . . . can I never stop you two quarrelling? Aren't you pleased that I'm going to be married to such a wonderful mixture of toughness, of hesitancy and shyness—yet with that certain . . . wasn't it oomph . . . I told you about?'

"The Colonel said: 'Say, listen, where have you been hearing words like oomph?'

"She said: 'I don't know. I think it must have been in one of Mr. O'Malley's books. I've read three over the week-end. Now, Cyrus, let me give you some more tea. And don't you think that you ought to congratulate me?'

"Cyrus said: 'Look, Georgia, the idea of you being married and happy appeals to me a great deal, but before I congratulate you I want to see this O'Malley guy. Now when I come to think of Red O'Malley's books and the way he writes I think this hombre is too tough for you. I'd like to take a look at him '

"Georgia said sweetly: 'Would you really like to do that?'

"Chavenix nodded. She pointed to Roland Giradot. 'The cream of the jest is, Cyrus, that is Red O'Malley. Roland Giradot is Red O'Malley.'

"There was a long pause; then Chavenix said under his breath: 'Jeez . . .!'

" 'His publishers told me all about it,' said Georgia. 'For years Roland here had been writing the rather delightful and charming books and those lovely poems which appealed to him so much. But alas nobody wanted to buy them. So he took another name and wrote a very different sort of book. He called himself Red O'Malley, wrote some very tough stories of which the public in all countries of the world cannot have enough, and made himself a fortune.'

"She turned. She said: 'Roland, I think you're the most marvellous person in the world. You have everything. Not only that, you understand women. You knew that as Roland Giradot you weren't doing at all well with me. You had enough brains to meet me in the shrubbery last Thursday night as Red O'Malley.' She smiled. 'I liked that a lot.'

Giradot said in the softest voice: 'Georgia . . . darling . . .!'

"Chavenix said: 'So here's a fine kettle of fish. You say he's really not tough. How can an egg turn it on and turn it off—soft one minute and tough the next—that's what I want to know?'

"Giradot said: 'That's a very pertinent question, Chavenix. I'd like to explain that to you. When I'm writing one of my normal books I think of myself as Giradot. I'm affected by the atmosphere of the book I'm writing. I find I'm a very meek sort of individual; that I'm not very good at'— he looked at Georgia—'making love; that I haven't a great deal of confidence in myself.'

" 'Yeah . . .?' said Chavenix. 'Well, just tell me how you manage to get tough.'

" 'I will,' said Giradot. 'When I feel I want to be a little tough I just think of myself as Red O'Malley. I just think about the last book I wrote as O'Malley or the one that I'm planning to write as O'Malley.'

"Chavenix said: 'That's hooey. It's not possible.'

" 'Isn't it?' said Giradot. 'Let me show you.' He got up. 'Now I'm Red O'Malley. . . .' He walked across the room; put the fingers of his left hand inside the collar of Cyrus Chavenix's tunic; yanked him to his feet; planted a very smart upper-cut underneath the Colonel's jaw, and allowed his unconscious body to relax back in the chair.

"Georgia said softly: 'Darling . . . aren't you wonderful? Now be Roland and bring him round again. . . .' "

.   .   .   .   .

Mr. Woodpecker sighed. The afternoon sun was beginning to die. On the opposite bank, Krasinsky plucked a primrose and held it delicately to his nostrils.

He said softly: "See what I mean, Mr. Woodpecker?"

Marcel nodded. He got up. "Thank you very much, dear Mr. Krasinsky. I see what you mean." There was a new and firm timbre in his voice. He seemed at least two inches taller. There was something about Mr. Woodpecker which no one had ever seen before. He went on: "One of these fine days I'll be able to tell you——" He stopped because he found himself talking to nobody. There was no one seated on the opposite bank except a rather perky-looking sparrow which looked at him with its head on one side and with what Marcel thought was a twinkle in his eye.

Marcel shrugged his shoulders. He began to walk down the lane on to the main road. Half an hour afterwards at the railway station he went into a telephone box. He rang Miss Eulalia Swansdown's number. After a moment he heard her soft and attractive voice on the line.

He said: "Listen, baby. . . . this is Marcel. My train gets in at Victoria at about half past four. Be there to meet me. And you'd better wear that navy and white check coat and skirt I like so much and the blouse with a ruffle on it."

She said: "But, Marcel. . . ."

"Don't answer me back. Be there; otherwise I'll fix you. . . ."

Eulalia said in the meekest of voices: "Very well, darling."

Mr. Woodpecker hung up. He came out of the telephone box. He found a seat; lighted a cigarette; waited for his train, whistling softly to himself.

EPISODE NINE

Of Pastoral Blackmail

Cℛℛℛⅅ

Believe it or not, there is, not many miles from London, a hamlet rejoicing in the name of Mogador. The place took its name from the fact that, at one time, a Prince of Mogador, which your atlas has already told you is on the Moroccan coast, lived there; although why anyone having at his beck and call, so to speak, the atmospherics, glamour and other romantic benefits usually associated with Morocco, should choose to live in an English country hamlet is more than I can say.

But our interest in Mogador is due only to the fact that it was from an even smaller hamlet in the vicinity; from a cottage with an address "near Mogador", that my friend Eustace de Salen received a letter of invitation from Etienne Laroq—a letter written by him in one of his odd moods of self-satisfaction, asking De Salen to stay with him for a long week-end. Eustace supposed that Laroq wanted as usual to tell him the story of how he had brought off one of those nasty sinister coups in which he specialised.

Etienne said in his letter that he expected satisfactorily to conclude during the next week or so the business which had brought him to England, and that in spite of the last unfortunate affair in which he and De Salen had been associated, and over which he bore Eustace no ill-will, it might be amusing for them to spend a few days together in the heart of the country.

Of Pastoral Blackmail

De Salen had reason to remember the peculiar characteristics in which Etienne Laroq rejoiced. He remembered him as a tall, slim and much too good-looking specimen of humanity of some thirty-six years of age, and his experiences during the early days of the Russian Revolution—he escaped from Petrograd in 1918 at the age of sixteen—had stamped upon him certain characteristics which were entirely bad.

Since these days Laroq had wandered about the world making an honest—or dishonest—penny here and there by such means as suggested themselves to his somewhat elastic nature. He had worked as an *agent* or spy for at least four different Governments and his services were always at the disposal of the highest bidder.

De Salen had always regarded Etienne as a subject worthy of the study of anyone who considered himself interested in the vagaries of human nature, and, although on the occasion of their last meeting Eustace had—with a certain amount of pleasure—handed over Etienne to a country policeman, and had the satisfaction of knowing that he was cooling his heels in a cell for a few days on a charge which my friend had very successfully managed to trump up against him, yet it was quite obvious from his letter that he had arranged in his own mind to forget this business and was prepared to be friendly again if Eustace so desired.

Having nothing very much better to do at the time, being somewhat bored with life, and considering that some more "close-ups" of Etienne might be useful, De Salen packed a few things and drove off in the direction of Mogador.

It was a beautiful summer's evening, and Eustace was so deep in contented thought that he failed to notice the fact that he was doing forty-five miles an hour in a restricted area until a glance in his driving mirror showed him a suspicious-looking car some hundred yards behind him. This, his guilty conscience assured him, must be a police car. He took a bend in the road, slowed down, and, seeing an open gate with a bridle path big enough to take the car, running across some fields, he swung the car in. Ten yards down the path there were some trees. De Salen pulled up behind this clump and got out of the car. Looking through the hedge he was able to see that his surmise about the road police was quite incorrect. The car contained an apparently innocent family probably on its way to Brighton.

He got back into the car, lit a cigarette and prepared to back on to the main road. Just as he was about to shift the gear-lever he observed, leaning up against a tree, an individual in a shepherd's plaid suit, smoking a small cigar and regarding him with a certain interest.

"Good evening," said the stranger pleasantly. "It is a beautiful evening."

De Salen agreed. There was something rather attractive about this loudly clad individual whose large watch-chain fascinated him.

"My name is Krasinsky," the stranger continued. "I hope that you will not consider me impertinent, Sir, but I have noticed that people—especially in England—are very anxious to do the right thing on every conceivable occasion. The idea of doing something which might appear to be a little incongruous, something not entirely indicated, seldom enters the scheme of life in this charming island."

De Salen sat back in the driving seat and lit a cigarette. Krasinsky was smiling at him most attractively. He waited.

"For instance," continued Krasinsky, "your idea at the moment is to get back on to the main road. The idea seems good to you because it is the habit of people to drive motor cars along roads and *not* across the countryside. I have noticed that the English people seldom drive cars across the country-side—except when inebriated. The Irish, on the other hand, often do things like that, which is one of the reasons why the Irish are such a supreme, poetic, gallant and entirely idiotic race who spend their whole lifetime endeavouring to obtain something which they do not want and with which they do not know what to do when they have got it."

"I follow your reasoning," said De Salen. "But may I ask what all this has to do with me?"

"Nothing at all, Sir," said Krasinsky. "Nothing at all' Except that I realise that you, being you, *must* of necessity drive your car back on to the road, that you have not sufficient romance, sense of adventure and *je ne sais quoi* to continue driving across the fields here merely so that you may find out what is over the other side of the hill."

He puffed at his cigar.

"No Englishman ever wants to find out what is on the other side of the hill," he said cheerfully. "And I wish you good-evening, Sir."

He took off his hat, with a little bow walked away and was lost to sight in a moment.

De Salen smoked his cigarette. The fat gentleman in the odd suit intrigued him. He began to believe that there was something in what Krasinsky said. After all it is quite true that English people seldom drive their cars along bridle tracks and across fields. Quite suddenly the idea of driving straight across the countryside appealed to Eustace immensely. It seemed that this was one of the things that he had always wanted to do, although the truth of the matter was, I suppose, that Krasinsky had intrigued him into doing something which, in ordinary circumstances, he would have considered insane.

Anyhow he thought he would try it. He started off and drove carefully along the rough path, avoiding odd pieces of flint which spelled potential punctures. After a hundred yards the path diverged into an even narrower one, which he could see ran through a little wood. Eustace was annoyed because it seemed that he must either turn round and go back on to the main road again, or drive through the wood as best he could in the hope of finding a roadway on the other side.

Just then it decided to rain. A few large drops fell. De Salen's car was an open touring car, and he had now to decide as to whether he would put the top up or chance the rain. He decided to take the latter course and to get on to a road as soon as possible.

He had just concluded these ruminations when he saw ahead a sight which, to say the least of it, was surprising.

Of Pastoral Blackmail

Standing under a tree some forty yards away was a woman, and whilst it is not unusual for women to stand under trees when it is beginning to rain, there were certain factors about this woman which aroused his interest, curiosity and admiration.

Obviously she was wearing an evening gown. It was of some black sheathlike shimmering stuff, and it had a train, although why a woman should wear a full-dress evening frock in the heart of a wood had yet to be discovered. She was wearing a short fur shoulder cloak, and as Eustace rattled and bumped towards her he could see that the amazing titian red of her hair made the whiteness of her complexion even more intense.

Altogether a very interesting situation, made even more interesting by the fact that she appeared to be crying!

De Salen negotiated the car in her direction as well as he could. He bumped over small hillocks, gulleys, fallen branches and all sorts of weird obstacles until he arrived in the little clearing where she was standing. By this time the drizzle had increased. He got out of the car, pulled up the top cover and fixed it, at a spot some ten or twelve yards from where she was standing. Having done this he walked over to her and got under the tree just as the storm broke in earnest.

"Good evening," he said. "Is there anything I can do for you? Can I give you a lift anywhere?"

She had dried her tears and when she looked at him Eustace saw that she was very beautiful. She had a small straight nose, a most desirable mouth and blue eyes. Her eyes were large and conveyed rightly or wrongly an expression of extremely injured innocence. Her figure was slim and very graceful. It was difficult for Eustace to guess her age. He put it down to somewhere between twenty-five and thirty.

When she spoke it was in good careful English, a language obviously not her own.

"There is nothing you can do for me, thank you," she said. "Why should there be?"

De Salen smiled.

"Oh, I don't know," he said. "It isn't usual to find ladies in evening frocks standing under trees in the rain in the middle

214

of the countryside at seven-thirty at night. I thought possibly something was wrong, that you might want a lift."

"Thank you, no," she said. "I am quite happy. I don't want a lift. I should be obliged if you would go away."

"Certainly," he said. "With the greatest of pleasure."

Eustace thought she was unnecessarily brusque. He was annoyed. Any man would be annoyed in like circumstances, mainly because his curiosity had been aroused and there seemed no chance of satisfying it.

"Well, I hope it keeps fine for you, Madam," he said. "This storm will soon be over. It is just a little summer rain, you know."

He got back into the car, drove through the clearing and along an open space between the trees. In front of him, about thirty yards ahead, he could see a narrow road. He pulled the car on to this and lit another cigarette.

De Salen was curious about the woman. After all, he reasoned, a woman doesn't stand under a tree in the middle of a little wood in some place near Mogador in an evening gown just to pass the time. Obviously she was waiting for somebody. A thought struck him.

He wondered if she could possibly be waiting for Etienne Laroq.

I should point out to you at this stage that my friend had never known Laroq to be in any part of the world very long without finding at least two or three attractive women somewhere in the neighbourhood. Laroq had a peculiar attraction for women. Eustace had never discovered what it was, or what particular brand of sex-appeal his was, but he told me that many members of the fair sex had been greatly concerned about Etienne to their eventual cost, because Etienne was the most untrustworthy person where women were concerned.

And it was this idea which made De Salen drive a little way along the road and then stop at a place where, shielded by some bushes, he could look back through the wood and see the mysterious lady. She was still standing there holding up her skirts with her left hand and smoking a cigarette. Eustace thought that, whoever he was, the male for whom she was waiting must be a lucky man. There weren't many women as beautiful as she who would condescend to wait for anybody—especially in a wood in the rain.

Eustace had just made up his mind to move on when he heard the sound of a car which seemed to be coming in his direction. Suddenly the noise ceased. Quite obviously it had stopped round a bend in the road on which he was waiting. A couple of minutes afterwards he saw a man walking through the trees towards the woman. He smiled to himself. It was Etienne all right.

Eustace realised what a lucky thing it was that he had met the fat fellow in the shepherd's plaid suit. Krasinsky had been right about the Irish. The Irish had something even if they did drive cars across the countryside on occasion!

.   .   .   .   .

As he drove along the narrow roadway Eustace wondered what devilment Etienne was at. He knew that there must be something financial attached to this business in some shape or form. Laroq, he knew, would not inconvenience himself by going out into the rain to meet a woman—no matter how attractive she was—merely for the fun of the thing.

He made up his mind to find out just what was going on, and, if he could, to throw a spanner into Etienne's machinery. Eustace was aware of, and disliked, Etienne's superb arrogance, his absolute lack of morals, his disloyalty to anybody or anything once they had served his purpose.

Half a mile down the road he found the cottage. It was an antique building, consisting of two or three old-time cottages knocked into one. It had been nicely retiled and repainted, and the garden that surrounded it made a splash of colour against the green trees, the coppices and thickets which grew in its rear behind a well-kept lawn. A white palisade fence ran round the place with a wide gate and a driveway up to the door.

Of Pastoral Blackmail

He drove in and rang the bell. As he expected the door was opened by Mavison, whose chilly countenance broke into a half-smile as he recognised De Salen.

"Good evening, Sir," he said. "We thought you'd be down. Dinner is at nine o'clock, so perhaps you will change now? I expect Mr. Laroq back at any minute now."

As he followed Mavison upstairs Eustace wondered just how much the old scoundrel knew about what was going on. Mavison—he was certain that that was not his name—had been in Etienne's employ for ten years to his knowledge, and a good many before that he imagined. Eustace had an idea that Mavison had committed some sort of crime in England, and then, rather than face the consequences, had gone off to Marseilles and joined the French Foreign Legion.

De Salen was also fairly certain that Laroq, who had served as an officer in the Legion for nearly three years, had picked Mavison up there, and probably arranged for his release before his time was up. At that time Etienne was very strong with the French Government, for whom he was working in some secret capacity—probably as *agent provocateur*, at which peculiar and dirty business he had no equal anywhere in the world— which would account for his being able to get the man out.

Mavison was a character. He was tall and thin and gloomy. He was an excellent servant and knew how to handle underlings. Also he had an extraordinary affection for Laroq and a loyalty to him that surpassed my friend's understanding. If ever a man disproved the proverb that no man is a hero to his valet it was Mavison, because knowing Etienne intimately, seeing him day by day, watching him at the peculiar and often nasty bits of business in which he specialised, and being able still to retain his affection for his master, was something which De Salen said he would never be able to understand.

As he splashed in his bath Eustace made up his mind as to how he would begin operations. The first thing to be done was to find out who was the mysterious woman in the wood— the haughty and titian-haired beauty who waited about under oak trees in rain-storms for Laroq.

He realised too, that it would be a very good thing to find this out, if possible, before Laroq returned. He got out of the bath, wrapped himself in a bath-robe and rang the bell. When Mavison appeared he asked him to bring him a cocktail and when he returned with the Martini Eustace opened the ball by asking a few questions.

"How does Mr. Laroq like this part of the world, Mavison?" he asked, as the man was about to leave the bathroom with his tray.

Mavison paused with his hand on the door knob.

"Very well, I believe, Sir," he said. "I have never known Mr. Laroq to be so well. He is in the pink of condition if I may use that expression."

"Isn't it a bit lonely about here?" asked De Salen. "I noticed on my way here that there were very few houses or cottages in this part of the world. But possibly there is a village behind the wood?"

"No, Sir," said Mavison. "There is no village nearer than Bevaston on the one side and Mogador hamlet right over in the other direction. Bevaston isn't very far away, and between it and this place there are a few houses straggling about the countryside."

"I used to know a Mrs. Vresey who lived in these parts," De Salen volunteered. "She had a house near here, I believe. Strangely enough, on my way down I thought I saw Mr. Laroq and her, walking along one of the bridle paths. I very nearly pulled up and waved to them, but I thought I might have made a mistake, so I didn't bother."

Mavison pondered. De Salen lit a cigarette casually, wondering whether he would fall into the trap he had laid. He did.

"I don't think there's any Mrs. Vresey about here, Sir," said Mavison. "I think it possible that you might have seen Mr. Laroq on the bridle path, but if you did I think the lady would have been the Italian lady—the Countess. She is the only lady who has been here since we have been down in the country."

"Oh yes," said De Salen glibly. "Of course, the Contessa—the Italian who lives over at the house towards Mogador?"

"No, Sir," said Mavison. "She lives at Bevaston, at the Grange House quite close to the Rectory, and she has only been in residence there for a few months."

"Oh well," said De Salen, "it doesn't matter."

He sent Mavison off for another Martini, feeling rather pleased that he had, at least, identified the woman.

And he had been just in time, for as Mavison disappeared De Salen heard Etienne's key in the front door.

.   .   .   .   .

It was quite obvious to De Salen that Laroq was very pleased with himself.

During dinner his conversation took a light and airy tone which indicated that life was good. They discussed everything, and Laroq related with his usual self-satisfaction his adventures since Eustace had seen him last. Apparently he had been getting into and out of trouble in three different countries, but as each time his operations had been financially successful, the trouble had been worth while.

Looking at him as he sat at the other end of the table with the candle-light playing on his white skin and long sensitive nose—he liked dining by candle-light and although it was still quite light outside Mavison had drawn the heavy curtains—Eustace thought that the situation of the world of today was made for people like Etienne.

Wars and rumours of wars, depressions, national and international troubles, created situations which, for him, were ideal. He was the supreme opportunist in mischief. Quite ruthless, he regarded people as so many oranges to be sucked dry.

De Salen wondered how he was going to start work on Etienne. He was perfectly certain that Etienne's meeting with the woman in the wood was part of some scheme, probably some evil scheme. He was also quite decided that Etienne had selected her as his next victim.

He remembered her big blue innocent eyes which had looked with apprehension at him when he had spoken to her. Such a woman would be fair game for Etienne.

Yet at the same time he realised the necessity for caution. Laroq had a brain that worked like lightning, and once he had a suspicion that Eustace was trying to upset his apple cart he would take good means to protect himself. However, he had to start somewhere, so De Salen took the bull by the horns. After Mavison had brought in the port and had gone he said airily:

"I hope you had a satisfactory interview in the wood, Etienne. I think she is very nice. I wouldn't have guessed that you had such attractive neighbours in these parts."

Laroq looked at Eustace across the table, his eyebrows slightly raised, one a little more than the other, a trick he had when professing surprise.

"Really, my dear Eustace," he said with a smile, "now how did you manage to see that? Surely you didn't come that way? You must have been right off the road."

"I was," De Salen confessed. "I got off the main road on the other side of Mogador. I'd been doing a little speeding and thought I was being followed by a police car. As I already have two convictions I thought I might try and miss a third, so I drove across a wide bridle path and managed by some good luck to get the car across that wood. When I got to the road on the other side I saw you going through the trees. Naturally I was intrigued to see you meeting such an attractive woman in such a charming frock in a rainstorm. Is she very nice?"

Etienne smiled.

"Quite charming, Eustace," he said. "Quite charming, but luckily not too brainy. She seems to possess all the feminine instincts for starting something that she can't finish as you would say, for which she must"—a mock dramatic note came into his voice—"pay the price."

"I see," said De Salen. "At your old blackmailing tricks again, eh, Etienne? You know one of these fine days you'll find yourself in prison."

"Possibly," Laroq replied, "but up to the moment, beyond one or two short incarcerations for so-called political offences in different countries, I have managed to keep out of durance vile. May I trouble you for the port?"

De Salen realised that as far as Laroq was concerned the conversation was at an end. He was surprised at this, because one of the main reasons for Etienne liking him about the place was so that he might boast of his different successful adventures. The fact that he was disinclined to talk about this most recent conquest showed De Salen that there was something quite important afoot, something about which he wished Eustace to know nothing.

"What was your idea in getting me down here?" Eustace asked Laroq as he passed the decanter round the table.

"Oh, I don't know," said Etienne. "You know, Eustace," he continued with a slow sarcastic smile, "I have always regarded you as a somewhat unintelligent Doctor Watson. You are, I know, discreet, and beyond the fact that I believe on one or two occasions you have done your best to upset little schemes of mine and failed dismally in the process, I like talking to you about my operations. I suppose this is one of the failings of the near-criminal," he went on with a grin.

De Salen said nothing. He realised with an inward smile that he'd upset more of Etienne's schemes than that worthy would ever know of.

"I see," he said as they lit their cigarettes. "So you believe that you are going to bring off a *coup*; some delicate operations are to be brought to a successful conclusion, and then when they're all over and finished you're going to tell me all about it. Is that it?"

"Something like that," said Laroq. "Now what about some billiards? I always think better when I'm playing billiards."

·   ·   ·   ·   ·   ·

They finished their game about a quarter past eleven, and Eustace paid Etienne the £1 that he had won. He thought it was rather clever of him to allow Etienne to win the £1—he could beat him at billiards any day in the week—but he did so because he thought it might put Laroq into a nice open frame of mind, in which he'd do a little talking. It did nothing of the sort.

A few minutes afterwards Laroq said that he was going to bed; that they would probably meet at breakfast, and off he went. Eustace told him that he would soon follow him, but as the night was fine he thought he might take a walk before turning in.

Once outside the house De Salen lit his pipe, walked on down the road to the cross roads where there was a signpost, and began almost automatically to walk towards Bevaston. At the back of his mind there was some idea of calling on the mysterious Contessa, of warning her generally against the machinations of Etienne and endeavouring to find out what was afoot.

Despite the lateness of the hour he thought that he might have a chance of catching her, because—and he was rather proud of this deduction—he reasoned that no woman was going to put on an evening gown for the purpose of meeting Laroq under a tree, and that the possibility was that she had intended going up to town to dine or to the theatre.

If his idea were correct then Eustace imagined she would be on her way back now and might arrive at The Grange about the same time as he did, the signpost having informed him that Bevaston was three-quarters of a mile away.

It was a lovely night. The short but intense rainstorm of the earlier evening had freshened the countryside after the heat. There was a good moon, and walking along the road on which the rain had successfully laid the dust, puffing at his pipe, Eustace felt very pleased with himself, almost like a knight errant who was going to the rescue of some beautiful and, of course, innocent lady.

At the same time he realised that he had to be careful in his operations, because if Laroq discovered he was trying to put a spoke in his wheel he would be quite merciless, and Eustace had no doubt would think up something special for him which would get him where it would hurt most.

Of Pastoral Blackmail

About ten minutes afterwards, round a bend in the road, standing back in some well-kept grounds, he saw an attractive house. He could see lights in two or three windows where the curtains were not closely drawn, and he came to the conclusion that this would be The Grange.

As he approached nearer De Salen saw that there was a breast-high wall running right round the property, and down on his left towards the back of the house there was a white gate in this wall. He thought it quite possible that this gate would be open, that it would be a short cut for him if it were, so he got off the road, cut across country through the trees towards the gate. He was half-way there when he saw it open, and through it came the Contessa. She was holding her short fur cloak closely about her and she made off in the direction of a clump of trees. He was most interested. It seemed a habit of this lady's to stand up under trees and wait for people.

Eustace altered his course so that he was walking parallel with her about twenty-five yards on her left, and kept carefully in the shadow of such trees and bushes as came his way. Presently she stopped. She stood under a large oak tree and looked about her. Eustace halted too behind another tree.

The night was quite still and presently he heard the sound of footsteps approaching. He looked round cautiously and saw walking from the direction of the road towards the tree where the Contessa was standing, a tall and well-built man. As he passed through a little patch of moonlight De Salen could see that he was wearing the well-cut uniform of a chauffeur.

And he wore this uniform with an air. His peak cap was set at an angle slightly over one eye, and there was something not unattractive in the thin bronzed lines of his face. Standing there watching him approach the Countess under the oak tree, De Salen wondered what the devil was afoot. He also realised the truth of the proverb that half the world doesn't know what the other half is doing, and he wondered whether Laroq was aware of the fact that the lady who he thought was so stupid was keeping another appointment so soon after his own.

At this moment Eustace heard a discreet cough from somewhere in his vicinity. Apparently these two were not the only actors in the comedy or drama that was being played. He stood quite still and looked cautiously about him. Away on his left, ensconced behind a large bush, his eyes following the moving figure of the chauffeur, was an individual who, to judge by the cut of his waistcoat and collar, was a clergyman.

He was short. He had a round and slightly humorous face, and the absence of any head covering showed a well-shaped pate covered with thin and curly grey hair. In his left hand, shielded by his fingers but with the lighted end towards De Salen, there was a cigarette. Eustace felt rather disgusted with him. He didn't approve of clergymen playing peeping tom on beautiful ladies in forests, especially when he happened to be doing the same sort of thing himself.

By this time the chauffeur had reached the oak tree. Eustace could see that he and the woman were arguing about something. In the moonlight her face was tense. De Salen realised that all this wasn't getting him anywhere, and he thought that he ought to take advantage of the situation to do something about it. Quite obviously something serious was afoot and as everyone else seemed so concerned he didn't see why he shouldn't take a little more practical interest in things.

He circled behind some trees and approached the clergyman from the rear. When he got behind him he touched him on the arm.

"Goodnight," he said, "and how do you do?"

The clergyman turned round and looked at him. He had the most benign face Eustace had ever seen in his life, and he seemed only mildly surprised to see him.

"I am very well, thank you," he said. "My name is Nicholas Houdthwaite-Jones—the Reverend Nicholas Houdthwaite-Jones—and I am the Rector of Bevaston. You're probably wondering what I am doing in this wood at this time of night, but the fact of the matter is I am very interested in the movements of my chauffeur who is over there talking to the lady.

"It is a most extraordinary thing," he went on, "but since he has been in my employ the attendance at the services on Sundays have increased wonderfully. He is a strange young man—an American, very good-looking. On two or three occasions I have watched him leave his quarters over the garage very late at night, and tonight I thought I'd try and find out just what he was at."

"It is very good of you to explain all that," said Eustace. He told the Rector who he was.

"Personally," Eustace went on, "I'm rather more interested in the lady. I have an idea in my head that she is being blackmailed, and I have another idea that we ought to do something about it. Don't you agree?"

As they stood talking behind the bush it occurred to De Salen that there was something vaguely ridiculous in the whole situation. Through a gap in the leaves he could see the chauffeur and the Countess deep in an intense conversation.

"We must certainly do something about it," he continued, and in a few words he told the Rector of the earlier meeting which he had seen between the woman and Laroq. He also gave him his idea of Laroq's character and his impression that he was up to no good. Just as he had finished the Rector put his hand on De Salen's arm.

"Look," he said, "Skendall is going off. Don't you think we ought to tackle him?"

Eustace looked up. The pair under the oak tree had parted. The woman walked towards the white gate in the wall leading to The Grange, and disappeared through it. Skendall, who had walked a few paces with her, stopped and lit a cigarette.

"I think you're right," said Eustace. "Let's tackle him."

They came out from behind the bush and began walking towards the chauffeur, who was standing there inhaling his cigarette with obvious pleasure. When they were a few paces from him he heard them and turned round. He was a very good-looking young man. There was something quite attractive about his face, except that Eustace thought his eyes were a little too close together. He was not at all perturbed to see them.

"Hey, Reverend," he said. "You're out pretty late, ain't you?"

"That's as may be," said the clergyman, "but this gentleman and I think that some explanation is due from you about this meeting with the Countess. You know, Skendall," he went on in the same benign voice, "it isn't usual for chauffeurs to have meetings with countesses at midnight in deserted woods, and it usually means trouble for somebody, and I don't want any trouble at the rectory."

"Don't you worry your head, Reverend," said the chauffeur. "And another thing," he went on, "I ain't the normal type of chauffeur, not by a long chalk, and can I help it if dames go for me in a big way?"

"You mean that the lady is in love with you?" queried De Salen.

"No, I don't, but she was."

Skendall turned to the Rector.

"You know, Reverend," he said, "before I came over here and took this job with you I was working in Rome. I was staff chauffeur at a hotel there.

"O.K. Well, that's where I met this dame and she was dead nuts on some guy over there, some Italian. They was engaged to be married or something. Well, this engagement sort of blows up. I was driving for a family that was living in the same hotel where she was, and I think she sort of fell for me on the rebound. You know what I mean. I reckon she was sort of playing around with me in order to forget this other guy.

"Well, to cut a long story short, she writes me a whole lot of letters. Then she goes off and I don't see her any more. O.K. Well, about three months ago I got a letter from some guy called Laroq—Etienne Laroq—and this bozo says that it's going to be well worth my while to come over here, and not only does he say this but he also sends my fare. He says that when I get over here maybe me and him can do some business together.

Of Pastoral Blackmail

"Well, I come over and just at this time you get that ad. of yours in the paper for a chauffeur, so I killed two birds with one stone by taking the job with you."

"And what did Laroq want?" asked De Salen.

"Nothing very much," Skendall replied. "He wants to buy them letters she wrote me and I'm goin' to sell 'em to him."

The Rector's mouth opened in astonishment.

"But you can't do that, Skendall," he said. "If this lady has written you some indiscreet letters in circumstances such as you have divulged to us, you couldn't possibly think of selling those letters to anybody else."

Skendall looked at his employer in amazement.

"Why not?" he said. "They're my letters, ain't they, and there's nobody can stop me selling them to him. I can do with two hundred and fifty quid."

De Salen turned to the Rector.

"I begin to get the idea," he said. "Laroq wants to buy the letters from Skendall here so that he can blackmail the Countess. Evidently she has got something that he wants."

And in his own mind De Salen was perfectly certain that he was right. He knew Laroq's technique, and he knew that he'd stop at nothing to get what he wanted.

"Look here," he said to the chauffeur, "I'm going to be perfectly frank with you. Mr. Laroq is a rather extraordinary individual. He's simply using you in order to blackmail that unfortunate woman with the foolish letters that she wrote to you. Probably she regrets writing them, probably she regrets the whole thing. You know the law in this country is very tough on blackmailers."

"You're telling me?" said Skendall. "But you boys have got me all wrong. I ain't blackmailing nobody, and it ain't blackmail for me to sell a set of letters that belong to me for £250 to some guy who wants to buy 'em. That's what I have been seeing the Countess about. I told her that if she liked to raise the ante and pay me a bit more I'd sell her the letters back again, but she says she ain't got the money, and anyway she thinks I ought to give the letters back to her, a thing which I am certainly not going to do.

"No," said Skendall, shaking his head quite definitely. "I reckon this job is quite an ordinary bit of business, and I reckon I'm going to sell those letters to the Laroq guy. After all, the Countess made use of me when she wanted to, didn't she, so I reckon this is where I am going to make use of her."

He stood in the moonlight, his uniform cap slightly over one eye, a smile on his handsome face.

"You know, Skendall," said the Rector, "it seems that you are a most unmoral person."

"Maybe," said Skendall, "I don't know what it means, but maybe I am. Anyhow that's the way it is. The point is if anybody likes to give me £250 for those letters they can have 'em, and if I don't get the dough by tomorrow morning I'm going to sell 'em to Laroq. I reckon I'm tired of this place anyway. I'm going back home. With that dough I could start a frankfurter stand some place, which is a thing I have always wanted to do. Well, goodnight, Reverend," he said.

He raised one finger to his cap, turned on his heel and walked off.

De Salen and the Rector stood there looking at each other.

"A rather difficult situation," said the Rector.

Eustace nodded.

"I'm inclined to agree with you," he said. "I wish I knew where your chauffeur kept those letters."

"I know that," said the Rector, "I've got them. Some little while ago he gave me a sealed packet which he asked me to keep in the safe. I expect that would be the letters."

"Well, in that case, it's easy, Rector," said De Salen. "We simply destroy them. That settles the whole argument."

"Oh, no, Sir," said the Rector. "Two wrongs don't make a right. The fact that Skendall is misbehaving himself is no reason why I should commit an act which, besides being obviously dishonest, is also to my way of thinking quite immoral. I shall most certainly *not* destroy the letters."

"All right," said De Salen, "if you won't destroy them, you won't."

They walked on in silence. Presently they came to the Bevaston Road and began to walk towards the village. Eustace imagined that they were going in the direction of the Rectory.

"No, Sir," said the Rector firmly. "I could not make it march with my conscience to destroy those letters. It would be wrong. They are the property of Skendall and he is, in fact, entitled to do what he likes with them. At the same time," he continued with a sigh, "I wish I could find some way of reaching his better feelings and getting him voluntarily to return the letters to this unfortunate woman."

"So do I," said Eustace. "Although obviously she's an idiot to have written them to him in the first place. I could spank that woman. She must be an awful fool."

"Most certainly she has been foolish," he said.

He stopped suddenly and looked at De Salen with a brightening eye.

"Look here," he said. "I've an idea. Let's go back to the Rectory and I'll get Skendall to come into the study and we'll talk this thing over again. We'll treat him as an equal—socially and morally. You," he went on, talking quickly with a certain excitement which had seized him as a result of the dramatic situation in which he found himself involved, "must supply the dramatic element. It must be your business to draw a picture which will reach Skendall's better and more humane instincts. You must show him what awful misery and unhappiness this Laroq can cause the Countess if he obtains possession of the letters.

"Then," continued the Rector, "at the crucial moment, just as Skendall begins to crack—I think that is the word that is usually used—I will make him another offer. I have saved up eighty pounds towards the restoration of the antique carving on the east wall of the Rectory which I regret to say was knocked down and quite ruined last month by a touring car driven by an inebriated Czecho-Slovak. At the crucial moment I will offer Skendall this eighty pounds if he will sell me the letters. Possibly he will consent, in which case the matter is at an end and we will return them to this unfortunate young woman."

De Salen considered the suggestion. Eventually:

"Well, Rector, I'll try anything once," he said, "but I can't see it working. This Skendall is as tough as they make them. He just can't see our point of view. He can't see that he is, in effect, making himself a party to a most immoral act. He's simply thinking in terms of two hundred and fifty pounds and a hamburger stand somewhere on Lower Broadway, and whether any amount of talk will reach his humane instincts, as you call them, is, to my mind, extremely problematical."

The Rector sighed once more.

"We can but try," he said bravely.

.   .   .   .   .

It was three o'clock in the morning, and De Salen and the Rector had put in two hours' work on Skendall without any effect whatever.

The night had become sultry, and in spite of the fact that the Rector had opened the French windows of his study they were all uncomfortably hot.

The Rector sat at his desk gazing despairingly at Skendall, who, coatless, his shirt collar unbuttoned, and a glass of the Rector's best port in his hand, lounged on the settee, his long well-shaped legs stretched out in front of him, a picture of poise, indolence and complete nonchalance.

"Say, listen, Reverend, an' you other guy," he said. "Why in the name of heck don't you see that you got this thing all wrong? What's the good of your tellin' me that what I'm doin' is screwy. Them letters belong to me, don't they? O.K. An' when it comes to morals let me tell you somethin'. I reckon it wasn't exactly moral for the Countess to go for me in a big way just because she was fed up with this Italian guy she had a shindig with—the guy she now wants to get married to. Another thing, there is a girl in New York who is also nuts about me, an' if I don't show up there pretty soon with enough dough to start up this hamburger proposition, well I reckon that she ain't goin' to sit around waitin'. She's just goin' to take a run-out powder on yours truly an' hitch herself up with a guy who runs a pump an' flat tyre business around the block. If I wanta get that girl I gotta get back quick an' I gotta get back with the dough."

He drew in his legs and leaned towards them.

"Listen," he said. "You guys talk about morals. Well, when I was comin' over here I told Lillah about this business an' she says: 'Go on, Tony, you go an' collect an' come back an' maybe I'll make an honest man outa you.'"

He stopped suddenly and a faraway look appeared in his eye. He brisked up as if the thought of the girl in New York had started a new train of thought.

He got up and walked over to the Rector's chair.

"Look, Reverend," he said, looking down on the incumbent, "you said you'd give me eighty pounds if I sold you those letters, didn't ya? O.K. Well, I reckon you trusts me, don't ya? I reckon you think I'm a good guy. O.K. Well, I'm goin' to show you somethin'. You get that eighty pounds an' you get the letters outa the safe an' bring 'em to me here. But I don't want any more talk or any more wisecracks outa either of you guys. I'm goin' to handle this business in my own way, see?"

The Rector got up.

"Very well, Skendall," he said. "We're in your hands, and I don't know whether I can trust you or not, or what you intend to do, but I'm going to take a chance."

He went out of the room. De Salen lit a cigarette and watched Skendall, who had walked over to the window and was looking out on to the moonlit lawn with a smile playing around his well-carved lips. De Salen didn't like this new phase at all. It seemed to him that Skendall was going to make sure of getting another eighty pounds on the deal and still go through with his original idea; that all their efforts had merely shown this enterprising Yankee chauffeur the strength of his position.

After some minutes the Rector came back. In one hand he held an ordinary foolscap envelope, the flap of which was stuck down with rather soiled stamp-paper edging. In the other he held some banknotes. He held both hands out to Skendall.

"There, Skendall," he said. "I'm going to trust you. I'm going to rely on the inherent goodness which, I know, is somewhere in you; the goodness that I thought I recognised when I gave you your job here."

Skendall grinned. He took the packet and the banknotes, placed the packet carefully in his hip pocket and counted the eight ten-pound notes, which he stowed away in his breeches pocket.

"Now," he said, "I reckon we can get down to cases. I reckon that we will all go up an' see this Laroq guy; but I want you two to know that I gotta handle this job in my own way. I got an idea—a big idea—an' maybe, if you two just stick around an' keep your traps shut, I can pull it off. Is that O.K. by you?"

"It's O.K. by me," said the Rector. "And I'm certain that it's going to be O.K. by this gentleman too."

De Salen nodded.

"I agree," he said. "I don't see that there's anything else to do."

"All right," said the chauffeur. "Come on, you bozos, let's get goin'."

.   .   .   .   .

De Salen says that he will never forget the scene at the cottage, or the expression on Etienne's face after they had knocked Mavison up, gained admission and sent for Laroq.

They grouped themselves like rival armies, Laroq, on one side of the dining-table with Mavison in his rear, regarding De Salen with a baleful eye, for he had already sensed, by the presence of Skendall, that Eustace had been up to something.

On the other side of the table the Rector sat. De Salen leaned up against the book-case on his right-hand side, whilst Skendall, his coat and shirt collar still unbuttoned, his hands in his breeches pockets, regarded Laroq with his usual cynical smile.

"Now, listen here, Mister Laroq," he said, "an' don't talk until I let you in on the set-up. These two guys—the Reverend and this other one—have been on to me about sellin' you them letters the Countess wrote me. They been tellin' me that the deal's immoral an' that I'm just an ornery durn son of a so-an'-so to let you have 'em because they reckon that you're goin' to blackmail the Countess some way or another with 'em.

"An' they mean what they say. The Reverend here has given me eighty pounds if I won't let you have the letters. He's prepared to do without mendin' the Rectory wall where some guy knocked a coupla dolphins off it when he was all tanked up, providin' the Countess can be O.K.

"All right," he continued, "an' that ain't all. On the way up here this other guy,"—he indicated De Salen with his thumb—"says he will add another twenty pounds, makin' a total of a hundred in all, if I will not sell you the letters, but will hand 'em over to the Rector so's he can burn 'em. Well, what are you offerin'?"

Laroq smiled. Sitting there, De Salen thought he looked rather like the devil himself, in a crêpe-de-chine dressing-gown.

"My original offer holds good, Skendall," he said softly. "In fact," he went on, "I am prepared to increase it somewhat."

He lit a cigarette carefully.

"I don't know what these two have been telling you, Skendall," he went on, with a malicious look in De Salen's direction, "but I should like you to know that you are perfectly within your legal rights in selling me the letters, and you will be a fool if you do not take advantage of my offer.

"Remember that young woman of yours who is awaiting you in New York—Lillah—isn't that her name? Don't you want to marry her before that other fellow gets her just because she is tired of waiting for the man whom she sent off to England with a brave smile to collect the shekels that will start that hamburger business? You know women, Skendall. Absence may make the heart grow fonder, but it also gives the other fellow the chance he's been waiting for."

Laroq paused artistically to allow the full import of his words to sink in.

"Hand over those letters to me, Skendall," he said, "and I will here and now hand you three hundred pounds—an increase of fifty on my arrangement with you, and," he continued, "I will give you exactly two minutes from the time I stop speaking to make up your mind. Consider, Skendall, I paid your fare over, but if you sell these letters to these two people here I shall certainly not pay your fare back to New York, which I will do if you accept my offer.

"If you take their hundred pounds you will arrive back in New York with about seventy pounds at best, and you certainly can't start a hamburger business with that. On the other hand if you take mine, I pay your return fare and you land with three hundred.

"Well, what are you going to do? What do you think Lillah would want you to do? You've got two minutes to make up your mind."

They all watched Skendall who, slowly bringing his hands out of his breeches pockets, brought with one of them the Rector's eighty pounds. De Salen's heart sank.

Skendall looked at the Rector, and pushed the notes towards him.

"I'm sorry, Reverend," he said. "Maybe you'll think I'm a lousy heel; that I oughta be shot for this. O.K. Well, you'll just have to excuse me for livin', that's all, because this Laroq guy has just said something that has sorta made up my mind for me. He just said what do I think Lillah would want me to do. Well, I know the answer to that one all right."

He fumbled in his hip pocket and brought out the packet of letters.

"This is what Lillah would tell me to do," he said, "an' I'm goin' to do it."

He grinned at Laroq.

"Listen you," he said, "hand over that three hundred and another fifty for my fare back home an' I'm goin' to give you these letters!"

Laroq smiled. His smile went from Skendall, on whom it rested pleasantly, then to the Rector, and on to De Salen where it rested for a moment charged with a cynical hatred.

He got up and left the room. Whilst he was away no one spoke, but Mavison—that ex-crook—looked at De Salen with an expression of mild triumph.

When Laroq returned he held the notes in his hand. He counted them out—seven fifty-pound notes—on to the table. Then he pushed them towards Skendall.

Skendall picked up the notes, stowed them away in his breeches pocket and threw on to the table the foolscap envelope. Laroq picked it up.

"Gentlemen," he said, "I think that our interview is ended."

He turned towards De Salen.

"As for you, Eustace," he said, "You can pack your bag and get out. You thought you were being awfully clever, didn't you? You thought you were going to upset my plans? Well, it seems that you were not sufficiently intelligent, and, for your especial benefit, you might like to know that before I am through with these,"—he held up the envelope—"I shall make twenty times the sum that I paid Skendall here for them."

Skendall grinned. Then, as Laroq was about to open the envelope, he produced a cigarette from behind his left ear and lit it from one of the candles on the table.

"You won't," he said to Laroq. "You won't make a durn nickel out of 'em."

Laroq was unperturbed.

"And may I ask why not?" he said.

"Sure," said Skendall easily. "I'm on to your game. You know durn well that the Countess has made it up with that Italian guy of hers and they're goin' to be married. I reckon you was goin' to stick to those letters until after she marries him next month an' then—knowin' that he's a rich guy an' that she'll have plenty of dough when she's his wife—you was goin' to work the black on her an' collect plenty outa her; otherwise you was goin' to tell her you'd send him the letters an' let him know that she'd been writing silly love-letters to a chauffeur."

He took a long puff at his cigarette and sent the smoke out through his right nostril most artistically.

"Now, I reckon that I am a straight guy," said Skendall, "an' I am a guy who always keeps his word, an' when I said I'd sell you them letters for the dough you paid for 'em I meant it, an' I've done it, but you won't use 'em to blackmail that dame, an' I'll tell you why."

Laroq was still smiling.

"Why?" he asked pleasantly.

"Looky," said the chauffeur. "All this evenin' I been tryin' to please everybody, an' I think I've done it. The Reverend here and this other guy don't want the Countess to get hurt an' they was prepared to pay for it like good guys. You wanted the letters—well, you got 'em. But all the evenin' I been trying to do what Lillah woulda liked, that is sell the letters so's we could start that hamburger stand an' get married, an' at the same time see that you kept your lousy hooks off that Countess dame who is a nice little thing anyway even if she is a bit inexperienced."

Skendall stubbed out his cigarette end, helped himself to another from the silver box on the table and lit it from the candle.

De Salen was watching Laroq. He was not looking quite so happy.

"Tonight when we was talkin' over this down at the Rectory," Skendall went on, "I gotta big idea. Now you tell me something," he said to Laroq. "What's the name of the Italian guy that the Countess is goin' to marry?"

Laroq rolled the name off his thin lips.

"The gentleman is called the Marchese Antonio della Dalda," he said.

"O.K.," said Skendall. "Well, it might interest you to know that my name is Antonio—Antonio Skendall. My pa was an Italian an' his name was Antonio too. So here's the way it goes.

"All them letters are addressed to 'Dearest Antonio,' an' here's the reason why you *ain't* goin' to use 'em to blackmail the Countess. Tomorrow morning, before I leave here, I'm goin' around to see that dame, an' I'm goin' to write her a letter. I'm goin' to say in that letter that the letters you got there *are ones that she wrote to this Marchese guy;* the ones that she gave me to post to him because I was the hotel chauffeur an' it was my job to clear the mail box. I'm goin' to say that I didn't post 'em, I opened 'em, an' that when I saw the name was the same as mine I kept 'em an' told you they was written to me. Then you bought the letters off me so' you could blackmail the Countess by pullin' some phoney story that the letters was written to me, an' that I took the dough just because you are a cheap son of a double-crossin' heel, an' how do you like that?"

There was a gorgeous silence. De Salen told me that he had never, in the whole course of his life, seen any face diffused with such sardonic rage as that which appeared on the countenance of Laroq.

He got to his feet, his fists clenched, and for a moment it looked as if he would spring at Skendall, who, still smiling, merely produced from his pocket a fist on which his eye dwelt lovingly for a moment.

When Laroq spoke his voice was hoarse with rage.

"Get out of here—all of you," he said.

They moved in silent triumph to the door. As they reached it they saw Laroq hold the foolscap envelope in the flame of one of the candles; watched the cartridge paper of the envelope crackle and burn, as he made certain that no one else, at any rate, should have the precious and useless letters for which he had paid three hundred and fifty pounds.

.   .   .   .   .

They halted outside the Rectory gates and regarded each other with approval. The Rector seemed tired, as if the strain of the Laroq scene had been a little too much for him.

Skendall, cheerful and unperturbed, produced a cigarette

and lit it with a match which he struck cleverly on the seat of his breeches.

"Well, Reverend," he said. "I reckon I'll be scrammin' off in the mornin', but I'll get around an' say so-long before I go. I greased the car to-day, an' gave her a tune up, so's she'll be O.K. for the next guy you hire to drive you."

The Rector nodded.

"I think you've done very well tonight, Skendall," he said. "Very well indeed, and I want to show you my appreciation."

He fumbled in his pocket and produced the banknotes which Skendall had returned to him.

"Here's the eighty pounds," said the Rector. "That's my contribution to the hamburger emporium which Lillah and you are going to open. Now don't refuse it. I really want you to have it."

Skendall took the money with a grin.

"Gee, Reverend," he said. "This is swell. An' will Lillah be pleased or will she? Well, I'm goin' to hit the hay. Goodnight, gents."

He disappeared round by the back way towards the garage. The Rector sighed.

"I think you and I ought to have a little drink," he said to De Salen. "Just a small one to pull us together after all this business. Don't you think?"

Eustace agreed. He wanted a drink badly. He was tired but very pleased with the defeat of Laroq, and was looking forward to seeing Mavison's face when he went back for his bag and car.

As they stood in the study, their whisky glasses in their hands, the dawn began to break.

"Don't you think, Rector," said De Salen, "that you were rather more than generous to Skendall? After all, he'd had a very good evening's work. I think that the extra eighty pounds you gave him was almost too much. After all . . ."

"I'm afraid you don't understand," said the Rector. "You see I gave him the extra eighty pounds just now as a sort of sop to my own conscience. I wanted to feel that I had actually

238

done something towards buying the letters from him, because you see I still have them—they're in the safe here, in the Rectory."

De Salen looked at him in amazement.

"But the packet you brought out here; the envelope you gave to Skendall; that he handed over to Laroq; that Laroq paid three hundred and fifty pounds for?" He paused for breath.

"There was only a folded circular in it," said the Rector with a guilty look. "You see when I left you and Skendall here and went to get the letters I wondered if I could really trust Skendall to play the game. When I opened the safe and saw that the letters were in an ordinary foolscap envelope stuck down with a stamp-paper edging I got an idea. So I got another foolscap envelope from my desk, put the circular inside and stuck it down with stamp-paper, making it look as much like the other as possible. Luckily for me no one thought of opening it and looking inside."

It was nearly two minutes before Eustace stopped laughing.

"So you realise, Rector," he said, "that if Skendall hadn't told Laroq the letters would be useless to him, just as he was in the act of opening the envelope, Laroq could have discovered the fraud and kept his money. As it is the silly ass has burned the envelope believing it to contain the real letters. What a marvellous situation!"

The Rector nodded.

"I think we'll burn those letters here and now," he said. "Then, tomorrow, you can call on the Countess and tell her that everything is all right."

He went off, and De Salen stood looking out of the french windows telling himself what a wonderful time he was going to have when he went up and told Etienne the truth. He wanted to see his face when he learned that he had paid three hundred and fifty pounds for a garden seed circular.

The Rector returned. Solemnly, their glasses in their hands, in the flame of a candle that the Rector produced from a drawer, they burned the letters one by one.

Somewhere outside a cock began to crow, and for some reason the sound brought back to De Salen's mind a memory of the portly individual in the shepherd's plaid suit who had intrigued him into driving across country instead of going back to the main road.

He hoped to meet him again one day.

Of the Dream of Erasmus Bellamy

About the time that the sun was considering the important business of setting, Mr. Erasmus Bellamy, who was tall and slim, extremely agile and good-looking, turned from the country road that bisects the village of Betchworth and disappeared into the cool recesses of the tap-room of The Running Dog—an antique hostelry that stands not far from Betchworth golf course.

It would have been obvious to the most casual observer that Erasmus was unhappy. His brow was clouded and the charming smile which usually decorated his handsome features was conspicuous by its absence.

By these portents the intelligent reader will already have gathered that Erasmus was in some sort of trouble. Being wise, the reader will conclude that it was either a matter of health, of money or of love, and in this case he would have been two-thirds right, for Erasmus Bellamy was in love and the matter was made extremely difficult by the absence of money.

He leaned against the bar and drank a half-pint of bitter beer from a pewter tankard, but the beer tasted sour although it was a very good beer. He stood there, sipping the drink, glowering at a lithograph of a contented cow which hung on the other side of the bar, and considered everything—including suicide.

Suddenly he became aware of the fact that there was another occupant of the bar. This individual, whose name, by the way, was Rufus Skeyne, sat in a dark corner of the bar to which the departing sunlight did not penetrate and regarded Erasmus with a sardonic smile. Erasmus returned the look with a certain curiosity. For some reason which he did not know he was curious about Skeyne, and this Rufus Skeyne was a peculiar individual. He was tall; well-proportioned. His face was sardonic, his eyes peculiar—a trifle reptilian—and invariably about his well-cut mouth there lurked a cynical smile. Nobody was quite certain as to what Rufus Skeyne did for a living, where he lived or, for that matter, anything else about him. In Betchworth village he was a man of mystery and not unpopular with the peasantry; in fact well-liked by some of them.

But Erasmus was interested because he was always running into this man. Often, walking across the fields or the golf course in the evening, dreaming soft dreams of his lady love, he would find himself in the proximity of Rufus Skeyne, who would be sitting under a tree regarding the landscape with a sardonic interest.

Erasmus continued to drink his beer. Then, lazily, Skeyne got to his feet; adjusted a crease in his well-cut riding breeches; came over to the bar.

He said to Erasmus: "I think it's very hard luck. . . ."

Erasmus turned towards him. He said sharply: "*What* is hard luck?"

Skeyne smiled. "My dear fellow, it's all over the village. The story goes that last night you went up to Wingrove Hall, saw the Squire and requested the hand of his beautiful daughter Belinda in marriage. It then goes on to relate how he was very rude to you; that he asked how a penniless upstart like you could consider marrying his daughter. Then you lost your temper. You two had a slanging match, after which the old boy had you thrown out. I think it's very hard luck."

Erasmus said: "And may I ask what business it is of yours?"

Skeyne shrugged. "Anybody's business is everybody's business in this part of the world. Personally, I think the old boy is, to put it mildly, a son of a bitch. And she's a lovely girl, isn't she? I've often looked at her and thought she had *something*!

Of the Dream of Erasmus Bellamy

You know what I mean—the way she walks and looks and smiles. And those eyes of hers . . . they're lovely, aren't they?"

Erasmus said: "Damn you, yes. But what have you to do with her eyes?"

Skeyne grinned. "Nothing much." He leaned against the bar. "I heard something else too," he went on. "I heard that the old man had just taken out a new and very big insurance policy on his cattle."

Erasmus said: "Yes? And what has this to do with me?"

Skeyne shrugged his shoulders. "Nothing, I suppose, except that I was thinking that two or three of the gates on the pasture land are very loose. One of them is so old that it might almost fall off its hinges. I shouldn't be surprised if some of the cattle strayed one night. A damned good job too. Well, good evening to you." He lounged out of the bar; threw an odd smile over his shoulder.

Erasmus finished his drink. He went out of The Running Dog; began to walk aimlessly towards the deserted golf course. He thought life was impossible—certainly impossible without Belinda. But what hope had he?

Near the eleventh hole he sat down beneath an oak tree; leaned against it. He looked at the blue sky, already darkening with the evening shadows. Suddenly, he became aware that he was not alone. Sitting almost next to him was a portly form dressed in a black and white shepherd's plaid suit, with a large gold albert stretched across his stomach. Erasmus' eyes, moving upwards, became aware of a good-humoured, round and very benevolent face. He was even more amazed to observe a dove seated on the left shoulder of this strange individual— a dove which seemed remarkably happy and entirely unperturbed by the aroma of the short cigar which the stout gentleman was smoking.

Erasmus said: "Good evening, Mr. Krasinsky."

Krasinsky smiled. "I am very glad, my dear Erasmus, that you have recognised me, although you are possibly unaware of where you saw me last. I am like that. I go everywhere, see everything and occasionally try to do something about it. Yourself for instance. . . ."

"Myself?" said Erasmus bitterly. "There is no hope for me. I am madly in love with the most beautiful girl in the world. Her father loathes me. My prospects are practically nil. Well, Mr. Krasinsky, how do you advise me in my position?"

Krasinsky said: "Advice is seldom very much good because when proffered it is not often taken. But I am interested in your case, my dear Mr. Bellamy, because you remind me very much of a young gentleman who was greatly in love, whose name was Esteban, and who lived in a warm country very far from these beautiful shores. Would you like to hear the story?"

Erasmus sighed. "Yes . . . why not? There is nothing else to do."

Krasinsky said: "It might be of use to you. I think you might find it interesting."

For some unknown reason, quite suddenly, Erasmus began to feel tired. Not an ordinary tiredness but a rather pleasant fatigue of the mind. His eyes grew misty and he fell asleep, or so he thought, as Krasinsky said:

"Listen carefully. I think the picture might amuse you. . . ."

Now Erasmus was slumbering deeply. He began to dream, and this is what he saw. . . .

.   .   .   .   .

Esteban came out of the shadow of the mangrove swamp; began to walk along the winding cattle track that led towards Bana.

He was tall, slim and rangy. His skin was tanned to the colour of liver. His face was long but with humour lines about the mouth. He had soft brown eyes; white, strong teeth. He walked with a swagger, the Spanish spurs on his cuban-heeled cow-boots jangling. He wore black, tight-fitting Spanish trousers, wide over his boots, with a broad, tarnished silver stripe down the sides; a blue shirt open at the neck; a black, tight-sleeved bolero. There were silver neck cords on his sombrero. The black, pencil-line moustache above his attractive mouth gave him a cynical and sardonic expression which was belied when he smiled and showed his white teeth. Round his waist he wore a five-inch-wide *gaucho* belt studded with medallions. Over this was a pistol belt with an American .45 automatic in a black holster on one side.

When he neared the coppice he whistled and the *pinto* walked out of the shadows towards him.

The horse looked rather like Esteban. It was a thin and rangy *pinto* and when you looked at it you thought that the high pommelled saddle with its cow-rope horn and Mexican back was too big for it. Esteban swung himself into the saddle with a lithe and easy movement. He skirted the coppice; put the *pinto* into an easy canter. He rode through the heat of the afternoon.

It was six o'clock when he arrived at the Anzanas' shack. The shack, built of forest logs, plaster and mud, was set in a remote clearing towards the edge of the forest. It was a secret place, near enough to the cattle grazing country to be dangerous—for the owners of the cattle.

Esteban dismounted; lighted a long, thin cigarro. He walked round to the other side of the shack. Olé Anzanas, and his brothers Pedro and Quincho, sat, swinging their legs over the edge of the broken-down veranda. Between them were two bottles of *cachasa*—one of them empty. They smoked brown, Spanish cigarettes. They looked bored, dirty and dangerous.

Olé said, his dark face wrinkling into a grin: "May the good saints preserve us . . . look who comes . . . !" He spat on the ground.

Pedro Anzanas said: "Good-day to you, Esteban. How my heart bleeds for you. We have heard your sad news!"

Esteban shrugged his shoulders. "You are entirely wrong, Pedro. My news is not sad. Merely a little postponement of my happiness, I assure you."

Quincho said: "Yes . . . ? Amigo, what madness persuaded you that da Silva would allow you to marry his daughter?"

Esteban sat down on the ground, cross-legged. Pedro Anzanas picked up the half-empty bottle of *cachasa*; threw it towards him. Esteban caught it adroitly; removed the cork; put the neck of the bottle in his mouth, and drank.

Then he said: "My good friends, you will listen to me. Business is very bad for everyone these days. It is practically impossible for a gentleman to make any easy money, but I have an idea."

Quincho said: "May the saints preserve us . . . ! Esteban has an idea . . . !"

Esteban shrugged his shoulders again. He said: "I am informed by my beautiful Pilar, who adores me, and who is stupid enough to have a father like da Silva, that three days ago da Silva, for a reason best known to himself, insured his newly bought cattle with an insurance society near Zusta."

Olé said: "Why should he do a thing like that?"

Esteban smiled. "Possibly he'd heard that you had moved to this district, Olé. Now, figure to yourself, my heart goes out towards da Silva even although he has refused to consent to my marriage with his daughter. I have an idea that he needs money. I would like to help him."

Quincho grinned. "*Madre de dios* . . . it must be wonderful to be helped by Esteban!"

Pedro Anzanas said: "Keep silence . . . this should be *good*."

"I assure you it is," said Esteban. "Briefly, my idea is this. You Olé, you Pedro, and you, Quincho, are also very short of funds. I understand cattle raiding has been a little difficult of late because always the *rurales* are looking for cattle thieves. That is of course unless one has enough money to square Mendanda, our respected police chief. But supposing that to-night somebody were to cut out five or six hundred of da Silva's cattle, drive them over the mountain into the valley, do you think that, having insured this cattle, da Silva would worry too much about reclaiming them?"

Quincho said: "Possibly not. Perhaps he would rather have the insurance company's money."

Olé nodded.

Pedro said: "There is reason in this."

Esteban went on: "My idea is that tonight you should drive

five or six hundred of the cattle over the mountain into Silver Valley. You three could do it easily. You are good *llaneros.*"

Olé said: "All things are possible to men of good heart. What do we get out of this? It is one thing to have six hundred head of cattle in Silver Valley, but another thing to dispose of them, especially if they are branded."

Esteban said: "Half of da Silva's cattle are not yet branded. They came in only a week ago. This is the reason why he has insured the herd. Anybody's brand could go on them. There is always a good market for unbranded cattle. In fact," continued Esteban airily, "I will go so far as to say that I will find a purchaser for them. And at a good price." He picked up the *cachasa* bottle; took another swig. He threw the bottle to Olé.

Olé flipped off his Mexican sombrero with the back of his hand. Underneath was a sweat-soiled bandana handkerchief. He loosened the knot, wiping the sweat from his forehead. "I think the idea is good," he said. "Tonight we take the cattle. Tomorrow they will be in Silver Valley. We will take only the unbranded. When the time comes Esteban can come to us with an offer." He looked at Esteban. "Is this agreed?" he asked.

Esteban got up. He shook a little dust from his trouser leg. "My friends, I know I could rely on you. You shall hear from me. *Adios,* and may the saints preserve you."

.   .   .   .   .   .

When the evening shadows lengthened Esteban came down the trail that leads from Zusta. He dismounted and took a track by the side of a little wood. On the corner, standing beneath the tree where they had always met, stood Pilar da Silva.

Pilar was tall and slim and curveful and beautiful. When she smiled her oval face was illuminated and her white teeth flashed.

Esteban kissed her hands. He said: "Now for me the sun has come out. How is it with you, my Pilar?"

Her face became serious. "Esteban, I am worried about my father. Last night by some means the corral gates were left open. Over six hundred head of cattle are gone. He is almost beside himself."

Esteban cocked one eyebrow. The movement gave his face a pleasant Machiavellian expression. He said: "But, *carissima*, surely the cattle are insured?"

She nodded her head. "That is so, but they were unbranded, because my father has been ill and occupied, and that is what makes it serious. He says that because the cattle are not branded the insurance company will be angry and suspicious. You know they insist always on stock being branded. Today, Señor Pravis, his lawyer, came to see him. Pravis said that it would be a good thing for my father to offer a reward immediately; to deposit five hundred dollars for the reward with Señor Mendanda, the Chief of Police—the reward to be paid to anybody who could give any information as to where the cattle are. Pravis said this would give the insurance company confidence in my father."

Esteban said: "A good idea. Has he put in the claim on the company?"

She nodded. "He has reported the loss to the company's agent in Bana. He has claimed the insurance."

"That is excellent," said Esteban. "No one, I suppose, my sweet, knows anything about the cattle?"

She shrugged her shoulders prettily. "You know that in this part of the world there are lots of cattle thieves. It is almost too easy for them."

Esteban put his arm about her. He led her slowly back towards the track down by the side of the wood.

He said: "Return to your home, Pilar. Have confidence. All will be well."

She turned towards him. "I would care about nothing if my ather would allow me to marry you."

Esteban smiled. He made a grandiose gesture with his right hand—an all-embracing gesture. He said: "Have faith, *cara*. Have faith in Esteban. *Adios*, my little chicken."

He watched her until she was out of sight. Then he returned to the spot where he had tethered his *pinto*; mounted; rode off in the opposite direction.

It was eight o'clock when he arrived at the small adobe hut in which old José, an ancient range-rider, lived. He found José in the main room of the hut leaning over a bottle of *cachasa*. José was old and fat and grey-haired, but there was the same cunning twinkle in his eye, the same broad smile of welcome.

He said: "God be with you, Señor Esteban. What brings you to my poor abode? I am ashamed of it, but everything I have is yours."

Esteban sat down on the rickety stool. He said: "If that is so, my friend, we will start off with the *cachasa*."

José pushed the bottle across the table. Esteban took a long swig.

He said: "Listen, my old gaucho . . . times are hard and I think that a little happiness should come into your life. How would you like some money?"

José wrinkled his nose. "I would like it very much. How much money, Esteban? And what do I have to do for the money this time?" He grinned wickedly.

Esteban said: "Figure to yourself, my José, last night six hundred head of unbranded cattle were stolen from da Silva's corral on the other side of the *mesa*. They have disappeared."

José shrugged his shoulders. "Why not? Since I was a little boy cattle have been disappearing in this country."

Esteban nodded. "Precisely, my friend. Last week the cattle were insured and da Silva thinks that the insurance company may be suspicious because they were unbranded. So, in order to regain the company's confidence, he has deposited a reward of five hundred silver dollars with Mendanda, the Chief of Police, for information as to the whereabouts of his cattle. You, José, will go at once to see Mendanda. You will give him information about the cattle."

José said: "For all that money I would give information to the devil himself. What do I tell Mendanda?"

"You will tell Mendanda what is in effect the truth. You will tell Mendanda that last night was a lovely night. You could not sleep so you mounted that ancient *pinto* of yours and rode over the *mesa*, and you saw Olé, Pedro and Quincho Anzanas driving da Silva's cattle towards Silver Valley. There is, as you know, a canyon at the end of the valley which is an ideal hiding place for a herd, and that is where the cattle are. You will demand the reward."

"But of course," said old José. "Naturally."

Esteban said: "Listen. Mendanda will know that what you say is probably true. He will know that Olé, Pedro and Quincho are amongst our most expert cattle thieves. He will suggest to you that he will pay you half the reward and keep the other half for himself. You know Mendanda?"

José shrugged. "Who doesn't?"

"Very well," said Esteban. "You will agree to this. You will take the two hundred and fifty silver dollars, and I shall call on you tomorrow morning and collect half. Is it agreed?"

José got to his feet. "My good friend, Señor Esteban . . . I am already on my way. The prospect of such riches pleases me immensely. I shall be drunk for six months."

Esteban said: "Good, José! When you die may your grave be covered with flowers for ever."

"A superb thought," said old José. "When you leave me the sun disappears. God go with you, Señor Esteban."

.   .   .   .   .

The shadows had lengthened into darkness when Esteban threw the reins of the *pinto* over its head on to the ground and walked to the Anzanas' shack. Olé, Pedro and Quincho sat, their legs dangling over the broken veranda, passing a bottle of *cachasa* one to the other.

Olé said: "Good evening, Esteban. The night is better for your presence. Salutations, my friend."

Esteban said in his pleasant voice: "There is a little trouble, but nothing of importance."

Pedro said: "Always in the lives of great men there is trouble. What has happened, Esteban?"

Esteban shrugged his shoulders. "Consider, *amigos*, that last night some wastrel, who should have been better employed, observed you driving da Silva's cattle over into Silver Valley. Unfortunately, in order to regain the confidence of the insurance company, da Silva has deposited five hundred silver dollars with Mendanda as a reward for information about the cattle. Therefore, this wastrel, who observed your movements, will go to Mendanda, our esteemed Chief of Police, to claim the reward."

Quincho scowled. "Thus do the adverse fates affect the lives of hard-working men such as we."

"Now what, Esteban?" asked Olé.

Pedro said: "If I knew who this dog was I would slit his throat. There is nothing worse than an informer."

Esteban squatted on his heels, carefully evading his long spurs. He said: "Be of good cheer. A little thought and all is made easy. Olé, you know the police corral beyond the Zusta road—the corral which our Chief of Police built for wandering cattle?"

Olé nodded. "I know it well."

"It is empty," said Esteban. "So, when it is a little darker, you and Pedro and Quincho will ride to Silver Valley and drive da Silva's cattle into the police corral. You see?"

Olé began to laugh. "This is very good . . . !" He turned to his brothers. "Understand, my brothers, we are to be public benefactors. We find da Silva's cattle which had wandered because somebody had left the corral gates open, so we drive them into the police corral. Esteban, you are a great man." His face became serious. "But what about us?" he asked. "We are to be public benefactors. We save da Silva a great deal of money. We get nothing. All our time and energy is sacrificed for the public good. Are we to do good work and get nothing for it?"

Esteban said: "Listen to me. When this informant goes to Mendanda and informs him that he saw you stealing da Silva's cattle, Mendanda will never think for one moment that the cattle have been driven to the police corral. So what does he do?"

"It is obvious," said Olé. "He will arrest me, my brother Pedro and my brother Quincho. He will throw us into that filthy jail in Bana."

"Precisely," said Esteban. "So you go into jail wearing the expressions of martyrs. When you have been there a few hours

I will arrange that the cattle are discovered in the police corral, and you, who are public benefactors, have been thrown into jail like common cattle thieves. And Mendanda, in order to save his own skin, in order that the whole population of Bana shall not laugh at him, will pay you the half of the reward which he has kept for himself. He will give you two hundred and fifty silver dollars. This I will arrange because you are my friends and because I have always loved you."

Olé got up. He said: "Come, my brothers, we have work to do. The Anzanas family have always been in the forefront for the public good. We will drive da Silva's cattle into the police corral. Esteban, as always I rely on you."

Pedro said: "Me also. . . ."

"So be it, *amigos*," said Esteban. "When I leave you the moon goes out. I am desolate."

Pedro said: "For us it is worse. Life is miserable when you are not within the range of our eyes."

.   .   .   .   .

The next morning, on his way to Bana, Esteban called at the hut of old José and collected a hundred and twenty-five silver dollars. These he divided and slipped into his boot tops. He rode leisurely towards Bana.

At ten o'clock he entered the office of Cardona, the insurance company's agent, at the end of the little street. Cardona looked up enquiringly.

He said: "Good morning, Señor Esteban. Can I guess what brings you here?"

Esteban nodded. "Señor Cardona . . . always I have had a great appreciation of your mentality. Always I have said to my friends there is no greater representative of an insurance company than Señor Cardona. Always he has the good of his principals at heart."

Cardona nodded. "I am grateful for your good opinion."

Esteban crossed his legs; listened to the pleasant jingle of his spurs as he did so.

He said: "Señor Cardona, information reaches me that a

large number of the cattle of my esteemed friend and, I hope, prospective father-in-law, Ramon da Silva, have disappeared. I understand that he has already made a claim against the insurance company. Is that true?"

Cardona nodded. "It is indeed true. The sum involved is considerable. It is perhaps unfortunate that the cattle were un-branded."

Esteban said: "Possibly there were good reasons for this. Da Silva has been ill and occupied. At the same time the insurance company will be forced to pay. It would be bad publicity for them if they didn't."

"True," said Cardona. "They will pay eventually."

Esteban nodded. "Señor Cardona, I wish to do you a good turn because I have always liked you. I can save you and the company a great deal of time and money. When I leave here I propose to call on our respected and esteemed Chief of Police, Mendanda. I propose to give him certain information, as a result of which I assure you, Señor, da Silva's cattle will be returned to him and the claim which he has made against the insurance company will be withdrawn."

Cardona smiled. "This is very pleasant news. You are indeed my friend, Señor Esteban. My principals on the mainland will be intrigued and thrilled at the news which I shall send them."

Esteban raised one finger. "One moment, Señor . . . you will agree with me that the lowest *peon* is worthy of his hire. Is it not so?"

Cardona shrugged his shoulders. "Indeed yes . . . depending of course upon what the hire is."

Esteban said: "Would a great company such as yours miss a paltry two hundred silver dollars? Is this too much for a herd of cattle to be returned?"

"I don't think so," said Cardona. "I have no doubt that when the cattle are returned to da Silva they would willingly pay you the two hundred dollars."

Esteban rose. He stood looking sorrowfully at Cardona, his expression a mixture of misery and outraged dignity.

Of the Dream of Erasmus Bellamy

He said: "So you doubt my word, Señor Cardona. You tell me that the company will pay me this paltry sum *when* the cattle are returned. Perhaps you will be good enough to explain to me why I, Esteban, should trouble to interest myself in their business when they do not trust me. Perhaps you would care for me to wash my hands of this matter. Do you consider that I came into your office to be insulted? You will understand," he added softly, "that people who know me will inform you that I have killed a man for less than this."

Cardona said: "Señor Esteban, I assure you that you mistake me. Never for one moment have I doubted your integrity. In order that you may know this; in order that you may understand my affection and esteem for you I tell you that out of my contingency fund I will pay you the two hundred dollars at once, trusting in your word."

Esteban said: "Your words give me great pleasure. How wonderful is friendship and understanding and trust. Give me the two hundred dollars and I will sign a receipt."

Outside, in the narrow alleyway that led from the main street out towards the *mesa*, Esteban deposited the two hundred dollars in the bags concealed beneath his saddle flaps. He tethered his *pinto* to an adjacent rail; turned back into the main street; walked towards the white adobe one-story building that housed the Chief of Police. He went through the doorway into the hot, evil-smelling hall; crossed it; opened the door on the other side. He closed the door softly behind him.

Mendanda, Chief of the Bana Police, sat back in his chair, his feet on his desk. He was dressed in a dirty white shirt; stained blue linen trousers, kept up by a piece of lariat rope round his waist. His sombrero was tilted over his eyes, a long cigarro hanging from one corner of his mouth. There were holes in the soles of his canvas shoes and his ankles were dirty.

He said: "God be with you, Esteban. It is a long time since I have seen you."

Esteban sat down on a stool in front of the desk. "I have been busy. I have been away from here. Many things have kept me, but when news comes to me that there is a possibility of trouble for my friend Mendanda then I come to you immediately. As you know, I am your friend."

Mendanda spat out of the window. "This is great news for me. Your smile is like sunshine to me. Take anything I have." He spat out of the window even more artistically than before. "Tell me, Esteban?"

Esteban said: "There are unkind people in Bana. Hear everything. It seems that by some means the corral gates at da Silva's were left open. A herd of cattle strayed. You have heard about this?"

Mendanda nodded. "Did they stray?" he asked. "I have been told that Olé, Pedro and Quincho Anzanas were seen driving these cattle to Silver Valley—their usual place of hiding. I have had an information lodged before me. This morning I have arrested them. They are in the jail. When I accused them of this offence they said nothing." He shrugged his shoulders. "They did not even offer me any money not to arrest them, which I regard as being very suspicious."

Esteban said: "Mendanda, you will listen to me. You have been tricked. As you have just said, if Olé, Pedro and Quincho had been concerned in stealing these cattle they would have offered you money not to arrest them. The fact they have not done so is, as you say, suspicious. This is a plot against you."

Mendanda cocked one black eyebrow. He said: "So . . . tell me the plot."

Esteban said: "Some fool must have left da Silva's corral gates open. The cattle strayed. News of this came to Olé. He knew perfectly well that if they stole the cattle suspicion would fall on them, *so they did not steal the cattle.*"

Mendanda leaned forward; his lazy eyes were interested. He said softly: "I see. What did they do?"

Esteban said: "For once they decided to be honest citizens. They have driven the cattle into the police corral—the purpose for which you built it." He grinned wickedly at Mendanda. "Now they are going to bring an action against you for wrongful imprisonment."

Mendanda said: "It appears to me that there are no longer any saints. It appears to me that there is no longer any justice in the world that this thing should be done to me. I do not like this."

"Listen, my friend," said Esteban. "Why worry? It is so easy."

Mendanda leaned down and opened the desk drawer. In the drawer was his pistol belt, and a box of cigarros. He threw one across the desk to Esteban, who caught it deftly. He said: "Tell me, Esteban."

Esteban said: "It is as simple as this. Da Silva deposited five hundred silver dollars with you—a reward for information about the cattle. Have you paid it out?"

Mendanda said: "Yes and no. There are no secrets between you, my friend, and me, and you know that for a person of my integrity my pay is very small. I gave the informant two hundred and fifty dollars. I thought I was entitled to the balance."

Esteban nodded. "Listen to me, Mendanda, these people Olé, Pedro and Quincho may make trouble for you, more especially as they will say it was your business to know whether the cattle had been driven into the police corral or not, even although it is such a long way away and you have not had time to go there. Do this: Release them. Tell them that you wish to apologise to them; give them the two hundred and fifty dollars reward. As you know, I am friendly with them. I will get fifty dollars back for you."

Mendanda shrugged his shoulders. He said: "Everybody in Bana makes money except myself. I get only fifty dollars."

Esteban said: "No. This is my plan. You will send one of your *rurales* to inform da Silva that his cattle are safe and you will inform him that because of my great regard for him I have volunteered to put his brand on the cattle before they leave the police corral, so that the insurance company will be satisfied." He shrugged his shoulders gracefully. "I am not certain," he continued, "how many cattle are in the police corral, but if, for the sake of argument, there are six hundred head it may be that I will only brand five hundred and three, because after all some of the cattle may have run wild when Olé, Pedro and Quincho were driving them to the police corral."

Mendanda said: "I see. So that leaves ninety-seven head in the police corral. What then?"

Esteban said: "I have a purchaser. You and I are good friends. Always there has been great honesty between us. When I have sold the ninety-seven head of cattle I will divide the money with you, Mendanda, because you are my friend; because our interests are mutual."

Mendanda swung his feet off the desk. He opened another drawer; produced an iron ring with a dozen solid keys dangling therefrom. He threw the ring across the table to Esteban. He said: "Let them out. Tell them to come quietly to me and I will give them two hundred dollars, reserving only fifty for myself as commission."

Esteban picked up the keys. "So be it . . . *adios*, Mendanda. When you die the world will be lonely for me."

Mendanda said: "Go in peace, my friend. When the door shuts behind you a cold wind enters my heart."

.   .   .   .   .

When the hot afternoon sun disappeared in the west, Esteban came down the Zusta trail. Pilar da Silva waited by the tree. She came towards him.

She said: "How wonderful is life. My father is so pleased. This morning Olé, Pedro and Quincho Anzanas drove back the cattle. It seems they had strayed; had been driven into the police corral. He is a little annoyed because some are missing." She smiled at him archly. "He's pleased with you too for your kindness in putting his brand on the cattle before they left the corral. You must have worked hard."

Esteban shrugged his shoulders. "For your father I would do anything. Yesterday right through the broiling sun we four worked on the cattle. Nothing is too much for my Pilar." He put his arm about her. "I have news for you, my sweet. You are to be my wife."

She looked at him, her eyes glowing.

Of the Dream of Erasmus Bellamy

"Always, as you know," said Esteban, "the good will of your father has meant much to me. When he told me that some of his cattle were missing I was able to supply the deficiency at a very cheap price. Some unbranded cattle which I bought last month will be delivered to him tomorrow. Not only that," he said, "but listen to this, light of my soul. He has decided that it would be safer for him and his house that I should be his overseer. He has agreed that you shall be my wife. Now he knows that no longer will his cattle stray; that everything in his house will be at peace. Come, *cara*, let us go home."

They wandered down the pathway towards the main track, Esteban's *pinto* trailing behind them. After a little while, Esteban threw away his long cigarro; began softly to sing an old Spanish love song.

. . . . . .

Erasmus Bellamy awoke with a start. Already his mind was full of ideas. His usual smile appeared on his countenance. He turned to thank Mr. Krasinsky for his kindness, but found he was alone. It seemed that the portly philosopher had disappeared into thin air.

Erasmus got up. He began to walk. His hands were in his trouser pockets and he was whistling quietly to himself. His brain was busy. As he moved through the gate that leads from the golf course to the old Betchworth coach road he became aware of Rufus Skeyne who was lounging down the road, his hands in his breeches pockets.

Skeyne said: "Hello, Mr. Bellamy. . . ."

"Tell me, Skeyne," asked Bellamy, "what was in your mind when you talked about the insurance that the Squire has just taken out on his herd of cattle?"

Skeyne shrugged his shoulders. "I thought you might be interested. I could have half of that herd in one night if I had somebody to help me."

Erasmus said: "Meaning me?"

"Meaning you. . . ."

Erasmus said: "It would be wonderful, wouldn't it?"

Of the Dream of Erasmus Bellamy

"Of course it would be. We could pull this off easily. You would have money and, with a little thought, it might even be possible for you to marry the beautiful Belinda."

Erasmus asked: "What do you mean by that? Do you think he'd take it lying down?"

The grin on Skeyne's face was more cynical than ever. "He'd have to take it lying down."

Erasmus stopped suddenly. He became aware of a new quality in Skeyne's voice. He asked: "Why?"

Skeyne smiled. "He is my father. My mother was the housekeeper up at the Hall. He'd never do anything to me. He couldn't."

Erasmus thought of Esteban in the dream. He smiled back at Skeyne. He said: "Rufus, I have a feeling that in a few months' time you are going to be my half-half-brother-in-law. Let us go to The Running Dog, drink a pint of beer, and go into details. . . ."

EPISODE ELEVEN

Of the King of Tarragona

⟨✺⟩

One summer's evening I decided to take a walk towards Cannon Street, which is, as everyone knows, an important artery in the life of the City of London.

After seven o'clock in the evening the City is more or less deserted, and the atmosphere of the place seems peaceful, vaguely ponderous and a little self-conscious—somewhat akin to the atmosphere created by a bench of country Justices of the Peace after the Clerk of the Court has left them and they must perforce do a little thinking for themselves.

So, in the evening, the City (bereft of its hurrying crowds of junior clerks, "walking messengers", top-hatted financiers and hook-nosed members of the Stock Exchange, whose eager hurryings either denote a rise or fall in this or that stock or else that someone has suddenly thought of another rude story—a process to which, I am told, all successful stockbrokers are addicted) somehow shrinks into itself and produces as a sublimation of its empty inferiority the peculiar atmosphere to which I have referred.

Twenty-five yards from the place where Cannon Street merges into King William Street is a passage into which I turned, because years ago, when youth sat impudently upon me, I worked in a lawyer's office in the vicinity and would, on occasion, becoming tired of "*all that messuage and tenement marked on the plan hereunto attached and coloured pink,"* find an excuse for wandering down Bolt Passage and exploring the many odd little turnings that ran out of it.

It was on one of these occasions when I was playing truant from my desk that, in a very narrow and somewhat dark alleyway, I discovered a chemist's shop. Above the *facia* the words *John Hybelthoms, Chymist*, were painted, and in the window were displayed three great glass urns, one filled with a golden liquid, one with a rich blue and one with a peculiar greenish coloured fluid which, I thought then, must of necessity have been—even if only by virtue of its strange colour—most efficacious for the disabilities of the body for which it was intended.

On occasion I had entered the dark and musty shop. Once when someone had cut a finger badly, and on another occasion when a copying press had descended with unnecessary abruptness upon my hand. On each of these occasions I had been served by a very young man who possessed large luminous eyes, a pale damp skin, dark, dank hair, a preoccupied manner and a most distressing cough.

Also there was upon the right hand side of his neck, visible above his linen collar, a strange birthmark of the shape and colour of a ripe raspberry.

I can remember asking myself—with the unconscious callousness of youth—why the devil he did not do something about the cough, whose brassy resonance seemed to penetrate into the very corners of the shop and leave its possessor even more pale, more luminous, more gasping.

I did not then realise that the cough spelled tuberculosis and that the damp paleness of the thin cheeks and the luminosity of the dark eyes were but further symptoms of that unhappy disease.

As I walked along the alleyway, whose overhanging roofs shut out the dying rays of the summer sun, I began to compare these days with those; to visualise myself as a sprightly, cheerful and romantically inclined person, and to wonder what had happened to the sick young man who handed out, over the antique and dusty counter, those petty medicaments to which the junior clerkhood of that part of the city flew in times of cough and cold.

With an effort I remembered the name of the chemist's assistant (I was aided in the process by the very fact that of his three names two were common and one extraordinary)—Alfred Eustachio Jones. I remembered the day on which he had told me his names and talked with an ill-concealed air of regret of the necessity of his calling which kept him prisoner for nine hours each day within the close confines of John Hybelthoms' shop in the sunless alley.

I walked down the turning and up again, but I could not find the shop. It had gone and in its place were newly built offices with well-cleaned brass plates and an unshaven caretaker who stood at the door smoking a pipe and regarding me with a suspicious curiosity which asked what any normal person could want in that part of the world at seven-thirty o'clock in the evening.

I walked out of the alley, turned into Cannon Hill Lane, and into the hostelry which stood on the corner. *That*, at any rate, was still there, and, sitting in the corner of the small saloon bar, a pint pot clasped tenderly in one hand, his shepherd's plaid suit almost reflecting the last rays of the sun, sat Mr. Krasinsky, a cheerful smile upon his countenance.

I sat down by him.

"Good evening, my old friend," he said. "I observe by the slight touch of sadness that still clings to your countenance that you have been wandering about these lanes and alleys endeavouring to recapture from the days that have gone some slight indication of the mentality which was yours in 1912; of the glow of juvenility, the virility of step, the romantic aura and whatnot of youth, in order that you might draw, in your mind, some comparison between your state then and your state now. Am I not right?"

The waiter brought my beer. We lifted our tankards and drank. Out of the corner of my eye I saw that Krasinsky was still the same as he had been twenty-five years before when I had first met him in this same saloon bar, sitting in the same seat and wearing the same suit. Only his smile seemed a little deeper.

"You are, as usual, almost quite right, Krasinsky," I told him. "Just now I was wondering about Alfred Eustachio Jones, who served in the Chemist's shop in Meller's Alley. I was wondering what had happened to him. I was remembering his cough."

"Precisely," said Krasinsky cheerfully. "It was a most distressing cough, was it not? And his eyes were so large and his cheeks so pale. And do you remember that strange birthmark that shone upon his neck and looked like a raspberry?"

He took a great sup at his beer.

"Do you remember," he went on, "your visit, some ten years ago, to Tarragona?"

"Of course," I said. "But exactly what has my stay in Tarragona to do with Alfred Eustachio Jones, his cough or his birthmark?"

"Only this," he replied. "Do you not remember the day on which—after having been involved in a little *affaire* that necessitated your hurried absence from the sea-port for a day or two— hiring a motor-car and going off in the direction of Reus? Do you not remember the cemetery just outside Tarragona on the road to Reus where you stopped for water and where you saw that amazing and bizarre monument in good Spanish marble, picked out with a fine gold lettering?"

"I remember it quite well," I said. "But I still do not see what that has to do with Alfred Eustachio Jones."

"If you had not been in such a hurry and had inspected the far side of the monument," said Krasinsky, "you would have seen that it was inscribed:

'*In grateful and loving memory to the Señor Alfred Eustachio Jones, called The King of Tarragona, whose memory remains green in our hearts and whose soul rests with God.*' "

"Good Heavens, Krasinsky!" I exclaimed. "Do you really mean to tell me that Alfred Jones, one-time assistant in Hybelthoms' musty shop in the Alley, actually secured for himself that amazing monument?"

Of the King of Tarragona

He nodded.

"Such are the supreme surprises of our existence," he said. "And now if you will proceed to buy beer I will tell you the story of this monument and how it came to be erected. There is," he continued, "a moral to this story, but, speaking for myself, I have never been able to discover exactly what it is."

.   .   .   .   .

"You must understand," said Krasinsky, "that in the latter part of 1912, as the autumn wore on, my poor young friend Alfred Eustachio Jones became more and more despondent.

And there was every reason for his despondency. First of all his soul was sick and tired of the narrow outlook on life which came to him through the doorway of the shop in Mellers Alley, and secondly, looking into the future, there seemed for him no gleam of hope, no ray of sunshine, in fact, nothing at all except the possibilities of the sack and/or an early and uncomfortable death.

From his earliest days Alfred had come to regard himself as a complete failure. Born of desperately poor parents whose welcome to Alfred (his birth was the result of one of those unfortunate accidents which dog the amatory efforts of the most careful of couples) was of the most unenthusiastic kind, he grew up to consider himself a nuisance to all and sundry.

At the age of four, his parents having got themselves killed in a railway accident, Alfred was carried off by some well-meaning people—who professed to be interested in his welfare—to an orphanage, where, in return for a modicum of food and clothing, he did a great deal of hard manual work and was allowed to develop, at will, an inferiority complex of the most superbly acute description."

.   .   .   .   .

Krasinsky paused in his tale for a moment in order to delicately take a pinch of snuff which he carried in his waistcoat pocket, after which he addressed himself with gusto to the tankard of beer which had been brought at my order.

Of the King of Tarragona

I was wondering when I had first met Krasinsky. That I had met him in this hostelry, many years ago, I knew. But in the years, the actual day and the circumstances of our meeting had become lost. Somehow—and for the most mysterious of reasons—I associated my first knowledge of Krasinsky with the first sproutings of my imagination, when, at the age of fifteen or so, I had, like so many other very young men, planned to take the world by storm, and the hearts of many beauteous ladies by charm, chivalry and what-will-you. Somehow—again one does not know why—the memory of Krasinsky was bound up with my own memory of sundry charming mind reflexes of years ago, associated, invariably, with wine, with war, or with women.

Which, when I come to think of it, is probably the reason why so few men in these days meet Krasinsky. One knows that a meeting between him and a person entirely cynical, commercial, unimaginative, or merely ambitious, is impossible.

And I have often wondered why it is that the scurrying people of the City of London's midday hours—especially in the neighbourhood of Fleet Street—that "Street of Adventure" (where men so often mistake neurosis for "temperament," weak anger for "toughness", feeble jealousy for "critical ability", and where the truth is indeed so much stranger than fiction that the Literary Editor might well on occasion swap his pages with his News colleagues), do not sometimes consider the possibilities of a lonely walk at night through some of the dark alleyways that abound in the City, there to discover, on some red-letter day, the portly and check-clad figure of Krasinsky and to hear something of themselves as yet unknown; something remote from the crowded bar, or the harried news-room; something that might put a smile upon their lips and ease the fear from out their hearts.

·　　·　　·　　·　　·

Krasinsky said: "It was, as I have indicated, in the autumn of 1912 that life began to be almost impossible for Alfred Jones. He was now twenty-two years of age and his malady was, I believe, in an advanced state. He coughed continuously, and his employer, Mr. Hybelthoms, who was the sort of person who boasted that "he never stood any nonsense from nobody", had indicated that it might be a very good thing if Alfred proceeded to look for another job.

It was on a cold October day, and I had an idea that something of an amusing quality might happen in the Chemist's establishment. So, towards three-thirty in the afternoon, I was standing in the shop when Mrs. Larranbee (who was the wife of one of the partners in Larranbee, Hyde & Goteham) came in to buy a piece of sticking plaster for her husband, who had caught his finger on a pin in her waistbelt—they wore them in those days—and who had found the sharp side of her love in the process.

Mrs. Larranbee was a charming woman. She was well-dressed and of good height and figure, and it was perhaps the hand of fate that caused Alfred Jones to break into a desperate fit of coughing as she came into the shop. So racked was Alfred by the tremors which shook his frail frame that he was forced to support himself on the counter until the spasm passed.

Then he recovered himself and proceeded to serve Mrs. Larranbee with her sticking plaster.

He handed it to her and she put down the three pennies on the counter. She looked at Alfred and there was a suggestion of interest in her eyes.

"Really you ought to do something about that cough," she said. "It isn't any business of mine, *of course*, but I think you ought to see somebody about it. Have you a good doctor?"

Alfred shook his head. He was vaguely bewildered. In all his life no one, until now, had taken the slightest interest in him, and here was a lady—a beautiful lady—well-dressed, affluent, smelling delightfully of some rare perfume (he thought), concerned with whether he had a doctor—and a good one at that!

Mrs. Larranbee took a little notebook from her handbag and wrote down an address on a blank page in it. She tore out the page and handed it to Alfred with a charming smile.

"There is the address of my doctor," she said. "Please go and see him. I'll telephone him that he is to expect you. Good-day."

She walked out of the shop and left Alfred with his mouth open. But not for long. From his dark and somewhat smelly sanctum at the back of the shop Mr. Hybelthoms had observed the scene which had taken place.

Truculently he emerged and informed Alfred tersely that it was "not doing the business any good to have an assistant who was coughing himself to pieces and taking advantage of the good nature of customers". He informed Alfred that he could take a week's salary in lieu of notice and get out.

Alfred packed together his few belongings and left the shop. His heart was very heavy. He considered it would be extremely difficult for him to find himself another situation, especially having regard to the cough. He had no hope, and realised that he could not live on his savings for long.

It was next day that, fumbling in his pocket, he found the address of the doctor.

.   .   .   .   .

Doctor Erasmus Finegollen (said Krasinsky) regarded Alfred Jones in much the same manner as he would have examined a dying cod.

In the process he muttered some trite remarks about Mrs. Larranbee, whose hobby it was (and she derived an amazing amount of satisfaction from it) to send to Dr. Finegollen all sorts and conditions of odd people, whom she met in her daily life, for medical examination and such treatment or pre-scription as he thought fit.

The good doctor, however, seldom thought fit. He realised that the patients were sent to him because he was paid an "all-in" fee per annum by Mr. Larranbee (who thus cleverly pro-tected himself against his wife's promiscuous generosity in the realms of medicine) and because the process gave Mrs. Larran-bee a glow not to be compared with that following several small ports. Once she had sent the patient to the doctor her interest waned quickly, so that all the physician had to do was to inform the patient that there was nothing wrong with him and send him about his business.

By this means everyone was kept happy, including the patient, who—like the rest of his kind—could always " do " with a free medical examination, and derived at least some mental satisfaction from being prodded by a real M.D.

But, and we must be fair to the doctor, the medico could not, in common honesty (and certainly without rupturing his oath of Hippocrates in half a dozen different places), inform the unfortunate Alfred Jones that there was nothing the matter with him. He baulked at that.

Instructing the trembling and rather frightened Alfred to replace his shirt, the doctor sat down in his large and comfortable consulting chair and addressed himself to Alfred.

"I don't like the look of you at all, Jones," he said gloomily. "In fact I don't think you've got a chance. You're tubercular. You are in a bad way. I don't see that anything in this country is going to do you any good. In fact," continued the medico, placing his finger tips together, "if you don't get out of England you're a goner."

Alfred said nothing. He seized his braces with an expression of outraged dignity.

"Even if you do get out of here and go to a good climate," continued the doctor, "you'll only last six months. But if I were you I'd get out. And I know where I'd go."

Doctor Finegollen permitted himself to look upwards at the ceiling, and a smile curved his lips. He was thinking of something.

"Have you got any money?" he asked.

Alfred nodded.

"I got seventy pound saved up," he said. "I been saving all my blinkin' life thinkin' that one of these fine days I'd 'ave somethin' to spend it on, an' now just when I made it up to seventy pound last Saturday, you tell me I'm a goner. It's bloody awful, that's what it is."

The doctor nodded. Then suddenly there came upon him

one of those flashes of fine humanity which ennoble the existence of the most cynical of people. He leaned forward and
pointed a thin forefinger at Alfred.

"You listen to me, my boy," he said. "Have you ever heard
of Tarragona? Of course you haven't. All right. Well, the year
I qualified I was going out there. I was to be appointed medical
officer to a big shipping firm in the Port of Tarragona. I made
enquiries about it, Jones. I tell you it's a wonderful place. Hills
running down to the sea, lizards crawling up ancient walls, pipes
of port on tumbrils on their way to the sea-front, lovely women,
veiled in mantillas, riding through the town in fiacres in the
twilight, guitars playing at night under high, iron-barred windows."

The doctor shrugged his shoulders with an expression of the
most extreme regret.

Alfred, carried away by the physician's obvious sincerity,
forgot himself, his disease and his braces.

"Well . . ." he said finally. "Why didn't you go?"

The doctor smiled. It was an unhappy smile.

"Two nights before I was due to sail," he said bitterly, "I
went to a party. It was a farewell party given for me. I drank
more than was good for me. I met Mrs. Finegollen."

He paused and an expression of the most vindictive rage
passed over his face.

"I stayed here and married Mrs. Finegollen," he hissed. "*I
stayed here and married that woman!* I, who could have dallied
with *señoritas* under the palms, who could have thrown my hat
into the ring at the bullfight, who could have spent the day in
celestial dalliance with wine and women. I stayed here and
married that *camel* when I could have gone to Tarragona!"

His voice broke in suppressed passion.

"Crumbs," said Alfred with feeling. "Is she a rorty one?"

The doctor smiled whimsically.

"Rorty," he muttered, "is not the word for it."

He swung round on his chair and faced Alfred, who was
again fumbling with his braces.

"You take your seventy pounds and go to Tarragona," cried

Doctor Finegollen. "I tell you the climate's wonderful. It has everything a climate should have. You'll probably last a year there. Everything's as cheap as dirt and you can live like a fighting cock on nothing a week. You can get there for ten pounds—I'll tell you how. Well—what about it?"

He leaned still farther forward, his eyes searching Alfred's. It seemed that the whole being of the good doctor was, at that moment, bound up in the going (or not) of Alfred to Tarragona. So much so that his personality, expressed through his large and ox-like eyes, seemed to hypnotise the consumptive in the most extraordinary manner.

"Blimey!" said Alfred. "I'll do it. I'm goin' to Tarragona!"

His grip upon his reluctant braces became firm and determined.

An expression of the most extreme satisfaction came upon the face of the doctor. He took up his telephone and called a number. After a minute he spoke into the instrument and when he spoke his voice was charged with appalling vindictiveness.

"Augustina," said the doctor. "I shall not be home to dinner. I shall probably not be home until midnight. Possibly I shall not come home at all tonight.

"I am going," he continued with unholy glee, "to see a young friend of mine off to Tarragona. *And I am going to see that he gets there.* Do you understand, Augustina? *He* is going to get there. *He* is not going to be trapped *en route*—like some people I know—by an old frump who's laying for a young husband. *Good*-night, my *dear!*"

He hung up the instrument. Then he opened a drawer and took out a bottle of port. Upon the bottle was a shipper's label and on it was the word "Tarragona".

He filled two glasses, and together the old man and the young drank the rich wine.

"Alfred," said Krasinsky, "felt much better."

.   .   .   .   .

When more beer had been brought Krasinsky looked at the clock and then at me.

Of the King of Tarragona

"I propose," said he, "having regard to the time, which is drawing on apace, and the fact that I have an appointment with a dog-fancier in Marylebone shortly, to omit a full description of the circumstances of the arrival of Alfred Eustachio Jones at the port of Tarragona.

"Let it suffice that he was taken ashore by the third officer of the tramp in which—owing to the good offices of Doctor Erasmus Finegollen—he had arrived. This officer, filled to the brim with the kindly traditions of the merchant service and about seventy *pesetas'* worth of strong wine, not only arranged for Alfred to be lodged in the house of an acquaintance in the town, but was also able, before he sailed back to England, to secure for the slightly bemused Jones a post as assistant to the local teacher of languages—one Señor Eralio Pinosas—who agreed, in return for being taught English by Alfred, to teach him the rudiments of Spanish, a process in which our young hero secured the greatest advantage because Señor Eralio spoke a most excellent Castilian whereas the colloquial English taught to him by Alfred was of the most rudimentary description, mixed with some rather extraordinary Cockney expletives.

The days, the weeks and the months went by, and it is almost impossible for me to convey to you the amazing change which took place in Alfred. It was apparent that Doctor Finegollen had been more than right in his remarks anent the peculiar properties of Tarragona.

The sweet soft dry air, washed clean by the salt breezes of the sea, mixed with the rarer atmosphere which came down from the hills, flowed into the lungs of Alfred to soothe and heal them.

When six months had passed no one who had known him in the old days would have recognised the erstwhile chemist's assistant. His shoulders had broadened and his puny paunch had disappeared. His long thin legs had taken unto themselves a certain grace and his white and sickly skin was tanned to a shade of the richest brown.

With that amazing aptitude for language which so many of

London's Cockneys possess he had acquired an ability to talk and even write most excellent Spanish.

So, upon this particular night in May 1913 let me present to you a new picture of Alfred Jones as, clad in a tightly fitting pair of black trousers with a silver piping, a green silk shirt beneath a short jacket of black, a black silk handkerchief about his throat caught in an old silver ring, and a sombrero hat with a silver cord, smoking a long rattail cigar, he walked with a touch of swagger from the house of Eralio Pinosas towards the Café of the Six Stars, where with the sweeping courtesy acquired with the language, he greeted sundry acquaintances and ordered for himself a pint of Tarragona wine.

He sat there under the shade of a yellow awning and pondered on life. His mind, leaping back into the recesses of the past, visualised Mellers Alley and the musty shop of John Hybelthoms, with himself, complete with cough, behind the counter.

"Blimey," said Alfred to himself. "Ain't life marvellous? Sometimes I can't sort of think that I'm me."

And on more than one occasion he had looked into a mirror to identify himself with the departed Jones of the London days by the one sign that remained—the large raspberry birthmark which still showed dark against the tan of his throat— a birthmark which—it must be admitted—had been the target of kisses from the soft mouth of more than one fair charmer of Tarragona, whose successful attempts to beguile our Alfred into the pleasant ways of love had completed his education in no uncertain manner.

He was about to finish his wine when he observed approaching him the portly and expensively clad figure of the Señor Tendo Jose Gonzales, who took off his hat with a most pleasant and charming gesture.

"I believe that I have the honour of addressing the Señor Alfredo Jones?" enquired Gonzales.

Alfred rose with alacrity.

"This is a pleasant day for me," he said. "This day on which

Of the King of Tarragona

I have the honour of meeting the Señor Tendo Gonzales is a day which will always be marked with a red letter in my life."

They both bowed and sat down, and after the exchange of some more courtesies, Gonzales said:

"Señor Jones, you will of course realise that I am a man of extreme delicacy and honour. You will know too that I have the biggest and most important shipping and export business in Tarragona. The fact that my rival, Señor Concepcion de Pira, believes that *his* is the most important export and shipping business in Tarragona is of course *merely* a belief."

Gonzales lit a cigar and smoked silently for a few minutes.

"Señor Jones," he went on, "I have a proposition for you, and one which I hope will interest you. I believe that at the moment you are engaged as a teacher of English in the establishment of the worthy Señor Eralio Pinosas. This appointment, though no doubt giving ample scope to the intellectuality which I am sure is yours, seems to me to be unworthy of an individual of your ability.

"I had it in my mind to suggest," said Gonzales, "that you should resign your present appointment and take one with me. I have a growing business with England, and it is necessary that I should have in my office a gentleman who is able to deal with my correspondence with that country. Señor Jones, if you would consent to accept this appointment I shall be happy to pay to you the sum of 250 *pesetas* each week."

Alfred caught his breath. Here was riches. But he smiled and said nothing. The salary was so much greater than the job.

"You would perhaps consider," continued Gonzales with a charming smile, "that the emoluments of this appointment are strangely large. I intended that they should be because"—and he smiled ingratiatingly—"there is another unworthy idea which I would like to bring to your notice.

"But first of all it is necessary that I should know whether you agree to accept my offer of employment."

Alfred blew several smoke rings and then smiled at his companion.

"Tomorrow," he said, "when I find myself working in the office of the Señor Tendo Gonzales, I shall realise that the rest of my life has been entirely misspent, and that I have previously not known any happiness whatsoever."

Gonzales smiled.

"Excellent, my friend," he said. "Now listen to me. I have told you that the Señor Concepcion de Pira is my rival. Very well. Tomorrow night I would suggest to you that at about this time you take a walk with a friend to the Café of the Two White Pillars, which is a café frequented in the evening by de Pira. In a loud voice you will inform your friend of the fact that you are now working in my office and of the liberal salary which I am paying you. I suggest that you also inform your friend that you consider me to be the greatest and most important shipper in Tarragona. Do you understand, Señor Jones?"

"Perfectly," murmured Alfred.

"And what will be the result?" said Gonzales with a cunning smile. "I think you will find, Alfredo—for I would like to call you that because I realise that you are my friend—that within a day or so de Pira will approach you. He will suggest to you that it is a perfectly simple matter for you to work for him as well as for me. He will suggest to you that you allow him to pay you a salary even larger than the one you are receiving from me, but he will ask you to keep the matter as a personal thing between yourself and himself.

"I suggest, Alfredo, that you immediately agree to his proposal.

"And then what will happen?" went on the good shipper, with an expansive smile. "You will be working for us both and you will find that the next thing that de Pira will request of you is that you furnish him with a list of all my English accounts, for which he will probably offer you an increase in salary. You will immediately agree to this, and you will furnish him with a list which I shall give you. It will consist merely of those small buyers who do not pay their accounts, or who are generally a nuisance.

"But to me, dear Alfredo," said Gonzales glowing with good-fellowship, "you will bring a full and complete list of *all* the British accounts of my good friend and rival de Pira.

"In this way," concluded Gonzales, "you will achieve for yourself a reputation as a great man of affairs in the neighbourhood. You will receive two very excellent salaries. You will become a figure of the greatest importance in the life of Tarragona, and what is more, dear Alfredo, you will be my friend, and only my innate modesty prevents me from telling you that friendship with Gonzales is a most important attribute in the life of any man."

Alfred rose to his feet, and bowed gracefully.

"Señor Gonzales," said he "—or may I be permitted to call you Tendo?—I am at your service with joy and gratitude. I accept your offers, your plans and your friendship. This evening is the first occasion in my life on which the stars have ever twinkled or on which I have known true joy. . . ."

But to himself Alfred said: "Blimey!"

. . . . . .

Krasinsky called for more beer.

"It was now September in the year 1913," he said, "and I would like to tell you that mere words are quite inadequate to describe the appearance, the status, and the atmospherics which surrounded Alfred Eustachio Jones.

Gonzales had been right in his surmise that de Pira would, on hearing of Alfred's engagement to work for his rival, promptly offer him even more money to work for *him* and to disclose to him the names and addresses of Gonzales' best customers.

And so to Alfred life became as a burbling and very pleasant stream. He spent his days wandering between the office of Señor Gonzales and that of Señor de Pira. He supplied lists of unimportant customers to de Pira and lists of still more unimportant customers to Gonzales. From both of them he received something like seven hundred and fifty pesetas a week—which

275

is somewhere in the region of thirty pounds English money—
and, if you knew anything of Tarragona in 1913 you will realise
that this sum was indeed riches.

"Alfred had burgeoned—I think that is the word—like a
flower in summer," Krasinsky went on. "He was now the
picture of health. He walked with a swagger. His trousers were
tighter than those of any *hidalgo* and his shirts were of rich silk.
A red and yellow bandana handkerchief, bound around his
head, with the loose ends flapping jauntily under his sombrero,
gave him the appearance of a well-built, wicked, handsome and
extremely attractive bull-fighter.

By now his Spanish was perfect. His wink was the most
expressive in Tarragona. It was more than a mere flutter of the
eyelid. It was a superbly fluctuated invitation to feminine
challenge.

Small wonder then that one night, at a festa held in the
Café of the Two Pillars, attended by his many friends, someone
called him the name by which he was afterwards known—The
King of Tarragona!

Alfred acknowledged the compliment with a smile, and,
standing there, he permitted himself to think that he had a star,
that like Napoleon he was a man of destiny. There passed
through his mind a mental picture of Doctor Erasmus Finegollen, and he raised his glass and drank a silent toast.

. . . . .

"It was next evening," Krasinsky continued, "that Alfred
received an urgent summons from Gonzales. He found his
employer seated in the flower-filled glass-house at the back of
his mansion. Sweet perfumes filled the air, and from somewhere
near came the tinkle of a softly played guitar. There was no
light inside the place, but by the brilliancy of a perfect moon
Alfred was enabled to observe the stress of emotion upon the
face of Gonzales.

Sweat gleamed upon the brow of the Spaniard and his eyes
were round and very wild.

He motioned Alfred to a rustic seat.

"Alfredo," he said hoarsely. "You are my friend, and you know that I am a man of honour. By now you have learned of the sacredness of our Spanish family life; of the inviolability of our women: of the innate purity of our wives; of that amazing and fearful vengeance which we wreak upon such low and foully disposed persons as endeavour to seduce away from her husband the love, the mind or the person of a wife.

"Look then upon me," muttered Gonzales, "and observe a man racked and pulled apart by the torture of the devil; impaled upon a stake of love; ruined by desire and tempted by friends. Do you hear, Alfredo?"

Alfred tweaked his right ear.

"I hear, Tendo," he said. "And who is the lady?"

Gonzales looked about him like any conspirator who plans to throw a bomb at midnight.

"The Señora Juanelita de Pira," he hissed. "She burns me. She boils my blood to excruciating temperatures. She haunts my waking hours and despoils me of sweet sleep. How terrible it is that the wife of my rival de Pira should be able to do this to me by merely existing."

He swore a deep oath.

"But now it is finished," he said. "Alfredo, I am desperate. As you well know I have never spoken to this lady who has produced such passion in me, but yesterday, as she drove through the square, I looked at her. From my eyes I despatched a message of the most fearful and enduring love. She regarded me for a second and I thought that I saw, within her modest and violet orbs, something more than interest.

"I have said that I am desperate. Very well, I will chance everything. For, Alfredo, as you well know, if de Pira should suspect that another man had even looked at his wife in an amatory manner, he would demand the revenge that every true Spaniard would desire. He would kill me as sure as my name is Gonzales.

"Therefore, Alfredo, listen carefully."

Alfred nodded. He knew what was coming.

"Alfredo," Gonzales went on, "you are my friend. You are more to me than a servant. I have need of you. You have the run of the de Pira establishment. You can deliver the letter which I have written to Juanelita. You can bring her reply to me, and, if all goes well, you may arrange for this exchange of correspondence to continue. You will do this for me, my friend?"

Alfred got up.

"Tendo," he said, "you may consider it done."

Gonzales sighed.

"Alfredo," he murmured. "Your salary is doubled."

·   ·   ·   ·   ·

In the twilight Alfred walked in the flower garden behind the Gonzales summer-house. Young vines hung upon the trellis work and a little breeze came from the sea.

Behind a bank of flowers he came upon the Señora Amarelza Gonzales. She was tall and slim and willowy. The classic curves of her body showed plainly through the thin gown of cream silk which sheathed her and from which her tiny red-heeled shoes peeped out. Her raven hair, piled high and set off by a Spanish comb, crowned the beauty of her face. Her black eyes gazed moodily upon Alfred.

He swept off his sombrero.

"The richest flower in this garden of sweet scents is the Señora," he said. "May joy be with you."

She turned upon him.

"Señor Alfredo," she said, "I see in your eye an understanding, and in your carriage and presence the person of a *caballero*. I throw myself into your hands. In you I place my trust. More, in your mercy I place the honour of the family of Gonzales. Help me, Alfredo!"

Alfred nodded.

"Is it possible that you are unhappy?" he asked.

His smile was sympathetic.

"Alfredo," she said, "I am decimated by a love as wicked as it is impossible. I desire nothing so much as the things which

278

are denied me by every rule and right. I am torn by the passions of the most wicked of women. I grovel before myself, yet I am greatly attracted by the very wickedness of my thoughts. I ask —I demand—your help, Alfredo."

Alfred cocked one eyebrow.

"De Pira?" he asked.

She nodded her head.

"De Pira is fat but fascinating," she said softly. "I have never spoken to him, but yesterday, on my journey to the seafront, I looked at him. He returned my look and there was something in his eyes that spoke to my heart."

"And you wish me to deliver a letter?" asked Alfred.

"Yes," she said. "That would be easy for you to do. Take the letter which I shall give you to him, and bring me the reply. If all goes well, you, in the sweetness of your heart, may act as a permanent postman. Is this too much? Is my demand too great?"

Alfred shook his head and smiled.

"Amarelza," he said, "you may consider it done."

.   .   .   .   .

Krasinsky looked at the clock, the hands of which were moving inexorably towards the time when the raucous cry of 'Time, gentlemen, please' would interrupt our talk and empty our tankards.

"All this then," said Krasinsky, "took place in the month of September 1913, and it was in the following June, on an evening such as only the summer of Tarragona can produce, that Alfred Eustachio Jones, called 'King of Tarragona' by all who knew him, walked contentedly along the esplanade road that runs along by the bottom of the foothills and looks out over the sea.

On his left the trees, the flowers, the shrubs of the rolling foothills, presented an exquisite picture, made more beautiful by the sunset. To his right the ocean, supremely blue, rolled blissfully in towards the shore. The road was quiet and deserted.

There was peace over the countryside and in the heart of Alfred.

"It was almost impossible to believe," Krasinsky went on, "that this gallant figure which strode so easily, so manfully, along the road, was that of the one-time puny, cough-racked chemist's assistant.

He wore his usual tight-fitting black broad-cloth trousers with the silver lacing at the sides, a shirt of blue silk, a short white jacket and his red and yellow bandana handkerchief tied about his head. In his hand he swung a white sombrero.

He whistled. He was happy. Looking out over the sea, his eyes, striving to see backwards into the past, saw in the clouds a picture of the dusty shop of John Hybelthoms in Mellers Alley in the City of London. He stopped and stood looking out over the sea.

"Gor-blimey," he said. "It's been worth it. It woulda been worth it for an hour, a day or a week."

And although he did not realise the fact Alfred gave thanks to God.

.   .   .   .   .

The summer stillness brooded over the house of the Señor Tendo Jose Gonzales. Out on the patio he sat, whilst his servants, one by one, came to him and congratulated him upon the birth that day of a son and heir. Gonzales smiled pleasantly as each retainer spoke, and nodded his head in thanks. But there was a faraway look in his eyes.

When the good wishes and congratulations were over, he rose and walked to his room at the back of the house. He opened a drawer in an old desk and took therefrom an antique Spanish horse pistol which had belonged to his great-grand-father, and which, in spite of its age, was still extremely efficacious. He looked at it and fingered it lovingly. After a while he loaded the pistol with a round duelling ball and a charge of black powder.

He drank a glass of wine; then, taking his sombrero, he left the house and walked slowly in the direction of the mansion of the Señor Concepcion de Pira. But he did not reach it.

Of the King of Tarragona

At the bottom of the esplanade road where the *Guadagua* road meets the path that runs over the foothills, he met de Pira. They took off their sombreros to each other and smiled graciously.

De Pira spoke:

"Gonzales," he said, "friend of my youth, I was on my way to congratulate you on the birth of your son. May good looks, fortune and all blessings come upon his head and upon your house."

"De Pira," replied Gonzales, "I thank you from the bottom of my heart. I have the best of reasons for knowing that the blessings which you wish for my son will probably be his. And the strange thing is that I was on my way to your house, there to wish that every good thing in this world and out of it should be bestowed upon the son who was born to your wife but five days ago. I bow before this charming infant, and wish him all the goodness in this world and the next."

They shook hands. De Pira looked at Gonzales and saw the whimsical expression in his eyes. He saw also the butt end of the horse pistol which protruded from the bolero pocket of his friend.

Gonzales, returning the look, saw the same strange expression in the eyes of his rival. He observed too the bulge in the right hand summer jacket pocket of de Pira, a bulge which denoted the shape of a large revolver.

These two Spanish gentlemen stood for a moment, each one smiling at the other with that urbane courtesy for which their race is famed.

Suddenly, upon the soft air, came the sound of an old Spanish song. They turned and saw walking towards them, swinging his sombrero and singing merrily, the brave figure of Alfred Eustachio Jones.

They shrugged their shoulders and walked towards him smiling."

. . . . .

The clock struck.

"Time, gentlemen, please," roared the potman.

Krasinsky finished his beer and got up.

"The time has come when we must part, my friend," he said. "It is perhaps a pity that life is continuously interrupted by somebody calling 'Time, gentlemen, please' at inopportune moments."

We walked out into the street, through the passage on the other side and into Mellers Alley. We were both looking at the spot where the shop of '*John Hybelthoms, Chymist*' had stood.

At the end of the passage Krasinsky stopped. He held out his hand towards me. I took it and thrilled as I always have thrilled (and hope I always shall) at his touch.

"Goodnight, Krasinsky," I said. "But you have not quite finished your story. You have not yet explained why it was that Alfred Eustachio Jones, having recovered from his tuberculosis, should die. I suppose he had not truly recovered, that some germ still lurked in his system."

Krasinsky smiled.

"You are wrong, my friend," he said. "Jones did not die of tuberculosis. He died of two well-aimed bullets, one from the antique horse pistol of Señor Tendo Jose Gonzales, the other from the modern revolver of Señor Concepcion de Pira. The local physician, for a small gratuity, certified that death was due to the heat. After which it only remained for Gonzales and de Pira to erect the superb monument which still stands in Tarragona to the memory of Alfred."

"I see, Krasinsky," I said. "I think I can guess why they killed him."

"Of course you can," said Krasinsky. "I thought it unnecessary to tell you that both the son of Gonzales and the son of de Pira were born with a raspberry birthmark on the right side of the neck.

"*Au revoir*, dear friend. We shall meet again."

I stood looking after him until his check suit became merged in the shadows of the night. Then I turned into Cannon Street.

Of the King of Tarragona

I walked slowly westwards thinking of Krasinsky, of Alfred Eustachio Jones, and of the years that fly past us, each one a little quicker than the one before.

And as I walked it seemed to me that the dome of St. Paul's resolved itself into the handsome and ornate monument that I had seen in the cemetery on the Reus road in Tarragona on the way to the hills.